Praise for Lisa Lutz

'Lisa Lutz has put her two-year stint as a private investigator to inspired use . . . Fast-paced and funny' *Daily Mail*

'An addictively entertaining read' *Cosmopolitan*

'Hilarious, outrageous and hip. Izzy Spellman, PI, is a total original with a voice so fresh and real, you want more, more, more. Lisa Lutz has created a delicious comedy with skill and truth. I loved it' Adriana Trigiani

'Fast-paced, irreverent and very funny' Curtis Sittenfeld

'Very funny but sometimes surprisingly touching and never played entirely for laughs' *The Times*

'Hilarious' *Daily Express*

'Part Bridget Jones, part Colombo, Lisa Lutz's resilient PI Isabel Spellman emerges as a thoroughly unusual heroine in her delightful, droll debut novel' *USA Today*

About the author

Lisa Lutz attended UC Santa Cruz, UC Irvine, the University of Leeds in England and San Francisco State University – although she still does not have a degree. She spent most of the 1990s hopping through a string of low-paying odd jobs – including a two-year stint at a San Francisco private invesigation firm – while writing and rewriting the screenplay for *Plan B,* a mob comedy. After the film was made in 2000, she vowed she would never write another screenplay. Lisa has not had a permanent residence in over two years

Visit www.lisalutz.com.

Revenge of the Spellmans

LISA

POCKET
BOOKS

LONDON • SYDNEY • NEW YORK • TORONTO

First published in the US by Simon & Schuster, Inc., 2009
First published in Great Britain by Simon & Schuster UK Ltd, 2009
This edition first published by Pocket Books, 2010
An imprint of Simon & Schuster UK Ltd
A CBS COMPANY

1 3 5 7 9 10 8 6 4 2

Simon & Schuster UK Ltd
1st Floor
222 Gray's Inn Road
London WC1X 8HB

www.simonandschuster.co.uk

Simon & Schuster Australia
Sydney

A CIP catalogue record for this book is
available from the British Library

B Format ISBN 978-1-84739-384-5
A Format ISBN 978-1-84739-982-3

Printed by CPI Cox & Wyman, Reading, Berkshire RG1 8EX

For David Hayward

Revenge of the Spellmans

THERAPY SESSION #19

[Partial transcript reads as follows:]

DR. RUSH:[1] Two weeks ago you mentioned that you were being blackmailed.

ISABEL: Did I?

DR. RUSH: Yes.

ISABEL: Must have slipped my mind.

DR. RUSH: Would you like to talk about it?

ISABEL: Nah.

DR. RUSH: Well, I'd like to talk about it.

ISABEL: It's really not that big a deal.

DR. RUSH: Do you know your blackmailer?

ISABEL: I'm in the process of narrowing down the list of suspects.

DR. RUSH: How does your blackmailer communicate with you?

ISABEL: Anonymous notes.

DR. RUSH: What do they say?

ISABEL: I *really* don't want to talk about it.

---

[1] Dr. Sophia Rush—Therapist #2.

DR. RUSH: If these sessions went according to your plan, you'd sit here in silence for an hour eating your lunch.

ISABEL: *One time* I asked you if I could eat lunch. *One time.*

DR. RUSH: Tell me what the gist of the notes is and then we can move on.

ISABEL: "I know your secret. If you want to keep it you will meet my demands."

DR. RUSH: So, what's your secret?

ISABEL: I thought we were moving on.

DR. RUSH: We are. To what your secret is.

ISABEL: [sigh] My blackmailer knows where I live. At least I think that's the secret he or she is referring to.

DR. RUSH: Where do you live?

ISABEL: I don't want to lie to you, Dr. Rush.

DR. RUSH: I'm flattered.

ISABEL: I don't want to tell you the truth, either.

DR. RUSH: Are you being serious, Isabel?

ISABEL: I sense judgment in your tone, Doctor.

DR. RUSH: Right now I'm just confused. The judgment part will come later.

ISABEL: You're funnier than Dr. Ira.[2]

DR. RUSH: My couch is funnier than Dr. Ira.

ISABEL: See?

DR. RUSH: You really aren't going to tell me where you live?

ISABEL: If it makes you feel any better, most people don't know where I live.

DR. RUSH: My feelings don't come into play here.

ISABEL: It's nice to have one person I don't have to worry about.

DR. RUSH: Are you getting enough sleep?

ISABEL: No. But I drink a lot of coffee and take the bus, so things even out.

DR. RUSH: Why can't you sleep?

ISABEL: I've got a lot on my mind.

---

[2] Dr. Ira Schwartzman—Therapist #1.

2

DR. RUSH: [impatiently] For instance?

[Long pause.][3]

ISABEL: Something strange is going on with my brother.

DR. RUSH: We're not talking about your brother.

ISABEL: It's my therapy. I thought I got to choose the topics.

DR. RUSH: Let me ask you a question: Have you been hired to investigate your brother?

ISABEL: He's family. You don't need a paycheck to investigate family.

DR. RUSH: I'd like to return to the topic of blackmail.

ISABEL: Why?

DR. RUSH: Because it's a clearly defined stressor in your life.

ISABEL: It's not that stressful. I'd really like to switch topics now.

DR. RUSH: If you can come up with a topic as good as blackmail, I'm game.

[Long pause while I pretend to think of a worthy subject.]

DR. RUSH: I'm onto you and your long pauses.[4]

ISABEL: Okay. I'm being bribed by a political consultant.

DR. RUSH: Seriously?

ISABEL: Yes.

DR. RUSH: Why?

ISABEL: Because he thinks I know something. But I don't know anything . . . yet.

DR. RUSH: What does he think you know?

ISABEL: If I knew that, then I'd know.

DR. RUSH: [sigh] Is this bribe incident connected to the blackmail?

ISABEL: Absolutely not.

DR. RUSH: What makes you so sure?

ISABEL: The bribe is serious. The blackmail is child's play.

DR. RUSH: I need you to be more specific.

---

[3] I've found the long pause an excellent way to pass time in therapy. Until this session, I thought it had gone unnoticed.

[4] For other surefire ways to kill time in therapy, see appendix.

3

ISABEL: My blackmailer is making me wash cars and go to the zoo.

DR. RUSH: Go to the zoo?

ISABEL: It was supposed to be SFMOMA,[5] but I thought I could go to the zoo instead. My mistake. My point is they are entirely unconnected.

[Long, long pause.]

DR. RUSH: [sigh] Bizarre forms of blackmail, bribery, secret residences. The odds of all of this happening to one person, Isabel—

ISABEL: It sounds worse than it is.

DR. RUSH: Let's look at this from a different perspective. Your imagination has gotten you into trouble in the past. That's why you're in therapy. You can't deny that you tend to put a paranoid slant on most things you observe.

ISABEL: That was the old me.

DR. RUSH: Are you sure?

ISABEL: I've made progress, Dr. Rush. Lots of progress.

[Long, long pause.]

ISABEL: Haven't I?

---

[5]San Francisco Museum of Modern Art.

Part 1

UNRESOLVED ISSUES

Two months earlier . . .

THE PHILOSOPHER'S CLUB

Tuesday

An unknown male—approximately fifty-five years old, with an almost full head of gray hair, a slight build, an even slighter paunch, and a weathered but friendly face, garbed in a snappy suit and a not-unpleasant tie—walked into the bar. He sat down at the counter and nodded a silent hello.

"What can I get you?" I said.

"Coffee," Unknown Male replied.

"Irish coffee?" I asked.

"Nope. Just the regular stuff."

"You know, they got coffee shops, if you're into that sort of thing."

"It's three in the afternoon," Unknown Male replied.

"It's still a bar," I responded, and poured a mug of the stale brew. "Cream and sugar?" I asked.

"Black," he answered. Unknown Male took a sip and grimaced. He pushed the mug back in my direction and said, "Cream and sugar."

"Thought so."

Unknown Male put a five-dollar bill on the bar and told me to keep the change. I rang two dollars into the cash register and put the remaining three into the tip jar.

"You Isabel?" Unknown Male asked.

"Who's asking?" I replied.

7

"Ernest Black," the less-unknown male said, stretching out his hand. "My friends call me Ernie."

I shook it, because that's what you do, and then picked up a dishrag and began drying some glasses, because that's what bartenders do.

"I heard you used to be a detective," Ernie said.

"Where'd you hear that?"

"I was in here the other day talking to Milo."

"You and Milo friends?" I asked.

"We're not enemies. Anyway, Milo said you used to be a detective."

"Private investigator," I corrected him, and dried some more glasses.

There was a long pause while Ernie tried to figure out how to keep the conversation going.

"It looks like you're a bartender now," Ernie said.

"So it seems."

"Is this like a career path or more like a rest stop on a longer journey?" he asked.

"Huh?" I said, even though I understood what Ernie was getting at.

"I'm just wondering, are you planning on doing this bartender thing long-term or do you think you might go back into the PI business somewhere down the line?"

I casually put down the glass and the dishrag. I reached over the bar and grabbed Ernie by the not-unpleasant tie he was wearing and leaned in close enough to smell his stale coffee breath.

"Tell my mother that if she wants to know my plans for the future, she should ask me herself!"

Wednesday

My dad walked into the bar. Albert Spellman[1] is his name. I'd been expecting him. Three o'clock on Wednesday is his usual time. He likes an empty bar so he can speak freely.

---

[1] For an incomplete dossier on Dad, see appendix.

"The usual," Dad said, mostly because he likes feeling like a regular. Dad's usual is a five-ounce glass of red wine. He'd rather order a beer or whiskey or both, but his heart condition and my mother prohibit all of the above.

I poured the wine, slid the glass in his direction, leaned on top of the bar, and looked my dad in the eye.

"Mom sent some guy into the bar yesterday to pump me for information."

"No, she didn't," Dad said, looking bored.

"Yes, she did," I replied.

"Isabel, she did that *one* time two months ago and she never did it again. I promise you."[2]

"You have no idea what she's doing when you're not watching her."

"You could say that about anyone," Dad said.

"But I'm talking about Mom."

"I'd like to change the subject, Isabel."

I sighed, disappointed. I was not interested in the subject my dad had in mind.

"If you'd like to talk about the weather, I'd be alright with that."

"Not the weather," said Dad.

"Seen any good movies?" I asked.

"Haven't been getting out much lately," Dad said, "what with work and all. Oh yes. *Work.* That's what I'd like to talk about."

"I don't want to talk about work."

"You don't talk. You just listen. Can you do that?"

"I distinctly recall you telling me that I wasn't a good listener," I replied. "So, apparently I cannot do that."

"*Isabel!*" Dad said far too loudly, but who cares in an empty bar? "We are having this conversation whether you like it or not."

In case you were thinking the definition had changed, a conversation

---

[2] Mom hired a recent graduate from the American Conservatory Theater and armed him with a tape recorder and a list of questions to casually integrate into the conversation. For example: 1) Have you ever been in therapy? 2) Is it helping you? 3) Do you plan on being a bartender forever? 4) Are you seeing anyone right now? 5) How many tattoos does he have?

usually involves two people exchanging words, a back-and-forth, if you will. My dad provided a brief lecture that went something like this:

"You are a licensed private investigator. That is your trade. And yet, for the last five months, all you have done is serve drinks and collect tips.[3] You have refused to work at a job for which you are highly qualified, which used to give you some real purpose in life. I spent seven long, hard years training you at that job, teaching you everything I know while you talked back, nodded off, screwed up, broke equipment, slammed my hand in a car door,[4] lost me clients, and cost me a fortune in car insurance. Seven long years, Isabel. I can't get those years back. They're lost to me forever. Do you know how much more pleasant it would have been to have hired a nice responsible college student looking for a little excitement in his or her life? Someone who didn't insult my intelligence on a daily basis or leave cigarette butts and empty beer cans in the surveillance van, someone who said 'Yes, Mr. Spellman' instead of rolling her eyes and grunting? Can you imagine how my life might be different?[5] How my health might be improved?[6] Five months ago, when you took this 'temporary'[7] job, you promised your mother and me that you would start actively thinking about your future, which is directly connected to *our* future, because it's connected to the future of this business we have built not just for us, but for you. So, tell me, Isabel, after five months of serving drinks and over two months of seeing a shrink, are you any closer to making that decision?"

I'm not usually one who follows the adage "Honesty is the best policy," but my dad's speech exhausted even me, and so I decided to go with the very short truth.

---

[3] Not true. I've done all sorts of other things, like go to movies, take strolls in the park, drink coffee, drink other stuff, eat food, sleep, etc.

[4] That was an accident and he knows it.

[5] These kinds of questions one should never answer. So I didn't.

[6] He's laying it on thick now, working the guilt angle.

[7] Finger quotes.

"Nope," I said.

Dad sucked the last drop of alcohol out of his wineglass. He searched the empty bar as if he were looking for assistance. He made brief eye contact, but he couldn't hold it. The disappointment was evident. Even I felt some sympathy.

"Sounds like you could use a real drink, Dad," I said as I poured him a shot of Maker's Mark. "This will be our little secret."

Thursday

Thursday is my day off. I wake, read the paper, and drink coffee until noon. Maybe run an errand or two and surf the Internet, prowling for sites that amuse and educate. I kill time until I meet my old[8] friend Morty[9] for lunch. We used to meet at the same Jewish deli every Thursday, until I explained that, as a nonsenior citizen, I am not obsessed with maintaining unbreakable habits. Morty argued that he wanted to go to the same deli every week because he knew he liked the food and could be sure of an enjoyable meal. I argued that it's better to mix things up. And won. A good thing, as I was getting seriously tired of Morty trying to convince me to get the tongue sandwich.

This week I persuaded Morty to meet me at Fog City Diner[10] on Battery Street downtown. I took public transportation, but Morty drove his giant Cadillac and was at least twenty minutes late.

"Where were you?" I asked when he finally sat down at the booth. Morty is typically five minutes early for everything, so it was the obvious question.

"Got lost on the way over," Morty said.

"But you have a navigation system."

"I turned it off."

---

[8] Old in the literal sense. He's eighty-four.

[9] Mortimer Schilling, retired defense attorney. For more information, see appendix.

[10] A San Francisco landmark. Easy to locate. Serves a mean black and white milkshake.

"Why?"

"I can't stand that thing. Always barking orders at me."

As Morty studied the menu with his usual dedication, I studied Morty with a more critical eye than usual.

The third button from the top dangled from his threadbare cotton shirt. The lapel sported a food stain. His hair appeared stringier than usual and his glasses reflected like a car windshield after a brief drizzle.

"Hand over your glasses," I said.

"But then I can't see the menu," he replied.

"You're going to order a tuna melt and a cup of decaf like you always do in restaurants that don't serve pastrami."

I held out the palm of my hand until Morty relinquished his eyewear. I dipped my napkin in my ice water and cleared the grime from the lenses. I returned his glasses and warned Morty that driving under such a condition was highly dangerous. Morty nodded in agreement the way somebody does when he wants you to stop talking. The waitress swung by our table and took our orders. Morty opted for the meat loaf and gave me a smirk of rebellion. He still ordered decaf, though.

"How's Ruth doing?"

"Fine, I suppose."

"As her husband, shouldn't that be something you know?"

"She's in Florida for the week."

"Doing what?"

"Visiting her sister."

"Why didn't you go with her?"

"What's with the third degree?"

"I'm making conversation, Morty. These are all reasonable questions."

"I'm not moving to Florida!" Morty suddenly shouted.

"Who said you were moving there?" I asked.

"There's no way in hell."

"Got it."

"Now let's change the subject."

"Does Ruth want to move to Florida?" I asked, not changing the subject at all.

"She wanted to move to Italy twenty years ago and that didn't happen," was his response.

"What have you got against Florida?"

"Don't get me started," Morty replied.

The conversation pretty much ended there. Morty picked at his meat loaf and sulked his way through lunch.

As we exited the diner Morty offered me a ride home and I accepted. I noticed a dent on his Cadillac's front left fender and asked what happened. He shrugged his shoulders in a What-difference-does-it make? kind of way. He then pulled out of the parking space without checking his rearview mirror and just missed a cyclist who swerved in the nick of time. Morty didn't notice a thing. A few minutes later, he completely ignored a stop sign, and a short time after that, he started two-lane driving on Van Ness Avenue, until someone in a Mini Cooper laid into the horn. Morty's response was, "Relax, we'll all get there eventually."

After Morty dropped me at the house, I debated how soon I should contact the authorities. If today was an accurate representation of Morty's driving, he was a regular menace to society. I opted to give him one more chance; everybody has an off day.

Friday

A middle-age man walked into the bar followed by a teenage girl. The man appeared angry, the teenager defiant. Meet my sister, Rae, and her "best friend," Henry Stone.[11]

Three bar stools divided them. Henry unrolled the *New Yorker* magazine he was carrying under his arm and began reading. Rae dusted off the already-

---

[11] Once again, if you've failed to read the previous two documents—*The Spellman Files* and *Curse of the Spellmans* (both available in paperback!)—and you need further background information, see appendix.

dusted-off counter and said, "The usual." Her usual is a ginger ale followed by a reminder that she's not actually supposed to be in a bar since she's only six-teen (and a half!) years old. I poured Rae's ginger ale and served Henry his usual club soda. I waited for the unusual stretch of silence to end. Rae watched Henry out of the corner of her eye. He studied his magazine with rapt attention, uninterested in—or at least pretending quite well to be uninterested in—the rest of the room. As an act of what appeared to be mimicry, Rae pulled out her geometry textbook and gave a performance of rapt attention. Hers failed where Henry's succeeded. She checked him out of the corner of her eye, wait-ing for some acknowledgment of her presence. Rae downed her ginger ale and smacked the glass on the counter, making her presence impossible to ignore.

"I'll have another," she said.

"Does somebody want to tell me what's going on?" I asked as I served her second round.

"Nothing. Henry just needs to chillax," said Rae.

"Do you have any response to that?" I asked Henry.

"Isabel," he said, "this is a bar. Not a soda shop. Adults come here to get away from children. I could have you shut down for serving minors."

"Rae, go home," I said, sensing that Henry needed some space.

"I don't think so," was Rae's response.

"I tried," I said, turning back to Henry.

Henry finished his club soda and asked for something stronger. I sug-gested 7UP, but he had bourbon in mind, which meant my sister had done something terribly wrong. I was intrigued.

"What did you do?" I asked Rae after I served Henry his Bulleit.

"Tell Henry," Rae said, "that what I did, I did for his own good."

"Did you hear that?" I said to Henry.

He looked up from the magazine and said, "Hear what?"

"Um, Rae said that what she did, she did for your own good."

"Well, you can tell your sister that it was not her decision to make."

"What did he say?" Rae asked, even though Henry's response was per-fectly audible.

"You're kidding me, right?" I asked.

"What did he say?" she insisted.

"He said it was not your decision to make."

"Tell him he'll thank me later."

Henry returned to his magazine and continued pretending that Rae existed in some parallel universe where only I could see and hear her. I decided to play along for the time being, since I had to admit I wanted the scoop.

"She said you'll thank her later."

"Tell her I won't. Tell her she's forbidden to come to my house ever again."

"You can't be serious," she said. Apparently my translating skills were no longer required, because this was directed at Henry's back.

"Oh, I'm very serious," he replied, finishing off the last of his bourbon. I was shocked when he pointed to his glass and asked for another, but I assumed this meant further information would be forthcoming, so I served the drink and eagerly awaited the rest of the story.

I'll spare you the long, drawn-out argument and give you the basic facts. Henry, for the last five months, had been dating a public defender for San Francisco County named Maggie Mason. Maggie has an apartment in Daly City—not the quickest commute to the superior court building on Bryant Street. Henry lives in the Inner Sunset. It's only natural that Maggie would spend time at Henry's home and not the other way around. Two months ago, she got a drawer in his house; one month ago, she got a shelf in his pantry.[12] Last week Henry made a copy of his key and gave it to her in a jewelry box. My sister, convinced that Henry wasn't really ready to take the next step, took it upon herself to change the locks in his apartment a few days later. How my sister had access to his home and how this act of subterfuge went unnoticed by the neighbors, I cannot explain. Suffice it to say she did not deny her role in this particular drama. I'm sure you can imagine what happened next: Maggie arrived at Henry's house after a long day

---

[12] Henry's diet veers toward extreme health consciousness. If you want any food with flavor in his house, you really must bring your own supplies.

of work. She tried her key and it failed. She interpreted events the way any woman might: Henry gave her the wrong key, which was a subconscious or passive-aggressive communication that he was simply not ready. What had not occurred to Maggie was that my sister was playing saboteur in their relationship. Certainly there had been moments of tension between Maggie and her boyfriend's odd version of a "best friend," but Maggie had failed to see Rae's outright hostility. None of this escaped Henry's notice.

"Tell your sister," said Henry, "that she is no longer welcome in my home."

"We're back to that again?" I asked.

Rae's response was not the wisest. "I have a key," she said, rolling her eyes.

"I had the locks changed this morning!" Henry replied to my sister at a volume I did not know his voice was capable of.

"Total waste of money," Rae replied.

Henry finished his second drink, stood up in a huff, and said in his most threatening tone, "Mark my words, Rae: This isn't over." Henry nodded a silent good-bye to me and left the bar.

Rae nervously folded her cocktail napkin in quarters, then eighths, and attempted sixteenths. Her defiance softened and worry lines crinkled her smooth brow.

"He's really angry, Rae."

"I know," she replied.

"I've met Maggie. She seems nice. What do you have against her?"

"Nothing," Rae said. "It's just that if somebody doesn't do something about it, he's going to marry her."

Saturday
1400 hrs

A lawyer walked into the bar. Sorry, there's no joke here. It was my brother, David,[13] sporting three-day-old stubble and casual attire—cargo

---

[13] For David's dossier, see appendix.

pants, sneakers, and a GUINNESS IS GOOD FOR YOU T-shirt, which I'm almost positive was mine. My point is, David's ensemble was in direct conflict with his usual dress code. It was as if he were wearing a costume for someone planning a day at the park. Instead of ordering what was advertised on his shirt, David asked for a Bloody Mary, just to make me work. I added extra Tabasco and pepper, just to make him suffer.

"What are you doing drinking on a Saturday afternoon?"

"My vacation starts today."

"Some vacation," I replied, scanning the surroundings for emphasis.

"I leave for Europe on Monday."

"For how long?"

"Four weeks."

"Nobody tells me anything," I said.

"It's a last-minute thing," David replied.

"You traveling alone?" I asked.

"No," David said in a way that indicated the discussion was over. I, of course, did not agree to the inexplicit request.

"So, who are you traveling with?"

Familiar with my questioning tactics, David stayed his course. "I was thinking I should have someone watch my place while I'm gone, and since you live in a dump,[14] I figured I wouldn't have to pay you."

"Not that you couldn't afford to."

My brother handed me an envelope, leaned across the bar, and kissed me on the cheek. "The key and instructions are in there. I leave for the airport around ten A.M. on Monday. Don't enter the premises until at least ten thirty, in case I'm running late. I will return exactly four weeks later in the afternoon, so make yourself scarce by noon of the third Monday from this Monday. Got it?"

"Don't you want me to hang around so you can bore me with all your travel photos?"

---

[14] Indeed I do.

"Not really," David replied. "Now, behave while I'm gone," he said, raising a stern eyebrow. Then he left.

I cracked the envelope the second David exited the bar. As promised, it contained a key and a typewritten sheet of paper.

RULES FOR ISABEL WHILE STAYING IN MY HOME

Do . . .

- Take in the mail every day.
- Take out the trash when the bag is full. Put garbage bins on the sidewalk Thursday evening.
- Reduce, reuse, and recycle. Try to make this world a better place.
- Sleep in the guest room.
- Sophia cleans on Tuesday. Tidy up before she comes.
- Water all indoor plants. There are instructions next to each plant.

Do NOT . . .

- Mess with the sprinkler system. It's on a timer.
- Add porn sites to the Favorites list on my computer.
- Use my electric toothbrush. I don't care if you buy a new head.
- Throw any parties.
- Sleep in my bed.
- Move any furniture.
- Drink any of the following booze[15]:
  —J. Walker Black Label
  —Glenlivet 18 Year
  —Grey Goose Vodka
  —Rémy Martin VSOP

After I recovered from the insult of the list, I phoned David to clarify a few matters.

---

[15] Namely, the good stuff.

"Did you forget to include your itinerary?" I asked.

"No," David replied. "I'm not sure where I'll be."

"How will I reach you if there's an emergency?"

"Just call my cell phone."

I hung up the phone without any more answers than when I started. There was only one thing I could say for certain: David was lying to me. About what, I couldn't say.

As I contemplated my brother's suspicious behavior, the afternoon regulars began to arrive.

Clarence Gilley strode in shortly after four. He pretends he's on a schedule when it comes to drinking. Four o'clock is his start time and if he shows up any time after that he says, "Sorry I'm late. It won't happen again." I like Clarence. He tips well, tells me a single joke each visit, and then he remains silent, studying the sports section of the *Chronicle* for the next four hours.

Saturday's joke: *An amnesiac walks into a bar. He asks, "Do I come here often?"*

1700 hrs

Mom[16] walked into the bar. Whatever my father lacks in good looks, my mother makes up for it. Mom is petite and elegant with long auburn hair that comes straight out of a bottle. From a distance, she appears years younger than her age. In fact, Clarence whistled when my mom entered the bar. (Although I can't say for sure that he was responding to her and not to some alarming news from the world of sports.)

Like my father's, Mom's "casual" visits to the Philosopher's Club were thinly veiled interrogations. To my parents' credit, though, they managed

---

[16] Olivia Spellman. For brief dossier, see appendix.

to mix things up just a bit. This is a close approximation of my conversation with my mother that day:

ISABEL: What can I get you?

OLIVIA: A daughter with a purpose in life.

ISABEL: Sorry, we're all out. What's your second choice?

OLIVIA: I can't decide between a club soda and a real drink.

ISABEL: I'd prefer you had a real drink.

OLIVIA: Fine. I'll have a gimlet.

ISABEL: But just one drink. Then I'd like you to be on your way.

OLIVIA: I'll leave when my business here is done.

[The drink is served; the patron takes a sip and grimaces.]

OLIVIA: It needs more booze.

ISABEL: When I serve it to you with more booze, you say it needs more lime juice. Has it occurred to you that you just don't like gimlets?

OLIVIA: I used to love them.

ISABEL: Sometimes we need to accept change.

OLIVIA: Is this what you're getting out of therapy? Learning to embrace your inner bartender?

ISABEL: I'm just doing my time, Mom. That's all.

OLIVIA: Tell me something. Do you talk about me with Dr. Ira?[17]

ISABEL: We talk about everyone in my life at one time or another. It's possible I haven't mentioned Bernie[18] yet. But I'm sure it will happen eventually.

OLIVIA: Are you blaming me for all of your troubles?

ISABEL: No. Actually, I've been blaming David.

OLIVIA: Fair enough.

[Mother/patron crinkles nose when she takes a second sip of her gimlet. Daughter/bartender sprays an ounce of club soda into her drink.]

---

[17] Um, yes!

[18] See appendix.

ISABEL: Try it now.

OLIVIA: That's much better. How do I order it if I need to?

ISABEL: You don't. But if you have to, call it a gimlet watered down with soda.

OLIVIA: Very nice.

ISABEL: So, I'll trade you one honest answer for one in return.

OLIVIA: Agreed.

ISABEL: Did you send some guy into the bar on Tuesday to drill me for information?

OLIVIA: I did that once two months ago. Will you let it die already?

ISABEL: So, that's a no?

OLIVIA: Yes, it's a no. My turn?

ISABEL: Shoot.

OLIVIA: Are you dating anyone right now?

[Long pause.]

ISABEL: No one to speak of.

OLIVIA: What are you hiding?

[Another significant pause.]

ISABEL: Milo and I hooked up a few weeks ago. It's been awkward ever since.

OLIVIA: That's so gross, it's not even funny.

ISABEL: Yeah, you're right. I thought it might be funny, but when I said it, I just felt nauseous.

OLIVIA: In what direction are you heading, Isabel?

ISABEL: Nowhere, at the moment.

Sunday

Milo walked into the bar, which isn't all that unusual, what with it being his bar and all. I usually cover my afternoon shifts solo so Milo has more time off, but Sunday afternoon we always work together and take stock of the inventory. I've known Milo going on ten years now; he's been my employer for only five months of those. Bar owners' expectations differ from other employers': Show up on time, don't steal, make the right change, and don't be too generous with the booze. Most nights, I'm at least three for four.

While I cleaned glasses, Milo did the *San Francisco Chronicle*'s crossword puzzle, which he considers to be some form of actual work. (Something about keeping his mind sharp being good for business—don't quote me, I wasn't paying attention.)

"What's a four-letter word for a lunch staple?"

"Beer," I replied, because how is Milo staying sharp by asking me to do his crossword puzzles for him?

"That's not it. It has to be something you eat."

"Fish."

"It's not fish. Fish isn't a lunch staple in any place I know."

"I still think it's fish."

"Soup!" Milo shouted as if it were a different four-letter word.

"Congratulations," I said. Frankly, I was happy to know he could get at least one clue in the puzzle. Another minute passed in peaceful silence. But then it was over.

"I was talking to a friend of mine the other day," Milo said as he hung his coat on a rack behind the bar.

"Fascinating story."

"Give it time. It gets better."

"And then what happened?" I asked with rapt interest.

"He was telling me about this time he went into a bar, was making casual conversation with the bartender, and the next thing he knows, the bartender for no good reason tries to strangle him with his own tie and accuses him of having some kind of conspiratorial relationship with her own mother."

"I'm sure he's recovered by now."

"Not completely. There are a few lingering side effects."

"For instance?" I asked, playing along.

"He's got a closet full of ties—a regular clotheshorse, this one—and yet he's afraid to wear all of them. Used to be his signature look. Now he's got to figure out a whole new thing."

"Tragic story."

"Izz, he don't know your mother. We were conversing the other day, he has a situation, he needs a detective, he'd rather not pay an arm and a leg like your parents charge, so I mentioned you might be able to help him out."

"I have a job, Milo."

"This isn't a career, Izzy."

"For you it is."

Milo tossed his newspaper on top of the bar and sighed dramatically. "I'm cutting your hours to three days a week. It's time for you to get back in the game or find an entirely new game that doesn't involve serving booze."

"How much are my parents paying you?"

"Nada."

"I don't approve of your random use of Spanish."

"Ernie's gonna drop by again today. He's gonna tell you about his problem. You're going to offer him your services. You'll both negotiate a reasonable price. You'll do a good job for my friend."

"And if I don't want to?"

"I'll trim your hours some more."

1800 hrs

As promised, Ernie Black returned to the bar.

His problem was the kind of problem you hear about all the time, at least in my line of work—or my previous line of work. Scratch that. In every line of work I've known,[19] the suspicious wife (or husband) comes up often.

At the age of fifty, Ernie met the woman of his dreams. She applied for a receptionist position at the muffler shop he co-owns with his brother,

---

[19] Namely, the PI and bartender lines.

they dated for six months, decided to test their relationship on a four-day vacation in Reno, Nevada, and by the second day, decided to wed. Her name was (and still is, I presume) Linda. Maiden name: Truesdale. She has red hair, brown eyes, and is covered in freckles. I took note of this fact because redheads are easy to follow. Depending on Ernie's financial situation, I thought I just might cut him a break.

This was Ernie's first marriage and he wanted it to work. But women had always been a mystery to Ernie and so he tried to solve the mystery through cheap self-help books. When I first met with Ernie (well, the second time) he was reading a battered paperback titled *Women: Everything You Ever Wanted to Know and More*. He had recently finished a chapter on secrets and realized that his wife had a few.

I asked for the hard facts first, not wanting to be influenced by Ernie's interpretations. To begin with, his wife would often disappear for hours at a time and use a flimsy excuse for her absence. Ernie never pressed her on this issue because he didn't want her to feel smothered. Then there were the expensive items of clothing and perfume that would show up after these unexplained excursions, with no dent on their mutual credit card. The money had to come from somewhere. Those hours that passed without him—she had to be doing something. Ernie had a feeling he didn't like in the pit of his stomach, but he told himself that he was imagining things. It wasn't until last weekend, when he cleaned out the garage and found a shoebox full of $3,000 in cash, that he decided to look at the matter more closely.

I then asked Ernie what he thought might be going on and he handed me a handwritten sheet of paper that listed, in descending order of preference, his list of possibilities:

A) Nothing's going on. Everything has a simple explanation.
B) Linda has a shoplifting problem.
C) Linda is having an affair with a man who gives her money and gifts.
D) Linda is having an affair and she has a shoplifting problem.

While I was no expert on Linda, I decided that Ernie should leave with at least a shred of hope. I told him that option D was extremely unlikely. Then I asked him a question my mother always asks whenever we consider taking on a domestic case.

"Ernie, if we do find out that your wife is having an affair, what will you do?"

Ernie consulted his shoes for the answer: "We'd have to go to marriage counseling, I guess."

His reaction was calm, which was what I was looking for. You can't predict human behavior, but I would've bet a week's wages on Ernie being a peaceful man. So I decided to take the case.

Then we talked money. Ernie didn't have much of it, so it was a short conversation. I would be on call for the next time his wife planned an excursion. I cut my usual rate by half, which is 75 percent less than what my parents would charge for the same work. Ernie was getting a deal, but the job seemed easy enough.

It didn't mean anything to me—I'll tell you that right now. So don't get any ideas. There was no significance in me doing a favor for a friend of Milo's. A few hours of watching a redhead didn't mean I was back in the game. That's what I told myself, at least.

THERAPY SESSION #10

(THERAPIST #1: DR. IRA SCHWARTZMAN)

[Partial transcript reads as follows:]

ISABEL: This week has pretty much been the same as any other week.

DR. IRA: So nothing of interest happened?

ISABEL: No. It was a dull week.

DR. IRA: I see. And how do you feel about that?

ISABEL: Good. Very good.

DR. IRA: So there's nothing you'd like to discuss?

ISABEL: Not really.

DR. IRA: Are you sure?

ISABEL: Let me think about it.

[Long pause.[1]]

ISABEL: I thought of something.

DR. IRA: Go on.

ISABEL: Only two more weeks.

---

[1] This might surprise you, but I'd grown quite comfortable with these extended silences in Dr. Ira's office. A fifty-minute session is a fifty-minute session. There's no wiggle room. Long silences kill time. Silence means less work. This I have learned.

DR. IRA: Excuse me?

ISABEL: Only two weeks left until the final session of my court-ordered therapy.

[Dr. Ira consults his notes.]

DR. IRA: Indeed you are right, Isabel.

ISABEL: So our time is nearing its end.

DR. IRA: Should I interpret that to mean you plan to discontinue therapy after your final session?

ISABEL: That was my plan.

DR. IRA: [disappointed] I see.

ISABEL: We should do something to celebrate.

DR. IRA: What do you mean?

ISABEL: What's customary for celebrating the end of therapy?

DR. IRA: There is no custom.

ISABEL: I was thinking of bringing in a cake. I should probably order it now, if we want anything decent.

DR. IRA: I think it would be better if we just focused on the next few sessions.

ISABEL: You're saying no to cake?

DR. IRA: I don't feel that cake is appropriate.

ISABEL: Why not?

DR. IRA: Let me ask you a serious question, Isabel: Do you think you've made any progress?

HOW I ENDED UP
IN THERAPY

About a year and a half ago, I briefly moved back in with my parents, into the attic apartment where I've lived most of my adult life. During that brief phase of regression, I had a bird's-eye view of a suspicious neighbor's activities. Let's call the neighbor John Brown, because that, it turns out, is his real name. To make a long story[1] short, I began investigating the suspicious neighbor maybe more than I should have—or more than society deems acceptable. A restraining order was filed (against me) and the next thing you know I was in some serious legal trouble. (You met my octogenarian lawyer just a few pages back.)

Having a restraining order filed against you is one thing; violating that restraining order puts you in an altogether different boat. To anyone contemplating a ride in said boat, let me make a friendly suggestion: Don't do it. Just let it go.

Anyway, back to how I ended up in therapy. You see, my retired-cop father had some connections and so did my ancient lawyer, so they convinced the district attorney that court-mandated therapy was the appropriate way to deal with "someone like Isabel."[2] I was required to see a

---

[1] *Curse of the Spellmans*—now available in paperback!

[2] My dad's actual word choice.

psychologist or psychiatrist roughly once a week for three months. I was given three months to begin therapy, and I took my sweet time. In retrospect, I should have been more proactive and found my own shrink;[3] instead, my mom found one for me. I have only lukewarm words to say about the shockingly mild-mannered Dr. Ira, but this I can say for certain: He was not the right shrink for me.

Eleven weeks and three days after my court ruling, I made an appointment for the following Monday at eleven A.M. My dad phoned me on my way to the session to impart some information he thought I should have.

"Sometimes they don't talk right away," said my dad. "So don't just sit there and give the doctor attitude. You might have to talk first. Okay?"

"Who is this?" I replied.

My dad sighed and said, "Don't blame me for all of your problems, either."

"I won't," I said. "I plan on blaming Mom."

Dr. Ira Schwartzman's office was (and is, I presume) located on Market Street, right by the exit to the Montgomery Street BART and Muni station. It seems my mother thought convenience was the most important factor in finding me a therapist. The office was unlike the shrinks' offices you see in movies and television. The waiting room could fit inside a decent-sized closet. It contained two cloth chairs and a wooden coffee table. The furniture was marred by age—coffee stains, frayed edges, worn wood.

Dr. Ira Schwartzman opened his office door.

"Isabel?" he asked.

"That's me," I replied as I got to my feet.

---

[3] I intend nothing derogatory by using the word "shrink"; it's just faster to type than the alternatives.

The doctor invited me into a room not much bigger than the waiting room. The furniture was superior to the waiting room furniture but similarly outdated. What the office lacked in cinematic authenticity Dr. Ira Schwartzman certainly made up for in his physical being, from the comfortable loafers and tan corduroy trousers to the white oxford shirt and the brown sweater with patches on the elbows. Dr. Schwartzman had one of those kind, wrinkled faces that give you the sense that you could tell him anything and he wouldn't judge you. Unfortunately, it was my plan from day one not to tell him a thing.

Dr. Schwartzman sat down in his comfortable leather chair, snapped a tiny cassette into a tiny tape recorder (he should really update to digital), and asked me if I minded if he recorded our session, explaining that sometimes he likes to revisit some topics to figure out a better way to help his patients. I told him it was alright and pulled out my own palm-sized digital recorder and asked him if he minded if I, too, recorded the proceedings. Dr. Ira seemed pleased, which I assumed meant he thought I was taking the whole therapy thing seriously. I didn't want to lower his expectations at that moment, so I just switched on my recorder and launched into my introduction.

THERAPY SESSION #1

[Partial transcript reads as follows:]

ISABEL: Dr. Schwartzman—is that what I should call you?

DR. IRA: Most of my patients call me Dr. Ira.

ISABEL: Dr. Ira it is. So, you know why I'm here, right?

DR. IRA: Why don't you tell me?

ISABEL: I have to come here. If I don't, I could go to prison. This seems better.

DR. IRA: So you're here to avoid prison? Is that what I'm hearing?

ISABEL: Yes.

DR. IRA: Is there another reason?

ISABEL: I think that's a pretty good reason.

[Long pause.[1]]

DR. IRA: How does it feel being required by law to seek therapy?

ISABEL: Not great.

DR. IRA: Can you elaborate?

ISABEL: I think that states it pretty well.

DR. IRA: Is this your first time in therapy?

ISABEL: Yes, totally.

---

[1] The first few times are extremely awkward. Ride it out. It gets easier.

[For approximately ten minutes, Dr. Ira launches into what seems like a scripted exposition about the rules of therapy. If I threaten to hurt anyone, he can report it to the police, blah, blah, blah. Then the real work begins. When he was finished, our session continued.]

DR. IRA: So is there anything you'd like to discuss?

ISABEL: I can't think of anything.

DR. IRA: Well, why don't you tell me about your family?

ISABEL: They're pretty ordinary, really. Just like any other family.

WHERE WAS I?

That was how my therapy began. I'll spare you sessions two through nine
(you'll thank me later, or not, if you like). Suffice it to say I lied to Dr.
Ira about my family, which I'm sure you've guessed already if you read either
of the previous two documents or glanced at the appendix. If not, you don't
know much about me, so maybe I should mention just a bit more.

I am a licensed private investigator who has been working for the family business, Spellman Investigations, since the age of twelve. No, that is
not a typo. It sounds fun, I know. But after decades of having your boy-
friends investigated, your bedroom searched, your phoned tapped, your
vehicle tracked, and your every move documented, it gets old. In my family,
we don't ask questions; we investigate.

After the trouble I had last year, I decided to take an extended break
from the family business. It was my job that got me into trouble, so I
figured a temporary career change might solve some of my problems.
Unfortunately, my job skills were limited, so I began working at a bar, the
Philosopher's Club, which used to be my own personal watering hole.

I assumed bartending wasn't bad work if you could get it, but I didn't
know that on a good night I could earn $200 in tips. Sure, you have to be
on your feet the whole time, but you don't have to sit on your ass in a car
for eight hours waiting for someone to leave when you know he's not going

to leave. I'm not saying that I saw a future serving drinks for a living, but I am saying it was a nice change of pace. I liked not having my parents as bosses. I liked not being concerned with what other people were doing besides what they poured down their throats.

I needed a change and I got it. As for therapy . . . I'll admit that with Dr. Ira, I didn't give it my all. I saw therapy as a punishment—which it was. There's no way I could call it anything else. So, like I would any punishment, I thought I'd simply endure it. My point is that it never occurred to me I could get anything out of therapy. At least it didn't until long after Dr. Ira decided to take a stand.

I moved into David's house on Monday at 6:00 P.M. Within the first twenty-four hours, I slept in his bed, used his electric toothbrush (I changed the head), moved the chaise longue closer to the television, drank a single shot of each liquor on the do-not-drink list,[1] and visited exactly one porn site just for the sake of his browser history.

David occupies a restored three-story Victorian all by his lonesome. Even for a married man, or a married man with two children, a couple of dogs, a cat, and a giant tropical fish tank, his 2,500-square-foot home is a lot of space, especially for anyone accustomed to San Francisco living. I made plans that week not to make plans so I could fully enjoy my brief time living in the lap of luxury.

I suppose I should mention my own living situation.

For the first eighteen years of my life, I occupied a single room on the second level of the Spellman family residence, located at 1799 Clay Street in the lower Nob Hill district of San Francisco. For the next ten years I resided in an attic apartment (approx. 700 square feet) at the very same address. At the age of twenty-eight, I decided that it was time to move out of the family home and began subletting a one-bedroom apartment (approx. 650 square feet) from Bernie Peterson, a retired police lieuten-

---

[1] Even though I'm a firm believer in not mixing booze.

ant who was friends with my uncle Ray (now deceased). Last year when Bernie was having marital difficulties, he decided to move back into that apartment. After months of being an unwelcome guest in an assortment of locations, I eventually realized that I had to find a place of my own with a lease in my name. That is when I moved into my current residence—a studio apartment (350 square feet) in the Tenderloin. My bachelor apartment is sandwiched between two other bachelor apartments, one occupied by a sixty-five-year-old retired schoolteacher with a snoring problem (Hal) and the other inhabited by a thirtysomething woman who I can only assume is a hooker; either that or she does a lot of entertaining. I don't sleep well in my apartment, and frankly, asleep is the only condition in which I don't feel like complaining about my apartment. Perhaps that explains why I was so pleased to have four weeks of vacation from my real life.

After I found some time to unwind and reorganize David's liquor cabinet,[2] I began my preliminary investigation, which consisted of ransacking my brother's office looking for some sign of foreign travel preparation. My theory was this: David is a type A, education-obsessed individual who would not consider traveling to a foreign land without taking a serious crash course in its language, culture, and key sightseeing attractions. I was looking for at least a minor collection of *Italian for Beginners* tapes and travel literature. What I found was a gun.

It wasn't in an obvious location. I should mention that. It was taped to the underside of the bottom right drawer on his desk. This was confusing for a number of reasons:

A) David has never been the gun-toting type, or even the taping-a-gun-to-the-bottom-of-a-desk-drawer type. B) David doesn't like guns; he's more of a pepper spray kind of guy. C) I knew there was a C, but frankly, the discovery of the gun was so alarming that I couldn't come up with a C at that moment.

To be honest, I had no idea what the gun meant, if anything. I was only sure of two things at the time of my discovery: David wasn't in Italy, and my investigation was far from over.

---

[2] Details to follow.

THE END OF THE ROAD

A side from my brother and my new client, Ernie Black, I had one other investigation that was perhaps the most urgent of all—a matter of life and death, come to think of it.

Morty and I agreed to have lunch that Thursday at a diner on upper Market Street. Since Morty and David both live in Russian Hill, I knew I could ask him for a ride without raising suspicion.

My octogenarian friend swung by at 11:45 A.M.—another sign of aging, I've noticed, is the taking of meals earlier and earlier in the day. Before I got into Morty's Cadillac I took a moment to inspect the exterior of his vehicle. I spotted a scratch along the front fender and another small dent on the rear bumper. Oh, and the car was filthy, which normally isn't the sort of thing I'd comment on, but Morty is not the kind of guy to drive around in a grimy car. It was simply yet another sign of neglect.

I got into the Cadillac, removed the glasses from Morty's head, and cleaned them.

"How do you not notice that they're dirty?" I asked. "They're right in front of your eyes."

"I have more important things on my mind," he replied, snatching the glasses out of my hand, returning them to his head, and pulling onto the road without checking his rearview mirror. Fortunately, no one was coming. But you can only get lucky so many times. On the fifteen-minute drive, Morty broke about half of the traffic laws out there—most significantly running a stop sign at twenty-five miles an hour and making a left turn without using his turn signal (a particular pet peeve of mine). By the time we were entering the restaurant, I'd determined that my objective during lunch would be to identify a person who had the power to take away Morty's driver's license.

"Is Ruthy still in Florida?" I asked.

"As far as I know," Morty replied.

"When is she coming back?"

" 'When hell freezes over' is her current plan."

"I see," I replied, realizing that the situation was far worse than I'd imagined. "Who is your emergency contact while she's out of town?"

"What? I don't know."

"I assume it's your son, the cardiologist."

"Sure. I guess so. He's in the south of France for the summer with his new girlfriend."

"If he's in France, he can't be your emergency contact. What other relatives do you have in the area?"

"What's with the third degree, Izzele?"

"I just think I should have the number of your emergency contact."

"My grandson. Gabe."

"You should give me his info. Do you have your phone book on you?"

Morty pulled his black book from his breast pocket. "He owns a skate shop south of Market. Here's his number. I'm sure you won't need it. I don't have plans to break my hip anytime soon."

"No one plans to break their hip," I said.

"Bah," Morty replied.

Gabe Schilling's skate shop was flanked by a high-end fashion boutique and a comic book store in South Park. I felt obliged to handle this matter in person to be sure it was taken seriously, so I drove to the shop after lunch.

I asked the pimply young male at the counter if Gabe Schilling was in. He stared at me as if I were a tax collector.

"May I ask what this is regarding?" he asked, with mock formality.

"It's a personal matter," I replied in the same tone.

The young male shifted his head toward the back of the store and dropped his professional demeanor.

"Dude, you have a visitor."

Another male in his mid- to late twenties with sloppy brown hair, tanned skin, and grease on his fingers, which he was wiping off with a rag, came to the front of the store. Unlike the kid at the counter, who I later learned was his employee, Gabe—Morty's grandson, ex–professional skateboarder (smashed his knee in a career-ending accident), current entrepreneur (one skate shop open in San Francisco, another on the way in the North Bay)—didn't eye me with the same suspicion. He smiled. It was warm and oddly familiar. He had pieces of Morty in him, I realized later, just not enough to make him seem, well, pickled or something.

"Hi. I'm Isabel Spellman, a friend of your grandfather's."

Gabe's eyes turned upward, consulting his memory. "You're Izzele? The one who goes to jail?" he said as if he were speaking to a celebrity.

"Most people call me Izzy."

"What can I do for you?"

"When was the last time you were in a car with your grandfather behind the wheel?"

"I never let him drive. He's a terrible driver."

"He's worse now."

"How much worse?"

"If he were my grandfather, I would have confiscated his keys already. But he's yours. Just go for a drive with him. If you survive, you can make up your own mind."

CASE #001[1]

CHAPTER 1

Ernie Black insisted this would be the easiest job of my career. His wife worked at his muffler shop, went to a book club now and again, occasionally took in a movie with a neighbor friend, and handled domestic duties. A couple of times a month, Linda claimed to be having lunch or shopping or both with a very old school friend named Sharon Bancroft. The friendship seemed odd for a number of reasons, but mostly because of the disparity in their social status. Sharon was married to a congressman from a well-to-do San Francisco family. "Old money," Ernie said, rubbing his thumb and fingers together. Ernie had never met Sharon, even though the women had met in grade school. But Ernie always found Sharon suspicious and he never quite understood how a politician's wife found so much time to spend with a muffler shop owner's wife. Ernie seemed a little too conscious of status for my liking, but he was older— fifty-five, according to his credit report—and maybe things like that mattered more where he came from.

Ernie gave me his wife's vital statistics so that I could run a background check if need be. But he insisted it was unnecessary. Ernie just wanted to make sure his marriage wasn't in trouble. If all she was doing during her

---

[1] This was in fact my first case as an independent contractor.

long absences was having lunch with an old friend, then Ernie could rest easy. All he wanted to know was whether his wife was having an affair or shoplifting or dealing drugs. Once I had the answer, case closed.

In light of Ernie's recent suspicions, I asked him if he'd ever followed his wife to see whether she was, in fact, only having lunch. He responded, "No, I'd never do that."

I'm fascinated by ethical distinctions like that.

On Thursday evening, after a three-hour search of David's home, just when I was about to call it a night, Ernie phoned to inform me that his wife had made plans the following day with *Sharon*. He said the woman's name as if she were an imaginary friend. We would soon find out. I agreed to be in front of his residence the following morning at 10:30 A.M.[2]

I've said this before: Surveillance is boring. Don't let the movies fool you. Watching an ordinary person live his or her life in real time is usually uneventful. They don't do things all that differently from you or me.

Linda Black exited her home at 11:10 A.M. and got into her vehicle—a ten-year-old Honda Civic. Linda was indeed a redhead, although patches of color had begun to fade near her brow. She wore her hair long and wavy, clipping it in back with a single barrette. She was approximately five foot six and slim but not skinny. An even pattern of freckles ran across her entire face. From a distance she appeared to be in her midthirties. Upon closer viewing, her real age (forty-five) was more evident. She had not shied away from the sun; through my binoculars I could see deep wrinkles framing her eyes. You could count the creases in her forehead. Still, the end result was attractive. She seemed comfortable in her skin.

Linda drove from her home in San Bruno (south of the city) to downtown San Francisco. She parked her car in the Macy's parking lot and took the elevator to the top floor. She had an hour-and-a-half lunch with the

---

[2] Linda was scheduled to leave at 11:15.

woman Ernie described as Sharon Bancroft (who appeared to be a cinematic stereotype of a congressman's wife).

I estimated Sharon's age to be within a few years of Linda's, but she'd aged less willingly. She was pale, with the skin tone and facial expressions of a porcelain doll. I concluded that Botox was her drug of choice, maybe along with diet pills, judging by her emaciated frame and the way she picked at her salad at lunch.

Even if I weren't investigating the women, I might have noticed that they were mismatched. I saw no evidence of opposites attracting. The women seemed uncomfortable with each other, their conversation strained.

After lunch, the women shopped. More accurately, Sharon displayed items for Linda, and Linda shook her head. Eventually Sharon wore down Linda's protests and bought her a scarf. The women exited Macy's and separated in the parking lot. Once Sharon was out of sight, Linda reentered the department store and returned the scarf for a store credit. Upon later examination of a similar scarf in the store, I learned that it cost close to five hundred dollars.

Something was amiss between the two women, but I couldn't say at the time whether it warranted an investigation. I was curious about their relationship, but it was hard to say what an investigation could uncover. There's only so much you can learn about someone through surveillance.

To save Ernie some money, I opted against an official report and simply called him to relay the facts of the day.

"So she was doing what she said she would be doing?" Ernie asked, sounding disappointed—not with his wife, but with himself.

"So it appears," I replied. "But I'd like to at least continue the investigation one more day, just to be sure. Call me the next time she plans another outing with Sharon."

"Okay," Ernie said.

"One more thing, Ernie. Why would Sharon buy your wife a five-hundred-dollar scarf? Is her birthday coming up?"

"Her birthday isn't for a while. May eighteenth. A five-hundred-dollar scarf?"

"Yes," I replied. "That seemed a bit odd."

"Rich people," Ernie said as if that explained everything.

"Right," I replied. "I'll talk to you later, Ernie."

That night I worked a shift at the Philosopher's Club. My dad walked in early on, ordered a drink, and instead of griping about my current state of apathy, started griping about his back. There was something showy about his delivery that put me on guard.

"Maybe you should go to a doctor or a chiropractor or something," I said, trying to be helpful.

"No, it's not that bad."

"Okay. So get some rest."

"I just need a little something to ease the pain. You know what I mean?"

"I'm not sure what you're getting at, Dad. But I don't have a prescription drug connection anymore, if you're looking to score some Vicodin."

"First of all, Isabel, Mom has a huge stash of emergency pain medication from all the dental work she had last year.[3] What I'm getting at is that it would be nice to use David's hot tub. Hand over the key and I'll leave it under the frog[4] when I leave. You won't even know I was there."

"Don't you have an extra key to David's place?"

"No. He never gave us one. I think he didn't want you and Rae to have easy access to his house."

"Maybe he didn't want you and Mom to have easy access."

Dad ignored my theory. "Hand it over," he said.

I pulled the key out of my pocket and was about to relinquish it without securing anything in return, but I caught myself just in time.

---

[3] Mom always takes the prescription but never the pills, in some sort of sick test of her pain threshold. I've been meaning to mention this to Ex-boyfriend #9, Dr. Daniel Castillo, DDS.

[4] A porcelain garden frog given to David by our eccentric Grammy Spellman.

"I'll give you the key if you lay off the lectures for a month."

"Fine. But I'm making a copy of the key so I can use the hot tub until David gets back."

"One more thing," I said, still clinging to my leverage. "You make yourself scarce when I'm around."

"Deal."

JUDAS

I returned to David's home at three A.M., after my shift. I kicked the frog, found the key, and went straight to bed. In the morning I discovered that my father had left several damp towels on the floor in the bathroom and a sinkful of unwashed dishes. Too many dishes for an afternoon snack. I called him at ten A.M., after I got my first sip of coffee.

"What the hell did you do here, Dad? Have a hot tub party?"

"It wouldn't kill you to clean up after us for once in your life," Dad replied.

"Who's us?"

"Your mother and me. We decided to spend the evening at David's place."

"Why? You have your own house."

"David's is nicer and Mom likes cooking in his kitchen. Besides, she wanted to use the hot tub, too."

My call-waiting beeped, and frankly, this conversation was over.

"Next time, clean up after yourselves. I've got to go."

Morty was on the other line. "Hello," I said.

"You rat!" Morty shouted.

"Hi, Morty."

"You tattletale. You snitch. You Judas."

"No need to waste the entire thesaurus."

"How could you tell my grandson to steal my car?"

"He took your whole car? I just told him to take your keys."

"But why?"

"You're a menace to society, Morty. You could kill yourself or someone else."

"Izzele, I've been driving for eighty-four years."

"Check your math," I replied, since Morty is exactly eighty-four years old.

"I've been driving seventy-two years, and other than a fender bender or two, and that one time I totaled the car on a light post during a windstorm in the late eighties, I haven't been in an accident."

"Then what's with all the new scrapes and dents on your Caddy?"

"Why don't you mind your own business for once? This conversation is over."

Morty hung up before I could get in another word. Five minutes later he called back.

"Where are we having lunch today?" he asked.

"You still want to have lunch with me?"

"I have to eat, don't I?"

Morty had arranged for his own transportation to Moishe's Pippic.[1] He figured my recent betrayal of trust earned him the restaurant pick for that week. When I arrived, he and his grandson, Gabe, were already seated at a back table.

"You're late," he said to me, not removing his eyes from the menu. A menu he has memorized, I might add.

I checked my watch. "Only five minutes."

"Being on time is a courtesy. It shows respect."

---

[1] In English this means "Moishe's belly button." Appetizing, huh?

I sat down opposite the two men and waited for Morty to simmer down. He didn't.

"I'm not sure if formal introductions are in order since you've already met, but I'll keep my manners. Isabel the Snitch, meet my grandson, Gabe the Car Thief." Morty then turned to Gabe and in the friendliest tone suggested, "The pastrami here is out of this world."

"Why are you being nice to him?" I asked. "He's the one who stole your car."

"Because he's family. You expect family to disappoint you."

While Gabe delivered our orders at the counter, Morty stared at his menu, pretending to ignore me.

"Stop looking at the menu. You already ordered."

Morty slapped the menu onto the table. "How am I supposed to get around now?"

"San Francisco has a fine public transportation system."

"You want me to take the bus?!" Morty shouted. "I'm extremely old; by the time I get to the bus stop, I might be dead."

"Well, if you keep driving . . ." I stopped myself short. "Look, Morty, if you need a ride someplace, call me. I'll help out when I can. I'm sure Gabe will help you out. You can always call a cab, too."

Morty's fast boil was slowing to a simmer. It was time to learn whether any progress had been made on his wife's return from Florida.

"When's Ruthy coming home?" I asked.

"Only god and Ruthy have that answer. And neither is talking to me."

"Have you called her?"

"Of course I've called her. What do you take me for? She won't speak to me. She says if I want to talk I can get on a plane and talk to her in Miami."

"Then maybe you need to go."

Out of the corner of his Coke-bottle glasses, Morty caught Gabe returning to the table with our drinks. My old friend shot me a threatening glance and changed the subject.

"Are you crazy, Izzele? I'm not taking up bingo. I've better things to do with my time," Morty said, louder than necessary.

Over lunch I learned that Gabe was none the wiser about his grandmother's extended vacation. Morty lightened up on the verbal attacks. By the end of his pastrami sandwich he was in relatively decent spirits. We parted on almost-friendly terms and I reminded Morty that he should call me should he need my services as a chauffeur.

RAE'S WAR

L ate afternoon on Thursday, a storm rolled in. Rain blanketed the city and violent winds snapped tree branches and knocked down power lines. The conditions were ideal for a quiet night in my brother's luxurious home, hunting for more murder weapons or evidence of his current whereabouts. That was my plan, at least, until my sister showed up. Rae had apparently walked the full mile and a half from 1799 Clay Street to my brother's house. Her hair was soaking wet, her yellow raincoat was beaded with water, and her sneakers made a sloshing sound as if she'd been wading in a swimming pool.

"It's brutal out there," Rae said, pushing past me.

Since my sister has a driver's license and qualified car privileges, I asked the obvious question: "Why didn't you drive here? It would make it so much easier to ask you to leave."

Rae ignored the question and comment and removed all of her wet clothing, including her socks but minus her jeans, which were soaked at the bottom. She looked over at David's fireplace and said, "We need flames." She then began loading kindling into the fireplace. She balled up some newspaper, lit a match, and tossed it on the heap. Then, without checking to see whether any of her flames stuck, she got to her feet, appearing as if she had just discovered the meaning of life.

"Oh my god, we can make real s'mores," Rae said, and ran into the kitchen. "If he doesn't have marshmallows, I'm going to kill myself," she added.

I studied Rae's fire-making project, shouted toward the kitchen, "You have to open the flue, you moron," and relit the kindling.

I entered the kitchen to find Rae searching David's pantry with crime-scene meticulousness. No shelf, no corner, no crevice, no unlabeled jar went unchecked. A solo package of graham crackers was stashed behind a can of emergency coffee.[1] From David's freezer she retrieved a half-eaten tube of dark chocolate pastilles. Rae hopped down from the stepladder she was using and said, "I know he's got marshmallows around here some-where."

"What makes you so sure?"

"Because he's got graham crackers and chocolate."

"You had to search long and hard for those items."

"That's only because he hides the stuff."

"From you?" I asked, amused that David was Rae-proofing his house.

"No," Rae replied, rolling her eyes. "From himself."

"Explanation required."

"He buys candy or other junk food and then he comes home and puts it in some random place—sometimes not even the kitchen. Something that's well sealed he might put in the hall closet or behind the dishes, or—I don't know. I haven't found all of his hiding places. Then he tries to forget where he put it."

"But why?"

"So he won't eat it," Rae said, as if it was the most obvious of answers.

"Then why does he buy it in the first place?"

"He likes candy. If he really needs a fix, he wants it around. But he doesn't want it out in the open where he'll eat it all the time."

---

[1] David doesn't make a habit of drinking coffee out of a can, but he keeps several units on hand in case of a natural disaster.

"That is so weird," I said.

"He's weirder than you think," Rae replied, and then shouted into the air. "I know where the marshmallows are! Open the garage door."

I pressed the button in the foyer and Rae quickly threw on her raincoat and stepped halfway into her sneakers. She ran into the garage and came back a few minutes later holding a bag of marshmallows sealed inside another airtight bag.

"Near his camping supplies. I knew it," Rae said.

Since Rae had already catalogued the hiding places in my brother's home, I decided to consult her on the sly.

"During your s'mores hunt, did you notice anything out of the ordinary?"

"Can you be more specific?" Rae asked.

"Anything out of place?"

"Why are you asking?"

"I'll put that fire out right now."

Sometimes a threat is the only thing that gets my sister talking.

"He's missing some camping supplies. That's all I noticed," Rae said.

While I contemplated David's missing camping equipment, Rae began toasting her marshmallows in the fire. The phone interrupted our respective activities.

"I'm not here!" Rae said.

"Where are you?" I replied as I headed for the phone.

"Not here," Rae replied with more conviction.

"I'm not lying to Mom and Dad for you."

"Just let me have my s'more and I'll be on my way."

"Hello," I said, picking up the receiver.

"Is Rae there?" Mom asked.

"She just left."

"I know you're lying. Listen to me carefully, Isabel. I don't care how you do it, but don't allow Rae to leave. She's outdone herself this time," Mom said without a hint of humor.

"I think she went to a friend's house," I replied, quickly switching my allegiance. I wanted Rae to stick around so I could uncover her crime. "No, no. I don't know which friend," I said into the receiver.

"We'll be right there," Mom said, and hung up the phone.

"Sure, I'll call you if I hear from her, but that seems unlikely. Okay, bye," I said to the already dead line.

"They bought it?" Rae asked, not quite believing my act.

"I think so," I replied, not wanting to oversell it. "What did you do this time, Rae?"

Headlights flashed through the front window and a car engine roared in the driveway.

"Did Mom call from the cell or from the house?" Rae asked.

I double-checked David's caller ID. "From the house."

"They couldn't have gotten here that fast," she said, stuffing the s'more and a few extra graham crackers in her pocket. Rae crept toward the window and peered out beneath the blind. She promptly jumped to her feet and grabbed her sneakers and raincoat by the front door. "No matter what, Isabel, just stall him for ten minutes, okay?" Rae raced through the kitchen.

"Stall who?"

"Henry!" she shouted, and then I heard the back door open and slam shut.

The doorbell rang. It was indeed Henry Stone.

"Hey, Henry. Nice to see you," I said pleasantly, hoping he was not as angry as he appeared.

Henry pushed past me and said, *"Where is she?"*

"She's not here," I replied, and then suddenly realized the better response would have been "Where's who?"

"I can smell the burnt marshmallows. Don't lie to me."

"Okay. Sorry. She was here and then she left," I said, and then deposited Rae's leftover in the trash can. "You look like you could use a drink, Henry."

"I think that's a good idea," he replied.

I served Henry the good stuff without hesitation. Then I poured myself a shot from a bottle of Jack Daniel's that had my name on it.[2]

"Your sister is ruining my life," Henry said as he sank into David's couch.

"Please continue," I said, suddenly realizing I was borrowing a phrase from Dr. Ira.

"You won't believe what she did this time."

As it turns out, I did believe it. But you can decide for yourself. Here's the story:

After the lock-changing incident was followed up by Maggie helping herself to some of Rae's candy stash and my sister swapping soy milk for Maggie's regular milk, Maggie decided to handle the "Rae situation" on her own. Without discussing her plans with Henry, the assistant district attorney used her office's resources to acquire my sister's cell phone number. She left a brief message on Rae's voice mail, having noted my sister's habit of zoning out when speeches get too long. "Meet me at the Dessertery on Polk Street at four P.M. sharp. This is Maggie."

Out of curiosity, Rae showed up, albeit fifteen minutes late. Maggie knew their meeting wouldn't go as planned when she told Rae to order anything on the menu and my sister asked for decaf coffee. Black. Maggie then suggested that perhaps the two of them could come to an understanding. Rae said she was listening. Had Maggie gone straight to her terms, which were indeed reasonable, the two women might have been able to work something out. However, Maggie began with what she believed to be a harmless preface, in which she implied that my sister's interest in Henry was more like a "crush" than (as Rae had

---

[2] Literally—my name is taped to the label. David keeps the bottle around specifically for me.

described it) a "lifelong friendship that is ultimately a meeting of two like minds."

Rae responded appropriately for someone guilty of neither jealousy nor unrequited love.

"Ewwwww," she said as loudly as one can say that word and still give it the proper tone of disgust. She then tossed a quarter on the table and said, "We're done here."

Two days later, Rae, knowing that Henry and Maggie had dinner plans that night, logged on to Henry's e-mail[3] and begged out of their evening plans. She then phoned Henry's office, claiming to be Maggie's secretary, and canceled their plans from Maggie's end. Rae's plan was discovered straightaway. It was unlike Henry to cancel a date via e-mail. In fact, the only person Henry makes plans with or communicates with primarily in that fashion is Rae.

When Henry finished his tale, or rather Maggie's, I asked the obvious question.

"Why did she toss a quarter on the table?"

"I know. I thought that was strange, too," Henry replied.

"Do you think she was paying for the coffee?"

"Maybe."

"When was the last time a cup of coffee cost a quarter?"

"She's been watching a lot of old movies lately," was Henry's answer. Then he changed the subject. "I need you to do me a favor," he said.

"Shoot."

"I need you to take care of the Rae situation."

"Why me?"

"I ask myself that question every day," Henry replied.

"Have you tried reasoning with Rae?"

"Have you?"

"Okay. I get your point. I'll have a talk with her."

---

[3] No. No one knows how she got the password.

"Talk to Maggie, too. I need a neutral third party negotiating this peace settlement. Here's her card," he said.

I studied the card as a stalling tactic. There was something on my mind, but I was debating whether to bring it up.

"You must like this Maggie woman."

"Call me crazy, but I tend to date people I like."[4]

"Ouch. I'm going to let that remark slide for now. Remember, you need me."

"Sorry. I've got a headache."

"Is it serious?"

"Nothing aspirin won't cure."

"No. With Maggie. Is it serious?"

"You have a strange way of asking questions. Seems like an unfortunate quirk for a private investigator. I hope you're better with strangers."

"I am."

"Good."

"So are you refusing to answer my question?" I asked.

"It could be serious one day. I don't know. If it were, would you have an opinion on the subject?"

"Are you asking if I have an opinion?"

Henry's spirits were not up to the task of an indirect conversation with me. "No, Isabel, I'm not asking if you have an opinion. Thank you for taking care of this matter for me. Excellent bourbon," he said, placing the empty glass on the bar and taking his leave.

Okay. For those who have read documents one and two, you might be thinking that I do have an opinion—a strong opinion—on the subject of Henry Stone and that perhaps this was a missed opportunity to voice that opin-

---

[4] I believe Henry was referring to a few of the individuals on my list of ex-boyfriends (see previous two documents for details, if you're curious).

ion. It's true. I have an opinion. For the time being, I'm going to keep it to myself.

Five minutes after Henry left, my father showed up looking for Rae. When I explained that she had left at least a half hour ago, my dad decided to make the most of his visit and used David's hot tub. After Dad relaxed his muscles, he decided to relax his mind in front of David's television. He even had the nerve to make casual conversation.

"So how have you been?" he asked.

"Can't complain," I replied, turning up the volume on the television.

Dad shouted over the laugh track. "Anything new?"

"I've almost completed my court-ordered therapy."

"I'm proud of you, Isabel." Dad said that line as if he were struggling to make it sound legitimate.

"For what?" was my response. The therapy was court-ordered; it wasn't like I set out on my own to sort out my troubles.

Dad stared at the television, hoping an answer would come to him. "Well," he said, "you didn't get into any more trouble in the meantime, did you?"

I turned to my father, perplexed. He's not exactly the kind of man to congratulate you on your misdeeds (or absence of misdeeds, in my case). I must have looked guilty rather than confused, because then he said, "You didn't, did you?"

"Noooo," I replied, and turned the volume up even more.

Another long silence extended through more bad television, accompanied by desperately encouraging laugh tracks. A commercial came on and I muted the sound.

"Seen any good movies lately?" Dad asked.

Having endured what I believed was more than a fair amount of small talk, I reminded my father of our agreement at the bar the other day, and he reminded me of all the times I had broken my word. My plans for the evening (searching David's house) were derailed by Dad's visit, but I wasn't going to let him interfere with my sleep. I phoned Mom, who phoned Dad, and finally my father was on his way. I went to bed near one A.M. As I drifted off to sleep, I contemplated reasons why David might have a gun the way some people might count sheep.

NO GOOD DEED

My phone rang at dawn the following morning. I don't know about you, but I like at least six hours of sleep a night.

"Hello?"

"Izzele. Morty here. I need a ride."

"What time is it?"

"Six A.M."

"Where do you need to go this early?"

"Nowhere. But at ten this morning, I have an appointment with your friend the dentist. I thought you could drive me."

"Why are you calling me at six A.M.?"

"So you don't make other plans. Can you drive me?"

"Sure. Okay."

"Be here at nine," Morty said.

"But your appointment is at ten."

"I like to be early."

"I don't."

"You know, the new Caddies have just come out. I could hop on over to the dealer this afternoon."

"How would you get there?"

"I'd take a cab. And then I'd leave with a brand-new four-door sedan with my name on it."

"I'll see you at nine," I said, and hung up the phone.

I tried to sleep in, but the universe was conspiring against my rest, or at least the Golden Gate Disposal and Recycling Company was. I can sleep through many things, but the piercing jingle of bottles smashing against one another is not one of them. By 6:45 I gave up on sleep.

"Isabel, what a pleasant surprise," Daniel said when he saw me and Morty enter the examination room. Ex-boyfriend #9, Daniel Castillo, DDS, gave me a warm kiss on the cheek and asked what I was doing in his office.

"She's my driver," Morty said as he seated himself in the chair.

"Are you two related?" Daniel asked.

"No," I replied.

"I'm her lawyer," Morty said.

"Lawyer?" Daniel repeated, seeming confused.

"I kept her out of jail. She owes me."

"Hey!" I shouted. "What about attorney-client privilege?"

"I'm confused," Daniel said. "Are you now working for Mr. Schilling?"

"No," I replied. "He's just not allowed to drive anymore."

"I still have my license," Morty said, giving me the evil eye. "There has been no official ruling." The last sentence was directed at Daniel.

"I see," Daniel replied, deciding that further questions were probably a bad idea. "Shall we begin the exam?"

Daniel put the bib on Morty and angled the chair back.

"Can you do anything about his teeth-sucking?" I asked.

"Mr. Schilling, try to floss after every meal. Or at least once a day."

"Ahhh onnn uck ayyy eeth," Morty said while the scaler and mirror were in his mouth.

"What? I can't understand you," I said.

"He said he doesn't suck his teeth," Daniel replied.

"He also makes this weird clicking noise, like his dentures are loose or something."

Morty once again mumbled something incomprehensible, and I turned to Daniel for translation.

"Can you go sit in the waiting room, Isabel?" Daniel asked.

"Is that what he said?"

"No. It's what I said."

Twenty minutes later, Morty left the exam room and immediately made that teeth-sucking noise.

I turned to Daniel for at least sympathy, but I got none. I guess dentists hear a wide variety of teeth-related noises all day long. I suppose you get used to it. Daniel said good-bye and gave me a list of family members who needed to make checkup appointments. He said something about getting together sometime; his wife[1] would love to have me over for dinner—the usual awkward ex exchange, although in this case I got a free toothbrush.

Upon exiting Daniel's office, Morty insisted that I take him to the store to do his weekly grocery shopping. Having never gone to the supermarket with my ancient friend before and therefore not knowing whether his ten-minute study of the decaf coffee selection, his intimate dance with the grapefruit, and his long-winded discussion at the deli counter were the true habits of an old man whose wife was on the lam or whether it was payback, I let our four-and-a-half-hour excursion (door to door) slide for the time being. However, after I dropped Morty off at his house, I decided to do a little research to be certain how to cope with my new responsibility in the future. I dropped by Gabe's skate shop.

---

[1]Don't get me started.

This time, Gabe was alone at the counter, doing something to a skateboard—no, I don't know what. The closest I've come to skateboarding is smoking pot with someone who did.

"Izzele," Gabe said, much to my annoyance.

"I'd hoped you'd stop calling me that."

"It's good to have hope. To what do I owe the pleasure?"

I leaned on the counter, suddenly feeling too tired to stand upright. "Have you ever been to a grocery store with your grandfather?"

"Sure. But it's been a while. He hates going to the store. That's why we set him up with an online delivery service. He just logs on to his computer."

"I knew it!" I said.

"Huh?" Gabe said.

"Morty's punishing me. I just spent three hours chauffeuring him to the dentist—we had to be early—and then an hour and a half in the grocery store, shopping for items that came to a grand total of forty-three dollars. Have you talked to your grandmother yet?"

I played along with Morty at the diner, but called Gabe with the inside scoop later that night. He agreed to intervene. "I'm afraid it's not very good news," Gabe replied.

Here's Morty and Ruth's conflict in a nutshell: For sixty years, Ruth Schilling, a sun worshipper at heart, lived in a city that is temperate but rarely toasty. She settled for yearly vacations in the desert or the tropics and bided her time. The Schillings made a deal. When Morty retired, they would move to a meteorological sauna. But when he turned sixty-five, he postponed his retirement another five years, then another five. Then he stuck a desk in their garage and took on a random client (like me) here and there—just enough to be able to claim he wasn't officially retired. Ruthy eventually hopped on a plane to Miami with her mah-jongg tiles, jewelry, and resort wear, and told Morty that she'd either see him in Miami or see a divorce attorney. But Morty wasn't budging and neither was Ruth.

Gabe and I compared notes and concurred that Ruth was 100 percent in the right. We therefore agreed that our responsibility in this matter was to convince Morty of that fact.

On my way to the car, after leaving Gabe's shop, I was poised to call Maggie and begin mediating the Rae situation when my mother phoned.

"I need you to come home right away," my mother said, sounding professional but urgent.

"Is it an emergency?" I asked.

Long pause. "Sure. Why not?" she replied.

I arrived at the Spellman residence fifteen minutes later.

My mother held an official-looking envelope in her hands. I'd already waited five minutes for her breaking news, and my patience was waning.

"Mom, I have to be at work in an hour. Either spill the beans or let me go."

My mother slid the envelope across the table. "You can't tell anyone. No one has seen it yet."

"What is it?" I asked, trying to place the return address.

"Rae's PSAT scores."

I opened it and studied the report. "This can't be right," I said.

SAT scoring has changed since my day, when 1600 was a perfect score. An essay question has been added, upping the total to 2000. Rae's score was 1795 (really, really high).

"I thought the same thing," replied my mom. "But I called the school. It was just a practice test, but the score is legitimate."

Mom kept talking, but I wasn't paying attention anymore.

"What was David's score? Do you remember?" I asked.

"Fourteen-eighty," Mom said.

"You are so weird, Mom. Why would you have memorized David's SAT score?"

"I checked his file[2] this morning. Yours, too, Miss Ten-Fifty."

In my defense, I was seriously stoned both times I took the SAT (and didn't break into quadruple digits on the first outing). However, my sister's score was shocking.

"If she is this smart, why is she scraping by with a B-minus average?"

"Good question," Mom replied.

"What are you going to do?" I asked.

"I don't know. But there are going to be some changes around here."

---

[2] There is indeed a file on each of the Spellman children. I wish I could say that these resemble scrapbooks, but they're really more like official dossiers—think fingerprints, not finger paintings.

PEACE TALKS

For someone officially off the job, my investigative endeavors had certainly picked up steam in recent weeks. Aside from the ongoing Ernie-Black's-not-very-suspicious-wife case (on hold until the wife actually did something suspicious), there was the mystery of the gun found in my brother's house, the mystery of my sister's surprise PSAT score, and finally, the mystery of why Maggie Mason was willing to negotiate with my tyrannical sibling.

Since Henry refused to negotiate with Rae, I was forced to play mediator in their dispute. But first, let me provide you with some background on the new couple.

Henry Stone and Maggie met on the job. Well, sort of. They met in the empty corridors of the Bryant Street criminal court building, where Maggie was roaming the halls with the stunned, aimless bearing of someone who had given up searching for a solution to her troubles. She'd been cramming for a murder trial for five sleep-deprived days.

When the trial was over—and her client was found guilty[1]—Maggie was looking forward to going home, crawling into bed, and staying there for a few days. The problem with that plan was her car: It wouldn't start. After

---

[1] "He was soooo guilty," according to Maggie. Not that she didn't wage an excellent defense.

a few failed attempts, Maggie exited her vehicle, opened the trunk, and pulled out a set of jumper cables. When she closed the trunk, she locked her keys inside. She didn't panic until she realized that she'd also locked the car door behind her, with her briefcase and cell phone inside. Maggie returned to the criminal court building, figuring that between cops and criminals she could find someone to break into her car. Henry Stone found her first.

Maggie searched the hallway with the jumper cables tossed over her shoulders like a mink stole. She was exhausted and her heart wasn't in the hunt. She sat down on a bench outside one of the many courtrooms and rested her eyes.

Henry approached the tired woman in the suit and jumper cables and asked if she needed assistance.

Henry borrowed a slim jim from the police department and broke into Maggie's car. He gave her battery a jump start and Maggie gave Henry her card.

"I owe you," she said.

A week later, they had their first date.

Five months later, I was meeting Maggie at a coffee shop across the street from her office at the Bryant Street courthouse to play mediator in her negotiations with my sister. I ordered a coffee and sat by the window, waiting for the two parties to arrive. Maggie waved at me from across the street.

On the surface, Maggie appears attractive, confident, and maybe a little conservative. As I watched her cross the street, her bearing made her almost a cliché of a high-achieving professional in her midthirties. Her gray suit and white shirt were tasteful but bland. What I liked most about Maggie was how the surface was so deceiving. Up close you might notice that she buttoned up her jacket so that you couldn't see the wrinkled shirt beneath. You might also notice that even though her hair is a shiny dark brown, several thick strands of gray have begun to emerge and she seems in no hurry to cover up this fact, even though it's the only solid evidence that she's past thirty. You might also notice that she's a compulsive foot-tapper and that if she notices you noticing, she'll try to stop.

Maggie apologized for being tardy and asked if I needed anything. I said no. Maggie suggested a refill and took my cup without further discussion. She placed her own order of a cappuccino, loaded it with three packets of sugar, and returned to the table with a giant oatmeal cookie.

"Help yourself," she said as she broke off a large piece of the cookie. "I have to get all my sugar consumption in when Henry's not around," she explained, not that eating a cookie requires explanation.

"Agent Stone. Twelve o'clock," I said, nodding my head at a man in split-toe oxfords hiding behind a newspaper.

Maggie turned and recognized her boyfriend's impeccably shined shoes. Henry, overhearing our conversation, folded the newspaper and quickly approached the table for his final debriefing.

"Remember," he said to Maggie at low volume, "always maintain eye contact. Otherwise she'll sense weakness. Be clear on your nonnegotiable points. And don't forget: The Marshmallow Rule[2] isn't on the table. Good luck."

Henry kissed Maggie on the cheek and returned to his concealed position in the corner.

Maggie checked her watch. Rae was already ten minutes late—a blatant sign of disrespect. Maggie dusted cookie crumbs off her skirt and then was distracted by another minor crisis.

"Damn it!" she said. The hem of her skirt was held together by a safety pin. "I wrote myself a note a couple weeks ago to fix that. Shit. Now I know why my boss was staring at my knees all morning. She thinks I'm a slob. 'Nice skirt,' she said. I actually said, 'Thank you.'"

Okay, so Maggie is a little bit neurotic, but in the kind of way that makes neurotic sound more like a benign genetic characteristic, in the

---

[2] Yes, I asked. Apparently, Henry no longer allows marshmallows in his home since they are one of the primary ingredients in a few of Rae's favorite and messiest recipes.

vein of detached earlobes or tongue-rolling ability, rather than a personality disorder that might require psychiatric intervention.

I decided to offer Maggie a helpful suggestion. "Next time you're at Henry's place, just leave the skirt out. By morning, your hem will be as good as new."

"I don't like it when he touches my clothes," she whispered. "You wouldn't believe how many shirts of mine he's ironed."

"Really? I think I'd look at it as a perk. Kind of like dating a dry cleaner. Wouldn't you make the most of that?"

"She's here," Maggie said, eyeing the front door.

Rae entered, wearing a black overcoat and a scarf. She looked older than I'd ever seen her before, almost like a sixteen-year-old. Her sandy blond hair was pulled into a messy ponytail and her girlish freckles had started to fade. She wore a stoic expression to mark the seriousness of this event. When the negotiations began, I had some trouble controlling my own amusement. Anyway, I recorded it all so I wouldn't forget the details.

THE NEGOTIATION

[Partial transcript reads as follows:]

ISABEL: Who would like to begin?

MAGGIE: Rae, first let me apologize for dipping into your Halloween stash.

RAE: I worked hard for that.

ISABEL: You shouldn't be trick-or-treating at your age, anyway.

RAE: I thought you were the impartial mediator.

ISABEL: Let's not drag this out. Rae, what's your first demand?

RAE: I want to watch *Doctor Who* at Henry's house every week.

MAGGIE: Why? This whole season is a snore.

[Long, hostile pause.]

ISABEL: Maggie, do you agree?

MAGGIE: No problem.

ISABEL: Your counter?

MAGGIE: I would like it if she didn't change the locks on me and Henry again.

ISABEL: She agrees to that. Anything else, Rae?

RAE: I'd like to have a constantly replenished supply of candy in my usual
    hiding place.[1]

---

[1] The hiding place where Maggie discovered the Halloween candy.

MAGGIE: Anything in particular?

RAE: Licorice, Hot Tamales, Jolly Ranchers, peanut M&M's, Milk Duds, and some dark chocolate. I hear it's good for you.

[Maggie hands Rae a piece of paper and a pen.]

MAGGIE: Write it down.

ISABEL: Maggie, your counter?

MAGGIE: I'd prefer it if you didn't swap soy milk for regular milk again. That stuff's disgusting.

ISABEL: Okay, if everyone is in agreement, I think we can call this meeting a success.

Rae passed her list of junk food supplies to Maggie with a cold formality. I could only assume that the tension would ease over time—or at least I hung on to some remaining shreds of hope. My sister asked me for a ride home and I passed her the keys and told her to wait in the car.

When Rae exited the café, Henry revealed his presence once again and approached the table.

"I better run," he said, kissing Maggie, this time on the lips. I stared out the window during this exchange. Henry thanked me for my services and departed. I put on my coat and thanked Maggie for her patience.

"You must really like him," I said.

"I do," she said convincingly. She then wrapped her cookie in a napkin and stuffed it in her pocket. "There's something I was hoping you could help me with," she said, sounding embarrassed.

"What is it?" I asked.

"I think someone is spying on me."

"Really?" I replied cautiously.

"I know. I sound like some conspiracy theory nut, but . . . my credit report has been run recently. Some previous coworkers and friends tell me they've been getting phone calls about me."

"What kind of calls?"

"My secretary said someone called asking about my schedule for the weekend. She claimed to be from a charitable organization—my secretary couldn't catch the name. But she didn't offer any more information, and that was it."

"When did the phone call happen?"

"A few days ago."

"I'll start with the credit report and we'll go from there," I said. However, I wasn't terribly concerned for Maggie's well-being. In my mind, Rae was suspect numbers one, two, and three.

Maggie suddenly realized she was fifteen minutes late. For what, she did not say. She thanked me again and raced out of the café. She jaywalked across the street without looking in either direction and, from my vantage point, cheated death.

In an hour's time, I had returned the source of so many people's troubles to the Spellman residence. Rae launched into a hearty complaint about the silent treatment she was receiving from Henry Stone.

"Not one word in the last week. Do you have any idea what it's like to have your best friend pretend you're invisible?"

"I don't. However, I've never stalked, harassed, and terrorized my best friend. So I wouldn't, would I?"

"Whatever," Rae replied, and then got up and poured herself a bowl of Cocoa Puffs.

My mother returned home as Rae finished up her afternoon snack. My sister threw her dirty dish in the sink, mentioned that she had homework to do at Ashleigh's[2] house, and asked if she could take the car. Our mother handed her the keys and told her to be home by eleven since it was a school night. I waited until Rae was out the door before I spoke my mind.

"What are you doing letting her take the car? She should be grounded after what she did to Henry and Maggie."

---

[2] Ashleigh used to be Rae's only other friend besides Henry, but in the last year her social network has greatly expanded.

"Oh, right," Mom said as if she'd forgotten to pick up eggs at the grocery store. "Slipped my mind."

If I had more energy for troubles not my own, I would have launched into a lengthy discussion with my mother about her lax parenting techniques. When I was a kid (and, yes, it does trouble me that I'm already using this phrase) I wouldn't get the keys to the family car after vandalizing someone else's property.

The truth was that my mother had other things on her mind. Brochures were now scattered across the table. Upon closer inspection, they were propaganda for Ivy League and a few other esteemed universities.

"Is that for Rae?" I asked.

"No, it's for you," Mom replied. "I refuse to give up hope."

I ignored the sarcasm. "Where'd you get those?"

"I went to a college fair. In light of Rae's test scores, there is no way in hell she's getting out of earning at least a four-year degree. At *least.*"

"She wants to run the business, Mom. She's not interested in anything else."

"She can run the business after she goes to college. By that point, she might have changed her mind."

"You can't force her to go to college."

"Oh yes, I can," Mom replied with an air of deep assurance.

"Okay, then," I replied, eager to escape whatever drama was unfolding. I didn't escape fast enough, however.

"I wouldn't kill myself over this negotiation if I were you," Mom said.

"Excuse me?" I said.

"It looks like things might be getting serious between Henry and this woman, no?"

"Maybe."

"And you're alright with that?"

"Yes."

My mother attempted a meaningful look; I did my best to pretend not to notice.

"Let me tell you something, Isabel. If you just sit there and do nothing, one day it will be too late."

"What business is this of yours?" I asked.

"I'm your mother."

"It's my life. You're just a member of the audience," I said, getting up to leave.

"Well, I want my money back!" Mom shouted after me as I headed for the front door. "Because this show sucks!"

CASE #001

CHAPTER 2

I'm sure by now you're wondering what happened to that lone case I was working on—the Case of Ernie Black's Not Terribly Suspicious Wife Who Probably Wasn't Cheating on Him. The next day, Ernie called me and mentioned his wife was seeing her friend again—the rich wife of the congressman. Ernie hinted that maybe there was an untoward relationship between the two women. It was starting to feel like he was grasping at straws because he couldn't live with the unknown (believe me, I know the feeling). Had my second day on the job gone the same as my first, Ernie would have paid me his hard-earned three hundred bucks[1] and we would have parted ways for good. But then things got interesting.

On Thursday afternoon, Linda Black met Sharon Bancroft for lunch at the Mark Hopkins hotel. I couldn't observe the actual luncheon part of the afternoon since I wasn't sure how the maître d' would take to a woman in blue jeans and a T-shirt occupying a table and drinking only water or coffee (remember, this is a bare-bones investigation—any extra costs, like a pricey lunch, would have to be preapproved by the client, and it was too

---

[1] I was giving him a special deal. Don't think I'd charge you the same.

late to go home and change clothes). So I sat in my car, across the street from Linda's car, and read the newspaper for the next hour and a half.

Don't worry. That wasn't the interesting part.

Linda and Sharon exited the Mark Hopkins hotel in tandem. Sharon passed her ticket to the valet, who retrieved her shiny new Jaguar. The women said their good-byes in the driveway. I watched Sharon half smile and give Linda a kiss on the cheek. The redhead started backward a few times, indicating that she was ready to leave, but Sharon continued to talk. When Linda finally made her escape and began walking the few blocks to her car, a sense of calm seemed to wash over her face. If my binoculars weren't deceiving me, that is.

I turned on the ignition and waited for Linda to pull out of her parking space. She was an easy tail, completely unaware of her surroundings, no sense that there was any reason that someone would follow her, which points to someone who is either overly confident or has nothing to hide. I had decided in that moment, as I watched Linda check her rearview mirror for traffic, that the only mystery here was why Linda was friends with Sharon. It was my plan to go home and inform Ernie that he could feel confident in his wife's faithfulness.

Linda pulled her Honda Civic north onto Taylor Street. As I veered onto the road after her, I was cut off by a light blue Nissan with darkened windows. Since it's always wise to keep one car length between you and your subject, I decided against laying into the horn. Linda turned left onto Sacramento, followed by the rude Nissan, followed by me. It looked like Linda was going to continue up to Van Ness Avenue and make a left, heading for the freeway—her usual route. Ernie and I agreed I should save him money at all costs, so I phoned him and asked if his wife was planning on returning home after her lunch. Ernie said Linda had just called him. She was on her way home. Since I was only a few minutes from my own home, I saw no point in continuing the surveillance.

Linda signaled for a left turn when she reached Van Ness. The Nissan was still right behind her and also signaled. The Nissan had made a U-turn on Taylor Street between California and Sacramento streets. Since California and Sacramento run parallel, there's no logical reason for the Nissan to have made a U-turn when it could have simply turned right onto California and reached the same destination. As much as I wanted to go home, this surveillance wasn't over.

The Nissan stayed on the Honda's tail from Van Ness and Sacramento all the way to Linda's residence in Burlingame. Linda never noticed her pursuer, and the pursuer never noticed me. Linda parked in her driveway; the Nissan parked a few doors down. I noted the license plate number on the Nissan and debated whether to phone Ernie or not. I opted against it, since I couldn't figure out how to ask him, without causing alarm, why someone else might be following his wife.

I returned to the Spellman household to run the license plate. Slipping past what sounded like a very serious family meeting in the living room, I gathered scraps of the conversation, including "future," "no choice," "education," and "important." I ignored Rae's pleading look and entered the office. Family conflicts had eaten up enough of my leisure time.

It took me five minutes to learn that the Honda-tailing Nissan was registered to a Robert Goodman. A common name. It could've been anyone, but I felt a tic of familiarity.

Robert Goodman?

Bob Goodman?

Bob Nogoodman, as my Dad used to call him.[2]

Bob, for a sporadic eighteen months, had been a part-time employee of Spellman Investigations. His tenure with the firm ended at least five years back, when my mother discovered that his surveillance reports were pure

---

[2] I agree, not terribly clever.

fiction. Unfortunately, Bob had few skills beyond surveillance, or, more specifically, sitting on his ass all night long.

I made a photocopy of Bob's personal information from the file and noticed a Post-it in my dad's handwriting that said, "If he doesn't answer his cell, try the 500 Club."

This might seem a little too easy, but Bob used to consider the 500 Club his own personal living room. I drove straight to Seventeenth and Guerrero, hunted for parking, and found a space adjacent to Dolores Park. When I arrived, Bob was sitting at the bar. I ordered a beer, waited a beat, and then slipped into my ploy.

"Bob? Is that you?" I asked as I guided my beer and my behind over to the bar stool next to him. Bob couldn't place me at first, so his preliminary expression was one of suspicion. Bob had never been a friendly man. Did I mention that before?[3] Then Bob remembered me.

"Oh, hey there, Izzy," Bob said without a gram of excitement.

"It's been a while," I said.

"I guess."

"How long has it been?"

"A while," said Bob, staring at the game on the TV.

"What have you been up to?" I asked, hoping to draw him into some kind of conversation.

"Nothing much."

"Are you working?"

"I'm retired."

"Right, but I thought you did some freelance stuff—security, PI work . . ."

"Not lately."

"Really?" I asked, trying to contain my skepticism.

"Really," Bob replied, finally making eye contact. He was growing suspicious. I wasn't sure how much steam I had left before the conversation would be officially over.

---

[3] Consider it mentioned.

"So, what have you been up to?" I asked.

"This and that."

Bob certainly had no reason to deny being employed. Unless, of course, his employer insisted that he sign a confidentiality agreement. Now all I had to do was find out who Bob was working for, who hired them, and why. Piece of cake.

I returned to my parents' house (once again sneaking through the window) and ran a credit report on Bob, hoping it would reveal his current employer. But Bob's primary income was from his pension, and no current employer was listed. As I slipped out the window, I began to contemplate an innocent scenario that could explain why two private investigators were surveilling one Linda Black.

DAVID'S SECRET

That same night, when I finally had David's place to myself, I poured myself a drink from the bottle of Jack Daniel's with my name on it and roamed the sprawling residence, searching for either more incriminating evidence or at least something that could explain the gun.

After an hour and a half, all I'd found was a snack-sized bag of M&M's in the back of a file cabinet and an unopened box of Red Vines in the linen closet. I thought about the "Do NOT" list, especially its "Do not sleep in my bed" dictum, and decided to refocus my investigative energies on the bedroom. I had already checked between the mattress and the box spring, rummaged through the storage bins on the top shelf of his closet, searched for false bottoms in his dresser drawers, and even scanned the floor for loose boards. Nothing.

I was about to give up on the bedroom when I grabbed a flashlight and crawled under the bed. There was nothing on the floor, but when I twisted onto my back I found a notebook stuck in the slats of the bed frame.

I'll be honest: I was hoping for something juicy like a diary, although in retrospect the idea of my brother having a diary is rather disturbing, so I guess in the end it was a good thing. Besides, even I would be racked with guilt over reading someone's diary. Not that I wouldn't do it, but I would certainly feel bad about it.

What I found was a notebook resembling a ledger. Inside I found something unexpected. It was a handwritten spreadsheet of dates, sporting events, point spreads, bets, wins, and losses. It was in my brother's handwriting and there was no way to see this notebook as anything but a gambler's record. But, obviously, the gambler was my brother, and based on the record of wins and losses, he was losing big.

I spent the rest of the evening trying to contemplate a scenario that didn't paint my brother as a compulsive gambler. The following morning I decided to give myself a break from the David investigation and involve myself in a much more enjoyable activity.

"DO NOT THROW ANY PARTIES . . ."

As you may have gathered, it was my plan to break every rule on David's "Do NOT" list. The party was the one rule I was most looking forward to breaking. However, good parties usually involve a celebratory occasion, and since birthdays, New Year's, and every other booze-oriented holiday were either long past or far away, I had to arrive at an altogether different festive theme. And then it occurred to me—a theme more festive than any other I could think of: the end of my court-ordered therapy.

I planned the party on a Friday morning. The modest guest list included the following individuals: Petra, Morty, Gabe, Daniel (Ex-boyfriend #9, the dentist) and his wife, Len and Christopher, Milo, Mom, Dad, and Rae. My paltry list of invitees confirmed a long-standing opinion of my brother's—I don't have enough friends my own age.

As if to confirm that fact, I then phoned Henry (age forty-five) to see if he and Maggie wanted to attend. The conversation went like this:

ISABEL: I'm having a party on Sunday to celebrate the end of my therapy. Want to come?

HENRY: Will Rae be there?

ISABEL: Yes.

HENRY: I respectfully decline.

ISABEL: She'll behave, I promise.

HENRY: You can't promise that.

ISABEL: I'd be happy to uninvite her.

HENRY: I'll think about it.

ISABEL: Bring Maggie, of course.

HENRY: She's on a camping trip.

ISABEL: Oh. Good. I mean, not good. But, then you know there won't be any Maggie-and-Rae conflicts. Okay, bye.

I hung up the phone and reminded myself that I was supposed to look into the credit file breach for Maggie and I had completely forgotten. I wondered what Dr. Ira would say about that. Was I being passive-aggressive? (See, I learned a few things in therapy.) I decided it was best not to bring up any new material for my final session and simply made a mental note to look into the Maggie matter as soon as possible. But first, I had a party to throw.

My best friend, Petra, arrived early with booze and snacks. I promptly marched her up the stairs into the bedroom and then the closet and demanded that she tell me what was amiss.

"Huh?" was her first reply.

I realized that she'd require more information for an informed inspection, so I mentioned my suspicions about David actually being in Europe. "Can you just look through the closet and see whether the right clothes have been taken for a European vacation?"

"I'm not sure I'm comfortable being your informant," Petra replied.

"How about a drink?" I said. "Would that make you more comfortable?"

I think Petra's own curiosity got the best of her. She gave David's wardrobe a quick peek. Then she focused on the suits, quickly filing through them.

"His Hugo Boss is here," she said.

"Intriguing," I said, although I wasn't entirely clear on why it was intriguing.

"He wouldn't go to Italy without that suit," she said.

"Why?" I replied.

"Because he's madly in love with it."

"Creepy," I said. "Could he be cheating on it with another suit?"

"It's possible," she replied. "But unlikely."

"Do you notice anything else?" I asked, realizing that Petra was itching to get out of the bedroom.

"It looks like some blue jeans are missing and some hiking boots. If that's all, I need to start making the Magic Punch,"[1] Petra said on her way out of the bedroom. I contemplated the missing suit for a few minutes, but then the doorbell rang and I realized that my revelers were going to require some attention.

Like most parties—or at least my memories of them—my End of Court-Ordered Therapy Party is best portrayed as a collage of incongruous moments. Here's how I remember it, upon reflection:

I.

[Rae, upon passing Gabe in the hallway:]

RAE: Who are you?

GABE: Gabe.

RAE: That means nothing to me.

---

[1]For recipe, see appendix.

GABE: I'm Gabe Schilling, grandson of Mort Schilling.

RAE: The old guy?

GABE: Yes.

RAE: I can see the resemblance.

GABE: Thanks.

RAE: You always go to parties with your grandpa?

II.

[As Petra came upon my mother in the kitchen:]

PETRA: Oh, hi.

MOM: Hi, Petra. How have you been?

PETRA: Okay. You?

MOM: I'm looking for toothpicks. Know where I might find them?

PETRA: Third drawer on the right.

[Awkward silence.]

III.

DAD: Tell me the truth.

LEN: Listen to me carefully. I'm about to tell you something extremely important. Pleats are over. Do not wear pleated pants under any circumstances. Do you understand me?

DAD: That means I'd have to buy an entirely new wardrobe.

CHRISTOPHER: Just new pants. The shirt is not so bad.

LEN: The shirt is okay, but I'd get rid of the shoes.

DAD: I don't know if I can do all that.

CHRISTOPHER: Baby steps. Get rid of the pleated khakis.

LEN: Deal?

DAD: Deal.

IV.

RAE: Why did you invite Daniel?

ISABEL: Because he's my friend.

RAE: You should only have to see a dentist once every six months. They shouldn't be invited to parties.

ISABEL: You're lucky you were invited.

RAE: I know there are some Red Vines hidden around here somewhere. Have you seen them?

ISABEL: No.[2] Why don't you just eat the party food?

RAE: [Some adolescent noise I can't spell.]

V.

MORTY: What?

MOM: Can I take your sweater?

MORTY: I already had one, thanks. It was delicious.

MOM: How about I refresh your drink?

MORTY: No, but I could use another ginger ale.

VI.

GABE: We should do something sometime.

ISABEL: That's so vague.

GABE: I'll try to think of something more specific.

ISABEL: Okay. But it can't be illegal because I can't handle any more court-ordered therapy.

GABE: That certainly narrows down our options.

ISABEL: Don't I know it.

---

[2] Lie.

VII.

HENRY: Rae, stop offering me junk food. If I'm hungry, I'll find something to
   eat on my own.

RAE: I'm being hospitable.

HENRY: Take your hospitality somewhere else.

RAE: Dude, you need to relax.

HENRY: How many times do I have to tell you to stop calling me "dude"?

RAE: A couple hundred times and maybe I'll stop.

VIII.

MILO: Come on, tell me what's in the punch.

PETRA: No.

MILO: Please.

PETRA: Never.

IX.

DANIEL: Very interesting crowd, Isabel.

ISABEL: Uh, thanks, I guess.

ROSA.[3] [to Daniel] Don't you think Isabel would be perfect for Mark?

DANIEL: That's a terrible idea.

ISABEL: Trust me, it's a bad idea. But thanks.

ROSA: [to Daniel] How about Jonah? He's so sweet.

DANIEL: I'd like him to stay that way.

ISABEL: Hey, I'm still here.

DANIEL: I think a congratulations is in order. Three months of therapy. You
   must be a new woman.

ISABEL: No, not so new.

---

[3] Daniel's neurosurgeon wife.

ROSA: I know! My friend Jack. He's very cute.

ISABEL: Excuse me. I need to get some more Magic Punch.

I considered my ECOT[4] party a smashing success. By the end of the night, I could almost feel the three-month cloud of therapy giving way to a clear sky. The next day I would say good-bye to Dr. Ira for good and I could barely contain my bliss.

---

[4] End of Court-Ordered Therapy.

GOOD-BYE, DR. IRA

THERAPY SESSION #12

[Partial transcript reads as follows:]

ISABEL: So this is good-bye.

DR. IRA: For you and me, it is.

ISABEL: Of course, just for you and me. Who else would it be good-bye for?

DR. IRA: There's something I need to talk to you about.

ISABEL: Right now you're wishing I brought in that cake, aren't you?

DR. IRA: No, I'm not. Listen, Isabel. There's a form that I need to fill out for the court, acknowledging that you've complied with the terms of your sentencing. I'm having some trouble filling out that form.

ISABEL: I'd be happy to fill it out for you and you could just sign it.

DR. IRA: I must admit that I've failed you, Isabel.

ISABEL: Don't say that, Dr. Ira. I think you've done a great job.

DR. IRA: We haven't begun to crack the surface of what makes you tick.

ISABEL: You underestimate yourself, Doc. A crack was made. Maybe even a dent.

DR. IRA: I don't believe so.

ISABEL: Have you been talking to my parents?

DR. IRA: As I've explained to you on numerous occasions, I do not talk about our work here with other people.

ISABEL: So, you admit work was done.

DR. IRA: [sigh] Isabel, please, I'm doing this for your own good.

ISABEL: What *are* you doing, exactly?

DR. IRA: I've arranged with the court for you to continue therapy with another doctor. It's hard for me to admit this, but I just was not the right therapist for you. My colleague, Dr. Sophia Rush, may be better suited for treating you.

ISABEL: But I'm done with therapy. According to the court documents, I just had to complete twelve sessions.

DR. IRA: Not anymore. Now you have another twelve sessions to complete— twenty-four total.

ISABEL: You can't be serious.

DR. IRA: You'll thank me later.

CASE #001

CHAPTER 3

I never did thank Dr. Ira. After my unfortunate therapy session, I returned to David's house, to the aftermath of a party that now seemed to mock me. I collected the errant bottles and cans and dropped them in the recycling bin. I cleaned a few unwashed glasses and dishes and scanned the room for other evidence of merriment. David wouldn't be home for a week, but his housekeeper was something of a snitch and I've learned from experience that she can't be bought.

As I finished up my strategic cleaning, my cell phone rang.

"Hello?"

"I'm bored."

"Who is this?"

"Izzele, did I ever tell you how annoying that is?"

"Sorry. Hi, Morty."

"I'm bored. Get me out of here."

"Where do you want to go?"

"I don't care. Anywhere. Just hurry up."

Morty is not the easiest octogenarian to entertain. Other than lunch, I have no idea what sort of leisure activity appeals to him. However, the last time I mentioned a game of shuffleboard at the community center, my aged friend went through the roof, so I opted against anything so geriatric. I decided to kill two birds and bring Morty along on my off-the-books surveillance.

Now would be a good time to tell you about my plan. After I got the feeling from Bob that the surveillance on Linda might be more involved than I previously imagined, I decided to put a tail on Bob to see if he led me to his employer. I planned my next surveillance outing for the following Monday, not knowing at the time that I'd have company. I told Morty I'd pick him up at 11:15, but I couldn't find my car until 11:35.

Allow me just a moment to enlighten you about the state of parking in San Francisco. There is none. There have been nights I've returned home and hunted for close to an hour for a space, only to expand my perimeter to nearly half a mile from my residence. In theory, my parking life should have improved during my stay at David's place, but since he left his own car in the garage and offered his driveway to a neighbor with long-term house-guests, I was out on the streets. This particular day, I thought I'd parked my car on Eddy between Hyde and Leavenworth. I found my car on Geary and Hyde with absolutely no memory of parking it there.

I honked my horn in front of Morty's house—there's no sound reason why Morty deserves door-to-door service. Besides, even after I was twenty minutes late, he made me wait another five minutes.

"I thought I should make a pit stop before we hit the road," Morty said as he got into the car. "I brought something for us to nosh on, just in case."

"Buckle up," I said.

"I invited Gabe. When he heard we were going on a stakeout, he just had to come along. He lives in the Mission, right on the way, so don't tell me it's inconvenient."

"You don't just invite someone along on surveillance. It's not like going to a movie."

Morty paused to think about it. "Actually, it kind of is."

89

We drove five minutes to Gabe's house. Morty rang the buzzer since he had to "use the little boys' room" again. It occurred to me that the time span for which Morty was capable of sitting in a car without a restroom break was most likely two hours on the outside. The drive to Burlingame was at least a half hour. This surveillance would be short-lived at best. As Gabe and his grandfather returned to my car, I reworked my plan. I made a right turn at Sixteenth and Mission and headed back north.

"Where are we going?" Morty asked, concerned that I had changed my mind.

"I need to get something at my parents' house."

"You should have thought of that sooner. Now we're going out of the way."

"Morty, when I agreed to bring you along on this surveillance, what was rule number one?"

"No singing?"

"That was rule number four."

"No dental noises?"[1]

"That was number three."

"Oh yeah. No complaining."[2]

"Thank you. I need to pick up a GPS from my parents' house, okay? I wasn't planning on using one, but since you have to pee all the time, we might not be able to stay on the subject for very long."

During the ten-minute drive to the Spellman residence, Morty regaled Gabe and me with a detailed medical discussion of his prostate issue. The speech ended with the following inspirational wisdom for his grandson: "Kid, don't think this won't happen to you. God willing you live to eighty, you have a ninety percent chance of having this very same problem. *Ninety percent.* You can just forget about sleeping through the night."

Thankfully, I reached my parents' house and was able to escape the car

---

[1] Specifically, teeth-sucking.

[2] In case you were curious, rule #2: no deli meats in the car.

and the prostate Q & A that followed the lecture. I double-parked down the block and handed Gabe the keys.

"Why don't you park in the driveway?" Morty asked. "It's empty."

"Because I don't want my parents to know I was here," I replied as I exited the vehicle.

I casually slipped along the side of my parents' residence. Remember, there's a window there with easy access to the office. I keep a milk crate nearby to ease entry. I stepped on top of the crate and listened for voices. The office appeared empty. I pushed the slightly ajar window up and threw myself over the windowsill. I toppled headfirst into the office a bit more clumsily than usual and banged my elbow on the heater.

My parents own two GPS devices, which come in handy for tracking individuals and picking up a lost tail. They're less useful if you're more interested in what the person is doing than where he or she is doing it. I opened the drawer where we house the equipment and noticed that one of the devices was already missing. I took the remaining GPS and hoped that its absence would go unnoticed. I needed the instrument just long enough for Bob Goodman to show me who he was working for.

Thirty minutes later, Morty and I were sitting in my car, parked a block away from Ernie's house. I had just sent Gabe on a research-and-reconnaissance mission. For reasons I never did establish, he'd brought his skateboard along on the surveillance. This worked in our favor. He skated down the block toward the Black residence, hunting for a car with a man sitting in it. Along the way, Gabe flipped his board a few times.

"It would never work out," Morty said with an air of authority.

"What are you talking about?" I asked.

"You know."

"I really don't."

"You and Gabe. It would never work."

"Where did this come from?"

"First of all, if you two were to last, you'd have to convert."

"To what?"

"Judaism. And that requires some studying and I know how you hate that."

"Don't you think you're rushing things?"

"Secondly, you still got it bad for that cop."

"I do not!"

"You should give the cop your number," Morty said, like he always says.

"He has my number."

"Give it to him again."

"That's enough, Morty."

Morty, apparently, doesn't understand the saying "That's enough." So he continued: "Thirdly, I don't know how his mother would feel about him dating a woman with a criminal record. And fourthly—"

Gabe skated back to the car. I had to figure out a threat that would silence the old man. "Unless you want to spend the rest of your days taking the bus or hailing cabs, you will mind your own business," I said.

"I think he likes you, Izzele, so let him down easy when the time comes," Morty said, and then pantomimed locking his mouth shut and throwing away the key.

"Did he say something to you?" I whispered right before Gabe got back into the car, but Morty was fully committed to his pantomime act.

Gabe seemed to enjoy his little adventure. He reported the facts like a professional: "A male, anywhere from fifty to fifty-five years old, about thirty pounds overweight, wearing a Raiders cap and driving a late-nineties Nissan with a Raiders bumper sticker, was parked two doors down from the Subject's residence."

"Morty, I'm going to need your help. Are you game?"

"What's my cover?" Morty asked, followed by a wink.

If I had been with Rae, we'd already be on our way home, but I was dealing with amateurs. I made it simple for them: "Morty, you distract the guy in the car while Gabe places the GPS device on the vehicle."

In response, they came up with an impressive number of questions.

"What does the car look like again?"

"It's blue. But just look for the car with a man sitting in it."

"What does the guy look like again?"

"It will be the only blue car with a man sitting in it."

"How long do I need to stall him for?"

"As long as it takes Gabe to attach the GPS."

"What if he makes me?"[3]

"Okay, so you got that out of your system now?"

"Yes, I do. Now what's my cover?"

"Just pretend you're old and lost," I said. "Scratch that. Just pretend you're lost."

"Where do I want to go?"

It wasn't pretty, but Morty and Gabe completed their assignment. Bob, who was never famous for his observational skills, had no idea that a GPS device was now safely attached to his car.

Since the GPS would be doing most of my work for me, the Schilling men and I decided to get lunch. While Morty was in the bathroom, Gabe and I planned our subtle integration of the Florida conversation. The final execution went something like this:

MORTY: How's the turkey?

ISABEL: Dry. Just the way I like it. Is the pastrami to your liking?

MORTY: Better than ever.

GABE: Better than, say, Cheerios?

MORTY: What are you getting at?

GABE: On average, for how many meals per day are you eating a bowl of Cheerios?

---

[3] Morty just wanted a chance to try out PI lingo. He was not actually concerned.

MORTY: Are you spying on me?

GABE: I had my eye on your recycling.

MORTY: Mind your own recycling.

ISABEL: That can't be healthy, Morty.

MORTY: Sometimes I slice up a banana in it.

GABE: Maybe you could slice up some broccoli, too, or maybe some zucchini.

ISABEL: Gross. I'm trying to eat here.

GABE: You can't tell me you don't miss Nana.

MORTY: Of course I miss her.

ISABEL: You call your grammy "Nana"?

GABE: You call your nana "Grammy"?

MORTY: I'm ready for a subject change.

GABE: Me, too. We know about the deal between you and Nana.

ISABEL: I thought you were a man of your word.

GABE: As a lawyer you must realize you are in breach of contract.

MORTY: That's enough out of both of you.

ISABEL: Fifty-five years of marriage and this is how you repay her.

MORTY: [furious] The discussion is over.

GABE: No, Grandpa, it isn't. You're moving to Florida whether you like it or not.

MORTY: That's it.

At this point Morty put his sandwich down, wiped his hands on his napkin, and walked out of the deli. If he were a cartoon character, steam would have been coming out of his ears. A few minutes later Morty returned to the deli and asked Gabe for cab fare. He did it with as much dignity as could be expected under the circumstances. Then he made his final, less dramatic, exit.

After Morty exited the deli on hostile terms, Gabe provided further details on what I discovered was a very firm deal made between Mr. and Mrs. Schilling. As far as I could tell, Morty was indeed in breach of contract.

Gabe and I then worked out a plan to nudge—no, steamroll—the man into moving to Florida. Essentially our strategy was to cut him off. It would be hard, but once Morty realized that he had no one in this city, he would go kicking and screaming.

Then Gabe suggested a movie. We picked up a discarded *SF Weekly* from an empty table and scanned the listings. Gabe pulled a quarter from his pocket and said, "Heads or tails. Winner chooses the movie." I chose tails and in a typical illustration of my luck, the quarter landed with George Washington faceup.

"Let me get a look at that quarter," I said, just to be certain. After inspection, I agreed it was a legitimate piece of currency.

Gabe chose a foreign film. I won't provide the name because I have no particular interest in sharing with you the torment that I endured for the first forty-five minutes. At the forty-seven-minute mark, Gabe turned to me and said, "I'm bored."

"I'm even more bored," was my reply.

"Want to make out?" Gabe asked as if he were suggesting another bowl of popcorn.

"Or we could just leave," I said, intrigued by the offer but too fore-warned by my previous conversation with Morty to entertain it in any way.

We left. I'll tell you more about Gabe later. Now it is time to update you on the Rae/Maggie/Henry Stone situation.

THE RAE/MAGGIE/HENRY
STONE SITUATION

About a week or so after I had coffee with Maggie, she left a message on my voice mail asking me whether I had looked into her breached credit report. I immediately raced over to the Spellman offices and ran her report. As you probably know, credit reports are tagged every time there's a credit inquiry. The tags are most often from lenders or landlords, and my hope was that if I saw the tag, I would be able to prove who was checking Maggie's credit.

Her credit was excellent, in case you were wondering. Less than 5 percent average balance on her credit cards and only two inquiries in the past year. No liens, no bankruptcies, no dirt whatsoever. Whoever looked was disappointed. The "whoever" was ALLCORP Corp. Yes, it is a redundant name. A little joke of my father's when he created the dummy company to use whenever our investigations required a credit inquiry. Most people don't keep track of their credit reports, and this tiny tag from something that sounds legitimate would most likely go unquestioned.

As I'd predicted, the culprit in the mini Maggie investigation was Rae. She must have pulled the report before I stepped in to mediate. It was typical fare for my sister; she wanted dirt on her archenemy du jour. I phoned her just to confirm.

"Rae, were you investigating Maggie?"

"A little bit," Rae replied nonchalantly. "You know, before the negotiation. We're getting along much better now."

"I'm glad to hear it."

I didn't mention this to Maggie right away, fearing that the mere mention of another attack from my sister might bring about another battle. However, a few days later, whatever was simmering had been removed from the burner and tossed in the bin.

My sister has the ability to make friends and enemies with the flip of a switch. About a week after my initial negotiation with Henry, Rae, and Maggie, I received a phone call from Henry asking for my assistance.

When I arrived, Maggie and Rae were seated on Henry's couch, watching a movie.

"I'm bored," Rae announced.

"Give it time," Maggie replied.

"When is it going to get funny?" Rae asked.

I circled behind Henry's couch and, to my surprise, discovered that my sister and Maggie were watching *The Pink Panther* (the original 1963 version, of course).

"We need better snack food," Maggie said, wisely.

"Something salty," Rae said. Inspector Clouseau, speaking to a colleague, spun around a globe in his office and then leaned on it for support, crashing to the floor.

"I just don't get it," Rae said in response to the brilliant on-screen pratfall.

I turned to Henry, hoping for an explanation.

"What's going on here?"

Henry pointed at Rae—seated on his couch—as if she were in the midst of committing a criminal act.

"I can't get her to leave."

"Have you asked?"

"I can't ask because I'm not speaking to her."

"Please don't tell me that you asked me all the way over here to tell Rae to leave."

Maggie checked the cupboard. "No chips," she said. "Only pretzels made from spelt. What has enriched flour[1] ever done to you?" she then said as she tossed the bag back into the cupboard with a look of distaste on her face.

"Maggie won't relay messages," Henry replied to my question, ignoring Maggie's. He then turned to the sink and began washing the three dishes that remained.

Maggie shoved Henry out of the way and grabbed the sponge and plate from his hands.

"Stop it now! I'll do my own dishes," she said with mock indignation.

Henry spun around and spotted Rae putting her feet up on the coffee table. Briefly abandoning his vow of silence against my sister, he shouted, "Rae, get your feet off the coffee table!"

Rae removed her feet and said, "Oh, so *now* you're talking to me."

"Isabel, I don't want her here all day watching movies," Henry said. "And how is it possible that she's never seen *The Pink Panther*?"

Maggie placed a clean dish on the rack and asked me, "Were you raised by wolves?"

"That's one way to look at it," I replied, but that wasn't the full story.

The Pink Panther franchise is hands-down my father's favorite canon in film.[2] But no one likes to watch movies with Dad because of his habit of interacting with the TV. Dad has most of the Pink Panther films memorized, and so he likes to perform different roles, depending on his mood. Maggie finished washing the last dish in the sink and made a silent show of it to Henry to be certain that he registered her accomplishment. She then slipped on her shoes and coat.

---

[1] Henry refuses to keep overly processed grains in his home. Refined wheat flour (aka, regular old white flour enriched with vitamins) he claims is evil. I still can't tell you what it ever did to him.

[2] Minus *Trail of the Pink Panther* and all the loosely connected films not starring Peter Sellers.

"I'll go to the store," Maggie said. "Keep watching, Rae. I've seen these films at least ten times each."

"What a complete waste of time," said Henry.

"Keep your opinions to yourself," Maggie replied.

"I'll walk with you," I said to Maggie. "I could use the air."

Once outside, it was my plan to inform Maggie of the results of my investigation. I was reluctant to mention it to her since a week had passed without incident. But Maggie had other topics on her mind that day.

"Sometimes he drives me crazy. Always hanging up my sweaters and putting my shoes by the door. All those stupid household rules."

"Just ignore them. That's what I do."

From my perspective, the silence that followed was an awkward one, but I couldn't speak for her. To be honest—which I'm not all that often, or at least not to the extent that I'm about to be, so do me a favor and don't expect this kind of honesty in the future—the whole Maggie/Henry relationship was hard on me. The fact that my sister was now making friends with Maggie was even harder. Sure, on some level it made everyone's life easier, but it also made their relationship (Maggie and Henry's) seem more permanent. The hardest part of all was that I liked Maggie. I tried not to, but I did. No matter how I turned the situation around in my head, the only solution was for me to get over Henry.

And so, right then and there, I got over him. That was it. I was moving on. Perhaps you don't believe me. But seriously, I was over him. Like that.

"Nice job solving the Rae situation," I said, breaking the silence and the debate going on inside my head.

"I learned to speak her language," Maggie replied.

"Cash, television, and junk food?"

"That's it."

I hopped around a puddle and then stepped over a single tennis shoe and a bra.

"What happens on these streets when I'm asleep?" Maggie asked.

"You do not want to know," I replied.

"Your shoe falls off and you don't notice? You decide one shoe is enough?"

"Maybe you find a better pair of shoes," I suggested.

"But why is there only one?"

"The other is probably kicked in a drain somewhere."

"One of many possibilities," she said, seeming distracted by much more than used personal items.

Then it was time to break it to her. "It was Rae," I said. "The person who ran the credit check and asked the weird questions was Rae. Premeditation, of course. You've got nothing to worry about now."

"Are you sure?"

"Yes. Aren't you relieved?" I asked.

"No, actually. I'm not," Maggie said, furrowing her brow and looking more than concerned.

"Why not?" I inquired.

"Rae may have been behind the phone calls and credit check, but now I'm being followed, or at least I think I'm being followed. Maybe not. I'm not sure," Maggie said, sounding as if she was beginning to doubt her sanity.

"What kind of car?" I asked, already cataloguing the family vehicles.

"I think an SUV one time and the other time a gray sedan. It was at night. I could only see headlights, really. Rae only drives your mother's Honda, right?"

It wasn't Rae. That was obvious. Suddenly Maggie's troubles seemed more troubling.

"Have you received any threats?"

"Nothing like that. Not yet, at least."

"Do you have any idea who it might be?" I asked, happy to refocus my mental energy.

"Not exactly. But I defend a lot of criminals, so the suspect pool is deep," Maggie replied.

"The next time something happens, give me a call. In the meantime, try to come up with a list of potential suspects from your client base and maybe we'll start looking into them."

"Thanks, Isabel. Let's keep this between you and me, if you know what I mean," Maggie said. Translation: Don't tell Henry.

"No problem."

Maggie and I returned to Stone's residence equipped with an afternoon's worth of movie-watching junk food. I decided to join in on the rest of the film festival since I couldn't think of anything better to do that day. Plus, I really enjoyed the look of disappointment on Henry's face when he realized that he could not enforce the Reading Rule[3] on a party including two full-grown adult women. Four hours later (revisiting *The Pink Panther* and *A Shot in the Dark* reaffirmed my opinion that the latter is far superior; Rae agreed, being particularly fond of Clouseau's houseboy, Kato[4]), as my eyes adjusted to something other than a television screen, Henry pulled a wool coat from his closet.

"You left this here last week," he said, handing it to me.

"Thanks," I replied, looking it over.

"A couple of the buttons were about to come loose," he said. "I fixed them."

Indeed he did. I turned to Maggie when Henry was out of earshot. "That, my friend, is how it is done."

Four hours after Henry's original phone call, I accomplished the task originally asked of me: I extracted Rae from his residence.

On the ride home (Rae had taken the bus to Henry's place), Rae turned to me with an oddly apologetic expression.

"I like Maggie," Rae said. "There, I said it. I'm sorry. But I can't help it. She's just my kind of person."

---

[3] For every hour of television watched, Henry makes Rae read for an hour. He has been known to enforce this rule on adults as well.

[4] Spelled "Cato" in subsequent films; no explanation.

"I like her, too," I replied.

"You do?"

"She's great. What's not to like?"

"I'm confused," said Rae. "Aren't you jealous? Because Mom says you got a thing for Henry."

"First of all, Rae, you keep that to yourself or I will make your life a living hell. And second of all, sometimes things don't work out the way you want them to."

"I don't know about that. Things usually work out exactly the way I want them to," Rae said with more conviction than you could possibly imagine.

SPELLMAN TROUBLES

As I exited David's house to make my shift at the Philosopher's Club, two men approached, one in a suit and tie and the other in a cardigan over a button-down shirt. Both were well groomed and appeared professional, except the man in the cardigan wore an extremely flashy pinky ring, which I found distracting and incongruous.

Pinky Ring Guy did the talking.

"Hi there. Is David home?"

"Are you a friend of his?" I asked.

"I'd say we're friends," Pinky Ring Guy said, although he didn't sound all that friendly. "Are you David's friend?"

"I'm his sister," I coldly replied. Something wasn't right about these guys, especially the one with the pinky ring. Actually, I had no business forming an opinion about the suited guy, since he hardly spoke. I could fault him for the company he kept, however.

"I didn't know David had a sister," Pinky Ring Guy said.

"You must not know him very well. Listen, I got to run. Is there something I can do for you?"

"Know when David will be back?"

"Nope," I replied.

"Tell him Joe's looking for him."

"Joe who?" (Always try to get a last name.)

"He'll know," Apparently Joe said. "Nice meeting you, sweetheart."

The two suspicious gentlemen walked away, although they appeared, oddly, to be on foot, making it impossible to take down a license plate. On my way to the Philosopher's Club I left a detailed message for David on his voice mail. And then I killed the rest of the afternoon serving drinks and concocting theories about my brother's relationship with Apparently Joe. Until my dad walked in, that is.

I served Dad his usual glass of middling red wine and waited for him to file some kind of verbal complaint against me. Instead, he picked up a discarded newspaper and pretended to read it. I knew he was pretending because his eyes met only the headline. Eventually he put down the newspaper and spoke.

"One of Rae's instructors accused her of cheating on the practice SAT. And another teacher supported her accuser," Dad said, seeming genuinely troubled.

"On what grounds?"

"That Rae is a mediocre student and nothing in her academic history would support her having scored that high."

"How does someone even cheat on the PSATs anymore? And why cheat on a test that's just a trial run for the real thing?"

"I don't know. They think she's clever enough to cheat with her access to surveillance gadgets, but not smart enough to score in the ninety-fifth percentile."

"What does Rae say?"

"Nothing. She won't confirm or deny."

"What do you mean she's not confirming or denying?"

"It's hard to explain," my dad replied, although he did try to paraphrase some of Rae's reactions to the accusations. But it's probably best if you hear it from the source. I'll get to that shortly.

After my dad finished his wine, he slipped five dollars on the counter and said, "You want to have lunch next week, Isabel?"

"Why?" I asked.

"No reason."

"Yeah, right."

"Seriously, Isabel. I'm just asking you to lunch."

"There's got to be an angle."

"Forget it. Have a nice evening, Izzy."

Dad left. An hour later Rae arrived. I served her a ginger ale and tried to get to the bottom of the situation.

"Did you cheat on the SATs?"

"The PSATs,"[1] she corrected me.

"Answer the question."

"Where are you getting your information?"

"Dad."

"Interesting," Rae replied.

"So?" I asked, leading once again back to the original question.

"I'm sorry. Where were we?"

"Why have you been accused of cheating?"

"Why is anyone ever accused of anything?"

"Why are you talking like this?"

"Like what?" she replied.

Out of frustration, I resorted to an ultimatum. "If you don't answer my question, I'm going to ask you to leave."

Rae finished her drink in a single gulp and left a dollar on the bar.

"Don't expect a tip," she said as she made her exit.

An hour later my mother called on her cell phone. In the most venomous tone, she said, "The next time your father asks you to lunch, you say yes." Then she hung up on me.

The rest of the day I had only one thought in my mind: *Is this really my life?*

---

[1] She pronounces them "Psssats."

CASE #001

To the naked eye, Linda Black wasn't doing anything wrong. But she must have been doing something to have two private investigators following her. I decided against telling Ernie about my latest information. I kept an eye on the blue Nissan's whereabouts over the next few days. If Bob's car was idling outside of Ernie's muffler shop or home, I wouldn't bother leaving the house, but on the rare occasion Linda (followed by Bob) ventured somewhere else, I'd pick up the tail. Other than the bank, lunch with a local female friend (not Sharon), and a trip to the library (where Linda used the computer but did not check out any books), the only location Mrs. Black visited was a mailbox center to check her mail.

I called Ernie that evening to ask about the rented mailbox.

"What rented mailbox?"

So Ernie didn't know about the mailbox. Ernie also couldn't come up with a plausible explanation for why his wife might require the mailbox.

It occurred to me that his wife might have some financial issues that she was hiding from him. I asked Ernie who handled their finances. Linda, of course. He didn't know how his business would have survived without her. Ernie was floored by the mailbox discovery. But his mind was still on Linda having an affair, so he molded this new information to fit his fears.

"Maybe she's using the PO box to communicate with her lover," Ernie said.

"Probably not."

I tried to get Ernie interested in the money situation, but he wasn't. Since I wasn't ready to inform Ernie about the second investigation on his wife, I asked for Linda's Social Security number and date of birth and offered to do a quick check on her finances. He didn't see what that had to do with anything, but I pushed and he agreed.

And that's how I learned that Ernie and Linda were not legally married. This took a few days to confirm. Linda Black's credit reports bore the name Linda Truesdale—according to Ernie, his wife's maiden name. Also according to Ernie, this was Linda's first marriage. But since Ernie wasn't the sharpest tool in the shed, or at least not the most suspicious, I decided to check their marriage license, which should contain each party's birth name, location of birth, and previous marital history.

I phoned Ernie to verify the location of his wedding. They traveled a short distance up the coast, stayed at a beach hotel in Marin County, and were married by one of Linda's friends, who just happened to be a minister of the Universal Life Church.[1] The wedding took place in Marin County, but there was no record in Marin. The couple lived in San Mateo County. There was no record in San Mateo County. In between San Mateo and Marin you will find San Francisco County. No record there.

I phoned Ernie again to see if maybe I had misunderstood him.

"Ernie, when you say that you're married, do you mean you're married in the legal sense, or that in your heart you're married, or that you're married in the common law sense of the word?"

---

[1] For your own free online ordination, visit www.themonastery.org.

"I mean I'm legally married with a marriage license and all that stuff."

"Could you get me a copy of your marriage license, Ernie?"

"I'm sure it's around somewhere."

"How about your tax returns?"

"Linda handles all that."

"But you should still have access to them, right?"

"I'm sure I *could* get that stuff for you, but why?"

"It's important, Ernie. I'll explain later. Just bring whatever you can by the bar sometime this week, okay?"

Two days later, Ernie dropped by in the afternoon. I served him club soda with a splash of whiskey. He's not an afternoon drinker, he informed me, as if I would consider that a credit to his character.

Ernie had never been a fan of paperwork, filing, government documents, or proofs of existence. Ernie liked working on cars, buying suits, and taking short vacations in which relaxation—not education or experience—was the key ingredient. Ernie was a simple, likable man. He was probably even a very good husband, or at least was trying to be, based on the ridiculous literature he carried with him. (The latest tome under his arm was *How to Make Women Happy Even If It Makes You Miserable: A Guide for Men.*) He was also the kind of husband one could easily dupe if one were in the business of duping husbands.

My client had only an hour to visit with me while Linda was running the shop. Ernie ran home and pulled every file from their file cabinet and brought it to the bar. I told him to chat with Milo while I perused the box. The most significant piece of paper that he pulled for me was a marriage license. It looked legitimate enough on the surface; in fact, it was—or had been once. It would be difficult to prove, but what I was holding in my hands was a doctored copy of a marriage license, with the names and dates changed to fit the parties involved. This document surely existed for Ernie's benefit alone and therefore required minimal effort to create. I didn't say anything to Ernie at the time. How do you tell a man who thinks he's been married for five years that he's not married at all? I'm all for the sport of uncovering bad news, but I've never enjoyed being the bearer of it. For the time being I would keep my silence. I searched through the rest of the box to see what else I could find.

The tax returns were enlightening. Ernie and Linda filed separately. As an employee at Ernie's muffler shop, Linda received a W-2. A legitimate-looking W-2 sat in the file, but it was under Linda's maiden name, Truesdale. It seemed safe to question Ernie on the financial matters. I interrupted him and Milo, who were in the midst of griping about Sunday's game.

"Ernie, why do you and Linda file separate tax returns?"

"Linda has had some credit problems in the past and wanted to limit my liability. Something about the IRS coming after my business."

"Did Linda legally change her name from Truesdale to Black?"

"No. I mean, people call her Mrs. Black, but on her driver's license her name is Truesdale. She said she couldn't deal with all the paperwork of a name change."

A name change is a simple procedure with a legitimate marriage license; this detail I kept to myself. It's quite possible that Linda wanted to keep her maiden name but didn't want to offend her more traditional husband.

"Do you mind if I make a couple copies of things?" I asked Ernie. "I promise I'll shred everything when I'm done."

Ernie looked to Milo for the answer. His first question was unspoken: *Can I trust her?* Milo nodded and Ernie said, "I guess so."

As I headed for Milo's office, Ernie's second question was posed.

"What is it you're looking for?" he asked.

Ernie was a nice guy and I'd made mistakes before by assuming the worst about people. I didn't want to make one again. At least, I didn't want Ernie unduly suspicious of his wife unless I was positive those suspicions were justified.

"Maybe nothing," I replied. "Just being thorough."

That evening, I studied the financial data that Ernie provided. Ernie's tax return, which included his business income, appeared legitimate enough. Only a forensic accountant could prove otherwise. Linda Black-Truesdale's two-page 1040 required only basic math and probably took her approximately ten minutes to complete. She had one W-2, took the standard "married, filing separately" deduction, and that was that. The odd part to me was that the copy kept in the file was the original. I smudged the signature to be sure.

It was impossible to point suspicion in any one direction, but the most suspicious part of the story was that Ernie and Linda were not married and it appeared that Linda was going to great lengths to convince Ernie that they were. From a practical standpoint, this didn't make any sense. In the event of a divorce, Linda would have difficulty proving community property. It only made sense if she had something to lose. I did an asset search and nothing showed up in her name. I ran a credit check, thinking if she had a bankruptcy in her wake, she might want to protect Ernie from her credit problems. But her credit was impeccable. At this point my investigation was stalled. All I knew was that there was more to the story.

But the investigation got a jump start when Bob Goodman showed up at the headquarters of RH Investigations. This might not sound like a big deal to you, but you're going to have to take my word for it. It was big. In retrospect, it was the point of no return.

Part 11

REGRESSION

WRONG TURNS

It only takes one bad decision to turn your luck sour. But what if you make several in a row? Then it might seem like you don't know how to *not* make the wrong turn. Over the next few weeks I set in motion a series of events that would eventually lead to blackmail, felonies, political intrigue, a trip to the zoo, and family therapy. I could shoulder the blame for all the chaos that ensued, but I'm unconvinced that anyone else—given the same set of circumstances—would have behaved any differently.

The first event I should mention was my meeting with the deciding judge on my restraining-order case—the case that landed me in therapy. There was this minor issue I wanted to officially clear up. As you may recall from not too long ago, Dr. Ira was convinced he could force me to continue therapy with another therapist. Shortly after my final visit with Dr. Ira, I phoned Morty to see if a therapist could really alter the terms of my plea bargain at his discretion. Morty took Dr. Ira's claims more seriously than I did and scheduled a time for both of us to meet with the judge.

At ten A.M. on a Wednesday morning, I showed up at Morty's house to pick him up for our eleven A.M. meeting (the drive, including parking, is only twenty minutes). As it turned out, Morty and I never made it to the meeting with the judge. I found my old friend suited up, ready to go—and seemingly at death's door. Twelve hours earlier, when we spoke on the phone, Morty had been grumpy but fine; this morning he was coughing relentlessly, had trouble breathing, and when I finally convinced him to let me take his temperature, it was 103. I phoned Gabe and drove Morty straight to the hospital, where he was promptly admitted. Morty was put on a high dose of Tamiflu and slept the rest of the afternoon. The doctor reminded Gabe and me that the flu in the elderly is life threatening. Morty's prognosis was positive, but he would need some time to recover. Gabe called his grandmother, who had to concede a temporary defeat in her geographic standoff with her husband. Ruth hopped on the next plane to California.

The next day I phoned the judge and made a solo appointment to discuss my situation. The meeting got off to a bad start. I was twenty minutes late because I couldn't remember where I'd parked my car again and the judge didn't take well to my tardiness. But since I was there and he had a few minutes until his next appointment, he agreed to hear me out. I explained my side of things and then the judge asked me a bunch of questions that I must have answered wrong, because he decided in favor of Dr. Ira. I left the judge's office with an overall sense of doom. Even though it was my night off at the Philosopher's Club, I decided to go there to drown my sorrows.

And just when I thought my week couldn't get any worse, Milo fired me.

This was his flimsy explanation: One day Milo would like to retire. He would like to leave the bar in the hands of someone reliable, someone who understands that bartending isn't some passing whim but a contributing element of the social machine. I suppose in an attempt to rule me out as a potential heir to the Milo empire, he decided to go with a family member. His young cousin from Ireland would be flying out next week and starting immediately, full-time. There were a couple points in Milo's revelation that I had to take issue with.

"You're Italian, Milo. What are you doing with an Irish cousin?"

"My father was from Sicily. One hundred percent Italian. My mother, half Irish, half Italian. Do you want me to make copies of the Ellis Island paperwork for you?"

"What's this cousin's name?"

"Connor O'Sullivan."

"If ever I heard a phony-sounding name—"

"You be nice to him when he shows up."

"Why don't you fire that other guy?"

"Jimmy?"

"Yeah."

"Because Jimmy doesn't have a job just sitting there waiting for him."

"Who says I do?"

"Your parents come in here every week praying for you to come back to work. They're good people and you put them through hell."

"If I didn't know you better, I'd swear you were on the take."

"I wish I got an extra paycheck for dealing with you. You can work the rest of the week and then you're done," Milo said.

"So not fair," I said.

"Izzy, you've been killing time here long enough."

KILLING TIME

y days of unsupervised visits in David's home would soon be coming to a close. I destroyed much of that evening and the following day pretty much ransacking my brother's house trying to figure out exactly what kind of trouble he was in. There were no more visits from men with pinky rings and no more weapons. In fact, I never even found bullets for the gun.

To refresh your memory (and mine), I've jotted down a list of the incriminating evidence I have against my brother.

- A gun
- A ledger
- A visit from strange men

The obvious conclusion: David had a gambling problem. But if he had a real problem, it would follow that he was having financial problems. The goons wouldn't visit him unless David wasn't paying his debt. The glitches in that theory were that A) David wasn't exactly the compulsive-gambling type, and B) David has a lot of money; it would take a long time for him to go broke.

I couldn't locate where David kept his credit card bills, so I had to settle for hunting through the mail that had piled up on the kitchen table and selected a credit card bill that already had a crack in the envelope. I happened to hold it over a pot of boiling water, and then the bill accidentally dropped out of the envelope, and when I was retrieving it to put it back in the envelope, I happened to read it.

There was a charge for a meal at the Last Supper Club, a few gas station charges, and some clothing purchases, but he had paid the previous month's balance in full. There was no evidence of debt. I was missing something. But in 2,500 square feet of residence, I wasn't sure where else to look. I called the person who knew the house almost as well as David. And no, that person was not Petra.

"What?"

"That's not how you answer a phone," I said.

"Can I help you with something?" Rae said rudely.

"Yes."

"Then speak."

"Don't talk to me like that," I said, feeling my blood start to boil.

"Chillax, will ya?"

"I don't like word hybrids. How many times do I have to tell you that?"

"Let's recap this conversation," Rae said. "*You* called *me.*"

"The next time I see you, I plan to toss you out the window," I replied.

"I'll make sure to be on the first floor."

There was a brief pause while I tried to get my anger under control.

"I have a question," I said. "Ten bucks in it for you if you answer it correctly."

"I don't want your money."

"What do you want?"

"I want Henry to start speaking to me again."

"He's not speaking to you at all?"

"He says things like 'Get your feet off the table,' 'Shut the door,' 'Please leave,' that sort of thing. But nothing friendly."

"I'll see what I can do," I replied.

"Speak," she said.

"That is so obnoxious."

"I'm waiting for your question," Rae said impatiently.

"In your many hours of hunting for snack food in David's house, do you recall an unusual hiding place, something that would be slightly out of the ordinary?"

"What exactly are you looking for?" Rae asked suspiciously.

"I'm dying for some Milk Duds," I said sarcastically.

"Then don't look in the heating vent in the guest room," Rae said. "He stopped putting things there after the M&M fiasco . . ."

I'm sure Rae's story was fascinating, but I hadn't checked the heating vent in any room, so I ended the call, grabbed a screwdriver, and raced upstairs.

This was too easy. At least that's what I was thinking when I pried the vent off the wall and found a metal box inside with a latch, but no security beyond that.

I placed the box on the floor, unhooked the latch, and lifted the lid. I probably gasped when I saw what the box contained. I stared at the items at first, not totally believing what I was seeing. A syringe and a vial, a bag of white powder, another baggy filled with weed. I couldn't believe my eyes. I simply sat there on the floor staring at this box in utter disbelief. Perfect David could not possibly be a drug addict.

He couldn't. When my eyes stopped working, my nose kicked in. There was a familiar smell emanating from the box, but not the right kind of familiar. I know what marijuana smells like. This was something else. I picked up the bag of weed and brought it to my nose.

Oregano, that was it. I opened the bag of white powder, touched a bit to my pinky, and tasted it. Sugar. I picked up the vial and realized that the contents were carefully marked as saline. With the items removed from the box I could see the letters written on its base.

GOTCHA!

I had to give David credit. Thanks to his little game, I was no closer to solving the real mystery—his current whereabouts—than I was when I first moved into his place. You'll be happy to know, however, that I not only solved the mystery (eventually), but I also got my revenge. I should mention, however, that my revenge came at a cost. That night when I fell asleep in David's bed,[1] it would be the last full night of sleep I would get for the next month.

---

[1] His bed is way better than the one in the guest room.

THE PSAT PROBLEM

I spent the next afternoon working the Ernie Black case pro bono, which made the day just a waste of time, not money.

I surveilled Linda Black for four hours on her day off and learned that the redhead probably colors her hair, likes coffee, apparently frequents libraries, and bargain-shops. There was no shoplifting, nor were there any clandestine meetings. It was a perfectly dull day.

I returned to David's house in the evening. My plan was to spend the night restoring his home to its pre-Isabel state and doing some Internet research to catch him in a lie on his return the following day.

As usual, my plans were foiled by my family. I arrived at David's house only to find my dad in the hot tub, my mom invading the kitchen, and Rae roasting s'mores in front of the fireplace.

I promptly demanded that all parties evacuate the premises. Then I threatened to call the cops. My aggressive orders were met with the following responses:

RAE: Chillax. Can I interest you in a s'more?
MOM: Are you hungry, sweetie? I'm making grilled salmon.
DAD: [when he finally surfaced from the hot tub] I needed that.

Once I gave up my futile quest for a peaceful night at "home," I used the time to uncover the latest goings-on in the family.

"So, Rae, how are you handling the cheating situation?"

"I'm handling it," Rae replied.

"What does that mean?" I asked.

"She won't confirm or deny," my mother said plainly. Yet no one seemed concerned.

Dad jumped in to defend my sister. "She's agreed to take the test again under close supervision. And then she will be vindicated."

"Why don't you defend yourself like a normal person?" I asked my sister.

"Who is to say what normal is?" Rae asked in response.

"When did you start talking like this?"

"I have no idea what you're talking about," was Rae's only reply.

"Relax, Isabel. It will all work out," said my father.

"Where does all this trust come from?" I asked my parents.

"What has she done that's so wrong?" said Mom.

"You can't be serious," I replied, and launched into a litany of Rae's crimes over the last few years. I'll spare you the wordy diatribe and provide you with the bullet points:

- Harassed her uncle. Stole his property.[1]
- Staged her own kidnapping.
- Drove without a license. Ran a man over.
- Tried to buy booze and porn from local liquor stores.[2]
- Got wasted at a party.
- Masterminded a vandalism plot against the neighbor's front yard.
- Changed the locks on Henry's apartment.
- Played mind games with Henry's girlfriend.

"But she's never been incarcerated, has she?" Mom replied.

---

[1] His lucky shirt. Which she then held for ransom.

[2] Okay, so she was doing it to help the vice squad, but no one asked her to.

. . .

After dinner, Mom and Dad cleared the table and tried to make a run for it, leaving me with all the dirty dishes. I blocked the front door, locking the deadbolt for dramatic effect, and refused to back down. Mom cooked, so it fell on Dad to do the washing up.

Once the plates were loaded into the dishwasher, my dad decided to have a nightcap before their departure. My father was spending far too much time perusing David's liquor supply. I poured him a shot of my Jack Daniel's and told him to drink up and be on his way.

"Why does this taste different?" Dad asked.

"Not sure."

True answer: "Because it's eighteen-year-old Glenlivet" (approx. $80). A discriminating houseguest can do a lot with a funnel and some free time. In case you're wondering what happened to the JD, it's in the Glenlivet bottle.

Just when I thought I was within minutes of ridding David's house of the family, the doorbell rang.

My sister rushed to answer. Surely anyone on the other side of the door was more exciting than her own kin.

"What are you doing here?" she asked upon seeing Gabe.

"What are you doing here?" he asked in the same suspicious tone.

"I was making s'mores," my sister replied, as if that were the perfect justification for her presence. It was one thing for Gabe to accompany his grandfather to a party but another entirely for him to show up unannounced at the door of the home where he knew I'd be. I knew for sure this would raise all four of my parents' eyebrows.

Since I was in no mood to watch my parents interrogate a friend of mine, I tried to keep the reintroductions brief.

"Mom, Dad, you remember Gabe Schilling, Morty's grandson. My parents were just leaving."

"We were?" my dad asked.

"Yes," I replied.

"So nice to see you again," my mother said, holding out her hand. "How is your grandfather doing?"

"He's expected to leave the hospital in a few days. My grandmother just flew back to town, so his spirits have improved."

Mom and Gabe shook hands and then my father shook his hand and I tried to use body language to move everyone toward the door.

"Well, it was great of you to come by," I said.

Sadly, the only person taking my hint was Gabe. He returned to the foyer and said, "Oh yeah. Nice seeing you all again—"

"Not you," I said. "I'm trying to get rid of the rest of them. They've been here all night."

You might find this hard to believe, but even *that* line didn't get my family anywhere in the vicinity of the front door.

"In case you were wondering, Gabe, we raised her with better manners than that," said my mom.

"No, you didn't," I said.

"Can I get you anything to drink?" my dad asked.

Gabe turned to me for instruction.

"He'll have a Jack Daniel's," I said.

My mother sat down on the couch and patted the seat next to her for Gabe. Then Rae sat down on the coffee table across from Gabe and stared at him for a second too long.

"How old are you?" she asked.

"Twenty-seven."

"Can I see some ID?"

"Rae!" I shouted.

"Isabel, why does the bottle of Jack have your name on it?" asked Dad.

"Why are you still here?" I replied. Okay, so I didn't totally give up.

"Tell me about yourself, Gabe," said my mother.

While Gabe provided a brief bio that included his rise to fame as a skateboard star and ended with the responsible-small-business-owner part, my dad made a close and suspicious study of all the amber-hued liquors in David's bar. Dad tasted the Jack Daniel's, followed by the Glenlivet, and then he had a thimbleful of the Johnnie Walker Black Label.

"Isabel, how many of these bottles have you tampered with?" Dad asked.

"I don't know," I replied impatiently. "I lost track."

"God, Isabel. That's just so . . . what's the word for it?"

"Ingenious?" I offered.

"Rude," said my mother.

"Funny," said Rae.

"Unethical," said my dad.

That's when I flipped a switch. "Unethical. Really. Is it more unethical than, say, *cheating on the SATs*?" I asked rather loudly.

"Psssats," Rae corrected me.

"Innocent people defend themselves against unjust accusations. They don't evade all direct questioning."

"She's retaking the test next week," Dad calmly interjected. "Then everything will become clear."

Rae seemed decidedly uninterested in this part of the conversation. "Are you Izzy's boyfriend?" she asked.

"Get out. All of you. Before I call the cops!"

You might be surprised to learn that they actually left shortly after my final outburst.

The door shut and I breathed in a moment of completely divine silence. Gabe broke it.

"So, you're heading home tonight?"

"Unfortunately."

"Where do you live?"

"In the Tenderloin."

"Where exactly in the Tenderloin?"

"On the corner of Eddy and Hyde."

"I'll pick you up tomorrow at seven thirty P.M."

"I'm working tomorrow."

"I'll pick you up the day after that. Same time."

"For what?"

"Dinner and a movie. No coin-toss this time. You can choose."

"Is this a date?" I asked.

"Always a pleasure, Izzele," Gabe said, stretching out his arm for what appeared to be a handshake.

"Nice seeing you again," I said.

Gabe took my hand and kissed the back of it. The move was so casual and swift someone else might not have even noticed.

THE DISCOVERY

2005 hrs

Once I had removed all the witnesses, it was time to re-create the scene of David's bar before I got my paws all over it. I had drawn a line in chalk at the level where each beverage had once been, and refilled each bottle to said line, even if the beverage it contained did not correspond to the label.

After performing a treasure hunt for all my clothes scattered about David's home, I tossed them in a laundry basket and tossed the laundry basket in the trunk of my car. Dad did a decent job cleaning up the kitchen, so I didn't bother touching up his work. Besides, if David complained about the condition I left the kitchen in, I could always blame Mom and Dad. Same went for the bathroom. I left a brief note on the sink chronicling Dad's use of the hot tub.

2255 hrs

I ventured back to my Tenderloin closet, hunted for parking for twenty-five minutes, and, in three trips, managed to unload *everything* from my car. In my neighborhood, you don't leave a ball-point pen in your vehicle.

After the third time I walked up three flights of stairs carrying at least sixty pounds of stuff (I really don't know what it was that I needed so badly at David's house), I launched myself onto my bed (which doubles as a couch and a desk and a coffee table) and closed my eyes, hoping for a moment of rest before I began to unpack. As I lay there deciding that I could unpack in the morning, my cell phone rang.

"Isabel?"

"Yes."

"It's Christopher. Am I calling too late?"

"No, not at all." It was only 11:15. I like to think of myself as a night owl.

"Interesting party, by the way," Christopher said.

"Thanks. Next time I won't invite my parents."

"Be quiet," Christopher responded. "I love your mother. She's such a devil."

"You say that like it's a good thing."

"Darling, I need my beauty sleep, so I'll cut to the chase. I have a friend moving to the Bay Area and I wanted to know if your brother might consider renting out his in-law unit—if he doesn't already have a tenant."

"What are you talking about?" I asked.

"I want to know if your brother is renting out his in-law apartment. Frankly I don't know why you're not living there instead of the dump you call home."

"You saw David's house. He doesn't have an extra apartment and he'd never rent out a room to a complete stranger—or his sister."

"Isabel. Listen carefully. Your brother has a basement apartment. I don't know what condition it's in, but based on how he keeps the rest of the house, I'm sure it's habitable."

"No, he doesn't."

"Yes, he does."

"Christopher, you've gone mad."

"Izzy, darling. I know a few things. Take my word for it."

"Let me get back to you on this," I said, and quickly hung up the phone.

I slid into my sneakers, threw on a coat, and grabbed my car keys. In ten minutes I was back at David's place.

2330 hrs

There was only one door on David's entire property that I had not passed through. In his backyard, right next to his garage, was an entrance that I had always assumed led down to a musty unfinished basement filled with leaky pipes, cobwebs, and moldy wood. The door itself was in better condition than I recalled. There were two deadbolts, but I suspected both used the same key. Had I noticed it before, I would have considered it high security for an unfinished basement, but still, I gave David the benefit of the doubt. Maybe he kept financial records down there; maybe the basement offered another entry into the house. Legitimate reasons existed for extra security, but in ten minutes I'd learn the true reason.

I entered David's place and pulled a collection of keys he kept in the pantry. I tried each one on the basement door until I was successful. Before crossing the threshold, I pulled the key from the key ring, first noting its sequence in the mix.[1]

What I discovered behind that wooden door with paint chipping off the edges was a carefully refinished one-bedroom apartment, minimally furnished. It housed a bed, a dresser, a plush brown love seat, a small work desk, and a chair. The kitchen contained a modest amount of dishes and cookware, a vintage Formica table, and diner-style chairs. The wood floors were perfectly refinished, covered with a blue and gray patterned throw rug. This place was nice enough to live in.

0045 hrs

There's a locksmith my parents have used for years now who doesn't mind being woken up in the middle of the night if you throw him an extra fifty bucks. That overpayment also includes not asking any questions. I dropped by his apartment and had him make two copies of the key. Then I returned to David's house and replaced the original. I drove home, spent twenty-five minutes hunting for a parking space, and went to bed.

---

[1] I would need to return it to its appropriate place once I made a copy.

0220 hrs

I awoke suddenly to the high-pitched sound of Eva (my probably-hooker neighbor) laughing uproariously. Her john must have been a comedian. I banged on her door and the noise quieted down. I tried to fall back asleep but Hal's snoring, which I hadn't noticed earlier but now seemed as loud as Eva's laughter, kept me awake. I got up to get a glass of water and something on the floor seemed to run past me. I can't tell you what because I didn't look that carefully. I put my sneakers on and began packing.

0350 hrs

It seemed wise to do the bulk of the move in the early hours of the morning. I decided as I packed my clothes and assembled all my necessary electronic equipment that I would keep this move light. The rest of my belongings I could put into storage. After moving three times in the past two years, I'd learned to travel light. Two large suitcases and four boxes I transferred to my car in three loads. I drove to David's house, double-parked while I unloaded my things as quietly as possible, and then parked my car four blocks away.

0450 hrs

I entered the secret apartment, unpacked for two hours, and then got into bed, exhausted. Although I couldn't pinpoint a moment in my life when I had been more tired, and even though the apartment was quiet and the bed was comfortable, I didn't fall asleep until 8:00 A.M.

0905 hrs

I awoke unrested but resolved. I phoned the landlord of my Tenderloin closet and gave notice.

SQUATTING 101

I know what you're thinking: *This is surely a bad idea.* Maybe you're even judging me as well. So, before I get into the nuts and bolts of my surreptitious new living arrangement, allow me to defend myself.

If you have read the previous document,[1] then you know that last year, I came *this* close (picture a half-inch space between my thumb and index finger) to becoming homeless. I had moved out of my parents' attic (which we can all agree was a necessary change) and began subletting from Bernie Peterson (see appendix). Bernie then moved back into his/*my!* place, forcing me out onto the streets. Without any other options, I returned to my parents' home for a few days, only to be evicted because of the restraining order filed by their next-door neighbor. At that point, I had *no* place to live. Henry Stone took pity on me and let me share his two-bedroom apartment for a few weeks. But my own brother, who lives in a three-bedroom (plus den), two-and-a-half-bath house with a separate basement apartment, *not once* offered to share his home(s) with me.

To answer your questions: 1) No, I didn't feel guilty about moving into David's extra place without telling him. 2) Also no. I had no plans to tell him about it. 3) Indefinitely. I can be very careful when I'm motivated.

. . .

---

[1] *Curse of the Spellmans*—now available in paperback!

Adjustments had to be made, of course. But for the most part, I considered that the benefits outweighed the disadvantages. For instance, I purchased a camera to monitor my brother's comings and goings. I installed the hidden camera in his driveway so that I could keep tabs on safe entry and exit times through my computer. I got a post office box and had all of my mail forwarded. Indoors, my lifestyle adjustments were simple: I used headphones instead of speakers; I washed dishes and took showers during the day while David was at work; my cell phone remained permanently on vibrate. The cost difference between living in David's apartment and my previous low-rent existence was $900 per month. The satisfaction of pulling off this epic-level deceit: priceless. Now tell me you wouldn't do the exact same thing.

According to David's lengthy instructions, I was to vacate the premises by noon the third Monday from his departure. At 10:25 A.M. I made my first surreptitious exit of the secret residence and walked three blocks to the local corner shop for provisions. Of course, once I got to the shop I completely forgot what it was that I needed. Based on my foggy thinking, I decided coffee[2] was in order and tried to think of all the items that might come in handy should I have trouble making my exit. Remember, David's movements would be a variable I could not predict. I had to be prepared to camp out for hours. I picked up canned goods and a can opener and a few cleaning supplies. And then my mind went completely blank, so I purchased the items and headed over to a camera shop on Van Ness.

I'm not a surveillance equipment connoisseur; I've always found that type decidedly geeky. I purchased the same spy-cam that my parents own, albeit the latest model and the accompanying digital video recorder. The latter purchase maxed out my credit card (but hey, free rent).

I returned to David's house and spent the next hour setting up the system.

---

[2] Don't worry, the secret apartment was equipped with a coffeemaker. Oh, but I need filters. Thanks for reminding me.

At 11:45 A.M. I turned on my computer and watched the surveillance feed on the screen. Fortunately, David's wireless Internet worked in the basement.

12:25 P.M.: A red Jeep with a plastic top, covered in grime, pulled up in front of David's residence. David exited the vehicle in extremely casual wear (not the comfortable-casual one might wear on a long flight, but more hike or picnic or safari casual). His clothing, however, was secondary: There was a sling on his arm. The man in the Jeep, also in safari casual, grabbed David's luggage and walked him to the door.

The evidence on David had been firing in so many different directions that I couldn't even begin to make sense of this new development. I waited forty-five minutes and called my brother.

"Are you back?" I asked when he answered the phone.

"Yes. I'm back," David replied. "The house looks almost tidy."

"I did my best. So, how was La Notte Bianca?"[3] I asked. I had to launch into the inquiries before David had time to rest and prepare.

"I just missed it," David replied.

"Did you have to deal with any strikes?"[4]

"Nothing that interrupted my travels," David replied.

"How was Juliet's Birthday?"[5] I asked. "You were there for that, right?"

"I didn't go to Verona," David replied.

"I see," I said, losing steam. I'd studied for this interrogation, but apparently not enough. I was running out of material.

"Isabel?"

"Yes, David?"

"I have jet lag.[6] Can we do this later?"

"Okay. Welcome home."

---

[3] White Night. An all-night festival in Rome, the second Saturday of September, just before David's visit.

[4] Labor strikes are a fact of life in Italy. There are more strikes in Italy than in any other country. It's good to check before you travel.

[5] Celebrated on September 12 in Verona.

[6] He had something, but not jet lag.

CASE #001

CHAPTER 5

For the next two days, I lived in fear of getting caught. David stayed home to nurse his injury or his jet lag or whatever else required nursing, and I tiptoed around my new apartment, trying to find quiet activities that would keep me busy. You'd think this would have been a good time to catch up on some sleep, but my body couldn't adjust to the quiet of David's neighborhood, and no matter how tired I felt, how blurry my vision became, I could not sleep.

Ernie phoned me on day three of insomnia.[1] I slipped into the closet, where I was sure the sound wouldn't carry, and sat down on the floor.

"You got any news for me?" Ernie asked.

"I still have to look into a few matters," I replied, trying to remember what those matters were.

"Are you in a tunnel?" Ernie asked.

"No," I answered. I should have come up with some plausible explanation for the sound quality, but I didn't have it in me.

"So, Izzy, I need you to give it to me straight. Okay?"

"Absolutely, Ernie."

"Do you think Linda has got some other husband somewhere?"

---

[1] The phone was on vibrate, don't worry.

Sleep deprivation is just like being drunk, if you ask me. Suffice it to say, I found Ernie's last remark utterly hilarious. I put the phone on mute and tried to expel all the laughter out of my system.

When I was done, I calmly replied, "What would make you ask that?"

"You were looking at our marriage certificate, so I thought it had to be something about us being married."

"Don't jump to conclusions, Ernie. Let me do that."

"So, you don't think she's got another husband somewhere?"

"I doubt it," I replied.

"How sure are you?" he asked.

I proceeded to ask Ernie a few questions along the lines of how often he and his wife had been apart in the last five years, which led to me stating the obvious:

"Ernie, you and Linda haven't been apart more than, say, eight to ten hours at a time in the last five years. How on earth could she have another husband?"

"Good point," Ernie said.

"Has anything transpired in the last few days that you need to tell me about?" I asked.

It sounded for a moment like the phone had gone dead, but then Ernie spoke.

"Me and Linda got in a fight the other night," he said reluctantly.

"What about?" I asked.

"Socks and dishes and stuff."

"Excuse me?"

"She thinks I don't clean up enough after myself."

"Well, do you?"

"Probably not," he replied.

"Well, maybe you should just pick up your socks and do a few more dishes and then you won't fight about it anymore."

"It's something to consider," Ernie said. "Just let me know when you have any more details. I'm getting a little anxious."

I decided to put Ernie at ease. His fears were not the topic of this investigation, although I still didn't know what that topic was.

"Ernie, I'm almost positive it's not another man."

"Well, that's a load off my mind," Ernie said. "Call me when you know something."

"I will," I replied. But, as you know, it was a lie. I already knew something and I kept it from Ernie.

NEW DAVID

A few days after my brother's return, my mother demanded a family dinner—at David's house, now that she'd discovered its superiority to her own home. I bowed out with the fortunate excuse of having a shift at the Philosopher's Club (my very last shift). My mother said a pleasant good-bye and uttered something like "Maybe next time." Fifteen minutes later, Milo phoned and informed me that he would not need my services that evening. When pressed on whether my mother was behind his decision, Milo pled the fifth.

While I had observed my brother through a camera the last few days, I hadn't yet seen him in person. I waited for all the Spellmans to arrive before I made my exit and entrance. I figured their presence would provide enough distraction to keep any suspicious eyes off of me.

Through my hidden camera, I spotted my parents pulling up the driveway. I gave them ten minutes to get settled and then I slipped out of my new home, stealthily walked along the side of David's house, scanned the periphery for nosy neighbors, and then casually walked up the steps to David's house. I'd toyed earlier in the day with bringing a bottle of wine from David's own wine closet, but I decided that if this new living arrangement of mine was going to work, I would have to show some restraint.

My father opened the door. His forehead was creased a bit more than usual. The result was an expression of concern, but not with me. I entered and heard my mother in the kitchen interrogating my brother.

"Have you seen a doctor?" Mom asked.

"Yes, when it happened," David insisted.

"Have you seen an American doctor?"

"Yes."

"When?"

"This afternoon."

That was most definitely a lie; David had been home all day long.

"How much weight did you lose?" my mom then asked, continuing her investigation.

"Mom, calm down. I'm not dying," David replied.

"Sit down and start eating right away."

I followed my father into the kitchen and saw Rae seated in a chair staring at my brother as if he were a stranger. And it was then that I finally saw up close what was worrying my family.

Old David, the one of four weeks ago, had an almost blinding glow of health. He was the cover shot on a men's magazine. His skin was flawless, his posture perfect; his clothes often appeared as if they'd just been released from the dry-cleaning wrapper. But this man, slumped in a chair in his kitchen, looked like my brother if he had been living on the streets for the past four weeks. Not to mention the blue cast on his left arm in the canvas sling.

New David, approximately twenty pounds lighter, wore his clothes like a stranger. His Levi's hung off his hips; his T-shirt and sweater crinkled with the extra space. David's hair had grown longer and unkempt; he sported a beard, I suspect to hide his sallow cheeks—or because shaving is difficult when one's dominant arm isn't working. Bluntly, David looked unwell. My mother's concern, regardless of whether it was stronger than necessary, was certainly warranted.

After I took in the spectacle of my new and unimproved brother, it was time for me to comment.

"Some vacation."

"What happened to 'hello'?" David asked, commenting on my manners.

"Sorry," I replied. "Welcome back. It's so nice to have you home."

"Liar," David replied.

"How'd you break your arm?" I asked.

"He fell on the steps of the Vatican," said my mom. "Can you believe that?"

"No," I replied. "How much weight did you lose?"

"About fifteen pounds."

"In four weeks? That's so unfair."

"I had food poisoning," David clarified.

"Eating what?"

Pause. "Fish."

"What kind of fish?"

"Ceviche."

"Excellent answer. A dish famous for its food-poisoning potential."

"Speaking of food poisoning, I'm starving," said Dad.

"Me, too. I could eat an entire one-pound bag of M&M's," Rae chimed in.

While Mom cooked in the kitchen, Rae and my dad foraged through the refrigerator, looking for something to quiet their appetites. Finally David and I were alone and able to speak freely.

"Bravo," I said after a pregnant pause.

David smiled. He liked having his handiwork acknowledged. "I have to know: In what order did you find my evidence?"

"The gun, the ledger, the drugs. Nice touch with the basil."

"You didn't try to smoke it, did you?"

"You do something once when you're thirteen and nobody lets you forget it."

"I couldn't resist," David replied. "So, when did you decide I had a gambling problem?"

"After your goons dropped by. I'm guessing golf buddies?"

"Basketball."

"So, where were you? Because I know you weren't in Italy."

"Are you sure you don't want to go another round of Italian Internet trivia? I'd be happy to give you a few days to study."

"Seriously, David. You'd never go to Italy without your Hugo Boss suit. Word on the street is that you're madly in love with it."

"Whose word?"

"First, I'd like credit for not commenting on your bizarre relationship with clothing."

Rae returned to the living room with a bowl of pretzels and sat down on the sofa in between me and David. I wasn't interested in bringing Rae into my investigation, so I let the subject drop and pretended to be fascinated by David's phony vacation.

"There's only one person who had enough information about my wardrobe to know when a piece is missing. Was Petra here?"

"She came to the party," Rae said with a mouth full of pretzel mush.

"Rat!" I shouted.

Rae at least finished chewing before landing her retort: "Unemployed!"

"Cheater!"

Apparently sound travels farther in David's house than I thought. My dad promptly exited the kitchen and said, "Nothing has been proven yet!"

David turned to his bar for comfort and pulled a bottle of whiskey for a drink. After careful scrutiny of the liquor cabinet, which I had apparently restored too closely to its appearance at the point of David's departure, my brother grew suspicious and then certain.

"Isabel, when are you going to behave like a grown-up?"

"When you treat me like one."

Over dinner David was caught up on the latest goings-on in this ball of deceit we call a family. My mother became briefly suspicious when Rae asked David if he brought her back any Italian candy and David apologized and said it had slipped his mind, a violation of David's lifelong tradition of bringing Rae candy from all his vacation spots. However, even though I could see my mother's suspicion beat like a drum throughout the evening, she remained mute on the subject. I found this particularly annoying but true to form. David has always received the full spectrum of respect from my parents, which is totally unfair.

What sparked the most conversation during dinner was the extension of my forced therapy. David found great joy in this discovery, and whatever exhaustion his mysterious illness and vacation had caused, this particular topic seemed to have a salubrious[1] effect on him. Glowing as if he had won some great victory, David decided to add his two cents.

"You know, Isabel, maybe this time you should actually talk about your troubles."

I smiled sheepishly, allowing David his petty pleasure. I was going to inhabit his basement rent free. My victory was much sweeter.

After dinner, Rae informed David that his secret junk food stashes needed to be replenished. David left the kitchen and returned ten minutes later with an airtight container holding a mixed array of individual-sized candy. If David were fifteen years younger, I would have accused him of robbing a trick-or-treater. My sister wanted to know what secret hiding place she'd failed to discover and David refused to answer even when her pleas went beyond what would have been my breaking point.

Then Dad asked me to lunch. Well, first he asked David, who was really swamped that week, having just returned home. Then he asked Rae, who explained to Dad that during lunch hour she was usually in school, but if he wanted to give her an afternoon reprieve, she'd be happy to join him. Then Dad asked me. I watched Mom shift her head slightly and eye me from the other side of the room, so I didn't even think of saying no.

"Sure, Dad. Name the time and the place and I'll be there."

---

[1] One of Rae's PSAT words. I helped her study.

"There's no need for sarcasm, Isabel."

"Huh?"

"If you don't have the time or the inclination to have lunch with me, you can just say no."

"But I just said yes."

"Really?" Dad replied skeptically.

"Yes, really."

"What gives?" he asked, which was actually kind of annoying, and I was ready to change my mind. But then I took another look at Mom and decided against it.

"Well, Dad, right around lunchtime, I tend to get hungry. So, I figure you're buying, right?"

"Right."

"Why don't you pick me up from therapy tomorrow afternoon? I'll tell you all about it."

HELLO, DR. RUSH

THERAPY SESSION #13

My new therapist's office was located in the Avenues off California Street. The level of convenience was comparable, which I suppose my previous doctor considered, but this location made driving a reasonable option if I wasn't in the mood for public transportation. However, on this day I took the bus, since my father was picking me up.

I busied myself before, during, and after my session by making up a mental compare-and-contrast sheet between my two therapists. This I did in lieu of any real "work," which I would later learn was a term used to define the effort one puts into the uncovering and confronting of personal demons. It's not like I didn't think I had any demons. I did, but I could name them—and even provide an address and telephone number for each. As far as I was concerned, those demons could go to therapy instead of me.

Dr. Sophia Rush's waiting room had better magazines than Dr. Ira's. She also had a little self-serve coffee/tea station and a relaxing fountain, which I would later realize had less to do with relaxation and more to do with drowning out the sounds of therapy in the other room. She also had a cool key-code system for entering the waiting room, which I found very satisfying.

I was so preoccupied with noting the differences between Dr. Ira and Dr. Rush that any pre-therapy anxiety didn't surface until Dr. Rush finally made her entrance.

While I had no expectations or a preconceived visual concept of her appearance, my first reaction was *This can't be Dr. Rush.* I guessed her age to be forty-five based on the diplomas on the wall, but she was one of those really well-preserved forty-fives. Or an imposter. She was dark and Italian-looking and very attractive, yet I got the feeling she went out of her way to hide it, or at least didn't flaunt it. I doubt she had anything on her face other than moisturizer and her wardrobe was neither bland nor stylish. She wore simple, well-cut trousers, a plain but tailored crewneck T-shirt in a finer fabric than necessary, and a cardigan sweater. The result was something that wouldn't distract. Her office décor followed a similar code. It didn't strike me as empty and yet there was nothing in it that I found terribly compelling. By contrast, I could stare at the overloaded bookcase in Dr. Ira's office for hours, calculating its weak spots, debating whether it was secured to the wall, wondering how it would fall and if Dr. Ira would survive in the inevitable massive earthquake that has been hanging over our heads for years.

But that's enough talk about inanimate objects; let me get to the therapy session.

[Partial transcript reads as follows:]

DR. RUSH: Isabel?

ISABEL: Yes.

DR. RUSH: I wasn't sure if you'd make it.

ISABEL: I didn't think I had a choice.

DR. RUSH: We always have a choice.

ISABEL: I don't think so.

DR. RUSH: Sit down.

I sat down. So maybe she had a point. I had the option to not sit down, but that would have been awkward.

[Long pause.[1]]

DR. RUSH: I take it you're not happy to be here.

ISABEL: I served my time. I should be free by now.

DR. RUSH: Are you associating therapy with incarceration?

ISABEL: Not exactly.

DR. RUSH: Would you like to tell me how you do perceive your sentencing?

ISABEL: I know what I did last year was wrong.

DR. RUSH: I'd like to hear about it in your own words. I've only gotten this information secondhand.

ISABEL: In a nutshell, I found my parents' neighbor suspicious and couldn't stop investigating him. He filed a restraining order, which I broke. I admit that the charges against me were legitimate and I even thought that the original terms of my plea bargain were fair. But I met those terms. I saw Dr. Ira once a week for three months straight. You can't go around changing the rules. I mean, what if you decide after twelve sessions that I'm not cured and I need another twelve?

DR. RUSH: I can guarantee you won't be cured.

ISABEL: *Great.*

DR. RUSH: I don't cure people. I'm just a tour guide, so to speak.

ISABEL: Yes, but what happens when we finish the tour? Will you make me go on another one? I took a tour through Alcatraz once. It was fun. Doesn't mean I want to do it once a week, indefinitely.

DR. RUSH: Interesting that you bring back a prison-related reference.

ISABEL: My family doesn't go to museums. The tour options were limited. I suppose I could have gone with an aquarium analogy.

DR. RUSH: How about we make a deal?

ISABEL: What kind of deal?

DR. RUSH: I promise you that when your twelve sessions are up with me, we're done.

ISABEL: What's the hitch?

DR. RUSH: The next time you step through that door, bring an open mind.

---

[1] At this point in the game, I didn't find the pause in any way awkward.

LUNCH WITH DAD

My father picked me up from therapy and drove directly to No-Name Sushi[1] in the Mission. My dad's sudden and recent interest in longevity prompted a massive U-turn in his dietary habits. Sushi had not been a staple of my father's diet until very recently. I say this only because it justifies, or at least partially explains, his refusal to use chopsticks. Instead of using his fingers, Dad asks for a fork and knife, which makes sitting through a sushi meal with him a tad on the embarrassing side.

"What's new?" Dad asked, slicing into his salmon nigiri like a filet mignon.

Well, all sorts of things were new. I had a new therapist and now eleven more therapy sessions in my future. I had a new secret home. I had a new case I was working on. I even had new shoes, but somehow the adolescent in me surfaced and I found myself immediately on guard.

"Nothing," I said.

"Something has to be new," my father insisted.

"I'm not great with vague questions like that."

"Would you like me to be more specific?"

"Not really." Truth is, I'm not great with specific questions, either.

I was getting the feeling that Dad hadn't invited me to lunch because

---
[1] It seriously has no name.

he couldn't find anyone else to eat with. This lunch was supposed to be meaningful.

"Are you happy?" my dad asked.

See? I told you this would happen.

"If this is going to be one of those conversations, I'm going to need a drink," I said.

I ordered a large sake and downed two thimblefuls while holding up my pointer finger, instructing my father that he wasn't allowed to speak until I was done.

"What were you saying?" I asked after the second thimble.

My dad first looked annoyed, then disappointed, and then his expression suddenly shifted to some kind of sympathy/concern hybrid. Frankly, I was more comfortable with the first two expressions.

"Why is this so hard for you? Is it me? Or do you have this problem with everyone?" Dad asked.

"Oh, it's everyone," I said, but then I felt the need to clarify. "However, most people learn their lesson after one or two conversations with me and then quit with the honest and open communication."

"Now that you're back in therapy, maybe this is something you can work on."

"Sure," I replied. "I'll put it in the queue."

Had I wanted to answer any of my dad's questions with full disclosure, I had an endless supply of material. To refresh your memory: I had moved into my brother's house without his knowledge, I was recently fired from my primary source of income, one of my best friends was in the hospital and soon would have to move to Florida, and then there was the Henry Stone situation, which I really don't feel like going into right now.

After lunch, Dad offered to give me a ride home. My first response was, "Sure," because I never turn down offers of free transportation, but then I realized that I'd have to go to the home that Dad thinks is my home, and since I didn't want to go anywhere in that vicinity, I decided to take a Muni train instead. I kissed my dad on the cheek and almost made my exit. But then my father asked me the oddest question: "Do you want to do this again next week?"

MORE MAGGIE

Before my phone lost reception in the Muni tunnel, I got a call from Maggie. She wanted to meet me later for a drink. She had something to discuss. I agreed, since the time she suggested—happy hour—was a tricky time for me to enter or exit David's house.

I suggested we meet at the Philosopher's Club so I could get a peek at Milo's Irish cousin, heir to the Milo kingdom.

Connor, black Irish and handsome in a way that's so obvious it's annoying, stood behind the bar, regaling the two customers—Clarence and Orson—with some story about the potato famine or something. I'm pretty sure he was speaking English, but his accent was so thick, I could barely make out a word.

I sat down at the other end of the bar and waited for him to finish his story and serve the customers like he was supposed to. His story might not have been about the famine after all, since its close was punctuated by uproarious laughter. Connor made a silent motion to Clarence's and Orson's glasses, asking them if they were good for now, and then he made his way over to me, his left hand sliding along the bar the whole way. As if he was marking his territory.

"At can eye getcha, orgeous?"

"Excuse me?" I asked, although I could have translated.

"At urr ya drinkin?"

"Guinness," I said, because it really annoys Milo when I order that.

"My kinda girl," Connor said, and winked. As he pulled the pint, he looked me over and smiled.

"Ya wouldn't be Isabel, wouldya?"

"I wouldn't be if I had any say in the matter."

Connor served my drink, held out his hand, and said, "A pleasure."

Then Milo exited his office and shouted into our general vicinity, "You be nice, Izzy."

"I'm nice," I said very rudely to Milo.

"Let me tell you about this one here," Milo said, preparing to launch into some sort of long-winded character study of me. Fortunately, Maggie entered the bar and spared me the details.

She ordered a pint of something easier to pull and we sat down at a corner table, out of anyone's earshot.

"Thanks for meeting me," Maggie said while reaching into her purse.

"What's going on? Are you still being followed?"

"Oh yeah, but I didn't ask you here to talk about that."

"So, what's up?" I asked, maybe a little confused.

"I'm going to kill Henry."

Uncomfortable silence.

"But you haven't yet, right?" I asked.

"No, but I spend most days thinking about it."

"What did he do?"

"He cleaned my entire apartment while I was on a camping trip," Maggie said as if she were relaying the details of a sordid affair.

Long pause. "And . . . ?" I asked.

"There's no more. That's it," Maggie said, the tension mounting on her face.

"Does he not have a key to your place?"

"He has a key," she replied.

"Do you have strict rules about when he can come and go?"

"No. He also organized my sock drawer."

"Did it need organizing?"

"He replaced the herbs in my spice rack. Said something like 'They're no good after two years.' Bullshit. My mother's got spices that are twenty years old. Did I mention that?"

"You didn't," I replied. "I see how that might complicate matters," I added, just to be sympathetic.

"What am I supposed to do?" Maggie asked.

"I'm not sure I see the problem," the good me replied.

Now imagine a small Isabel on my shoulder in a red jumpsuit, carrying a pitchfork, whispering, "Break up with him, break up with him." You get the picture. I was keeping Devil Isabel at bay, but it wasn't easy.

"The problem is," said Maggie, still fuming so intensely you could practically see the smoke, "it's so passive-aggressive."

"How so?"

"It's like he's saying I don't know how to take care of my own home."[1]

Devil Isabel kept me silent a little too long. I was in a pickle here and I had to overplay my part to make sure I could release myself from guilt at a later date. All that aside, this is how I responded to Maggie's conflict. I think you will agree this was a mature, selfless, and accurate response.[2]

"I think Henry thought it might be nice for you to come back from your trip to a clean home. He's not judging you. I know Henry. He likes to clean. He can't stop himself. There's no agenda beyond that."

"He also goes through my pockets," Maggie said, her indignation dimming just a bit.

"I'm sure there's a reasonable explanation," I said.

---

[1] If I were Maggie, here's how I'd see it: He's doing the cleaning and I'm not. Who cares about motivation?

[2] Note to self: Mention this credit to your character in therapy.

"He's looking for crumbs," Maggie explained.

Long pause, waiting for the lightbulb.

"Oh, because you keep baked goods in your pockets!"

"Not all the time," she said defensively.

"Of course not," I replied.

"He says he doesn't want my pockets to get ants in them. It's never happened before."

"Well, better safe than sorry," I replied diplomatically.

Maggie gulped some beer, tapped her foot, stopped tapping, and then switched topics with as much grace as a drunken gazelle.

"I asked him if he wants to go camping with me sometime and he said he was willing to negotiate."

"Do you like opera?" I asked.

"I'm *okay* with it," Maggie said, wondering where *that* question came from.

"Under no circumstances are you to admit that you're okay with it. You'll need your hatred of opera as a bargaining chip."

"Oh, I see what you're saying," Maggie replied.

Maggie finished her beer shortly after I finished mine and asked me if I wanted another. I reached for my wallet; she gave me a look that I read as *Are you insane?*

"I'm buying," she said, and went to the bar.

In her brief absence I tried to work up a plausible reason for hating her, but I couldn't. In fact, I could only come up with plausible reasons for being friends with her. Of course, I was over Henry Stone, remember? I remember. So there's no problem here.

Maggie returned with two beers and a whole new subject.

"Now I'm one hundred percent certain that someone is following me."

"How often?"

"Not every day. I've noticed it a few times when I'm driving. Always a different car, though, and I've never been able to get a license plate. Also, my secretary mentioned that there have been a few more calls to my office and the person just wants to know if I'm at the office and how long I'll be there. She answered that question the first few times, but now we just make something up."

"Different cars. What kind?"

"It was at night. It was hard to see. Some kind of sedan, I think. I just had a feeling."

It's not unusual to be unable to identify a car during a nighttime tail. In your rearview mirror often all you can see are headlights.

As if reading my mind, Maggie said, "It's not Rae. That I know for sure. She was actually with me one of those times I was being followed and told me how to lose the tail. And the phone calls to the office. She already calls me and knows where I am."

"She does?" I asked, not realizing that Maggie and Rae's "friendship" had reached this stage.

"Henry still won't really speak to her, so she's replaced him with me."

Interesting, I thought. What was Rae's angle?

"Here's the plan," I said. "The next time you're being followed, call me with your current location and I'll try to track down your pursuer."

"Thanks," Maggie replied. "One more thing: Any chance you can convince your parents to buy Rae a car?"

My sister has virtually every Bay Area bus, Muni, and BART schedule memorized and yet she always, if given the opportunity, will demand the services of a personal chauffeur. My family has learned how to say no, for the most part, but Henry never quite got the hang of solidifying this particular rule. Instead, he acquiesced when the drive didn't take him too far out of his way and Rae would do her best to make it convenient for him. Ironically, Rae has no problem using public transportation to arrive at the source of her ride, but she resists it in terms of reaching her final destination. It was clear from the question that due to Henry's current policy of not speaking to Rae, by association, Maggie had become Rae's primary transportation victim.

THE YIDDISH PATIENT

I hadn't seen Morty in a week, since his release from the hospital. The doctor suggested keeping visitors to a minimum and I had hoped that some alone time with Ruth would suddenly solve all their problems. Although no one would accuse me of being a relationship expert, I'm almost always wrong these days. Morty phoned and told me he was feeling better, so shortly after my meeting with Maggie I decided to take the bus to his home in the Avenues.

What should have been a fifteen-minute ride turned into a two-hour ordeal. I fell asleep on the bus, only be awoken an hour later by the bus driver, who was changing shifts. Then I had to wait for another bus in the opposite direction.

When I arrived, Ruth met me at the door and smiled pleasantly, but the smile was masking an undercurrent of extreme annoyance.

"Good, you're here," she said.

"How's the patient?" I asked.

"On his deathbed, if you ask him."

Ruth led me into their bedroom, where Morty reclined, wrapped in blankets over a robe over pajamas. Newspapers surrounded him and the television was on at full volume.

"How are you feeling?" I asked sympathetically. His pallor had improved, but both his carriage and his voice were frail.

Ruth asked me if I needed anything and I declined. She didn't ask Morty, which I thought was odd.

"What took you so long?" Morty said.

"You know the buses in this city."[1]

"What'sa matter with your eyes?" he asked.

"What'sa matter with *your* eyes?"

"I'm old. Your excuse?"

"I haven't been sleeping well."

"Guilty conscience?" Morty asked.

"You should talk. How are you, really?" I asked, sitting down on the edge of the bed.

Morty lightened up on some of his sick act and said, "I'm not one hundred percent."

"You're eighty-four. Say good-bye to one hundred percent."

"I don't need your negativity in my current condition."

"What are you doing, Morty?" I asked suspiciously.

"I'm recovering."

"Bullshit."

"Watch your language, young lady."

"Ruth knows what you're up to. You know that, right?"

"Bah."

"What do you think is going to happen here?"

"Once she's back for a few weeks, she'll forget all about that Florida business." His voice then shifted to a whisper. "I got us symphony tickets."

"So what?"

"So I never took her to the symphony before."

"Did she want to go?"

"Yes. She used to have season tickets. Always went with a girlfriend."

---

[1] He doesn't know. That's what I was counting on.

"Some husband you are."

"I'm an adoring husband. Have you seen the rocks on her fingers?"

My phone rang, thankfully. I'm not sure how much more conversation with Morty I could have tolerated.

"Hello?"

"Izzele, it's Gabe. I'm here."

"Where?"

"In front of your apartment."

"Which one?"

"You have more than one?"

"Oops," I said, suddenly remembering that he was going to pick me up at my old place.

"You forgot about our date?" he asked.

"Sort of," I replied.

"Where are you?"

"At your grandpa's house. I'm sorry. I forgot what day it was."

Silence. More awkward than the therapy kind.

"Do you still want to go out?"

"Sure," I replied, thinking quickly. I didn't want to go back to a home where I no longer lived and I couldn't clue him in to my new living situation, so I suggested he pick me up at Morty's place and we go from there. Gabe agreed.

When I got off the phone, Morty had a number of comments for me on the overheard phone call. "Keep your opinions to yourself," I snapped before he managed a single word.

Morty once again locked his mouth shut and threw away the key.

"I like you better that way," I said.

Fifteen minutes later, Gabe arrived. While his grandson was chatting with his wife, Morty turned to me and said, "Psst," as if we were in some 1940s crime caper. I ignored him at first, but then he *psst*-ed again.

"What?"

In a cautious whisper Morty said, "Tomorrow, Ruthy is playing bridge with Ethel. Between six and nine P.M. Can you bring me a pastrami sandwich on rye from Moishe's?"

"You're unbelievable," I said, and made my exit.

GABE "DATE" #2

I apologized when I jumped into Gabe's VW Jetta, but I still got the cold shoulder. Fair enough. If I had told him about my new living situation, he would have understood how I might have upended my internal calendar. Everyone finds moving stressful. Unfortunately, one of the agreements I had made with myself when I decided to move into David's home unbeknownst to him was that I wouldn't tell anyone. My point is, I had trouble coming up with a legitimate defense. Matters only got worse when my cell phone rang. It was Maggie, and she had a feeling she was being followed. Maggie provided her current location—a gas station on Van Ness and Pine—but she couldn't tell whether her pursuer was anywhere in the vicinity. She would stall as long as she could until I arrived.

"Gabe, I need you to pull over and let me drive."

"Why?"

"It's an urgent matter. I'll explain once we swap places."

"Seriously?"

"Right now."

I have moments when I can be impressively convincing (family members are immune). Gabe pulled his car to the curb and we switched seats.

Within five minutes of Maggie's phone call, I was racing Gabe's Jetta down Geary Boulevard, which was almost clear of rush-hour traffic. Five minutes after that, as I approached the intersection of Gough and O'Farrell, I phoned Maggie and told her to take Van Ness south. I continued onto O'Farrell Street and reached the Van Ness intersection, pulling to a stop in the right-hand lane and turning on my blinkers—this is the sort of thing that drives me batty when I'm fighting traffic, but I figured it was time for my own cosmic payback. If I planned things correctly, Maggie would pass right by me and I, in theory, could close in on her tail.

My plan worked brilliantly. Maggie passed my vehicle, I waited for a few more cars to cross my line of vision, and then I pulled out onto Van Ness, cutting off a tan PT Cruiser (not a deliberate choice, but a pleasant bonus). I'd say there was nothing safe about my previous ten minutes of driving, but this move caused Gabe to finally speak.

"Now I see why we took my car."

I phoned Maggie as I was driving; Gabe's body language indicated that my multitasking was making him nervous.

"Relax," I said. "I've done this before."

Maggie picked up her phone. "Hello."

"Where are you going?"

"To Henry's place."

"Good," I replied. "Just make a few unnecessary turns to get there."

"Gotcha. I'm going to turn right on Hayes Street."

Maggie was six cars ahead, so her information was necessary, since it was dark and I had a few too many things to keep my eye on, not to mention traffic.

Maggie turned on Hayes. Within her vicinity a black Honda Civic, a yellow VW van, a gold Crown Victoria, and a Mercury Grand Marquis the color of smog made right turns. She crossed Divisadero and neared the park. Within five blocks we had lost the Honda Civic and the VW van. I suggested a right turn on Stanyan Street and all but the Mercury Grand Marquis dispersed in different directions. The Grand Marquis stayed on Maggie's vehicle for another half mile.

I asked Gabe to write down the license plate number of the pursuing car and then told Maggie we should all reconvene at Henry's house.

By the time the chase was over and I found a parking space, the adrenaline had drained from my body and I could feel that my eyelids wanted to close for a nap. I slapped my cheeks to wake myself up. Gabe gawked at me as if I were an alien from another planet.

"You scare me," he said.

"I have insurance," I replied.

Gabe wasn't sure what to make of the entire ordeal. The thrill of the chase appealed to his extreme-sports side, but my previous rudeness, followed by my bossy/sleep-deprived/unstable bearing, followed by the missing of the movie for which he'd bought tickets all resulted in a kind of stupor. I parked, but before we exited the vehicle, Gabe insisted on a full explanation for the car chase.

I provided one for him in detail. The edge to his mood had dulled some by the time we reached Henry's apartment.

Before I relayed any information to Maggie, I thought I should check whether she was keeping Henry in the dark or not.

"Ancay eway eakspay eelyfray?"[1]

"Esyay," Maggie replied.

Henry rolled his eyes and ignored us; Gabe looked at me as if I'd gone mad.

"I got the license plate number of the pursuing vehicle. It looks like a professional's car, but that's impossible to say. If it is, I should be able to find out who the person is working for," I said to Maggie.

"You think this is a professional surveillance? I figured someone I pissed off just hired a friend to follow me."

"I don't think so," I replied. "Whoever was driving knew what he was doing."

---

[1] Translation: Can we speak freely? (pig Latin).

Henry and Gabe stood awkwardly in the foyer.

I waved in the general direction of the men and said, "You've met. Remember? At my ECOT party?"

Henry turned to me and said, "If you ever want to take an etiquette class, it's on me." Then he turned to Gabe. "Nice to see you again."

They shook hands, and Gabe said, "I was just on a high-speed car chase," with almost no enthusiasm at all.

"Let me get you a drink," Henry replied.

When Henry returned with the drink, Gabe continued his quest for sympathy.

"We were supposed to be at a movie, but Isabel stood me up."

"Almost. Not completely," I replied. "So it doesn't count."

"I'm sure she had a lengthy and convoluted excuse," Henry said, showing just a little too much interest.

"No," I replied, defensively. "I just forgot what day it was."

Henry then turned to Gabe. "What were your plans?"

"The usual. Dinner and a movie."

"Why don't you stay for dinner?" Henry said.

"No, thank you," I said.

"Why not?" Gabe chimed in.

To make a short story even shorter, we stayed for dinner, which was awkward, I think, for everyone but Maggie. A retired skateboarder and a police inspector tend to have little in common. Since the only thing they had in common was me, I was the topic of most conversations. Since I have a tendency to disappoint, any discussion of me will eventually lead to a complaint. The only upside was that I was so exhausted, my mind wandered to a borderline-unconscious dimension and I missed most of the good jabs.

I woke from my stupor when Henry began commenting on my character. Apparently when I'm preoccupied with something, personal considerations don't come into the picture.

It was Maggie who came to my defense with these simple words:

"Henry, shut up. Not everyone has your attention to detail." There was a long pause, followed by "Thank god," which she mumbled at the very end.

As "dessert"[2] was being served, there was a knock at the door. A brief surge of anger flashed across Henry's face.

"Don't answer it," he said.

Gabe appeared confused and turned to me for an explanation, but I didn't have one. Maggie got to her feet and charged toward the door. Henry intercepted her in the foyer.

"No," he said grimly.

"Don't be such a sourpuss," Maggie replied.

"She's not allowed in my home," said Henry.

Okay, so now I had an explanation. I turned to Gabe. "My sister is here. We should probably give her a ride home. Thanks for dinner, Henry," I said as I took my coat off the rack. "I'll handle the Rae situation."

"Thank you," Henry replied.

"You need to chillax," Maggie mumbled at Henry. I realized she was probably spending far too much time with Rae.

Gabe and I slipped out of a narrow space in the doorway, aimed at not giving Rae entry into Henry's place.

"Why can't I come in?" Rae said, trying to push past me.

"Henry doesn't want you in his home," I said with maybe a little too much enthusiasm.

"Everyone has forgiven me but you, Henry!" Rae shouted from the other side of the partially open door.

Henry leaned into the hallway and said to Rae, "I don't care if the pope has forgiven you; I haven't."

Rae gave Henry the annoyingly confused face she often pulls when she's trying to play the innocent victim.

"I don't get it," she said. "We're not Catholic."

---

[2] Sliced fruit. Rae would argue: not dessert.

I shoved Rae down the hallway, insisting that the only personal transportation option for the evening was from Gabe (through me).

"I wanted Maggie to give me a ride," Rae said, disappointed.

"Sometimes things don't work out the way you plan."

"That's your trip," Rae said, which Gabe seemed to find more amusing than it was.

In truth, Rae was far less amusing than she used to be. What was cute in a little girl was not so charming in someone closing in on adulthood. Of course, I have no business griping about anyone's adolescent behavior, but there I was. Griping.

We dropped Rae off at the Spellman residence and I had Gabe drive to where my car was last seen, claiming that I had to check on the street-cleaning schedule. Obviously, I was trying to avoid a long walk home from my purported residence in the Tenderloin. Before I exited his vehicle, Gabe had a few minor things to get off his chest.

"Well, it's been interesting, Izzele," said Gabe.

" 'Interesting.' What does that mean?"

"Tonight was meant to be a date, but clearly it wasn't."

Great. So Gabe was one of *those* people who can voice his/her emotions without embarrassment. Why can't I make friends more like me? At least that was the thought I had at that very moment.

"If you think about it, I still think tonight qualified under the definition of 'date.' Plus, it was free and included a car chase," I unwisely replied.

And that was the end of the me-and-Gabe saga. His parting words: "I think you like me, but you're in love with that cop. We'll stay friends for the sake of Grandpa Mort."

Most men don't show Gabe's good sense. There was a part of me that wished I felt more for Gabe. I could think of no pure flaw in his character, and then it occurred to me that someone so delightful should not go to waste.

"Do me a favor and get a haircut," I said as I handed Gabe Petra's card. "You need one. You really, really need one."

Gabe stared at me like I was a lunatic but took the card. Then we said our good-byes. I walked in the shadows until I reached David's house. Only his bedroom light was lit, so I figured I had a fairly safe passage to the back of the house. I just had to be quiet with the key. I entered my dark home, tripped over my own backpack, brushed my teeth by moonlight, and fell fast asleep. Okay, I didn't fall asleep, but everything else was true.

JOB INTERVIEW #1

Most people who function in everyday society have had more than two[1] job interviews by the time they've reached the age of thirty-one, but working for the family has a few perks. For the most part, I've escaped this particular rite of passage; however, you might be surprised to hear that my very first job interview was for my position at Spellman Investigations. While I had been working for my parents for close to three years (off the books), my dad decided it was time they used me as a tax deduction. At this time, my father insisted on a formal meeting in which we played strangers (or, I should say, he played a stranger) and performed a mock—but very serious—job interview. In fact, I even had to write up a résumé for the occasion. If I am to be honest, I'm still bitter about that mandated charade to this day.

Allow me a brief digression to revisit that occasion . . .

Isabel, age 15

After Dad forced me to write a cover letter with an attached résumé and mail it, he called me from the office line on the home line and asked to

---

[1] There are two job interviews I mentioned here and then my meeting at a temp agency, which is more like a medical intake than a job interview.

make an appointment for an interview. Our conversation ended with the following suggestion: "Dress appropriately, Ms. Spellman."

Who's to say what appropriate is? My father was making me jump through hoops to get a job I already had. Remember, this occurred during the height of my rebellion. I wasn't going to play along without some form of subterfuge.

My appropriate dress was one of David's costumes from a Halloween past: black dress pants, a white short-sleeved oxford shirt with a pocket protector, a bow tie, dress shoes (David's stuffed with socks for comfort), and a plaid jacket that didn't quite fit the ensemble, but I liked its effect. I finished off the look by pulling my hair into a severe ponytail and putting on a pair of horn-rimmed glasses. I then grabbed David's briefcase, which I had already packed with the necessary props for the occasion.

At one P.M. sharp, I knocked on the door to the offices of Spellman Investigations.

My mother answered, holding her coffee cup. Sadly for her dress, she had taken a sip just before she saw me. The coffee cascaded out of her mouth and down her dress. She had the nerve to be angry with me for her own loss of control.

"For god's sake, Isabel, I just bought this dress," Mom said, allowing my entry.

"Good afternoon. You must be Mrs. Melman.[2] I'm Isabel. I'm here for the interview."

My mother rolled her eyes, which was pretty much all I had done for the two days after I learned of this ridiculous interview. She excused herself, wanting no part of this charade, which suited my purposes just fine.

Dad eyed my outfit, debating whether he should call the whole thing off then and there, but opted in that moment to continue with the show.

"Mr. Melman, a pleasure meeting you," I said.

---

[2] One of our neighbors at the time kept getting our name wrong. David and I started calling our mom and dad Mr. and Mrs. Melman when we were in the mood to annoy.

"It's Spellman. Have a seat, Isabel. Can I get you anything?"

"I could use a coffee," I replied.

"Refuse the coffee, Izzy."

"If you don't want to serve me coffee, then don't offer it."

"Just say 'No, thank you,' Isabel."

"No, thank you, Isabel."[3]

"Sit down," Dad said, this time in a far more hostile tone.

I sat down, placed the briefcase in my lap, and opened it. I had packed a lunch to keep me busy in case Dad got boring. I tucked a cloth napkin into my shirt and began dining.

My dad observed my behavior for a full thirty seconds, trying to map out his next move. He put his feet up on his desk and watched me eat.

"Are you enjoying yourself?" he asked.

"It's a pretty good sandwich, if I do say so myself. However, a cup of coffee would make it even better."

"That's it. Get out. I want you to go to your room, change into your normal, I-don't-care-what-you-think-of-me clothes, and come back into this office as Isabel, prepared for an interview."

"Dad, this is seriously one of the dumbest things you've ever asked me to do."

"Fifteen minutes," Dad replied. Then he got out of his chair, snapped my briefcase shut, almost snapping off my fingers in the process, and sent me on my way.

"Make it a half hour," I shouted upon exiting the room. "I'd like to finish my lunch."

Twenty-five minutes later

I returned to the office impersonating myself. I messed up my hair a bit more than usual and wore a sweatshirt with a stain instead of a clean one,

---

[3] I am well aware that this is an incredibly old joke.

and sneakers instead of boots, just to add a bit more mockery to this game. Dad scowled and sat down at his desk. The official interview went something like this:

ALBERT: Tell me about yourself, Isabel.

ISABEL: What do you want to know?

ALBERT: Anything.

ISABEL: Are you sure about that?

ALBERT: New question.

ISABEL: Thank god.

ALBERT: What do you know about our organization?

ISABEL: It's not very organized.

ALBERT: Wrong answer.

ISABEL: If you're feeling sorry for yourself right about now, remember that it's your own fault.

[Albert clears his throat, looks at his list of questions, and tries to move on.]

ALBERT: Why should we hire you?

ISABEL: Do I need to remind you that I already work here?

ALBERT: Tell me how you can contribute to our organization.

ISABEL: Please. Just let me drink the Kool-Aid.

ALBERT: That's it, Isabel. Get out of here!

ISABEL: It's been a pleasure meeting you, Mr. Melman.

JOB INTERVIEW #2

Rick Harkey, director of RH Investigations, has been an acquaintance of my father's since long before I was an ill-considered idea in anyone's head. Harkey and my dad shared similar paths—both ex-cops turned PIs—but their similarities end there. To begin with, Harkey and my dad are physical opposites. Harkey is tall, lean, and handsome in an aged-movie-star kind of way. His crowning achievement is his full head of silver hair. There's something not quite right about older gentlemen who struggle to hold on to their looks—they become even vainer than their high school counterparts, always boasting of their flatlining weight and regular haircuts. My study of this phenomenon is limited, but allow me to apply this one truth at least to Harkey: The man is madly in love with himself. In contrast, the only person my dad is madly in love with is my mom.

Harkey and my dad have history. The kind of history a kid figures out from listening in on conversations, observing odd parental behavior at parties said child wished she did not have to attend, and from flat-out questioning her mother years later. On the job, their personalities clashed. My father's affable manner and ease with both friends and foes got under Harkey's skin. Dad was well liked; Harkey was, at best, feared. Years later, when both men joined the PI community, they found themselves together at social gatherings more often than they'd have liked. It was at one of these PI parties, well before I was born, that Harkey met my mother. He just couldn't believe my big lug of a dad could get a woman so attractive and charming, and he made his disbelief well known. A few years later, at another one of those PI holiday parties—magnifying-glass key chains as party favors—Harkey commented once again on my father's extreme good fortune. Dad took all this ribbing with an ounce or two of humor, but he knew Harkey's heart was in the wrong place.

It wasn't until a few years later at yet another holiday event that Harkey crossed the line: He made a play for my mom. All Dad saw from the other end of the room was my mother throwing a drink in Harkey's face (I know, she's right out of a black-and-white movie), but when Dad got the inside scoop, which surely was my mother's watered-down version, the simmering tension turned to a boil. The two men could no longer be in the same room together.

As far as big cities go, San Francisco isn't so big, and neither is the PI community. Harkey knew who I was. We'd met on a few occasions and I'm sure that just as I knew him by reputation, he knew me. I was fairly certain I could use this bad blood to my benefit. I think you will be most impressed to see how much I had improved between my first and second job interviews.

I arrived at Harkey's office unannounced but knew that he would receive me with a warm welcome.

[Partial transcript reads as follows:]

HARKEY: My-my, Isabel. What a pleasure to see you.

ISABEL: Sorry I didn't make an appointment.

HARKEY: You are a tall glass o' water.

ISABEL: Thanks for noticing.

HARKEY: You've certainly filled out since I saw you last. Must be five or six years.

ISABEL: Are you saying I've gotten fat?[1]

HARKEY: No, no, no. You look lovely, Isabel. I'm honored by your presence.

[Note: I'm about to retch at this point but decide to push through.]

ISABEL: You're probably wondering what I'm doing here.

HARKEY: It did cross my mind.

ISABEL: I'm looking for a job.

HARKEY: Excuse me?

ISABEL: I'm sure you've heard about some of the troubles I've had recently. Everything is fine; my license is still intact, but the Parental Unit is holding a grudge. They won't give me any work. I've been bartending for the last five months. The money's fine but I'm itching to get back in the game. Know what I mean?

HARKEY: Your parents won't give you work?

ISABEL: Nope.

HARKEY: Really?

ISABEL: I'm serious. Can you help me out?

HARKEY: Right now I've got all the full-time employees I can keep in business.

ISABEL: How about part-time? I heard you were looking for some help around the office.

HARKEY: You're overqualified for the job I have available.

ISABEL: I just want to get my feet wet again. You understand, don't you? Besides, I can't work for my parents the rest of my life.

And that is how I began working for RH Investigations.

---

[1] I tend to be extra sensitive when I'm tired.

DAVID'S SECRET

The next morning when I arose after yet another night of no sleep, I discovered that I was all out of coffee. I cried[1] for about five minutes until I realized that David would have a fresh pot brewing and I could pretend I was in the neighborhood. I didn't even bother getting dressed. I threw on a jacket and sneakers, checked my computer camera, and made my escape. I stood on the sidewalk, scoped the neighborhood for any prying eyes, and then casually walked up the front steps to David's residence.

"Isabel," David said, and then he stared for a long while at my ensemble. "What are you wearing?"

"Pajamas," I replied. It's best to be honest.

"Is everything alright?"

"I'm out of coffee and I was in the neighborhood. Please tell me you have some brewing," I said, sounding maybe a little desperate.

David backed away from the door and allowed my entrance. He returned to his kitchen, where the *New York Times* was spread out across the table.

"Help yourself," David said, almost pleasantly. Then he added, "You know there are a number of coffee shops in your neighborhood."

"I know," I replied. But none this close.

---

[1] In my defense, I don't usually cry when I discover there's no coffee. Well, only once before.

I stood in front of David's coffeepot for a long while trying to figure out what was missing. There was something I was supposed to do next and I couldn't for the life of me figure it out.

"You need a cup," David said.

"Right," I replied, and then darted my eyes around the kitchen aimlessly.

David got up, opened the cabinet, and handed me a mug. I poured the coffee, but my grip and coordination were shaky. David watched carefully, cleaned up a spill, and put the pot back in place.

"You okay?" David asked.

"I've been better," I replied. Come to think of it, that statement was a little too true. I was sleepless, jobless, living in a basement apartment on the sly, in court-ordered therapy, and trying to solve one simple case to prove to myself that there was something, just one thing, that I could do right. Yeah, I'd been better.

I sat down at the kitchen table and pretended to read the paper while I drank the coffee like it was medicine. Then I drank another cup and then David made another pot. I looked at the clock: 8:45 A.M.

"Don't you have to go to work?" I asked.

"Taking the day off," David replied.

Now that the coffee had kicked in and my eyes and brain were working at about 40 percent, I could see that David's health was much improved since his return, which got me thinking again about where he was and why it was a secret. I decided that I needed the answer to this mystery as well. The thing is, people usually make sense. When they don't, I have to make sense of it to feel right. I'm not sure why, but it's always been that way.

"Why would you say you were in Europe when you were camping[2] probably not too far from here?" I asked.

"Because I want to live my life without someone else providing a running commentary," David replied.

---

[2] This was a guess. But the missing camping gear made it an educated one.

Hmmm, he had a point. Besides, I was feeling just a bit guilty or indebted about living in his apartment without him knowing, so I thought I should try to play it cool and give him some space. I did, however, need to obtain a few more particulars.

"The elaborate lie about a European vacation was just so we wouldn't know what you were really doing?" I asked.

"In a nutshell."

"Could you provide me with a few more details and then, I promise, not another word out of me on the subject?"

"Under one condition," David replied.

"What?"

"Tell me which booze bottles you tampered with so that I don't have to taste every single one."

"Deal," I replied.

For the next ten minutes, David, in honest, no-defenses mode (uncommon among the Spellman children), explained to me that in the year after his divorce he felt aimless and unsatisfied with his work and his personal life and was experiencing some kind of pre-MILFO.[3] At some point in the midst of this angst, David was leafing through a magazine at his accountant's office and saw an ad for a "life-changing" wilderness program. He tore the page from the magazine and spent the evening perusing the program's website.

The program offered a three-week excursion, the prospect of which both thrilled and terrified my brother. For five days you were instructed on how to survive in the great outdoors. Then you were dropped by helicopter in the middle of nowhere (namely Yosemite) and were expected to fend for yourself alone for the next two weeks. Equipped with a tent, a sleeping bag, canned goods, a guide to edible vegetation, one change of clothes, a kerosene lamp, a few fishhooks, and a couple other things I don't remember but I suppose I would if I were ever caught in a similar situation, David

---

[3] Mid-life freak-out. But David used the term "existential crisis" instead. Tomato/tomato.

was left to his lonesome. He described the first few days as utter agony. But then peace took over. Within a week of his abandonment he had figured out a daily routine and the hours passed effortlessly. A few days after that, he found some kind of inner peace or whatever. Then he broke his arm slipping on a bluff during a hike for food, which probably really tested that aforementioned inner peace. He made a sling out of his extra shirt and somehow managed to survive until he was "rescued."

My immediate response to this tale was, *Are you a complete moron?* But I've learned that my first response is often the one I should keep to myself.

"Were you scared?" I asked instead.

David seemed relieved that these were the first words to exit my mouth when he finished his tale.

"The whole time," he replied.

While I was sorting through the liquor cabinet, meeting my end of the bargain, David said, "We should go camping sometime. I think it would be fun."

That time I forgot and responded with the first thing that came to mind.

"Are you a complete moron?"

MAGGIE'S SECOND MYSTERY

All I wanted to do after my morning coffee was go back to bed, but since sleep wouldn't come to me in the middle of the night, I could assume I wouldn't find it in the middle of the day. Since the David mystery was solved, I decided to work on my other secondary case.

I had only the license plate number of the gray Mercury Grand Marquis that had pursued Maggie. I didn't want my parents to know I was investigating this matter, so I couldn't use their source for this research. Reverse license plate searches are a tricky deal. Often you can't get the vehicle owner's address, and the information is closely monitored. However, if you happen to be friends with a cop, that's another story.

It had been approximately six months since I last called in a favor with Sheriff Larson (Ex-boyfriend #10). I decided he was my best bet. Our relationship was brief and there was little attempt at friendship afterward, but he always managed to track down a criminal record or a vehicle registration for me, so I knew he'd come through.

Meanwhile, I hunted for the location I'd left my car the previous night. I had taken a shower and washed off the ink, but I distinctly remembered writing down Green Street and Taylor Street on my arm. However, in the vicinity of Green and Taylor, my car was not to be found. Just as I was beginning to panic about my own mental well-being, Larson called and distracted me.

"That was fast," I said.

"Your Grand Marquis belongs to a retired cop," Larson replied. "Tell me you're not investigating him."

"I'm not investigating him."

"You telling me the truth?"

"I swear. Do you have a name?"

"Pete Harrington. He lives at the Marina. You need his dock number?"

"No, thanks," I replied. "I know where he lives."

After a few more minutes of car hunting, I abandoned my search and hopped on the bus. I napped for an hour and missed my stop. I exited the bus, got on another bus going in the same direction, and set the alarm on my cell phone clock for forty-five minutes later. Miraculously, I got in another nap as my head bobbed against the grimy window. I almost felt refreshed by the time I exited the bus at the Marina.

Pete Harrington was a retired cop who lived on a houseboat. A long time ago he took me and David sailing. I'm not sure why, but I think he lost a poker game to my dad, who, hoping to educate, inform, or at least broaden my horizons, suggested that some of Pete's losses could be recouped by a day of sailing and, more importantly, babysitting. Pete owned the boat outright and his pension was solid, so he didn't need or want too much extra work, but every once in a while he'd do a job for one of the many PI firms in the Bay Area. Pete had no loyalty to any one firm, so I decided not to make any assumptions.

As I traveled down the dock, I spotted Pete, tanning his leathery skin in the unusually bright but still chilly San Francisco sun. It looked like he was sipping iced tea, but knowing Pete it was spiked with something, even though it was well before noon.

Pete didn't mind the interruption. He got to his feet, gave me a bear hug, and insisted that I stay for a cocktail. Pete served his cocktails in tumblers, so it took a while to finish. We caught up, enjoying the conversation, the sun, and the water, and I pretended very briefly that I hadn't a care in the world. As for the reason I paid a visit to Pete, well, I finally got around to asking about that when it was time to leave. I didn't want Pete to think this was anything but a social call.

"Pete, why did my mom hire you to follow that brown-haired woman who drives the dark green Subaru?"

"She never told me and I never asked," Pete replied.

The morning drink with Harrington and the bus ride prompted another lengthy nap. This time I rode the full route of the 49 bus (starting on Van Ness Avenue and North Point Street, all the way to City College and back to the lower Nob Hill neighborhood) and found myself, two hours later, approaching my parents' house. I purchased a cup of coffee at the corner shop and by the time I reached the Spellman residence, I think I could have passed a basic math test.

"Mom," I said, trying to invoke the tone of disappointment so often used against me, "why are you investigating Maggie Mason?"

"I'm not investigating her anymore. It's over," my mother replied, sounding more annoyed or frustrated than guilty.

"Why were you following her in the first place?"

"Looking for dirt. Why else?" Mom replied.

"I don't understand."

"Don't play dumb."

I had an inkling, but I wasn't committed to it. "Explain yourself, Mom."

"I found nothing," Mom said, taking a sip of her coffee and then spitting it back in the cup. "Yuck. I think that was from yesterday."

"Why are you disappointed?"

"Because she's great. I mean, *great.* She's smart, she's thoughtful, she's a bit of a nut in a good way. Completely addicted to Diet Coke. If you look in the back of her car, there are at least a dozen dead cans. She volunteers for Project Literacy and a soup kitchen and nobody knows about it. A homeless man lives in the foyer of her building. I asked him about her—his name's Jack—he said he's her doorman and she makes him peanut butter and marshmallow sandwiches."

"Gross," I said.

"That's his favorite," Mom continued. "And she tips well, he said. She always has food in her pocket; I don't know why that amuses me. And she's figured out how to make friends with Rae, which is no easy feat when Rae's set on taking you down. I don't know. There's something special about Maggie."

"Are you going to leave her alone now?" I asked.

"I have no choice," my mom replied. "There's *nothing* I can do for you here, Isabel. She's perfect. If I were Henry, I'd pick her, too. She's got a better job and she's less emotionally stunted."

"It might have been better for both of us if you never admitted your motivation."

"I agree," my mother replied.

"What am I going to tell her?" I asked. "I arranged to look into this matter for her."

"Since you're so willing to look into matters for people, why don't you just come back to work?"

"I'm not ready," I replied. "Now, what am I supposed to tell Maggie?"

"You don't have to tell her anything. I'll talk with her. Say something about how I needed to investigate her since she was spending so much time with my teenage daughter."

"You think she'll buy that?" I asked.

"If I sell it," Mom replied, and I knew she was right.

I got to my feet. I couldn't spend another second in that house. I did, however, have to get in my last words: "And you people wonder why I'm in therapy?"

By early evening, I was ready to return to David's and my house and get a good night's rest for my first day on the job at RH Investigations. There was one pressing matter, however, that I had to take care of first: find my car.

I toyed with the idea that it had been stolen, but stealing a ten-year-old Buick with three dents, a missing hubcap, and a duct-taped fender doesn't seem like the best use of one's time.

I searched for an hour, and just when I was about to give up, I found my car parked on Leavenworth at Green. I even had a ticket for parking during street cleaning. I wondered how this kind of mistake could be made. "Leavenworth" looks nothing like "Taylor," even if it's written on your arm. Since I found the car and it was safe to park in that spot until morning, I left it and returned to my house. Once again, I scouted the vicinity before scaling the perimeter fence and entered through the back door.

I slept a full three hours[1] until I woke up in a panic, hearing sounds by the exit that sounded almost like someone turning a key in a lock. I sat for fifteen minutes in a crouch with my ear to the door, preparing to jolt into hiding should I see the knob actually turn. You'll be happy to know that it was a false alarm. An hour later, after checking the video feed on my computer and practicing some deep-breathing exercises, I was back in bed, simulating sleep.

---

[1] So far my record in David's place.

CASE #001

CHAPTER 6

I was twenty minutes late for work because, well, David was late for work and I couldn't leave until he left. Rick Harkey was not pleased. I supposed the actual excuse wouldn't go over well, so I told him that my alarm didn't go off. Turns out that's not the best excuse, either. I've been late for work before, plenty of times. But I was always at ease disappointing my parents; having a mostly-stranger scowl at me was uncomfortable.

Harkey was also displeased with my wardrobe. He guided me into a small nook with a Formica table, a couple of chairs, a paper shredder, and a bulletin board and asked me to quietly read from a yellowed and worn piece of paper pegged to the far right corner.

DRESS CODE

- Men should wear suits or dress slacks with a dress shirt and a sweater.
- Women should wear skirts with nylon stockings or dress slacks with a blouse and/or a sweater.
- No T-shirts, no blue jeans, no sneakers, no sweatshirts, and no flip-flops or Birkenstocks.

When I finished reading, I came to the unavoidable conclusion that I would have to keep this undercover investigation as brief as possible. I was currently wearing blue jeans, boots, and a button-down shirt under a sweater with the tails hanging out. Harkey reminded me about the no-denim rule and then suggested I tuck in my shirt.

After my six-hour shift—filing via a numbered system that worked as security against my prying eye, and shredding an entire box of Harkey's five-year-old financial statements—I was almost looking forward to my therapy session. Only I couldn't tell Dr. Rush about my new job or my new home or anything, really.

THERAPY SESSION #14

[Partial transcript reads as follows:]

ISABEL: My car keeps moving.

DR. RUSH: That's what they do, those cars.

ISABEL: I mean, I park the car and the next time I go to drive it, it's not where I remember it.

DR. RUSH: Maybe you should write it down.

ISABEL: I tried that.

DR. RUSH: And what happened?

ISABEL: I took a shower.

DR. RUSH: Why don't you try writing on a piece of paper next time?

ISABEL: Okay. I guess that's sound advice.

[Long pause.]

DR. RUSH: Is there anything else you'd like to discuss?

ISABEL: Not that I can think of.

DR. RUSH: Think harder, then.

[Long pause.]

ISABEL: You don't have as much stuff as Dr. Ira.

DR. RUSH: It's been a while since I've been to his office, so I can't comment.

ISABEL: If you do go to his office, you might want to mention that he could use a new bookshelf and maybe he should bolt both bookshelves to the wall. You have a nicer office than Dr. Ira. I like the fountain and the coffee station in the waiting room. I also like your carpet better.

DR. RUSH: Stop stalling, Isabel.

ISABEL: Excuse me?

DR. RUSH: Did you forget what we talked about last week?

ISABEL: No. But what exactly are you referring to?

DR. RUSH: Therapy is not a place you go to kill time, especially if it's court-ordered.

ISABEL: I don't think that's what I was doing.

DR. RUSH: It seems that way to me.

ISABEL: How does that make you feel, Doctor?

DR. RUSH: Isabel, according to the revised terms of your plea agreement, you have ten more sessions with me after today. If the rest of this session goes like the first part, you'll have eleven sessions left. All I have to do is file some paperwork with the court.

ISABEL: You must really like paperwork.

DR. RUSH: You must really hate self-examination.

ISABEL: Well, yeah. Who doesn't?

DR. RUSH: Most people aren't as resistant as you are.

ISABEL: Really? So, I'm, like, already your worst patient?

[Long pause.]

ISABEL: Sorry. Refresh my memory. What am I supposed to do?

DR. RUSH: Just talk about something that's on your mind—but keep me and Dr. Ira out of it.

ISABEL: [sigh] There are a lot of things on my mind. I wouldn't know where to begin.

DR. RUSH: Let's start with your family.

Part III

PROGRESS

THE RANSOM

PART I

After therapy, I really needed a drink, so I took the Muni train to West Portal and stopped in at the Philosopher's Club. Paddy O'Brien[1] was tending bar as usual, so I ordered a beer and sat down at a table so he wouldn't think I was interested in having a conversation.

"How are ya today, orgeous?" Connor asked. Normally I wouldn't assume he was talking to me, but since the only other person in the bar was Clarence, I answered.

"Fine," I said, picking up a discarded newspaper to further discourage conversation.

"Eye ot ay etter or ya," he said.

"Huh?" I replied.

Connor approached the table and said something else, but I didn't pay attention. He placed a sealed business-sized envelope on the table, stamped and addressed to me care of the Philosopher's Club. There was no return address. I broke the seal on the envelope and found a piece of paper with letters cut and glued from newspaper and magazine print that read:

---

[1] Not his real name.

185

I Know yoUr litTle SeCret
If yoU waNt to KEep iT
You wiLL meeT mY demAnds
InsTrUctions TO FollOw

My first reaction was to mentally catalogue my many secrets. But I was tired and that was a lot of unnecessary work. Clearly my "secret" was my new living arrangement. My "blackmailer" was equally obvious. The note had Rae written all over it.[2]

I finished my beer and headed over to my parents' house.

Rae was in her room, supposedly studying for the PSAT retake on Friday to clear her name. I found my sister hanging upside down off her bed in the middle of what I can only assume was a fascinating phone call.

"No—it's not possible. I don't believe it. I'll never believe it. Well, maybe under those exact sets of circumstances, I might believe it. But right now . . . I don't . . . I better go. My sister is here and she's showing no signs of leaving. See ya tomorrow. Bye."

Rae sat up in bed, looked me over, and said, "You look unwell."

"I'm tired," I said, trying to muster a cold edge to my voice. Exhaustion slurred my words, so it didn't come off as I had hoped.

"You should try sleeping," Rae replied. "Or at least taking vitamins. There's a box of Froot Loops downstairs. Help yourself."

The non sequitur threw me and shifted the tone of the conversation in Rae's favor.

"I don't follow how Froot Loops relate to vitamins or sleep."

"They're vitamin-fortified," Rae explained.

"Don't push your drugs on me," I replied, feeling a surprising surge of hostility.

---

[2] Rae has left a distinctive pattern of blackmail in her wake. See original document, *The Spellman Files,* for details.

"What do you want?" Rae asked, losing her patience.

"What do *you* want, I think is the point."

"I want a new car."

"Be reasonable."

"A used car."

"*That's* what you want?" I asked, barely containing my outrage.

"And world peace," Rae said, fishing for what I was looking for.

"Don't play games with me, Rae."

"Are you stoned?"

"I'm here about the note."

"What note?"

"Your little blackmail letter."

"I stopped blackmailing people years ago."

"You're denying you wrote—correction, cut and pasted—the note."

"Izz, if you're being blackmailed, it's not me. If you want to provide me with the details, I can look into the matter for you."

My phone rang just in time. I needed to convince Rae that my situation wasn't urgent. Otherwise she'd have the leverage of having spotted a weakness.

"Hi, Morty," I said into the receiver.

"Izzele. Get over to my house right now. I have an emergency."

"Did you call 911?"

"Not that kind of emergency."

"Then you shouldn't call it an emergency. Where's Ruth?" I asked.

"She left an hour ago for a bridge game. Are you coming over or what?" Morty asked.

"Yes."

"Don't tell anyone," Morty said.

"Who am I going to tell?"

"Not one word!" Morty urged, and then hung up the phone.

"I have to go," I said. "But this isn't over, Rae. I'll be in touch."

"Get some beauty rest," Rae said as I passed through her doorway. When I was almost out of earshot, she mumbled, "You need it."

THE MORTY PROBLEM

Two weeks after Morty's return from the hospital, his health was mostly restored, although he didn't own up to that fact. Still in his ensemble of striped pajamas, terry-cloth robe, and severely worn slippers, Morty met me at the door and directed me into the kitchen. A single piece of paper sat on the table next to a cup of coffee and a half-eaten sandwich.

"What am I going to do?" Morty asked, standing back from the page as if it were an explosive object.

I picked it up. It was a divorce petition, naming Ruth Schilling as the petitioner and Mortimer Schilling as the respondent. My guess was that the document had not yet been filed at the court, so it was still in the threat category, like a loaded gun in a holster.

"She's bluffing, right?" Morty asked.

"I don't think so. If she's found an attorney, what would keep her from filing the paperwork?"

"I can't believe she'd do this to me. While I'm at death's door, no less."

"Knock it off. No one's buying the sick act anymore."

"What should I do?" Morty asked, weaving his hands together like a villain in a silent film.

"What do you mean?" I replied.

"What's my next move?" my old friend asked in all seriousness.

"Sit down," I said authoritatively.

Morty didn't budge, so I pulled a chair for him and repeated my demand. He sat.

"You're moving to Florida, old man. And if you don't, I can guarantee your children will toss you in a home and leave you there to rot. Ruthy has been with you for fifty-five years. You made a deal and you're going to stick to it. Got it?"

Morty's face flushed with anger, which soon faded into acceptance. He nodded his head sullenly.

"Get out of your pajamas and start packing," I said.

MY NEW JOB

DAY 2

I couldn't risk being late two days in a row, so I phoned David when I was ready to leave and asked him if he could look for my watch in the guest bedroom—which is located in the back of the house, where he wouldn't see me on my way out. However, David was still asleep (at 8:20 A.M.? The universe was turning upside down!), so I apologized for waking him and exited his residence with yet another David mystery to solve. Because of my own new work schedule, it was hard for me to keep track of David's work habits, but as far as I could tell he hadn't been at the office since his return.

I was having some trouble keeping track of the mess of mysteries in my head, so I tried mentally organizing them as I waited for the bus. Once the bus came, it was a different story. I grabbed the last open seat in the back by the window and took a quick nap, setting my phone to ring fifteen minutes later. Minimally refreshed but on time, I strolled into the offices of RH Investigations at 8:55 A.M., wearing a pencil skirt, boots, an oxford shirt buttoned to the top, and a cardigan sweater, with my hair in a severe bun. I would have looked really put together if all the clothes hadn't been heavily wrinkled.

I shredded files and answered phones for the first two hours. Harkey was the kind of employer who could be sitting at his desk doing nothing but drinking coffee and clipping his nails, and if the phone rang, I would have to walk from the back room to the reception desk and answer it. While I was out of Harkey's view, I inspected the office systems as best I could. The key to finding the Truesdale/Black/Bancroft files would be cracking the numerical filing system. I also needed some alone time with the files.

Fortunately, Harkey had a business lunch that day. He showed me a stack of files, told me to answer the phones, and jotted down his cell number should any emergencies occur. I could tell he was uneasy leaving me alone in his office, but he had a system in place that would take some time to crack. Besides, Harkey was arrogant enough to assume I couldn't decipher his simple code.

I figured I had ninety minutes tops before Harkey returned, so I got straight to work.

I picked up a file with the following number on the tab: 07.8547519.1. Inside was a file opened in 2007 that was clearly a background report on a man named Mark Hedges. The 07 surely referred to the year the file was opened. This simplifies purging files at a later date. Generally, a numeric filing system involves A) the date on which the file was opened, B) the name on the file, or C) on rare occasions, a random number (for security purposes) that must be cross-referenced against another list. I took a guess that the numbers after the year marker referred to the name on the file. So I looked back at the Hedges file. This was elementary-school code breaking. Allow me to explain Harkey's simple code system.

Each letter in the alphabet has a numerical representative that is either one or two digits. Each number corresponds to the letter's simple sequence in the alphabet. A is represented by 1 and Z is represented by 26.

To find the file on Black, Truesdale, or Bancroft (since I wasn't sure who Harkey saw as the true subject of the investigation), I pulled out a pencil and paper and worked out each potential file number. Then I searched for a numbered file corresponding with Truesdale (nothing), then Black (nothing), and finally Bancroft—where there was indeed a file. I pulled the file, made copies of its contents, stuffed them in my purse, then returned the file to the cabinet and checked the clock. I had fifteen minutes before I could expect Harkey to return from his lunch. I raced to file as many files as I could and then I misfiled a few, just in case I needed some fuel to get fired in the near future.

The investigation had Bancroft's name on it, but the true subject was Linda Truesdale-not-Black. The file consisted of a surveillance log, a background report, and a list of attempts to access her financial data. At the bottom of the log sheet there were references to MP3 files, which I assumed meant Harkey had some audio recordings connected to the case.

According to the log, they were on the XYZ drive, but when I checked the computer there was no such drive. This led me to believe that the files were being hidden. I just had to figure out where.

One hour and thirty minutes after Harkey's departure, I could hear his booming voice on his cell phone as he approached the office. I quickly escaped from the computer directory, returned to the file room, and made a show of dusting off the countertops.

INVISIBLE ISABEL

This new bit of information left me puzzled about how to proceed. When my shift ended at Harkey's, I decided to drop by my parents' house to come clean about my undercover investigation—and solicit some advice. When I arrived, Rae was seated at the kitchen table, books and papers splayed in front of her, pencil in her mouth.

"What are you doing?" I asked, even though the answer was obvious.

" 'Studying,' " Rae said, using finger quotes.

"For what?"

"The Psssat."

Then my dad entered the kitchen. I said, "Dad, I need to talk to you for a minute."

My father sat down at the table across from Rae and began eating some yogurt. I pulled a chair next to his and repeated my previous request. Dad ate his yogurt as if I were invisible.

Had my faculties been in normal operating condition, I would have recognized the unique stance of my father when he's giving me his finest bit of attitude. Instead, I stared at my dad as if he were some alien life form and then turned to my sister for a consultation.

"Something's not right about Dad. What is it?" I asked.

Rae briefly studied Dad's body language and said, "It would appear that he's not speaking to you."

"Dad, are you talking to me?"

No response.

"That's a dumb question," Rae said. "I mean, if he's not talking to you he's not going to answer the question, is he?"

"You ask him," I said.

"Dad, are you not talking to Isabel?" Rae asked.

"Isabel?" Dad replied. "Who is Isabel?"

Rae turned to me. "It's worse than I thought," she said.

Then my mother entered the room.

"Mom, Dad's not talking to me," I said. "Why?"

"I'm not talking to you, either," my mom said, except that she sort of was.

Since Rae was the only one fully recognizing my presence in the room, I decided to turn to her for an explanation.

"Why aren't they talking to me?" I asked.

"If I overheard things correctly, I think it's because you went to work for Rick Harkey. Why would you do that? That guy is such a tool."

Dad cleared his throat, cuing Rae to elaborate.

"And Dad's mortal enemy," Rae continued.

"Thank you," Dad said to Rae.

"I have an explanation," I said to anyone who was listening. "Is anyone interested in it?"

Dad finished his yogurt, got up from the table, and headed into the Spellman offices. Mom said, "You really screwed up this time, Isabel," and left the room.

"I have an explanation!" I said. "Does anyone want to hear it?"

"I do," Rae said, but I was already out the door.

The mile-long walk back to David's and my house seemed to take forever. My feet felt like lead and I wanted to punch the wind that was slowing me down. I longed for a three-hour bus ride, but I was going to settle for a bed.

I was going to learn how to sleep in David's place one way or another. I dropped into a drugstore and purchased some nighttime cold medicine.[1]

I slipped into my apartment unnoticed, got into my pajamas, and took the medicine.

An hour later, I was still staring at the ceiling—sleepy, but not asleep, bored and miserable because my mind couldn't focus on anything but the fact that I might spend yet another night conscious and useless. My phone buzzed and I was relieved for the break from my own thoughts.

It was Charlie. I mean Ernie. My client, remember? Well, I barely did, so I figured I should remind you.

"I'm just checking in," he said.

"Oh, good," I replied, trying to figure out whether I had any information for him.

"Any new leads?" he asked.

"Yes," I replied. I was working the case, so there had to be a few new leads. Right?

"I'm all ears," Ernie said.

"Yes. That's true. You do have big ears," I said (yep, out loud).

Ernie laughed. Thank god. I recovered and told Ernie I was working on a lead, but I had nothing I was ready to tell him. There was another long pause. I can't tell you whether anything was said during that time, but I do think I got in a very brief catnap. Then Ernie woke me.

"I bought *Cosmopolitan* the other day. You know, the magazine."

"Oh, good," I replied, and then I tried to say "cosmopolitan," but I couldn't.

"You okay, Izzy?" Ernie asked.

"I just took some cold medicine. That's all."

"Do you have a cold?"

---

[1] See, I am evolving. These drugs are legal.

"No. What were you saying?"

"My wife reads *Cosmo*—that's what they call it—so I thought that maybe it would give me some insight."

"Did it?" I asked.

"I read an article about things men do that make women mad."

"So, what are you going to do, Charlie?"

"Who's Charlie?"

"Ernie. I meant Ernie. What are you going to do?"

"I'm going to try to stop doing those things," he said.

"Good," I replied.

"I love my wife," Ernie then said.

"I know."

"I don't want her to leave me."

When I got off the phone with Ernie, it occurred to me that sleep deprivation was eroding my detective skills. I looked at the Bancroft file one more time and tried to envision what my next step in the investigation would be. No information that could explain why Linda was being investigated could be gleaned from the contents of the file. But that audio recording was suspicious; I knew I had to get my hands on it. I wrote myself a note on my arm: "MP3?" Then I took another dose of cold medicine and finally drifted off to sleep.

THERAPY SESSION #15

[Partial transcript reads as follows:]

ISABEL: There might be something seriously wrong with me.

DR. RUSH: I wouldn't say that.

ISABEL: Medically, not psychologically wrong—although I can understand the confusion.

DR. RUSH: Please elaborate.

ISABEL: I can't remember things. Last night I wrote myself a note on my arm. "MP3," with a question mark. This morning when I woke up I had no idea what it meant. Lately if I write on my arm it's to remind me of where I parked my car. See, another symptom. I never used to forget where my car was. Well, once or twice.

DR. RUSH: Are you sleeping?

ISABEL: Last night I took some nighttime cold medicine and I got a full seven hours.

DR. RUSH: If you need cold medicine to get to sleep, you should see a physician.

ISABEL: I don't *need* cold medicine to sleep. I mean, I can sleep on a bus without any assistance.

DR. RUSH: Excuse me?

ISABEL: I think it will just take some time to get used to my new apartment.

DR. RUSH: So you've moved recently?

ISABEL: Yes.[1] Oh, but I figured it out.

DR. RUSH: You figured out what?

ISABEL: What MP3, question mark, means.

DR. RUSH: What does it mean?

ISABEL: It was just a reminder to check something on the case I'm working on.

DR. RUSH: I thought you had taken a break from PI work.

ISABEL: I agreed to this one case, just to get my feet wet again and see how I felt about the whole thing.

DR. RUSH: What is the case?

ISABEL: A guy thinks his wife is cheating on him or shoplifting. It seemed nice and boring, but then it got a little bit interesting.

DR. RUSH: How so?

ISABEL: Someone else is following the guy's wife as well. That means she's doing more than cheating, or at least whoever is interested thinks so.

DR. RUSH: Are you obsessing again?

ISABEL: I'd say I'm extremely curious.

DR. RUSH: Is it going to become a problem?

ISABEL: The last time I got in trouble was for investigating someone I wasn't *supposed* to investigate.

DR. RUSH: A neighbor?

ISABEL: Right. But this time I've been hired to investigate this woman, and the case has taken an unexpected turn. I'd be a lousy PI if I just ignored the evidence right in front of me.

DR. RUSH: You have to find a balance. Can you do that?

ISABEL: Maybe.

DR. RUSH: Let's look at it a different way. Is the case in any way negatively affecting your life?

---

[1] Right here I decided to change the subject. I trusted doctor-patient confidentiality, but I didn't trust the doctor to keep her opinion about the new living arrangement to herself.

[Long, long pause.]

DR. RUSH: Are you pausing because you're genuinely thinking or are you pausing to kill time?

ISABEL: At first I was thinking and then I'm pretty sure I fell asleep for a few seconds. What was the question?

DR. RUSH: Has taking this job negatively affected your life?

ISABEL: Well, my parents are giving me the silent treatment. Although my dad is way better at it than my mom, as usual.

DR. RUSH: Have they done this before?

ISABEL: My dad didn't talk to me for a week after I sold his golf clubs on eBay.

DR. RUSH: Why did you do that?

ISABEL: He never golfed and I needed the cash.

DR. RUSH: I see.

ISABEL: And my mom said only a few words to me for three weeks after my expulsion from ballet class.

DR. RUSH: Why were you expelled?

ISABEL: Long story.[2]

DR. RUSH: Why do you think your parents are so angry with you this time around?

ISABEL: Well, they've been asking me to come back to work, and the next thing they know, I've taken an administrative position with a competitor they both despise. It's understandable.

DR. RUSH: I'm not following. Why did you take a position with a despised competitor?

ISABEL: Because he knows something about the case I'm working on.

DR. RUSH: Is that ethical?

ISABEL: It's in a gray area.

DR. RUSH: Shouldn't you be staying out of that area?

---

[2] Actually, it's not so long. During the three-month stretch at the age of twelve when I was forced to take ballet, I committed a series of pranks in which I took great pride. My crowning achievement, and the cause for my expulsion, was when I mopped the studio floor with vegetable oil right before class.

ISABEL: I'm not sure you can be a good investigator if you're not willing to break a few rules here and there.

DR. RUSH: Do your parents understand that?

ISABEL: Sure. But if they're not talking to me, then how am I going to explain myself?

DR. RUSH: Why don't you write them a letter?

ISABEL: Huh, I hadn't thought of that.

After therapy, I took the bus[3] back to "my" place and spent a quiet evening in, composing my letter of contrition to the Parental Unit. My "Dear Mom and Dad" letter touched on all the issues that I knew were the roots of their disappointment. It even included a wholehearted apology for all my past misdeeds. I would include the letter in this document, but it was too sincere to make for decent reading material.

That night I went to sleep without cold medicine. I got in about two hours until I woke from a nightmare involving David storming my apartment accompanied by about a dozen SWAT team members and a battering ram. I stared at the ceiling until dawn, planning my next bus ride.

---

[3] Had a nice twenty-minute nap.

CASE #001

CHAPTER 7

Early Tuesday morning, I dropped the letter in my parents' mail-box. I then took a detour before work. Robbie Gruber—a computer expert who runs a business named Call-A-Geek—has been Spellman Investigations' go-to guy for technical troubles for as long as I can remember having technical troubles. No one can sort out a computer problem better than Robbie. However, it comes at a cost.

I've seen Robbie bring my mother to the brink of tears and watched him and my father almost come to blows. Robbie tosses around the word "moron" like he has a daily quota to fill. He accuses you of being so dimwitted that you couldn't find an on/off switch without a map. His shouting will unnerve you so much that you won't be able to follow his simple instructions—"CONTROL! ALT! DELETE! HOW FUCKING HARD IS THAT!" And when your computer is restored to health and Robbie is packing his things to go, he will shame you into thanking him.

Robbie keeps his front door open (which doesn't seem wise when you have the kind of enemies he does), so I let myself in. When he saw me, he didn't say hello but rolled his eyes and continued doing whatever it was he was doing.

"Hi, Robbie," I said with a tone of perkiness I was sure would irritate him. "I need your help."

"I'm busy. Come back later," he replied.

I pulled up a chair and sat down next to him. "Nope."

I took the log sheet from my bag and put it on Robbie's desk, along with two twenty-dollar bills.

"I'll make it quick," I said.

"What?" Robbie said, finally making eye contact. Although I've noticed that it's not eye contact he makes. He looks at the spot just between your eyebrows. He can't stand to look you in the eye.

"Look at the log sheet," I said. "All the files are in their exact location except I can't find the XYZ drive. There is no XYZ drive when you look in the browser. I've also checked the individual computers in the office. Should I assume it's an external hard drive?"

"You lost a file on your own computer?" Robbie asked in a tone so condescending it would be impossible to duplicate.

"Not my computer. Someone else's. I'm trying to figure out why I can't find this folder when everything else is easy to access."

Robbie glanced at the log sheet and went back to work.

"Probably a hidden share drive," he said.

"What's that?"

"I'm not explaining that to you. You won't understand—I guarantee it. Just follow my directions and do not deviate from them in any way. You can't just use the network browser to search for the drive—it won't work, because it's a *hidden* drive, get it? Go to the Tools menu and choose Map. Network. Drive. Do I need to repeat that?"

"No, I'm recording you," I replied.

"After you Map Network Drive, type in backslash, backslash, computer, XYZ, dollar sign. When I say 'computer' I'm using a placeholder for the name of your file server. Don't type in 'computer' like a complete moron. And a dollar sign is just a dollar sign—shift-four. Got it? And you know what a backslash is, right? It's leaning backward, not forward. If you do exactly what I tell you, you should find your file."

"Are you sure?" I asked. "Don't make me come back here."

"Yes, I'm sure," Robbie replied, snatching the money off the desk. "Close the door on your way out."

The front desk at RH Investigations was backed against a wall and offered a clear view into Harkey's office if the door was open, so it followed that he had a clear view of me. With the door open and Harkey's eye on me whenever he didn't hear the click of the computer keys, my window of opportunity to search for the relevant files was limited. I decided there had to be a better way.

THE RANSOM

PART II

After exiting the offices of RH Investigations, I turned on my cell phone. There were five voice mail messages, as follows:

MESSAGE #1: It's me.[1] So I need the scoop on this Gabe guy. Great hair. Call me.

MESSAGE #2: Izz, it's Rae. So, Mom and Dad got your letter. They seem less mad. I'd be happy to facilitate a peace deal for a small fee. I'll be in touch.

MESSAGE #3: Izzele, it's Morty here. I just want to make sure I've thought of everything in regard to the whole moving to Florida business. Give me a call so we can put our heads together.

MESSAGE #4: Isabel, it's Gabe. I'm not sure what you did about Grandpa, but good job. Thanks. Oh, and your friend Petra gave me a great haircut. Um, yeah. Okay, that's all. Good-bye. Call me if you get the chance. I have something to ask you.

MESSAGE #5: Izzy, why am I getting mail for you at the bar? I thought we talked about this.[2]

---

[1] Petra is the only person who refuses to identify herself in voice mail messages.

[2] Milo calling.

Before I hopped on the train to the Philosopher's Club, I returned the call that required the least effort.

"Hi, Morty, it's Isabel. Listen to me very carefully: You have two choices. You move to Florida or you and Ruthy get a divorce. End of story. If you need help packing, give me a call."

I managed to fit the above words in between "Hello" and "Wait!"

Within twenty-five minutes of hopping on the Muni train (it was too crowded to sit, and therefore to nap) I was at the Philosopher's Club, reading the following letter in the customary ransom note format.

If You woUld liKe to kEEp yOuR
SeCRet, wAsH, dRy, and WaX YouR
FatHeR's AuDI THiS weeKeNd

If my blackmailer was Rae, she was trying to redirect suspicion toward my father. What was odd about this strategy was that she could only enjoy the status of puppet master but not reap any other rewards. If the note didn't have Rae written all over it, I would have accused my dad of the crime. Either way, it was disappointing, since I would have to spend at least two hours on a Saturday morning tending to his vehicle. I had to pay for someone's silence, but I'd rather pay that than rent. I blocked out Saturday morning on my schedule and hoped that it would silence my sister for a while. If not, I would have to retaliate.

Then I ordered a drink and sat down at the bar. Clarence misread my sluggish deportment as sadness and approached with the clear intent of improving my spirits. He said nothing but this:

"A skeleton walks into a bar. He orders a beer and a mop."

I didn't get it at first, but when I did, convulsive laughter took over—the embarrassing, unstable kind of laughter. When I finally came to I felt nauseous and needed a nap. I found my way to a booth in back and sprawled out.

"This ain't a motel! Wake up, Izzy!"

Milo, the human alarm clock, ruined my much-needed rest, and then he didn't stop to say hello. He turned to the Irishman, said something about going to the bank, reminded him not to let people sleep, and then left.

As I was trying to shake off my afternoon sleep-hangover with an Irish coffee,[3] Henry entered the bar. Alone. He sat exactly one bar stool over from me, as if he didn't even see that I was there.

I slid over to the next bar stool and said, "What's a guy like you doing in a place like this?"

Henry turned to me, surprised, and said rather angrily, "Where have you been?"

"Just over there," I said, pointing at my previous bar stool. "And over there before that," I added, pointing to the inviting booth.

"I dropped by your house two times last week. The first time I rang your buzzer at one A.M.—"

"What are you doing ringing my buzzer at one A.M.?"

"Let me finish."

"Okay," I said, studying Henry's demeanor. He was not himself that day.

"The second time, I woke up some guy who said you had moved. Where?"

"I can't believe they rented that place already. I bet the new tenant looked sleepy."

"Where are you living?" Henry asked.

Think fast. Think fast. Don't ruin this great thing you've got going.

"I'm staying with a friend for a bit. You know I was laid off here, so I need to save my money."

"What friend?"

"No one."

Connor approached and pointed at Henry's almost empty whiskey.

"An I get ya anooder?"

Henry said yes and slid his glass forward.

---

[3] I refused to give Connor the satisfaction of ordering it by name, so I said, "Pour me a cup of coffee and put some whiskey in it."

"You understood that?" I asked.

"Ow abut you, orgeous?" Connor then asked me.

"Would you please stop calling me that?[4] I'm good for now."

Henry sipped his refreshed drink and consulted the ceiling.

"Did you move in with that Gabe kid?"

"Are you crazy?"

"Then where are you?" he asked.

"I'm crashing at my friends Len and Christopher's place in Oakland."

"Why?" he asked.

"Because I don't have a job and can't afford rent," I replied. "And don't tell anyone named Spellman."

"Don't worry. I'm not talking to any of them."[5]

"Well, if you do end up talking to them, don't mention that I moved out."

Silence ensued, which, as I've explained before, I've grown quite comfortable with. But then I got the feeling that Henry maybe wanted to talk to me about something. There are hundreds of bars in this city, many near his home, any one of which he could patronize and drink alone in.

"How've you been, Henry?"

"Fine," he replied abruptly.

"How's Maggie?"

"I don't know."

"Why not?"

"I haven't seen her in a few days."

"Is she missing?"

"No."

"On the lam?"

"Are you capable of having a normal conversation?" Henry asked as he got to his feet. He was less angry than disappointed. It was one of those

---

[4] I couldn't help thinking he meant "gorgeous" ironically.

[5] The implication that the communication rift extended beyond my sister was intriguing.

rare moments when I had a brief picture of what it might be like to know me. I grabbed Henry's wrist to stop him from leaving.

"Wait," I said. "I'm going to try. I promise."

Henry gazed at me suspiciously and wondered what my angle was.

"Sit down," I said.

What followed was a long, awkward pause, because I wasn't even sure where to begin.

"Do you want to tell me what happened?"

"We broke up. That's all," Henry replied.

"I'm sorry," I said. "Are you okay?"

"I'm fine. Thank you."

"Do you want to talk about it?" I asked.

"No."

Another long pause followed. I would like you to note that my comments were all perfectly reasonable and noninflammatory. Further evidence that my social skills are improving. I finished my drink and pointed to the glass. Connor, who apparently can read people better than I can, refilled it silently to avoid disrupting the nonconversation Henry and I were having.

"Would you like me to tell you about my own troubles as a means of distraction?" I asked.

Henry turned to me and almost smiled.

"Yes," he said.

So I shared a few of my latest sagas with him: I told him about my trouble sleeping in a bed, but that the bus was working out for me. I explained that the constant sleep deprivation was messing with my memory in general, but especially in locating my car. I even told him that I took a job with my father's mortal enemy (although I provided few details beyond that point, since some of my activities loitered just outside of legal). Then I told him about the advances I had made in therapy. Henry asked for examples and I came up a bit short, but did recall that I had recently discovered the power of a carefully worded note and told him about my "Dear Mom and Dad" letter.

I was running out of distraction-worthy material, so I pulled out my coup de grâce, which I really wasn't planning on using, because the information would lead to follow-up questions. But since I'm the master of evasion, I figured I could risk it.

"And I'm being blackmailed," I said proudly.

Henry thought I was exaggerating, so I produced the latest note.

"What kind of dirt do they have on you?" Henry asked.

"I ripped off a liquor store in my early twenties. I'm sure it's one of my coconspirators."

Stone completely ignored my tall tale and held the note up to the light.

"It's Rae, of course," he said with great conviction.

"Maybe," I replied. "Although my dad has emerged as another suspect."

"When you're done with his car, mine could use a good wash and wax."

CASE #001

CHAPTER 8

O n my way "home," I phoned Petra and provided her with a newspaper-worthy bio on Gabe. She, in turn, provided the details of their budding romance, which had reached the stage of dating more than one night in a row but hadn't yet gone in the his-and-hers-tattoos direction. When Petra finished relaying every single detail of her previous night's rendezvous (and thanking me profusely), I solicited her services in the Harkey investigation. As usual, Petra was game for anything.

Petra arrived at the offices of RH Investigations at a quarter past twelve the following day. Dressed like a femme fatale from a 1940s film noir—red suit, hat, stilettos—she opened up her clutch purse and reapplied her lipstick.

"I have an appointment with Mr. Harkey. Please tell him Agatha Shveldenberger is here," she said.

"Shevelden—?" I tried to say.

"Shveldengerber," she said differently the second time around.

"Don't overplay it," I mumbled.

"I'm here for my appointment," Petra said loud enough for Harkey's ears.

"I need fifteen minutes," I said as quietly as possible, then, "Take a seat," at full volume.

I informed Harkey of his appointment through the intercom. A few minutes later, he led Petra into his office and shut the door. I quickly switched screens on the computer, followed Robbie's instructions, and after a couple of seconds, the XYZ drive appeared. I cross-checked the folders and began hunting for audio files with the number associated with the Bancroft case. There was no time to listen to the recordings, so I backed them up on a key-chain USB drive, closed all screens, and got back to work transcribing a recorded interview as quickly as I could. Petra and Harkey exited his office almost fifteen minutes to the second from when they entered.

Harkey walked Petra to the door and said, "I'm sorry I couldn't help you, Ms.—"

"A pleasure meeting you, Rick," Petra said, departing with the same dramatic flair that marked her entrance.

"Why is it that all the good-looking girls are crazy?" Harkey said after Petra was safely in the distance. "Present company excepted," he said with a disgusting wink.

"What's her story?" I asked.

"She believes her husband has been abducted by aliens.[1] I would have taken the job if she had any money. I *love* alien abduction cases. Anyway, she's broke. I told her I couldn't help her but suggested she contact Spellman Investigations."

Harkey returned to his office, enjoying his little joke. I spent the rest of the afternoon contemplating how I'd get myself fired.

After work I took the bus (I love the bus—have I mentioned that?) back to the general vicinity of my new home and hunted for my car, remembering that I had to move it for street cleaning. I walked to the corner of Green and Leavenworth, where my car was last seen, although, if you recall, I never remembered parking it there to begin with. After a twenty-minute hunt, I found it on Jackson near Leavenworth. I'd made certain to carefully

---

[1] Bravo, Petra. Bravo. For a partial transcript of their conversation, see appendix.

document my car's coordinates (on a piece of paper). The car was most certainly moved, and not by me. The good news: I wouldn't have to move the car for another four days. The bad news: Someone was playing games with me.

As I strolled over to my parents' house, I debated which piece of equipment I would pinch to further my investigation on the phantom who was relocating my car. I decided a hidden camera was the way to go and I pulled a small device (about the size of a quarter) that I could conceal in a seam of fabric over the driver's seat. I could hide the camera's receiver in the trunk. I put the equipment into my backpack and was about to exit through the window when I overheard voices in the next room. I couldn't resist listening in on what seemed like a slightly tense conversation:

DAD: So how do you think you did?

RAE: We'll find out soon enough.

MOM: You must have some idea.

RAE: I really think we should just wait and see the results.

DAD: I'm sure you did great.

RAE: There's nothing wrong with thinking positive.

MOM: Why do I get the feeling you're laying the groundwork for bad news?

RAE: It was harder than the last time.

DAD: How much harder could it be?

RAE: All I'm saying is to be prepared for anything.

At this point I heard footsteps approaching the office door. I really didn't want to make contact with my parents until they fully digested my apology letter, so I slipped out the same window I came in.

I returned to David's house, scouted the perimeter for signs of my brother, and slipped into the apartment. That night, I listened to the recordings I acquired from Harkey's office, which totaled over four hours. The conversations clearly originated from two bugs—one in Linda's car and one in Sharon's. Most of the recordings were nonnoteworthy. The women were typically alone and would occasionally sing along with the radio. The one-sided cell phone calls provided most of the content, but even they, for the most part, told me nothing. Sharon called her husband's assistant to make dinner reservations;[2] Linda called her husband and told him not to have meat loaf for lunch since that's what she was cooking for dinner. Sharon also phoned her decorator, trainer, and dog walker.

I suppose what was noteworthy about these recordings was that neither Sharon nor Linda knew that they were being recorded, and there was no logical reason why either of these women would plant a bug in her own car. Mostly they drove alone. My point: If Harkey made these recordings, he was breaking the law.

After listening to most of the audio files, I began fast-forwarding through them until I finally came upon something of interest:

LINDA: What are you afraid of, that I'm going to talk? I can't figure it out. I feel like I'm being paid off.

I reversed the recording to where the cell phone conversation began and transcribed the contents of the call. On a hunch, I checked Sharon's corresponding recordings to see whether a corollary conversation took place. I found something with the same date that sounded like a possible match. I transcribed that recording and merged the two transcriptions. What I got was enlightening, but not necessarily educational.

[The transcript reads as follows:]

LINDA: Hello?
SHARON: It's me. Did you get it?
LINDA: Yes, but I don't want it.
SHARON: Why not?

---

[2] Wouldn't it be simpler to call the restaurant directly?

LINDA: I just don't. I don't need those things. You don't need those things. How would I explain it to Ernie?

SHARON: Tell him it's a knockoff. He won't know the difference.

LINDA: Honestly, the idea of a purse costing two thousand dollars offends me.

SHARON: Do you know how hard it was for me to get it?

LINDA: What are you afraid of, that I'm going to talk? I can't figure it out. I feel like I'm being paid off.

SHARON: It was just a gift.

LINDA: It's not just a gift. I'm tired of the gifts. I'm tired of having things around I can't explain to Ernie. I'm tired of your guilt.

SHARON: You should have what I have. That's all.

LINDA: But why?

SHARON: You know why.

LINDA: What happened, what we did, took place a long time ago. I'm over it. You should be, too.

SHARON: We didn't do it. I did.

LINDA: Doesn't he get suspicious? All these gifts to your low-rent friend.

SHARON: Stop it.

LINDA: Well, doesn't he?

SHARON: He's asking questions. I don't know what he's thinking because he barely speaks to me.

LINDA: He thinks that I'm blackmailing you—that's what he's thinking.

SHARON: Well, he's always been paranoid. Sometimes I wish I left him years ago.

LINDA: You still can.

SHARON: No, it's too late. He'd find out for sure. And I'd lose everything.

LINDA: You don't need his money.

SHARON: That's my other line. I have to go.

My conscience wasn't clear about how I acquired this information, but the call confirmed that my suspicions were justified. Now I only had to figure out what I was suspicious of. Oh, and take down Rick Harkey for his violation of California Penal Code § 631(a) (eavesdropping), which makes illegal the taping of a private communication unless all parties consent. To be perfectly honest, the Harkey-takedown angle excited me more than whatever secrets Linda and Sharon were hiding. But that was just my bonus prize. I was still going to uncover their secrets.

CLOSE WINDOWS BEFORE WASHING

Saturday morning at ten A.M., I had to make a dangerous escape from David's house. My brother, like clockwork, goes for a nine A.M. Saturday run (five miles). I had just assumed he had departed when at approximately nine forty-five I exited our residence[1] and circled the perimeter, just as David was leaving through the front door. I quickly backed into some shrubbery and managed to go unnoticed, but it was an extremely close call, which sent my adrenaline surging.

On the way to my parents' house, I theorized about David's new un-clockwork-like schedule. Then it occurred to me that David might have actually quit his job. Or, even worse, gotten fired. Then I began theorizing about why he got fired. I had some interesting theories, but they seemed a bit too sensational to entertain.[2] Fortunately, hard labor quieted my mind.

After arriving at 1799 Clay Street, I filled a bucket with water and dish soap and began scrubbing my father's midnight blue Audi. Halfway through my lathering-up of the vehicle, Rae exited the house looking both curious and suspicious.

"What are you doing?" she asked.

---

[1] Note to self: Do not refer to it as "our residence" in David's company.

[2] See appendix.

216

"What does it look like I'm doing?" I replied.

"Washing Dad's car with the window still open. He's gonna kill you."

"Shit. Where are the keys?"

Rae pulled the keys from her pocket and tossed them at me. I opened the door, cleaned up the mess as best I could, turned on the engine so I could start the heater to dry the seat, closed the window, and continued my assigned task.

My sister studied me suspiciously.

"How much is he paying you?" she asked, as if no amount of money could get her to do the same.

I almost replied *Nine hundred dollars a month* but remembered my rule of silence.

"Nothing."

"Then why are you doing it?"

"It was dirty," I replied. The tone of my sister's inquiry indicated to me with almost complete certainty that she was not my blackmailer. The next logical choice was Dad. Therefore, when my father exited the house and questioned my activity, I played it like the knowing victim.

"Isabel, what are you doing?"

"Washing your car," I said, stating the obvious.

"Why?"

"You know."

Dad pretended like he didn't and said, "We got your note."

"I got *your* note," I said.

"What note?"

"Fine. If that's how you want to play it . . ."

"Excuse me?" said Dad.

"Can I assume you're speaking to me now?" I asked.

"Yes, I'm speaking to you."

"When I'm done with the car, I need to talk to you about something."

"I'll take you to lunch."

"What is it with you and lunch?" I asked.

"Don't forget the hubcaps," Dad said. "I like to see them sparkle."

. . .

My mom insisted that Dad and I have lunch alone, so we decided to go to a crepe place on Polk Street where she once claimed to have gotten food poisoning. My father made a big show of ordering the Greek salad. While my dad searched for all the nonvegetable items in his lunch, I told him about my discovery at Harkey's office. This was serious information: I caught his mortal enemy breaking the law. I half expected my dad to hoot and holler when I passed on this groundbreaking news.

Instead, Dad sat in contemplative silence, deconstructing cubes of feta cheese.

"This case you're working on," Dad said. "Are you going to be able to let it go?"

"Once I figure out what's going on," I said.

"Curiosity is a good characteristic for this job, but you need to strike a balance. Maybe you should get a hobby."

"Like what?"

"I have an idea. Why don't you come with me to one of my yoga classes? I find it very relaxing."

"Change the subject now, before I lose my entire lunch," I said.

"Sheesh. It was just a suggestion."

"Say something quickly to clear that image from my head."

My father rolled his eyes and consulted the ceiling: "Have you gotten everything you need from Harkey?"

Come to think of it, I had. I think. As far as I could tell.

"Yes, I think so," I replied.

"Give notice Tuesday," my dad said. He wasn't asking, he was telling. "But stay on good terms with Harkey."

"Why?" I asked, only hours into my plan of creating havoc with his files.

"I have my reasons," Dad replied cagily.

"Would you like to share?" I asked.

"No."

What followed was more awkward silence, which I'm sure I handled better than my father because A) I've been getting a lot of experience lately, and B) Dad was stabbing his salad with a little too much enthusiasm during the extended lull in conversation. Since I had a few more things to iron out, I spoke first.

"Are you going to stop blackmailing me now?" I asked.

"Whatever are you talking about, Isabel?"

Me: *sigh.*

"Really, is it going to be like that?" I asked.

Dad looked me dead in the eye.

"Listen to me carefully. I'm not blackmailing you in any way. If you are being blackmailed, however, that leads me to believe that you're doing something you shouldn't be doing. I would really like to know what it is."

"You're really not blackmailing me?"

"No!"

"No need to shout," I said. "But if you ask me to wash your car again, I'll know it was you."

My dad then started chuckling to himself.

"What's so funny?"

"I bet it's your mother. She's been nagging me to get the car washed for weeks."

With my blackmailer mystery solved and my brief, soon-to-be-ending employment with Rick Harkey out in the open, I began to feel my spirits lift. I even was able to picture myself getting a full night's rest. As I watched Dad try to catch a cube of feta with his fork, I made a short list of my current goals:

- Keep new home secret from David.
- Make sure Mom doesn't talk.
- Find out what's really going on with Linda Truesdale.
- Discover who's moving my car (and why).

If you've read either of the first two documents, for me, this is nothing. In fact, I almost felt like I had not a care in the world.

But then my dad threw his napkin on his plate and said, "One more thing."

"What?"

"You have one month to decide if you want to come back to work or not. If not, your mother and I are going to look into selling the business."

"What?" I asked.

"One month," my father replied. And that was the end of the conversation.

THERAPY SESSION #17

[Partial transcript reads as follows:]

ISABEL: How can somebody make a decision like that in one month?

DR. RUSH: Presumably, your parents figure you've had most of your life to make that decision.

ISABEL: Whose side are you on?

DR. RUSH: I don't take sides.

ISABEL: For this kind of money, you should.

DR. RUSH: That's not how it works.

ISABEL: Are you sure?

DR. RUSH: Why don't we talk about the decision itself rather than the timing of it?

ISABEL: I'd rather not.

DR. RUSH: Need I remind you that you have less than a month?

ISABEL: Are you sure you're not in on this with my parents?

DR. RUSH: Do you want me to give you the doctor-patient confidentiality speech again?

ISABEL: [sigh] I think three times is enough.

[Long pause.]

DR. RUSH: Let's move on to a topic you're willing to discuss.

ISABEL: Like what?

DR. RUSH: You've got a warehouse of material to pull from. You're telling me you can't think of anything?

ISABEL: Nothing off the top of my head.

DR. RUSH: Okay, then, I'll pick a subject.

ISABEL: Wait, wait. I've got something.

DR. RUSH: I thought so.

[Long pause while I think of a subject.]

DR. RUSH: I've got a least five topics, so start talking.

ISABEL: I'm being blackmailed!

DR. RUSH: Excuse me?

ISABEL: Wait, maybe I don't want to go with that topic.

DR. RUSH: Too late.

ISABEL: [sigh] So, I'm being blackmailed.

DR. RUSH: Really? I don't want to sound too excited, but this is a first for me.

ISABEL: Maybe I'm just the first patient to admit to being blackmailed.

DR. RUSH: I don't think so. My patients usually don't keep things from me. It sort of defeats the purpose. So, who's blackmailing you?

ISABEL: First I thought it was my sister, then my dad, and then my mom. Now I'm not so sure.

DR. RUSH: How do you not know who's blackmailing you?

ISABEL: Because I got an anonymous note.

DR. RUSH: Handwritten?

ISABEL: Of course not. Cut and glued from newspapers and magazines.

DR. RUSH: Seriously?

ISABEL: Yes.

DR. RUSH: What did the note say?

ISABEL: I think our time is up.

DR. RUSH: We have a few minutes.

ISABEL: We never have a few minutes when *you* say "Our time is up."

DR. RUSH: Because when I say it, it's true. Five minutes. Keep talking.

[Long pause, but not a five-minute pause.]

ISABEL: Okay, but I don't want to talk about the blackmail anymore. There's a more pressing matter on my mind.

DR. RUSH: More pressing than blackmail?

ISABEL: Yes.

DR. RUSH: Go on.

ISABEL: There's something strange going on with my brother. I have some theories; I'd like to run them by you.

DR. RUSH: [sigh] I think our time is up.

MAN TROUBLE

The following day, per my father's instructions, I gave notice at Rick Harkey's office. Our conversation went like this:

ISABEL: Dude, I have to give notice.
HARKEY: Can I ask why?
ISABEL: Well, mostly it's because you're a creep who has no personal or ethical boundaries. But it's also because of your crazy dress code and the fact that you made a pass at my mom ten years ago.
HARKEY: I'm sorry to see you go.

Sorry, that was my fantasy conversation. This was the real one:

ISABEL: Mr. Harkey, I apologize for the short notice, but today has to be my last day on the job.
HARKEY: Can I ask why?
ISABEL: Because my father says he'll never speak to me again unless I quit.
HARKEY: Is that all?

Dad had told me to use family as an excuse and it worked perfectly. I walked out of Harkey's office five minutes later. No hard feelings. Not yet, at least.

. . .

My undercover work with RH Investigations was done, but I continued working the Truesdale/Bancroft case. Ernie phoned me later that evening with something on his mind, although it took him a while to get to it.

"I've been helping around the house more, like we talked about," Ernie said.

"I'm glad to hear it," I replied.

"I even did my own laundry the other day."

"Excellent."

"Linda made pork chops the other night," Ernie said.

"I see," I said, not seeing anything at all.

"Pork chops are my favorite," he said.

"Well, that must have been nice," I replied.

"Do you see my point?" Ernie asked.

"Actually, I don't."

"We get along. I love her. For us, it's not that complicated. So my wife has a secret. Big deal. Shouldn't I just let her keep it?"

Ernie was asking the wrong person that question. I didn't know what to say. The case might have been over for him, but it wasn't for me.

"If you want me to stop, I'll stop.[1] But I'd like to continue the investigation just a little longer."

"Is there some new angle you're looking at?" Ernie asked.

"Sharon Bancroft. Something about her isn't right."

"You're not charging me to investigate the congressman's wife, are you?"

"Of course not. The rest of this is free of charge. It's just to satisfy my own curiosity."

"Do what you want," Ernie said. "Just let me know if you find out something that really matters."

"Thanks, Ernie. Do me a favor. The next time it seems like your wife is planning on meeting with Sharon, let me know."

---

[1] Yes, a lie.

"Sure," Ernie replied. "I've always had a funny feeling about that one."

"Don't forget," I said, and hung up.

I spent that evening at Morty and Ruth's house helping them pack. Gabe and Petra had arrived hours earlier and had already packed up all the books, tchotchkes, and family photos from the living room. The new couple was in the inseparable stage. While in normal relationship terms it was too soon for Petra to meet the grandparents, because Morty and Ruth would be en route to Florida within the week, Gabe couldn't resist an introduction.

I found Morty and Ruth in their bedroom, downsizing his winter wardrobe. Ruth put a black cashmere/wool blend overcoat in a donation pile by the door.

"That's my favorite coat," Morty said.

"It never dips below sixty degrees there," said Ruth. "You won't need it."

"So I'm going to spend the rest of my life in a sauna. We'll never even vacation someplace cool?"

Morty picked the coat off the pile and put it back on the bed. I watched them from the doorway.

"What can I do?" I asked.

"Isabel," she said. "Thank god you're here. I need a cup of tea. Listen, Morty has to cut out all the winter clothes from his wardrobe. We've been fighting all day. Talk some sense into him, okay?"

Ruth didn't wait for a reply; she simply exited the room. Morty rolled his eyes and gave me a look that I read as *This is all your fault.*

Morty opened his sweater drawer and said, "If I run the air conditioner really high, I can probably make use of some of these."

I wasn't willing to push Morty to the brink, so I agreed. I told him to lose half the drawer and then he was done. While Morty picked through and sorted his favorite sweaters, I scanned his ties and told him which ones had to go (for aesthetic reasons, not atmospheric ones). We'd been working in somber silence for about fifteen minutes when Morty stopped what he was doing and made what I hoped would be his final complaint to me before his departure.

"Oh, and thanks a lot for the shiksa with the tattoos," he said, rather annoyed.

"I've known her for years, Morty. I can vouch for her."[2]

"What's that crazy-looking thing above her eye?"

"It's just like an earring, but it's in her eyebrow instead," I replied, trying to make it sound as ordinary as possible.

Morty shook his head in sad disappointment. "I don't get you kids today. I just don't."

A few more minutes of silence passed. My friend's distaste for the task at hand was becoming toxic.

"Morty, there's no way around this. You know that, right?"

The old man looked up at me, lost. "Yes," he said, and then quickly looked away.

"Find a way to be okay with it."

A few hours later, we all went to eat at a local Chinese restaurant. Morty ordered all the foods that Ruthy usually forbids and she said not one word.

"How's the kung pao?" I asked.

"Deadly," Gabe replied.

"Pass the kung pao," said Morty.

I guess Morty still hadn't found a way.

Petra offered to give me a ride home as we were leaving the restaurant, but I turned her down. Since we were both, in theory, heading in the same direction, this raised some suspicion.

---

[2] If you've read the second document (*Curse of the Spellmans*—now available in paperback!), maybe you're thinking that I can't really vouch for her. But my theory is this: David made Petra feel too much like a grown-up. Gabe will always live in a state of boyishness. Petra, too, needs to pretend she can stay young forever. That's my theory and I'm sticking to it.

"Why don't you want to take a ride from me?" Petra asked.

"I feel like walking," I replied. I'm not known for the taking of exercise, but walking was as good an excuse as any.

"Really?" Petra replied skeptically.

"Yes," I said, fully committing to my act. "I need some fresh air." Then I committed even further and began walking.

After about ten minutes—when I was certain that all relevant parties had returned to their cars and evacuated the near premises—I hopped on the bus. It wasn't air I needed but a nice, long bus nap. I rode the Geary bus to the financial district and waited for the bus driver to wake me at the end of the line. Then I grabbed a cab to go home. No, this was hardly an economical form of travel, but at least I got some rest.

The cab dropped me on the corner of Jackson and Leavenworth, where my notes indicated my car was last seen. I roamed the streets looking for its new location. I found it on Clay and Jones, jotted down the location on my notepad, pulled the tape from the hidden camera (under a blanket in the trunk), and walked the five blocks back to David's and my home.

As I approached our street, I turned right around, since he was standing on his front porch, chatting with a male I recognized as a neighbor. Based on the noise level coming from David's place, he was having a barbecue or a party or something (and I wasn't invited!). As far as I could tell, at least a dozen people were loitering in the vicinity of the house. I had two choices: A) pretend I was in the neighborhood and crash the party, or B) go somewhere else.

SOMEWHERE ELSE

I finally got that walk I had been lying about. I arrived at the Spellman residence twenty minutes later to a scene of courtroomlike drama. My mother, my father, and Rae sat around the dining room table in stony silence.

"Hi," I said, after I let myself in through the front door.

My friendly hello was met with mumbled greetings.

"What's going on?" I asked, still all friendly.

The three parties involved in the sober proceedings stared at one another, as if not sure how to proceed.

"We're having a family meeting," my mother said.

Normally the words "family meeting" fill me with an unnatural dread, but normally family meetings are in my honor. Since I crashed this meeting, clearly I was living in that delightful off-the-radar territory. I cheerily sat down, looking forward to whatever kind of dirt might surface.

Mom and Dad glanced at me awkwardly and asked if maybe I could wait in another room for a few minutes until they were done.

I remembered that I had the videotape to watch and so I escaped into the office, snapped the tape into my parents' camera, and hooked it up to a computer. I had approximately twenty-four hours of low-quality video of my empty driver's seat to watch, or however much time passed between when I set up the camera and my car thief broke in. I ran the tape at a high-speed fast-forward that would skip hours at a time. Once I saw the car's location change, I watched the tape in rewind mode until I caught my culprit. I then watched the tape in real time with the sound on.

Rae, using a regular old key—she must have had a spare made—entered my vehicle and immediately made a call on her cell:

RAE: Hi, it's me. I just got to the car. Izzy must have some rich new boy-friend that she's keeping secret. She keeps parking around Russian Hill. I'm about ten minutes out. I'll be there in, like, fifteen. Who's drunk already? Madison? She's always drunk.

As the tape continued to roll, I watched Rae drive to a residence some-where in the Avenues, then get out of the car. Two hours later, she returned to the car with three very drunk teenagers in tow. I watched my sister pro-ceed to drive the first two semiconscious adolescents home and then pull the car to the side of the road while the third one presumably vomited. (The vomiting was off camera, but my sister's comment, "Make sure all your puke ends up outside the car," clued me in.) The rest of the action on the tape consisted of Rae collecting money for her chauffeuring services, driving back to the vicinity of her original theft, and approximately thirty-five minutes of hunting for a parking space. I disconnected the camera from the computer, returned it to my bag, and exited the office to find my parents now seated alone at the dining room table.

"Where's Rae?" I asked, ready for a fight. "I need to speak with her."

"She's upstairs, beginning what will be a very lengthy grounding," said my mother.

"What did she do?" I asked, my edge quieted a bit by the news of Rae's punishment.

"I still can't believe it," said my dad, shaking his head.

"We should just be grateful that these were practice tests and nothing will go on her permanent record," said Mom.

"Hello. I'm still here," I said.

"Rae's PSAT scores came in. They dropped by twenty-five percent."

"She cheated?" I asked.

"So it seems," my mother replied.

"How is that possible?" I asked.

My father shook his head again and again. "She won't say. Says she's willing to accept whatever punishment we dole out, but she won't reveal how she did it."

My mom appeared the most distressed. Her recent dreams of Rae's Ivy League education had come crashing to the ground. This new piece of information, illuminating yet another level of my sister's deceptions, left me dumbfounded. I would have to do some plotting before I could confront my sister. It was time to make my exit.

"You okay, Mom?" I asked.

"She's getting worse."

I felt sympathy and a touch of vindication. Rae has always been a volatile personality, but my parents let most of her questionable behavior slip through the cracks because, well, she was never as obviously bad as I was. But my rebellion was different; it was loud, obscene, and easy to recognize in both its motivation and expression. It seemed that the Unit was finally waking up to the potential troubles that lay in my sister's future. I could feel the crackdown coming.

As I was putting on my coat, my father said to my mother, "Should we cancel our disappearance?"[1]

"Definitely not," Mom replied.

"What disappearance?" I asked.

---

[1] In the Spellman household, "disappearance" means "vacation." It can also be used in its usual sense. (For full explanation, see appendix.)

"We were planning a weekend in wine country," my dad replied.

"Al, we'll figure something out. But I am not canceling that disappearance for her," Mom said.

"We'll talk about it later," Dad said as he walked me to the door.

"Tell me you took care of Harkey," Dad whispered in a conspiratorial tone.

"I didn't kill him, if that's what you're asking."

"You quit, right?" he said.

"I quit. I swear."

"Thank you."

"You're welcome," I replied.

"I hope you're thinking about what we talked about."

"Refresh my memory."

"Time is running out, Isabel. I want a decision."

"No problem. 'Decision' is my middle name," I said, sounding like a lunatic.

"Maybe next week we can have lunch."

"You still own a refrigerator, right?"

"One month. Use that time wisely."

Oh, I would.

I exited the house without relaying my recent discovery of Rae's car theft and return. There were lessons that my sister needed to be taught—lessons that would require careful planning. I had only one place to turn.

NEW INFORMATION

I walked up to Van Ness and Clay Street and hailed a cab to Henry Stone's place. I arrived shortly after ten P.M. to find a man in his PJs and a robe (not unlike Morty's recent habitual ensemble).

Henry looked surprised when he opened the door.

"Isabel," he said.

"Good, you remember me," I said.

"What's wrong?" Henry asked.

"A number of things," I replied.

"For instance?" he said.

"I thought you were the one with the manners."

"Excuse me?"

"Are we going to have this entire conversation in the foyer?"

"Is it going to be an entire conversation?" Henry said, finally turning back into his apartment, allowing my entrance.

"Can I offer you some herbal tea?" Henry asked.

"Sure, if you spike it with whiskey."

Henry decided not to bother with the kettle and poured two thimbleful glasses of whiskey. When he sat down on his couch next to me, I noticed that his gaze seemed a bit hazy, his bearing shaky.

"You look tired," I said.

"I worked a double shift yesterday," he replied. "Haven't slept in twenty-four hours."

"I'll get to the point," I said.

"Thank you."

"Rae has been driving my car without my permission," I said.

"Is that all?"

"And she cheated on the PSATs," I added, thinking, *Isn't grand theft auto enough?*

"She cheated on the PSATs," Henry repeated in a dull, annoyed tone.

"Do you want me to come back after you've had some rest?"

"You people cannot be this clueless," Henry said, closing his eyes.

"Excuse me?"

"She didn't cheat, Isabel."

"Yes, she did."

"No. She didn't," Henry said. "She *threw* the test."

"Huh?"

"She threw it, you numbskull. The original numbers were right."

"Are you sure? And make that the last time you call me a numbskull."

"Yes, I'm sure. Do you remember how many hours of SAT prep I did with that tyrant? I know what she's capable of, in both the good and the evil senses. When your parents started pushing the idea of a four-year university and forgoing the family business, she didn't like it and took action."

"Wow. This is some piece of information you have for me."

"Honestly," said Henry. "These days I don't like that kid so much."

Henry and I sat in a comfortable silence. In some other story, this would be when the heroine confesses her undying love. But, if you've been paying attention, I'm not exactly comfortable with expressing, considering, or even recognizing my own emotional landscape. But you have to agree, I took a step in the right direction. I invited Henry to be my accomplice in my sting operation against Rae, which is not unlike asking someone out on a date. If you think about it.

"Someone needs to teach her a lesson," I said. "Are you in?"

"I'm so in," Henry replied.

THE RANSOM

PART III

Henry needed sleep, so I left shortly after our plan was hatched. It was still too early to safely return to David's place, so I took yet another cab to the Philosopher's Club. It was packed with a postcollegiate crowd, in stark contrast to the few old regulars who usually show up in the afternoon. It had been a month since my firing, which from a purely business perspective seemed to have been a good idea. I had to give the Irishman credit; he was doing something right, although what, exactly, escaped me.

"Allo orgeous," he said when I sat down at the only empty bar stool. "Aht an eye etcha?"

"Guinness," I replied, hoping the conversation would end then and there.

As Connor pulled my pint, he reached under the bar and handed over an envelope addressed to me. I opened it and struggled to read in the dim light of the bar. Connor saw the effort I was making, and after he served my drink, he held a small flashlight over the paper. He certainly had a gift for customer service, not that the note improved my drinking experience. My blackmailer was at it again.

If U woUld LIKe 2
KEEp Ur sEcreT GO 2 SFMoMA
tHis WeEkEND

A brochure for the San Francisco Museum of Modern Art was also enclosed, along with a Muni map and explicit directions. I wasn't too worried, since I figured that my mother had bigger troubles and I might be able to negotiate this down to a slightly more desirable activity. I would call Mom in the morning to discuss.

I returned the letter to my bag and consulted my beer for answers. An oversized ex–frat boy with a booming voice began ordering for his posse of friends. I was in no mood for anything, especially loud people shouting into my ear, so I turned to Connor and asked him if Milo was in. Connor said something that didn't sound anything at all like "He's in the office," but I took that to be the gist. I slipped away from the bar and knocked on Milo's door.

"This ain't the bathroom!" Milo shouted through the wall.

I entered without an invitation.

When Milo saw me, he said, "Look what the cat dragged in."

"Can't you say something nice?"

"We've been missing you around here," he said reluctantly.

"That's what happens when you fire someone," I replied. I used an empty CD case as a coaster and put my beer on Milo's desk.

"How you been, Izz?" he asked. "Not great, based on the looks of you. You getting enough sleep?"

"Considering I don't have a job and I'm being blackmailed, I do okay."

"Glad to hear it," Milo said. He's known me too long to find the previous comment worthy of a follow-up question.

"What's going on with you?" I asked.

If you've read the previous documents you know that Milo has accused me of being self-involved. I'm working on that.

"I'm thinking about moving to Arizona."

"Why?"

"I'm in love."

"With a cactus?"

"No, Isabel, a woman."

"So where does Arizona come into all of this?"

"That's. Where. She. Lives," Milo said slowly, as if he were speaking to a four-year-old with ADD.

"How did you meet a woman who lives in Arizona?"

"Online."

"But you use dial-up."

"I'm patient," Milo replied.

I'll spare you the rest of the conversation, but suffice it to say that months back, Milo joined an online dating service,[1] began e-mailing a woman named Greta Grunch (I know, I know), and after a few months they decided to meet— first on her territory, then on his, and finally on neutral ground. How I missed this entire phase of Milo's life, I cannot say.[2] I'm sure he kept things from me in the interest of avoiding answering my natural follow-up questions:

- Are you practicing safe sex?
- How does her husband feel about you?
- Are you sure she isn't just trying to get her American citizenship?

The idea of losing another friend to a warmer climate dulled my mood. I listened to about twenty minutes of Milo gushing over his paramour and then I made my way back to David's house. I could hear a few of the remaining revelers chatting and listening to music indoors, but my careful scan of the periphery allowed my quick entry into the apartment. It had been a long day. I brushed my teeth and washed my face by moonlight, went straight to bed, fell fast asleep, and woke up two hours later to the sound of footsteps pacing overhead. When I finally realized that David wasn't planning a raid on his extra apartment, I took some nighttime cold medicine. During the half hour before the medicine took effect, I came to grips with the fact that my new living situation would probably not be viable long-term. I determined that I'd have to move. And then I remembered that I'd need a real job to do so. Shortly after that, the medicine kicked in.

---

[1] I will have you know that I did not once mock his use of the modern matchmaker.

[2] Of course, it could be that self-involved thing at work again.

THE RANSOM AND
OTHER STUFF

I n the morning I phoned my mother to try to negotiate down the museum visit to something a little more, well, fun.

"Could I go to the zoo instead of SFMOMA?"

"I think you have the wrong number," my mother said.

"How many times do I have to tell you that it's *not funny when you do it*?"

"Isabel?"

"Thank you," I replied.

"What are you talking about?"

"I don't feel like going to the museum; I'd rather go to the zoo."

"Have you been drinking?"

It was actually a reasonable question. My voice was hoarse and my throat was beginning to get sore. Was it possible that the cold medicine was giving me a cold?

I answered my mother's question: "It's nine A.M. Of course not.[1] Will you just answer the question?"

"What was the question again? Also, you should identify yourself when

---

[1] I always wait until at least noon.

you call people. It's more . . . adult. You know, there's no caller ID on the kitchen phone."

"Could I go to the zoo instead of SFMOMA?"

"I don't see why not," Mom replied.

"Thank you," I said. "And for being so agreeable, I'd like to share some dirt I've got on Rae."

"I don't know if I can take any more dirt."

"Okay," I replied. "Call me when you're ready."

"Don't hang up!" Mom shouted.

"Oh, are you ready?"

"Yes."

"Rae didn't cheat on the PSATs," I said.

"Yes, she did."

"No. She didn't. Henry says she threw the second test. She didn't like all that four-year-university talk, so she took action. She'd rather take a couple weeks of punishment now than four years of punishment later."

Silence.

"Mom?"

"Why can't I just find marijuana in her room and have the 'This is your brain on drugs' talk? I don't know what to do with this kid."

"You could ground her," I suggested cheerily.

"She's already grounded."

"Are you going to cancel your disappearance?" I asked.

"Now I'm not so sure," Mom said, but then she changed her tune. "No. No, I'm not."

"Then what are you going to do about it?" I asked. "I mean, you have to do something."

"Not sure. I need some time to come up with a plan."

"Well, if you need any help, call me."

"Just keep an eye on things this weekend. And when you're done doing whatever it is with the GPS, please return it. We only have two, you know."

. . .

I'd borrowed the one GPS, but had returned it. If the other one was missing, it was probably being used by Rae. It didn't take me long to figure out what she was doing with it. To double-check, I pulled up the map on my computer screen (I have the link to both GPSs on my computer) and there was the dot, parked right where my car was last seen. *Of course,* this is how she was able to find my car at a moment's notice. I should have figured it out, and I would have if there weren't so many other things in my life to figure out. The good news for me was that my own days of car hunting were over. And I had my revenge to look forward to.

CASE #001

CHAPTER 9

Other than continuing my surveillance on Linda Truesdale and Sharon Bancroft, I wasn't sure where else I could go with the investigation. One thing that I found a bit odd while looking at their vital statistics was that there was a three-year age gap between the two women. Usually childhood friendships are forged by people closer in age.

I had never asked Ernie about his wife's childhood, so I phoned him that afternoon to acquire some background information. Ernie continued to be a reluctant participant in my investigation. I couldn't help but admire him for that. Still, I got him to talk. Even if Ernie could stop investigating his wife, I couldn't.

I was intrigued to learn that Linda had grown up in the foster care system in Detroit. Her mother was a drug addict who abandoned her when she was five. She had no siblings or any other family to speak of. If the two women had met in school, it was an unlikely pairing. I needed more information. When the investigation began, it all seemed irrelevant; if you want to learn whether a wife is cheating on her husband, you don't look into her childhood for the evidence. But now I was convinced that this mystery I couldn't even name was tied to the past. I finally had concise questions to ask.

"Ernie, do you know the name of the school where Linda and Sharon met?"

"Probably had some president's name in it."

"Can you find out which president?"

"How would I go about doing that?"

"Well, you could ask," I suggested. But I realized that I wanted more information than the name of Linda's high school. For the next ten minutes I coached Ernie on how to interrogate his wife and gave him a page-long list of questions I wanted answered. Ernie told me he'd casually bring up the subject at dinner.[1] The following morning he called me with this information:

Linda went to Benjamin Franklin[2] High, which is where she met Sharon, in a Spanish class. And the tuna casserole was a big disaster, but Linda appreciated the effort.

"That's all you got for me, Ernie?"

"Linda doesn't like questions," was Ernie's reply.

Having known so few people in my life with an unqualified regard for privacy, I discovered a newfound respect for Ernie. I tried to imagine what life might be like without a current of suspicion running through me at all times. I traced backward in my life, hoping to pinpoint a time when that current wasn't active, but I couldn't remember it.

Respect or no, my suspicion remained and my investigation continued. Now that I knew where Linda had grown up, I was able to run a more complete background check on Ernie's wife. She was forty-five, and the criminal databases in Michigan go back only ten years. My parents have associates in different states with whom they trade local information. I dropped by the house, laid out the facts to Mom and Dad, and explained that I wasn't ready to let this case go. With all the information presented to them—the Harkey angle certainly helped matters—my parents agreed to cover the costs and, more importantly, sanction the investigation, allowing me access to their contacts.

---

[1] Ernie was cooking dinner that night. Tuna casserole. He got the recipe from a women's magazine that he picked up at the doctor's office.

[2] Not a president, Ernie.

. . .

Of course, once I laid out the few but incongruous facts, they couldn't help but begin offering their own angles. No Spellman can resist yanking on the loose threads that make a mystery, and despite our job's reputation, we know that mysteries are rare. I believed it was too soon to theorize about the secret that the women shared (which we agreed was the heart of the case) and whether that secret was even the reason behind Harkey's investigation. But my father cannot resist parlor games, and my mother can't resist being Dad's heckling audience. I'll share with you the least helpful portion of my afternoon:

DAD: I have an idea.

ISABEL: Why don't we hold off on the ideas until we have something to work with?

DAD: Let's say Sharon had a marriage before the congressman and Linda was his mistress. When they both discover the other person, they conspire to commit murder. Only years later, the body turns up—

MOM: [annoyed] Stop. That's mostly the plot to a movie[3] we watched on cable last week. Remember?

DAD: No.

MOM: Remind me to ask Dr. Fisher to do some kind of memory evaluation on you.

ISABEL: Mom, I hope you see the faulty logic in that.

[Long pause.]

MOM: Oh, right. I'll remind myself.

Once our "business" discussion came to a close, I got the lowdown on other family matters. I was delighted to learn that Rae was grounded for three months. Plus, in light of her recent PSAT scandal,[4] Rae's base-

---

[3] *Diabolique* (1996), starring Sharon Stone and Isabelle Adjani. A remake, of course.

[4] Which remained purely a "cheating incident" in the eyes of her unmoved guidance counselor.

line GPA (a B-minus standard set years ago) was raised to a B-plus. If Rae could not maintain the B-plus average, then she would lose the sort of privileges in the house that make life worth living for a teenager (television, telephone, Internet). And then, if she could not raise her grades after her first warning, she would lose the things that made life worth living for her in particular (anything containing high-fructose corn syrup).

As I was leaving the Spellman household, I announced my zoo excursion to see if I could get any company and also to ensure that my blackmailer knew I was meeting her demands. My dad took me up on my offer, which I regretted almost immediately.

While observing the delightful antics of the lemurs, Dad reminded me that my one-month clock to decide my entire future had ticked down to less than a month. As the giraffes snacked on leaves, Dad mentioned that he'd be willing to work in a retirement plan to sweeten the deal. As the African lion lounged about, which I suppose reminded my father of me, he said, "You can't just sit around and do nothing all day long." I then suggested lunch, since I figured the only time I could ensure he wouldn't be talking was while he was chewing.

After lunch, we spent another hour roaming the grounds, got sort of lost on our way out, argued over who was more responsible for our loss of direction, and when we were finally back in the car without the distractions of caged animals, I kept the conversation under my control. Since I was curious how they were going to handle the upcoming disappearance in light of Rae's grounding, I asked the obvious question:

"How will you monitor Rae's grounding when you're in a different city?"

"David's spending the weekend at the house with Rae."

"David?" I asked.

"You know, your brother. The handsome one."

"Why did you ask him?"

"Your mother thinks David and Rae should spend more time together."

"Why? Because I'm such a bad influence?"

"You're not part of the equation, Isabel. Don't make this about you."

"It's just strange that Mom would ask David to spend the weekend when she could ask me."

"If you think about it, it's not so strange."

"Why?" I asked, bracing myself for some new assault on my character.

"Well, the last time you and Rae stayed in the house together, you left a banana in the hall closet."

"Still with the banana!" I loudly replied.[5]

"Three weeks!" my dad shouted. "Isabel, it took us three weeks to identify where the odor was coming from."

Rather than continue defending myself over an honest mistake, I let the subject drop. No new subjects arose until Dad dropped me at my apartment. Unfortunately, this was very inconvenient for me, since A) it wasn't my apartment anymore, and B) I didn't even have the key to the foyer to fake it being my apartment anymore.

"Thanks, Dad. It's been fun. Tell Mom I wouldn't mind going to the aquarium next time, if this is thematically the way her blackmail is going to take us."

"I meant to say something earlier," my dad said. "I really don't think your blackmailer is Mom."

"You might have mentioned that before we spent three hours at the zoo."

Dad ignored my comment and pulled his wallet out of his back pocket.

"I know you're low on cash," Dad said, offering me a stack of bills.

"I'm okay," I replied, waving off the money. (I kind of was okay. Not paying rent really helps, and I did have a small amount of savings beforehand.)

"I know you're not. Your phone was shut off, which means your Internet was shut off. You can live without a landline, but—"

"Right," I said, remembering that disconnecting my utilities was a side effect I hadn't anticipated. Most people were in the habit of using

---

[5] If I had a dime for every time that banana incident was mentioned to me . . .

my cell number. Dad's one of those people who will call you on every number he's got.

"Don't be proud," my dad said, forcing the money into my hand.

I thanked him quietly and exited the car. Right before I shut the door, I heard, "You've got two weeks, Isabel. Two weeks."

Correction: I had two point five weeks.

DISAPPEARANCE #4

(THE WINE COUNTRY)

Friday afternoon, just after Rae got home from school, my parents packed their car and began the two-hour drive north from San Francisco to Napa Valley.

My mother asked me to keep an eye on Rae during the afternoon while David was still at work. I used this time to make contact with the Detroit PI—Gus Nordvent—to see what information he could come up with on Linda Truesdale. An hour later, Gus phoned me back.

"Your girl has got a record," Gus said optimistically as soon as I got him on the line. The truth is, PIs love finding dirt. For us, it's good news. Plus, it makes you feel more justified in getting paid.

"What did she do?" I asked.

"Wrote some bad checks when she was nineteen. A forgery charge when she was twenty. Looks like she was siphoning money from a restaurant where she worked. She's also got a juvie record, but, you know, that's sealed."

"Did she do time?"

"Four months in a minimum security."

"Anything else?" I asked.

"It looks like she's been a good girl since."

. . .

I hung up the phone and entered the kitchen. Rae sat at the Formica table eating a snack of pretzels and M&M's, studying a math test she'd gotten back with a score of 68 percent.

"So now you're throwing all your tests?" I asked.

"No," Rae replied, staring down at the exam. "I studied for this."

My sister then excused herself and said she needed a nap. I waited five minutes and circled the perimeter of the house, waiting for her to escape through the window. After ten minutes, I went back inside and tiptoed up the steps, opened her door, and saw her fast asleep. It occurred to me that if I was going to maintain an overnight surveillance on my sister this weekend I, too, needed my rest. I went downstairs and slept on the couch.

A few hours later, I awoke to the jarring sounds of pots and pans clanking in the kitchen. I got off the couch and found Rae ransacking the pantry.

"What are you looking for?" I asked.

"Something to make for dinner."

"Why don't you order in?"

"I feel like cooking," Rae replied.

David unlocked the front door just as I was about to take my leave.

"Warning," I said, "she's planning on cooking you dinner."

"I just ate!" David shouted at the top of his lungs.

Rae exited the kitchen.

"You can go now, Isabel," Rae said.

"Why are you trying to get rid of me?"

"I don't need two prison guards," she replied. Then she turned to David, staring at his un-lawyer-like ensemble, and said, "What are you wearing?"

"I just went to the gym," David answered, tossing his bag on the couch.

"Are you going to take a shower?" Rae asked.

"What's it to you?"

"I have a friend coming over for dinner," she said.

"What friend?" I asked.

"I thought you were leaving," Rae replied.

And so I left. I returned to my new home without any concern for David's schedule, had a snack, read the paper, dropped by the bar to borrow Milo's car, and returned two hours later to begin my stakeout outside the Spellman residence.

2000 hrs

I missed the arrival of Rae's unfortunate dinner guest. I should have known that the victim of Rae's cooking would be a surprise, since the usual suspects would never willingly consume a meal prepared by her.[1] The lights and shadows in the foyer and dining area indicated that Rae's company had not yet departed. However, the identity of the dinner guest was a shock, to say the least. Shortly after nine P.M., one Maggie Mason exited the Spellman home.

I had not seen or spoken to Maggie since our awkward dinner at Henry's house. I had considered calling her after I realized my mother was behind her "investigation," but when Henry told me of their breakup, I couldn't bring myself to make contact, as if I had to choose sides. I wondered if Rae's dinner invitation to Maggie was simply her way of retaliating against Henry's hostile stance. The problem with that theory is that it didn't explain why David was there.

I maintained my post for two more hours after Maggie's departure, but all I could see were the shadows of David and my sister watching television in the family room. They were in for the night, so I left. I returned to David's house, hunted long and hard for parking, and went to bed. Strangely, with David out of the house, I managed to sleep almost five hours straight. When I woke up, I told myself that this was caused by simple exhaustion—I'd been so tired that my body finally relented. I didn't acknowledge that I slept because my subconscious knew that at least that night I wouldn't be caught.

---

[1] For a list of Rae's past culinary experiments, see appendix.

Saturday I picked up my surveillance once again, only to spend another night observing my brother and sister watching television together in the family room. I phoned David to see what they had planned for the evening. I felt vaguely pathetic making this call from the cold discomfort of Milo's overly pine-scented Toyota Camry.

"What's up, Izzy?" David said upon answering the phone.

"Nothing. Just wanted to see how everything was going."

"Fine," David replied. "We're watching *Trail of the Pink Panther*."

"What would possess you to do that?"

"Because we watched the rest of the series last night and this is the only one left."

"But it's awful,"[2] I said.

"I explained that to Rae," said David, "but she wanted to see the entire oeuvre. And, to answer your next question, yes, she actually used that word."

"Did she pronounce it correctly?"

"No. But neither could you."

"Are you going to watch the whole film?"

"It's not so bad. David Niven is back. I like him."

"Who doesn't?" I replied. "How was last night?"

"Rae just baked some frozen hors d'oeuvres," he replied.

"You dodged a bullet."

I was expecting Maggie to come up somewhere in this conversation, but no luck. I played my cards close and didn't inquire.

"Was there a reason you called?" David asked.

"So, you're in for the evening?"

"Yes," David said.

"Okay," I replied, pausing for an invitation.

"Talk to you later," David said, and hung up the phone.

---

[2] It's basically a bunch of outtakes from previous films, but it's the last Pink Panther film starring Peter Sellers.

. . .

From the car I phoned Petra to see what she was up to, but the call went straight to voice mail and then I vaguely remembered that she and Gabe were going to a movie or skateboarding, or whatever it is the kids do for fun these days. Len and Christopher were at the moment onstage in a production of *The Vagina Monologues*.[3] I decided to return Milo's car to the bar. It was a Saturday night, which used to mean a dozen customers and maybe a short wait for a game of pool, and sometimes dead silence because no one put any money in the jukebox. This night, it meant there was one empty bar stool amid a sea of students, the requisite San Francisco hipsters, regulars, and Irish people from god knows where. If I put a song on the jukebox, I wouldn't hear it until hours later.

Connor and Jimmy tended bar. A young male playing the part of a fop—tweed coat, ascot, pink shirt—sidled up next to me.

"Hello there," he said, all friendly.

Connor then approached, pulled a letter from beneath the bar, and slid it in front of me. He eyed the fop and said, "Keep moving, friend, she's all wrong for you."

The fop didn't move. Connor smiled, but it didn't look friendly.

"Move along, now," he said. And suddenly Connor looked terrifying. The fop did some sort of medieval bow, which looked quite silly. Connor rolled his eyes and turned to me.

"A drink?" he asked, not waiting for a thank-you or anything.

"Why not?" I replied, and then I smiled. I love it when people move along.

Connor poured my whiskey and said, "I coulda sworn I'd go ta my grave without seeing Isabel Spellman smile. Thank you, orgeous."

For once, I could understand him. Sort of. Wisely, Connor didn't linger. He, too, moved along and served one of the many customers angling for his attention. I broke the seal on the envelope and opened the letter.

---

[3] Sometimes it's best not to ask. So I didn't.

I sAId GO to The MUseuM
NOt tHe zOO
GO 2 sFMOma thiS WEek or
Ur sECreT wILL B eXPOsed

The next time Connor passed my way, I asked when the letter had arrived. This one was delivered, not mailed. Connor said it came sometime in the afternoon—after four P.M. My parents were home packing at that time; Rae was either in school or in her room. While it was possible that one of them was still my blackmailer, I had to rethink matters. Was it possible that David knew?

All at once the noise, the people, and the smell of beer became unpleasant. I left the bar without checking on Milo and went to see the one person who always seemed to be on my mind.

DATE, INTERRUPTED

I expected to find Henry home that evening, since he was supposed
to be home later that night to be at the ready for our now-derailed
sting operation on Rae. I figured he'd be reading a book or something. I
didn't figure that, two weeks after being dumped by Maggie, he'd be in the
midst of another date.

It took me by surprise. I'm telling you this to explain my subsequent
behavior.

"Isabel, what are you doing here?" Henry said when he opened the door.

"I didn't feel like going home," I replied. "Are you going to let me in or
what?"

Sometimes I don't read body language very well. Since there was enough
space between Henry and the door frame for me to slip past, I entered his
apartment. In retrospect, I entered without invitation.

On Henry's couch sat a woman who had hair and was wearing clothes. I
think she must have been drinking something, but everything was a bit of a
blur. Her surprise and Henry's awkwardness upon my entrance clued me in
right away that I was interrupting a date.

"Hi," I said.

I think Henry then introduced us, but honestly, I couldn't tell you her
name.

"I'm Henry's life coach," I said, because it annoys Henry when I tell people that. Although I must admit, I got no joy from it this time.

The date, who I've reduced in my memory to a life-sized smudge, smiled uncomfortably and turned to Henry for an explanation.

"Isabel was in the neighborhood," he said.

"I'm sorry," I said, not sounding all that sorry. "Have I interrupted something?"

The Smudge smiled or frowned. Who can tell?

Henry said, "Yes, you have. Maybe you could come back tomorrow."

"But I have some important business to discuss with you now," I said.

"I'm sure it can wait," Henry replied.

"What makes you so sure?" I asked.

"It's getting late," the Smudge said. "I should go."

"Isn't it?" I said, agreeing enthusiastically.

"It's ten thirty," Henry interjected.

"She's got a watch," I said.

The Smudge stood, confirming her previously stated plans.

"A pleasure meeting you," she said to me, which I thought was inappropriately friendly.

"Likewise," I said for the first time in my life.

Another blurry exchange happened in the doorway as the Smudge made her exit. My vision cleared up when Henry returned to the apartment with a high-definition scowl on his face.

"That was incredibly rude," he said.

"Yes, she shouldn't have left so abruptly."

"What is the problem, Isabel?"

"Nothing," I replied, eyeing a plate of crackers on the coffee table. I had a sudden urge to pick up the crackers and hurl them at Henry, one by one, with a g-force never before experienced by a cracker. Then I had a separate urge to toss them on the floor and crunch them into the carpet with my shoe. Then, you'll be happy to hear, I had a sudden urge to hang on to whatever dignity I had left.

"I'm sorry," I said. "I shouldn't have interrupted your date."

I sat down on Henry's couch and eyed the plate of cheese and crackers with an entirely different urge.

"Are you hungry?" Henry asked.

"Yes."

"Help yourself."

I did.

As I was snacking on Henry's leftover date food, trying not to feel too sorry for myself, it occurred to me that I had for the first time in my life the perfect excuse to invite Henry on a social outing.

"I have to go to the museum sometime," I said. (Do you see where I'm going with this?)

"Why do you have to go to the museum?" Henry asked.

"I thought I could go to the zoo instead, but apparently I have to go to the museum."

"Still didn't answer my question," Henry replied.

"I know," I said. "So, do you want to go sometime?"

"Why not?" Henry replied.

It suddenly occurred to me that I should get out of his home as soon as possible. I'm always in danger of ruining things one way or another, so before he could inquire further about the motives behind my sudden interest in culture, I decided to make my exit.

"Thanks for the snack," I said. "I'll call you."

CASE #001

CHAPTER 10

On my way to Dr. Rush's office, Ernie phoned to inform me that Sharon and Linda would be meeting for lunch that day. I'm always looking for a good excuse to skip a therapy session, so I quickly switched directions, heading south on the 101 to Burlingame. I also phoned Dr. Rush to inform her of my change in plans.

ISABEL: Hi, Dr. Rush, I have to cancel my session today. Something came up with work. Sorry about the late notice.

DR. RUSH: Do you want to make up the session this week or next?

ISABEL: You wouldn't consider letting me slide for just this week?[1]

DR. RUSH: No. I wouldn't.

ISABEL: I see.

DR. RUSH: I have a twelve noon opening on Friday.

[Long pause.]

ISABEL: I guess I'll see you Friday, Dr. Rush.

---

[1] Yes, I really did think she'd let one week slide. Some people are very inflexible.

. . ..

My surveillance on Linda began outside the Black residence. At 12:35 P.M. she exited their home dressed in an outfit with a price tag that might have given her husband a heart attack—an outfit most likely gifted by Sharon Bancroft.

Forty-five minutes later, Linda and Sharon had a window table at Boulevard on Mission Street—one of the many fine San Francisco restaurants where I have not had the pleasure of dining. Since there wasn't much information I could cull from their lunch orders, I found a metered parking space two blocks away. I searched my car for reading material and found a two-week-old newspaper and a bit of poetry on an old coffee cup. I knew the lunch would last at least an hour, so I exited my car and walked two blocks to the closest newsstand.

I purchased a *Chronicle* and a pack of gum and grabbed a free *SF Weekly*. As I headed back in the direction of my car, I saw a black Lincoln Town Car with darkened windows pull into a red zone right in front of me. I'd started to walk around the vehicle when the back window rolled down and a grim but well-groomed man in a suit (at least a suit jacket—I couldn't at the moment vouch for the rest of his outfit) made eye contact.

"Ms. Spellman, we need to have a talk," he said.

"Do I know you?" I replied. (FYI, I didn't.)

"Please get in," he said. And then the driver got out of the car and opened the back passenger-side door.

In case you were wondering, the well-groomed fellow was indeed wearing pants. But his being fully clothed and having a driver didn't entirely soothe my sense of personal security. Obviously I wasn't just going to get into the car.

"Hang on a second," I said as I pulled my cell phone from my pocket and pressed the number three speed dial. I held up my index finger to let the well-groomed and fully clothed man know that I respected his time, but there was some matter I had to attend to first.

"Hi, Dad," I said into my father's voice mail. "I'm about to get into a black Lincoln Town Car on Main and Mission Street to have a chat with a man with a full head of brown hair, approximately forty-five years of age, with an excellent tan. The license plate of the car is XXXYYY.[2] If I don't call you back in—" I covered the mouthpiece on the phone and said to the man in the back seat, "How long do you think this will take?"

"No more than twenty minutes, I hope."

"If I don't call you back in twenty-five minutes, Dad, please call the cops. Okay, bye," I said, and hung up the phone.

"Where were we?" I asked as I got into the back of the car and sat across from the fully suited gentleman.

"Let me get straight to the point," he said.

"Do you have a name?"

"Call me Frank," he replied.

"Is that actually your name or just the name you want me to call you?"

"Frank" ignored my question, pulled a white envelope out of his breast pocket, and handed it to me. Inside was a stack of $100 bills. I counted slowly while "Frank" watched. There were fifty of them. You do the math. I'm sure it'll be faster than mine.

"I'm flattered, 'Frank,'[3] but I'm not that kind of girl. But even if I were, I'm not worth this kind of money."

"Ms. Spellman, I've seen your bank account. This money could keep you for a while."

"What is it that you want from me?" I asked.

"Information."

"I don't have any information. Do you?"

"Who hired you?" "Frank" asked.

"Who hired you?"

Long, awkward silence. As previously mentioned, I'm really comfortable with that these days; therapy has been good for me.

---

[2] No, not the actual license plate.

[3] Yeah, I used finger quotes.

"Is there any way I can compel you to cooperate?" Frank asked.

"Under the threat of violence, I'd sing like a canary," I said, tossing the envelope on the seat next to Frank.

"I'm not that kind of man," he replied.

"What kind of man are you?" I asked.

"Thank you for your time, Ms. Spellman."

On cue, the driver opened the passenger-side door, hinting not-so-subtly for my exit. I hopped out of the car and turned back to look at "Frank" one last time, to log him into my memory.

"What just happened here?" I asked.

"Watch your step, Isabel," was the last thing he said. The driver shut the passenger door and quickly pulled onto the road.

As I walked back to my car, I wondered just what kind of mess I had gotten myself into. An hour and fifteen minutes later, after the women had finished their fancy lunch and returned to their cars, I decided to follow Sharon home. While we both crossed the Golden Gate Bridge, my phone rang.

"Isabel! Isabel. Are you alright?" my dad said.

"Oops," I said. I had left the message but forgot to call him back. "Sorry, Dad. I'm fine."

"Give me the code phrase," he said.

"No, that's not my marijuana,"[4] I said.

"You almost gave me a heart attack. I picked up my voice mail, heard your call, and realized that it happened an hour ago. What's going on?"

"I'm fine, Dad. I'll call you later with some kind of explanation, if I can figure out what's going on. Bye."

I hung up as my dad was shouting my name. I followed Sharon to her Mill Valley home. The tony neighborhood in Marin didn't lend itself to long-term stakeouts. I tailed Sharon to see if anyone else was tailing her.

---

[4] We should probably update this phrase. I vote for: "Sorry, it won't happen again."

As far as I could tell, no one was. Sharon entered her home and I returned to the city.

On my return across the bridge, Milo phoned me.

"There's a guy at the bar asking around for you. What do you want me to tell him?"

"Tell him I'll be right there."

THE GUY AT THE BAR

I had assumed Milo was talking about Henry. Not sure why. Imagine my disappointment when I found Rick Harkey sitting at the bar, nursing a whiskey neat. As far as I know, Harkey has only two faces: the caricature of a good-hearted fellow (who will turn on you at a moment's notice) and the very real cruel bastard (who will turn on you at a moment's notice). Basically, they're both the same person; it's just the mask that's different.

Connor gave me a look when I entered the bar that I couldn't quite translate, but it seemed to indicate caution. I sat down on the stool next to Harkey and summoned a superficial but cheery demeanor.

"Rick, this is my bar. You're going to have to find one of your own."

"Isabel," he said, slowly turning to face me. Harkey, wearing a loosened tie, dark gray slacks, and a well-made oxford shirt rolled up to his elbows, was wearing his second mask. I hadn't seen it firsthand, so it was a bit unnerving. I could see the tight muscles in his arms twitch and his jaw clench as he spoke to me. He looked like a wildcat ready to pounce.

"What can I do for you?" I asked, trying to control the tension with excessive friendliness.

"You can tell me what you're up to, for starters," Harkey said. Even in the forgiving light of the bar, Harkey looked worn, older. I took pleasure in that, imagining it was all my doing.

"This and that," I replied with a toothy smile.

Connor approached as Harkey's fist tightened. I could tell the Irishman was keeping a close watch. He didn't like Harkey one bit. Who did?

"At urr ya drinkin, orgeous?" Connor asked.

I ordered a Guinness to keep Connor close by.

Harkey whispered, to keep the conversation private, "What do you know, Isabel?"

I whispered back, "According to my tenth-grade math teacher, less than nothing."[1]

"Do you want to be friends or do you want to be enemies?"

"I'm aiming for casual acquaintance."

"Don't fuck with me, sweetheart," Harkey said.

Connor made a big show of pulling the slow pint; he even whistled a bit. He was growing on me.

"Listen, Rick," I said at the same low volume, "I know you think you're holding all the cards here, but you're not."

Harkey smiled to suggest I was bluffing, but the smile was a bluff in itself. Connor served my drink.

"You're a guppy playing with sharks," Harkey said, tossing some bills on the bar.

"Maybe," I replied, finding the analogy particularly amusing. "I'm also a guppy with very sharp teeth."

"Still a guppy."

"A guppy who is tired of the guppy analogy, but, in keeping with it, can send one of those sharks to prison. And your kind of shark[2] wouldn't do so well in the pen."

"You think you have something on me?" Harkey asked, looking amused.

---

[1] Of course, I argued the mathematical impossibility of that statement.

[2] The ex-cop kind.

Then he let out a big mess of a laugh. Since people like Harkey have no real sense of humor, their laughs always sound fake even if they believe them to be real. I interrupted the guffaws to get him to shut up.

"Are you not familiar with California Penal Code section 631-A? It makes the taping of a private communication illegal unless all parties consent."

Harkey appeared confused until my comment registered and his color faded just a bit. I smiled. He kept his seemingly unmoved gaze on me, but I could see his insides twitching.

I reached for my beer, but Harkey grabbed my wrist and held it on the bar. His fingers tightened to just the point of pain.

"Sweetheart, I'd watch myself if I were you."

Connor then dug his fingers into Harkey's wrist.

"Sweetheart," he said to Harkey, "if you wan ta keep yar hand, I'd get the fuck outta here and not come back."

Connor looked downright scary. I wondered what kind of brawls he'd gotten into in his homeland. I was glad to have him on my side. Harkey loosened his grip, Connor loosened his, everyone held everyone's gaze, like a Mexican standoff, and finally Harkey turned on his heels and left the bar.

Once I caught my breath, I turned to Connor and smiled as friendly a smile as he'd ever see again.

"Thank you," I said.

"Sure ya know wat ur doin?" he asked.

"Nope," I replied.

I left the bar and returned to my new neighborhood, hunting for close to twenty-five minutes for a parking space that was within a mile of David's and my house. I jotted my car's location down in my notebook and headed toward our place. Lately, I had taken to keeping a pair of travel binoculars in my bag. I scoped the perimeter around the residence and noticed that David was in the midst of doing something resembling garage cleaning. Since it was Monday and David should have been at work, I decided to investigate.

The first thing I did was call his office from my cell phone.

"May I speak to David Spellman?" I asked.

"He's not in."

"When do you expect him?"

"I'm not sure. Can I take a message?"

"No, thanks."

David's vague receptionist made his extended absence (going on seven weeks now) all the more intriguing. Since I hadn't played the I-was-in-the-neighborhood game for a while, I thought I'd fake a drop-by and see what was new in the world of David Spellman—and maybe solve this mystery once and for all. Besides, my only other option was finding some way to occupy myself for the next few hours until I could go home.[3]

It's probably not wise to startle someone in the middle of a balancing act.

"What on earth are you doing?" I asked David as he stood on a stepladder and pulled a box from the top shelf of his garage.

"Ouch," he said, right before he toppled to the ground. Then when he made contact with the cement, he said, "Shit," then "Isabel!" then "What are you doing here?"

I waited to see whether my brother had any permanent injuries. If he did, I'd probably have made a run for it, but he was fine. Maybe a bruise here or there, but nothing that would cause any more guilt than I already had for living in his home without his knowledge.

"I was in the neighborhood," I said nonchalantly. I didn't apologize for causing the crash landing, because I've discovered that if you ignore things, sometimes the other party will ignore them, too.

"Why didn't you park in the driveway?" David asked.

---

[3] Note to self: Consider getting a hobby . . . or your own apartment.

(Normally if I'm in the neighborhood I park in his driveway, since parking in Russian Hill is brutal—I know, you know.)

"I found a space a few blocks away. Figured I should take it in case you were expecting company. Why aren't you at work?"

"Why are you dropping by when you think I'm at work?"

"I was going to sit on your step and mooch off your wireless."

"What's wrong with a café?" David asked.

"Not thirsty. Your turn: Why aren't you at work?"

"Taking the day off," David said, and then he proceeded to pull everything out of a yellowed file box.

"Just the day or many days?" I asked.

"I'm using up my vacation time," David answered.

"To clean your garage?"

The contents of the box were clearly relics of the past—a magic set from his tenth or eleventh birthday,[4] a stack of unopened baseball cards, a deflated football, and a rock collection. I have approximately ten boxes of stuff from my youth that will remain forever (or at least until the threat of destruction) in my parents' garage. I remember some seven or eight years ago watching David sort through his life's accumulation and reduce his early years to one box. My mother suggested his downsizing was over the top, but he insisted on simplifying his life when an interior decorator took over his home and defined his sense of style. I had a particular vendetta against this decorator since she made David give up a coffee table I gave him for his twenty-fourth birthday.[5] All this passed through my mind as David hunted desperately through the box, ignoring my question. I moved on to a more pertinent inquiry.

"What are you looking for?"

"My rabbit's foot," David said as if the answer was patently obvious.

---

[4] I remember burying his wand in a flower box, hoping that would end the nightly performances. I sadly discovered that a chopstick works just as well.

[5] I found it at a garage sale. It had a giant backgammon board beneath the glass.

"Why?" I asked.

"I don't know," David said, looking concerned. "I just have to find it."

"Is something wrong with you?" I asked, and then regretted the phrasing immediately.

"Isabel," David said with a tone of warning. "I'm having a bad day. No, I'm having a bad year. If you plan on being in my vicinity, you have to behave like a human being. Not like yourself."

"Ouch," I replied pleasantly.

"Got it?" David asked sternly.

"I got it," I said without an atom of attitude.[6]

Fortunately, my phone rang, which spared David the unhelpful suggestion I was currently forming into a sentence.[7]

"Hello?" I said. You're probably thinking in this day and age I should know who's calling on my cell phone, but some people still like to block their caller ID to keep you on your toes.

"Izzy, it's Dad."

Some of those people I'm related to.

"Hi, Dad," I said.

"Do you know whose car you got into today?"

"Nope. But he didn't kill me, which makes me think fondly of him."

"Frank Waverly."

"He looked more like a Jimmy to me."

"Does that ring a bell, Isabel?"

"No. But there aren't any bells around here."

"You don't keep up on current events."

"I'd like to skip over the traditional constructive criticism part of this conversation to where you tell me who he is."

"He's a political consultant."

"That's so cool," I said. "A political consultant offered me a bribe."

---

[6] I'm soooo going to mention this in therapy.

[7] "Why don't you buy a new one?"

"What?!" Dad shouted. "You didn't mention that."

"I just did."

"More details."

"Okay, he asked me to get in the car. He then handed me an envelope with five thousand dollars in it and asked me for information. Since I had no idea what he was talking about, I said no, which was a mistake, because it's more than enough money for me."

"Isabel, we need to talk about this. Come up with a plan."

"Dad, there's nothing to discuss yet, since I don't know anything."

"Come by the house."

"I'm busy looking for a rabbit's foot, okay? I'll talk to you later."

Dad's news was intriguing and required some follow-up investigation. None of which I could do unless I got inside my apartment, which meant I had to get David inside his.

As you may recall, I spent days searching David's house from top to bottom. I remembered not one but two rabbit's feet. I remember them because they seemed so out of place. A white one in the back of the junk drawer in his kitchen and an old soggy brown one in his office—third drawer on the right of his desk—that David had acquired on a Spellman camping trip (circa 1992) that all members wished to never duplicate again.

"What does it look like?" I asked.

"You don't know what a rabbit's foot looks like?" David rudely replied.

"You know they're not actually feet."

At this point, David was pretty much done with me. Like many before him, he pretended I wasn't there. To redeem myself, I entered his house and found the two rabbit's feet I recalled from my massive hunt.

I returned to the garage and opened the palms of my hands, presenting the offerings. David ignored the clean, white, faux foot and picked up the aged and soggy one as if it were a precious medallion.

"Thank you," he said, in awe. "How'd you find it?"

"How do you think?" I replied, hinting at the wild goose chase he'd prompted not too long ago.

"Finally some good comes out of your snooping. I'll make you dinner to celebrate," David cheerily replied.

I followed pod-David into his house and let him cook for me. His previous mood had lifted in an odd, unnatural way. I would have loved to have gone home to do some research on the new angle on the Bancroft case, but I had some research on my brother that I needed to handle first. I'd followed too many wildly opposing leads in the past few weeks to have any real objectivity when it came to David. I tried to erase all the previous sensational theories from my head and start fresh. All I knew for sure was that he had changed, and something was going on in his life to prompt that change. I stayed for dinner, ate his food, and asked whatever questions I could get away with.

David grilled fish on the porch, and I watched him while drinking a beer. I love cooking.

"How much more vacation time do you have?"

"A few weeks."[8]

"How was your weekend with Rae?" I asked, not all that interested in the Rae part.

"It wasn't so bad," he replied.

"What did you do?"

I was hoping the vague question would spark the answer to my one real question: What was Maggie doing there?

"We watched some movies, ate s'mores, she studied a lot—seemed unusually concerned about a bad test score—and, um, she invited this woman over. A new friend of hers."

"You mean Maggie?" I said. "Henry's ex-girlfriend?"

"Yes, do you know her?" David asked.

"I do," I replied.

"She seems nice."

"She is nice. Why did Rae invite her over?"

"I'm not sure."

---

[8] Bad news for me. I would have to be on constant guard.

"Strange, don't you think?"

"Well, yes," David said, turning his attention to the fish. Except that it seemed like he was showing me he was concentrating on the grill and not our conversation. At least that was my impression.

"What did you all talk about?" I asked.

"All sorts of things," David replied.

"For instance?" I asked.

"Maggie asked me if I'd buy Rae a car."

"Aha, now I have my explanation. It seems odd that Rae would think that having Maggie do her bidding would change the outcome."

"What's ridiculous is Rae thinking that somebody is going to buy her a car when she has close to fifty thousand dollars in a brokerage account."

"What?!" I shouted in utter disbelief. "What are you talking about?"

David furrowed his brow the moment he uttered that line, as if it were a not-well-kept secret and therefore one he forgot to keep. I could see him playing out the rest of the conversation in his head, trying to calculate how to withhold any further information.

"David," I said as a warning. "Just spit it out so you don't have to keep track of your lies at a later date."

David sighed and I waited in empty silence. I knew it was only a matter of time before he spilled the dirt, so I was patient.

"I only heard about it a year ago," David said as a preface, and we headed inside. "Rae has been saving all her life. She's incredibly cheap. Haven't you noticed? Most of what she earns goes into her savings account, and apparently six years ago she convinced Grammy Spellman[9] to open a brokerage account for her. It's in Rae's name, but a guardian typically has control of the money. Grammy gave Rae the password and she's been trading stocks online for close to six years now."

"I still don't understand how she got fifty thousand dollars."

---

[9] Here's what you need to know about Grammy Spellman: She and my Dad barely speak. But she's pretty good at sending a birthday card and a check to her grandchildren. She's the kind of grammy who would open a brokerage account for her granddaughter and keep it from her son.

"She started with savings of around five to ten thousand. Remember she's been earning a paycheck since she was eleven—and that doesn't include birthday and Christmas gifts."

"Or your hush money,"[10] I said.

"I haven't given her a cent in three years."

"Why would you?" I asked. "Forget it. Just explain how she parlayed five to ten thousand in savings into fifty."

"She bought Google and Apple stock at just the right time and then she sold it."

Dead, dead silence.

"I need a drink," I said, drifting over to David's bar. Out of habit I poured the Jack Daniel's, assuming it was the good stuff, and took a sip. It was like thinking you were drinking Coke and getting Diet Coke[11] instead. I'm fine with lower-grade bourbons; it's just not what I was expecting. Like everything else. I was exhausted by secrets, my own and others'.

I sat down on David's couch and stared at his wall while I drank my beverage. I had an uneasy feeling in my gut, but it got worse when David painted the full picture.

"Mom didn't want to tell you," he said.

"Everyone knew but me? Why?" I asked.

"Mom said it would upset you to know your adolescent sibling had amassed savings that beat your yearly income."

What my mother didn't understand was that her pity was the most upsetting thing. I made a show of lightly brushing off this information. I finished my meal, helped wash the dishes, and when I said I had to go home, I took almost no precautions when circling David's residence and entering through the back. It was almost as if I wanted to get caught, wanted to prove just how pathetic I really was.

---

[10] About three years ago, we learned that David had been giving Rae at least twenty dollars a week for no reason at all, other than to stay in her good graces.

[11] Please, no letters from the Jack Daniel's corporation!

THE LAST LUNCH
(WITH MORTY)

I planned lunch with Morty for the following day. I'd been waiting for David to leave all morning, but at eleven A.M. he was still home, and my usual safe midday exit would have to be a risky one. I checked the hidden camera in David's driveway one last time on my computer. Good thing I checked, since David was sitting on his porch, drinking coffee and reading the newspaper. I phoned David's cell to see if I could get him in his house. He picked up on the third ring.

"It's Isabel," I said.

"I know," said David. "What can I do for you?"

"I'm lost. Can you look something up on a map for me?"

"Sure, let me get to my computer."

Through my laptop, I watched David enter his house. I turned off my computer and made my way to the back door.

"I'm in the Dog Patch, around Cesar Chavez and Third Street."

"What are you doing there?" David asked.

"I'm casing the neighborhood for my next B and E."

"If you want my help, refrain from sarcasm."

"I'm supposed to meet Morty for lunch on Hopper Street."

"Hold on," David replied.

This is when I made my safe exit. You see, there is no Hopper Street. It would take David some time to realize this fact. I turned the corner at the end of David's block and walked up Hyde, closing in on the location of my car.

"There is no Hopper Street," David said, much sooner than I anticipated.

"Really? Hmm," I replied. "I better call Morty. He must have given me the wrong name. Okay, bye," I said, and quickly hung up the phone.

Since I last saw my ancient friend, he had not quit his habit of verbally equating moving with death. All events in the past week were accompanied by constant reminders that these precious moments we had together were coming to a quick and severe close.

This was my final private lunch with Morty, and I have to admit, I was pleased when my habit-obsessed friend wanted to try someplace new.

Morty isn't a fancy man, but when I met him in the foyer of Spork[1] he was wearing a suit with a sweater vest and bow tie. I kissed him on the cheek.

"Would it have killed you to wear a dress?"

"No," I replied. "But the mental injury would have been serious."

Morty gave his name to the maître d', who seated us promptly—remember, this is eleven thirty A.M. We were the first customers of the day.

After Morty and I were seated, I studied his ensemble more closely.

"How many layers have you got on there, Morty?" I asked. If ever someone was making a statement with his fashion, it was then.

"Undershirt, shirt, sweater vest, jacket," he said, counting on his fingers. "Four. Let me wear my clothes while I still have the chance."

"People wear clothes in Florida," I said.

"Today I'm not talking about Florida."

"Fine. What would you like to talk about?" I asked.

"I need to decide what I'm going to eat first."

---

[1] A high-end but casual restaurant in the Mission named in honor of the quasi-official utensil of the Kentucky Fried Chicken that used to reside in its place.

"Stop it," I said, referring to that annoying noise Morty makes with his teeth.

"You're hearing things," Morty replied.

Fifteen minutes later [2]

After our orders were placed, Morty took a business-sized envelope out of his breast pocket and handed it to me.

"My days are numbered, as you know," he said.

"Would you please stop saying that? It's annoying."

"Try being old. That's even more annoying."

. "You had no problem being old three months ago."

"Do you want to know what's in the envelope or not?" Morty asked, folding his arms defensively.

"Right now I'm about fifty-fifty," I replied.

"Fine, then give it back," he said.

I didn't, of course.

"Why don't I just open the envelope, and then you won't have to tell me what's in it?" I asked, breaking the seal.

"Wait. I must say something first. Put the envelope down," Morty said.

I lowered the envelope, but I didn't entirely release my grip.

"Put it down all the way," Morty repeated, getting annoyed.

I followed his instructions because, well, I had no choice.

"You know what's inside that envelope?"

"No. That's what I'm trying to find out," I said, attempting to move things along.

"Eighty-four years of wisdom," Morty replied, enunciating each word so I wouldn't miss them.

I stared down at the flat white envelope addressed to me. "Really?" I

---

[2] During the time it took Morty to make the life-changing decision of what to have for lunch, I read the menu from top to bottom—three times—and learned that Spork recycles their cooking oil as diesel fuel.

said. "Eighty-four years? You'd think eighty-four years would require a large box, or at least a thick manila envelope. Who knew you could fit eighty-four years into a four-by-nine-inch envelope?"

"Don't be smart," Morty said.

"Excellent advice. Is that in there?" I asked.

Morty's Last Words

Beneath the morbid title was a page-long bulleted list of his carefully chosen words of wisdom. I suggested that I could read the list in the privacy of my home, but Morty insisted that I review the list in his company in case I had any questions. So I did, reading each item out loud.

- If you ever have an unusual ache or pain, go to the doctor.
- Don't take any chances with your health.

"It was only a month ago that I found you at home with a temperature of one-oh-three," I said.

"I learned from my mistakes. You can, too," Morty replied. "Keep reading."

- Same goes for your car. If it's making a funny noise, go to the mechanic. Also, check the oil at least once every two months.
- Don't eat anything after the expiration date. Except pretzels. They're usually okay.

"Is this a joke?" I asked.

"A stale pretzel never killed anyone," Morty replied.

"Eighty-four years and this is your best material?"

"I wrote it this morning. Keep reading."

- When you get married, don't make any long-term verbal contract that you're not one hundred percent sure about.
- Make sure you have water on hand for the big quake. Also, know how to turn off the gas in your house. It was fires that killed the most people in the 1906 quake.

"Right," I said. "I totally forgot you were there."

Morty said nothing; he just gave me a dirty look and then another look that meant *I haven't got all day. Keep reading.*

- Stay away from new religions. They tend to be a lot of hoo-ha.[3]
- When you get old, start making friends with people younger than you so you always have at least one around.

Morty winked when I finished reading that line.

- Always tip well unless you don't plan on returning to the restaurant.
- Don't drink so much.
- Always double-knot your shoelaces.

"It's a shock you don't have a book deal with these kinds of gems."

"Shhhh. Keep reading."

"Do you want me to be quiet or do you want me to keep reading?"

I continued reading the list out loud. Occasionally I'd lower my voice when the waiter was in the vicinity. There's only so much public humiliation that I can tolerate.

- Get some fiber in your diet.
- Stay out of jail.

"Are you giving this list to everyone, or is this my personal medley of advice?" I asked. Frankly, it was hard to tell at that point.

"Keep reading," Morty said as if he'd said it one hundred times before.

If I had doubts about whether the list was generic or custom-made, the final three edicts cleared that up for me.

- Give the cop your phone number.
- Tell your dad that you're happy to take over the business.
- Let your brother know that you're living in his home without his consent.

---

[3] Yes, he actually wrote out "hoo-ha."

I asked repeatedly over an excellent lunch whether Morty was responsible for the series of ransom notes. His replies were as cagey as my sister's recent pseudodenials. You will find this impossible to believe, but I left lunch that day having no idea whether Morty was or was not my blackmailer. After I kissed him good-bye and promised one final farewell, I began to seriously contemplate a conspiracy.

Then Maggie called with her own conspiracy to discuss.

THE PHILOSOPHER'S CLUB

I took an unplanned nap on the Muni train and was woken by my father calling to inquire about the bizarre turn in the Truesdale case. I knew my father couldn't resist political intrigue. I explained to Dad that I knew nothing; then I explained it using different words, since the first time around it didn't stick. Dad asked a few more questions and reluctantly accepted that I wasn't holding out on him.

"If it makes you feel any better, Dad, right now I think that nobody knows anything."

When I arrived at the Philosopher's Club, Maggie was on her second beer and had dipped into her pocket provisions.[1] Connor served my usual whiskey without a word. He was really growing on me. I apologized to Maggie for my tardiness and joined her.

"You're going to think I'm paranoid," she said.

"I have no business judging people on that front," I replied.

As she sipped her beer, I could tell she was grasping for the words that would make her sound the sanest.

"I think someone's investigating me," she said. "Again."

---

[1] Twizzlers.

"My mom and Rae both promised me that they'd stop. And my dad is kind of busy, and it's not really his style."

"This time I don't think it's anyone in your family."

"Are you being followed?" I asked.

"Not yet."

"Is someone looking into your personal records?"

"I'm getting phone calls. Two so far."

"Harassing phone calls?"

"Not really. Both times it was a woman's voice and she asked me survey questions."

"Are you sure it's not just a survey?"

"I'm pretty sure. The questions aren't normal survey questions."

"For instance?" I asked.

Maggie pulled a notepad from her purse and reviewed her own scribbles, which, at least on upside-down viewing, were as illegible as hieroglyphics for one not schooled in hieroglyphics.

"She started with legal questions, asked me if I worked pro bono; then she inquired whether I believed in the legalization of drugs, and if so, which drugs."

"It sounds like it could be a legitimate survey," I interjected.

"Then the questions changed. She asked me if I was satisfied with my work. Then she ran off a list of leisure activities, including going to the beach, movies, camping, something else I can't remember, and asked me to rate my enjoyment of each one on a five-star scale. Then she inquired whether I was a dog or cat person."

"Really?" I said. "And how did you reply?"

"Cats give me the creeps. I'm a total dog person."

"What else?" I asked.

"The last question was the weirdest of all: She asked me about my favorite monkey, and when I said, 'Do you mean monkey as in rhesus monkey, or Monkee as in the band the Monkees?' she said, 'I don't know, let's skip that question.' That can't be a normal survey," Maggie said, looking for confirmation.

"Yes," I replied, confirming her suspicions. "I'll look into this matter for you," I said. And then my current nemesis arrived.

As far as I knew, it had been weeks since Rae had returned to the bar. But now she walked in and sat right down like a regular, oblivious to the fact that her sister and her new friend were seated at a table nearby.

I observed my sister for a moment before I approached. She threw her book bag on top of the bar with an air of frustration and casually ordered "the usual." Apparently Connor was familiar with her "usual," since he poured a large glass of ginger ale and placed it in front of her.

"Rough day?" he asked, which took me aback. Shouldn't this conversation have begun with "We don't serve minors in here"?

I quickly approached.

"What are you doing here?" I asked Rae.

"Unwinding," she replied, not even turning her head.

I sat down next to my not-yet-seventeen-year-old sister and then turned to Connor.

"You know, in this country the drinking age is twenty-one."

"She's drinkin' ginger ale," Connor casually replied. "When she's done, she'll be on er way. Right, Rae?"

"Right," Rae said, as if she and Connor agreed on almost everything. When Rae turned to look at me, she finally spotted Maggie.

"Just the person I was looking for," Rae said as she hopped off the bar stool and lugged her backpack over to Maggie's table.

"Five minutes and we're leaving," I said, to apparently deaf ears.

Rae sat down at the table and rummaged through her backpack, eventually pulling out a recently graded essay.

"I need a consult," Rae said.

"A legal consult?" Maggie asked.

"Hopefully it won't come to that," Rae said. "Look at this essay. Do you think it deserves a C-minus?"

As Rae passed the paper over to Maggie, I turned my attention to Connor. "Is Milo around?"

"He's in the office, sorting through his old files. He'll be happy to see ya."

We'll see about that, I thought to myself.

I entered an office that had been transformed from its previous dingy overload. A paper shredder sat in the corner with two tied bags of devoured documents. Milo was evidently on the cusp of reducing his life's accumulation to a single file cabinet. I sat down in the lumpy chair across from his desk. It's there more for show than anything else—Milo doesn't appreciate visitors in his office, hence the uncomfortable chair. It's an obvious dichotomy when you catch a glimpse of the lumbar support on Milo's ergonomic specimen.

"So, you're really leaving me?" I asked.

"I like how you're making this all about you."

"You could have called me."

"I told you I was moving."

"But I didn't believe you."

"I'm in love, Isabel."

"I figured it wouldn't last."

"That's very supportive. Thank you."

"So, what are you going to do about the apartment?"[2] I asked.

"Bernie says he wants to keep it in the family. Why? You want it back?"

This was an interesting offer. I wasn't sure how long I could keep my scam going and live with the accompanying sleep deprivation. Every day I felt my mind slipping more and more. Besides, visiting the museum on occasion is one thing, but if my blackmailer got any more ambitious

---

[2] Milo took over the rent-controlled apartment that I took over from Bernie, after Bernie took it over from me—but changed his mind. See previous document, *Curse of the Spellmans* (now available in paperback!), for details.

with his/her cultural initiatives on my behalf, I could see it becoming seriously inconvenient. And if David ever found out, I thought he just might kill me, or at the very least spend the rest of his days finding ways to torture me.

"Let me think about it for a few days."

"By the way, where are you living now?"

"In my apartment—you know, the crappy one in the Tenderloin."

Milo opened his desk drawer and passed me an envelope, an envelope addressed to me with NOT AT THIS ADDRESS—RETURN TO SENDER stamped on the front.

"Well, wherever you're living, you need to figure out how to get your mail," Milo said, clearly not wanting any of the details.

I decided to change the subject.

"When are you moving?" I asked.

"Two weeks. This Sunday, Connor's throwing me a good-bye party at the bar."

"How long have you been planning this party?" I inquired, curious that this was the first time he'd mentioned it. What if I hadn't shown up? Was he planning on saying good-bye to me at all?

"About three weeks. I sent you an invitation, but I guess it got lost in the mail," Milo said with an unnecessary amount of attitude.

The chair was digging into my leg and cutting off my circulation. I stood up, eyeing it with disdain.

"That's not a chair; it's a torture device," I said.

"This is an office, not a waiting room," Milo explained in defense of the chair.

"I guess I'll see you Sunday," I said.

Before I exited, Milo had to impart his own words of wisdom. Thankfully, his were relatively brief.

"Tick tock."

"Excuse me?" I said. "I don't speak clock."

"Time is running out, Izzy. One day, you got to grow up like the rest of us."

I'm not sure anyone would consider Milo all grown up—a career bartender skipping town to move in with a woman he barely knew. He was giving me advice? It felt like a new low.

"I wouldn't be so sure," I replied, although at that point I couldn't remember what statement I was replying to.

CULTURE 101

I drove by David's house on a reconnaissance mission. I didn't want to bother parking unless I was certain I could find safe passage into my apartment. I saw Maggie's car in the driveway. I assumed that Rae had insisted on a drop-off at my brother's house and then further insisted that Maggie come in for coffee, tea, or s'mores. Who knows?

I had time to kill and was at a loss for how to use it. At the moment I wasn't sure where to take the investigation. I'm not the kind of person who makes to-do lists, but if I was, going to the museum would have been on the list. According to the literature included with my ransom note, SFMOMA stayed open late on Thursday. It was Thursday. I phoned Henry.

"What are you doing?"

"Reading."

"Good. So you're not busy," I said.

"That's one way to look at it."

"I'll pick you up in fifteen minutes."

"Where are we going?"

"SFMOMA."

. . .

Forty-five minutes and twenty-four dollars later,[1] Henry and I strolled among the permanent collection. Henry liked to stop and stare for a long time at each piece. Me, I liked to grab all the free pamphlets I could get my hands on and attempt to memorize as many artists' works as I could, just in case my blackmailer decided that a quiz was in order.

I can't say that I was 100 percent bored, but Henry's extended viewing started to get on my nerves.

"Okay, let's move this show along," I said after I timed him staring at a Jackson Pollock[2] piece for thirty-four seconds.

An hour and a half later, Henry and I exited the building on Third Street and found a diner a few blocks away. Over a grilled chicken salad (for Henry) and a burger and fries (for me), we did what I suppose most people do after taking in some culture. I considered this practice overly time consuming: Look at art and then talk about art. I don't see why people can't look and talk at the same time.

"Now that wasn't so bad, was it?" Henry asked.

"It was okay," I replied. "These fries, however, are amazing. Are you sure you don't want to try one?"

Henry shook his head disappointedly. "Seriously, Isabel. Wasn't there one piece of artwork that you liked?"

"I guess I kind of dug that Rauschenberg guy."

"Which piece?"

"The one where he erases the other guy's drawing," I said.

"*Erased de Kooning Drawing*?"[3] Henry clarified.

---

[1] I paid for his ticket, since it was my blackmail.

[2] See, I was learning something.

[3] (1953.) Yes, that's really what it is. Rauschenberg erased de Kooning's drawing. The museum guard explained it to me. That's the kind of art I can get behind.

"That's the one," I said. "I probably would have liked it even more if I knew that de Kooning guy."

The remainder of our dinner conversation revolved around more familiar territory. Henry informed me that french fries don't count as a vegetable and I accused him of eating like a girl on a diet. Then we decided to stop arguing about food and I told him about Morty and Milo leaving me for warmer climates. Henry said that this sort of thing wouldn't happen if I made friends my own age. I ignored him for three minutes after that comment until he mentioned that we needed to review our plans for the sting operation.

The evening ended a few hours later when I dropped Henry off at his door. In case you're wondering (and I know you are), there was no goodnight kiss or confession of undying love. Okay?

THERAPY SESSION #19
(REVISITED)

[Partial transcript reads as follows:]

DR. RUSH: Two weeks ago you mentioned that you were being blackmailed.

ISABEL: Did I?

DR. RUSH: Yes.

ISABEL: Must have slipped my mind.

DR. RUSH: Would you like to talk about it?

ISABEL: Nah.

DR. RUSH: Well, I'd like to talk about it.

ISABEL: It's really not that big a deal.

DR. RUSH: Do you know your blackmailer?

ISABEL: I'm in the process of narrowing down the list of suspects.

DR. RUSH: How does your blackmailer communicate with you?

ISABEL: Anonymous notes.

DR. RUSH: What do they say?

ISABEL: I *really* don't want to talk about it.

DR. RUSH: If these sessions went according to your plan, you'd sit here in silence for an hour eating your lunch.

ISABEL: *One time* I asked you if I could eat lunch. *One time.*

DR. RUSH: Tell me what the gist of the notes is and then we can move on.

ISABEL: "I know your secret. If you want to keep it you will meet my demands."

DR. RUSH: So, what's your secret?

ISABEL: I thought we were moving on.

DR. RUSH: We are. To what your secret is.

ISABEL: [sigh] My blackmailer knows where I live. At least I think that's the secret he or she is referring to.

DR. RUSH: Where do you live?

ISABEL: I don't want to lie to you, Dr. Rush.

DR. RUSH: I'm flattered.

ISABEL: I don't want to tell you the truth, either.

DR. RUSH: Are you being serious, Isabel?

ISABEL: I sense judgment in your tone, Doctor.

DR. RUSH: Right now I'm just confused. The judgment part will come later.

ISABEL: You're funnier than Dr. Ira.

DR. RUSH: My couch is funnier than Dr. Ira.

ISABEL: See?

DR. RUSH: You really aren't going to tell me where you live?

ISABEL: If it makes you feel any better, most people don't know where I live.

DR. RUSH: My feelings don't come into play here.

ISABEL: It's nice to have one person I don't have to worry about.

DR. RUSH: Are you getting enough sleep?

ISABEL: No. But I drink a lot of coffee and take the bus, so things even out.

DR. RUSH: Why can't you sleep?

ISABEL: I've got a lot on my mind.

DR. RUSH: [impatiently] For instance?

[Long pause.]

ISABEL: Something strange is going on with my brother.

DR. RUSH: We're not talking about your brother.

ISABEL: It's my therapy. I thought I got to choose the topics.

DR. RUSH: Let me ask you a question: Have you been hired to investigate your brother?

ISABEL: He's family. You don't need a paycheck to investigate family.

DR. RUSH: I'd like to return to the topic of blackmail.

ISABEL: Why?

DR. RUSH: Because it's a clearly defined stressor in your life.

ISABEL: It's not that stressful. Can we *please* talk about something else?

DR. RUSH: If you can come up with a topic as good as blackmail, I'm game.

[Long pause while I pretend to think of a worthy subject.]

DR. RUSH: I'm onto you and your long pauses.[1]

ISABEL: Okay. I'm being bribed by a political consultant.

DR. RUSH: Seriously?

ISABEL: Yes.

DR. RUSH: Why?

ISABEL: Because he thinks I know something. But I don't know anything . . . yet.

DR. RUSH: What does he think you know?

ISABEL: If I knew that, then I'd know.

DR. RUSH: [sigh] Is this bribe incident connected to the blackmail?

ISABEL: Absolutely not.

DR. RUSH: What makes you so sure?

ISABEL: The bribe is serious. The blackmail is child's play.

DR. RUSH: I need you to be more specific.

ISABEL: My blackmailer is making me wash cars and go to the zoo.

DR. RUSH: Go to the zoo?

ISABEL: It was supposed to be SFMOMA, but I thought I could go to the zoo instead. My mistake. My point is they are entirely unconnected.

[Long, long pause.]

DR. RUSH: [sigh] Bizarre forms of blackmail, bribery, secret residences. The odds of all of this happening to one person, Isabel—

ISABEL: It sounds worse than it is.

---

[1] If you've found something that works, why quit?

DR. RUSH: Let's look at this from a different perspective. Your imagination has gotten you into trouble in the past. That's why you're in therapy. You can't deny that you tend to put a paranoid slant on most things you observe.

ISABEL: That was the old me.

DR. RUSH: Are you sure?

ISABEL: I've made progress, Dr. Rush. Lots of progress.

[Long, long pause.]

ISABEL: Haven't I?

Part IV

EVEN MORE
PROGRESS

CASE #001

CHAPTER 11

On my way home from therapy, I was followed. Since I usually park my car within several blocks of David's residence, and only the blackmailer knows where I live (presumably), I had to assume that someone—probably Harkey or one of his goons—had put a tracking device on my vehicle. To throw my pursuer off, I parked my car west of Van Ness near Broadway. This would put me in a different neighborhood than my usual and would confuse my tailer, until I could lose the tracking device. In case anyone was following me on foot, I didn't return "home" straightaway; I crossed Van Ness and entered a café on Polk Street.

If I know Harkey's logic like I think I do, he put a tail on me to derail my investigation. Either through intimidation or interference, he figured he could get me off the case. However, the tail confirmed that there really was something to investigate—so it had the opposite of its intended effect. Dr. Rush might argue that this was a perfect example of taking my job to extremes, but some truths have to be uncovered. I may have made some wrong turns in the past, but so far on this case I had no regrets. What I knew for sure was that I had to get to the truth before Harkey did.

I could only assume that the core of the Truesdale/Bancroft mystery rested in their distant past, mostly because I couldn't find any recent dirt on either of them. I'd had trouble locating any bank records on Linda, and tax returns are impossible to access. I had a feeling that Linda had money in her own personal account, but unless I could get a look inside that PO box, I'd never know. I needed to dig deeper. The only information I had from Ernie was where the women attended high school. Like so many other things in modern society, that information is protected by strict privacy laws. I couldn't get my hands on anything unless I bribed a school administrator, and I was keeping this investigation clean. Well, mostly.

I looked up both women on classmates.com,[1] and neither had registered under Benjamin Franklin High School. I searched the listings for the year Linda graduated and zeroed in on the person with the most recent activity. Her screen name was fairydust611,[2] which led me to the conclusion that she was either a unicorn-loving lunatic or a drug dealer, but I figured a drug dealer had better things to do than reconnect with her high school classmates. Lunatics are often far more forthright with their information than the sane, so this boded well for my investigation. I e-mailed fairydust611 and asked her whether she had been in touch with Linda Truesdale since high school. I explained that I was an old friend who lost her contact information in a fire (I figured fairydust611 would appreciate the sense of drama).

After I sent the e-mail, I ordered a coffee and scoped out the café, looking for signs of trouble. But all the patrons looked legitimate for this area of town, this time of day, and this sort of establishment. One of the problems with Harkey's business is that his surveillance guys look like surveillance guys. You can spot them from a mile away. Hidden in a car, they can slip past your periphery, stay on your tail, and maybe go unnoticed for hours. But on foot, they stand out like sore thumbs. This was one reason Spellman Investigations had a leg up on the surveillance business in the city. Sure, we often hired retired cops or security guys, but we also employed college students, part-time porn shop clerks,[3] and three women of varying ages and sizes (if you count me).

---

[1] A website dedicated to uniting people with their painful past.

[2] Could it be there were 610 fairydusts before her?

[3] Just that one time, but it seemed worth mentioning. I wonder what Jake Hand is up to these days.

While I waited for fairydust611's reply, I checked my e-mail:

To: Izzy Ellmanspay [I.Ellmanspay@gmail.com]
From: Henry Stone
Re: Rae
Message:
Isabel, please tell Rae to stop calling me. One message a night is
more than enough. And, I should add, not ONE of those messages
was an admission of guilt. In fact, she's never offered a sincere apol-
ogy for changing my locks or anything else she's ever done. Tell her
"I'm sorry you're angry" is NOT an apology. Also, don't tell me to use
call block, because she just borrows her friends' phones.
Thank you for handling this matter.
Henry

I e-mailed Rae, relaying the message, but I had a feeling it would fall on
deaf ears or blind eyes. Henry was mistaken in thinking I'd have any more
sway than he would, but I admired his hard stand against communicating
with Rae. One of these days I would have to try it myself. Sometime during
my e-mail game of "telephone," fairydust611 replied.

To: Izzy Ellmanspay [I.Ellmanspay@gmail.com]
From: Fairy Dust [fairydust611@gmail.com]
Re: Linda Truesdale
Message:
Howdy, Ms. Ellmanspay. I don't remember any Linda Truesdale at B.F.
High. Are you sure Truesdale is her maiden name?
Cheers,
Betty

I was happy to learn that fairydust611 had a real name and was quick
to reply. I shot her another e-mail straightaway.

To: Fairy Dust
From: Izzy Ellmanspay
Re: Re: Linda Truesdale
Message:
Betty,
Thank you for your quick reply. Do you remember a Sharon Meade?
She would have been two or three years behind you.
Thanks,
Izzy E.

I waited five minutes for another speedy reply but maybe fairydust611 had to cook meat loaf or dust off her unicorn statues. I slipped my computer into my bag, slung my backpack over my shoulder, and exited the café, scanning the pedestrians on every adjacent street corner to note whether I had a tail.

I crossed Van Ness Avenue, checking over my shoulder a few more times. As I approached my car, I could see no signs of a tail, so I decided it was time to reposition the GPS that was planted. I sat down on the curb, pretending to tie my shoe, and then I lay down on the cement and checked under the curb side of my vehicle. Rae's GPS was inside the back rear fender. The new one was just under the front right fender. After I removed it, I looked it over and found a small label: RH. Putting your initials on a tracking device you're using covertly? Behold the unique blend of arrogance and stupidity that is Rick Harkey. I was amused that he thought so little of me that I wouldn't figure out his method. But Harkey is famous for believing women are good for just a few things. I scanned the area one more time and placed the device on the cleanest car in the vicinity, figuring that was the one that got driven the most. Then I felt a short surge of elation as I imagined the inconvenience Harkey and his men would suffer at my hand. Then I started letting my mind wander, dreaming of further revenge, but I stopped myself. I had a few other worries that took precedence.

. . .

Fifteen minutes later, as I approached David's and my house, I saw a new car—specifically, a new Toyota Prius—in his driveway and decided to investigate. I knocked on his door.

"Why are you always in the neighborhood?" David asked when he saw me.

"I live here, didn't you know that?" I replied. *I know,* I'm becoming reckless. I blame exhaustion.

"I suppose you want to come in," David said, not seeming all that broken up about the idea. He was wearing something strange. Loose-fitting clothing in a fabric that looked all-natural or breathable or whatever. Ew. (Sartorial U-turns are always a sign of something—why shouldn't I be curious?) I refrained from commenting, which took most of the strength I had left, because I wanted to find out about the car first.

"Not if you have company," I said, nodding my head at the unknown vehicle.

"Something wrong with your neck?" David asked.

"Whose car?"

"Mine," he replied casually. It was an effort, the casualness. As if he were trying to convince me that the whole topic was casual and I shouldn't think twice about it.

"That's not your car," I said.

"Yes, it is," he replied. "Are you coming in or not?"

I followed David into his house. I was distracted by the car and the meaning behind the car and whether my brother was turning into someone new. I honestly didn't have any valid complaints about the new David—at least what I knew of him. Well, I could complain about the skipping-work part because it cramped my coming-and-going style, but that didn't seem fair. Still, there were motivations to uncover.

"Where's the BMW?"

"I traded it in."

"And why did you get a new car?" I asked, trying to maintain the casual air.

"I wanted to reduce my carbon footprint," David replied.

It was a reasonable response, but nothing is that simple with David—switching from a luxury sedan to a Prius signals more than just a whim of ecological conscience.

"Are you having a MILFO?" I asked.

"Why do you insist on reducing complex issues to simple terms? Sometimes people change without some sensational backstory to explain it. Sometimes people need to change and they're not even sure why."

Was it possible that my brother's mystery was no mystery at all, just some kind of vague life change prompted by divorce, age, and the Discovery Channel?

"My therapist would love you," was all I said.

"So, how is that going?" David asked, casually twisting the conversation over to me. Don't worry, I can't be twisted.

"Nineteen sessions[4] down; five to go."

"Have you discovered anything new about yourself?"

"Of course, but I'm prohibited by professional ethics from discussing what happens in therapy."

"No," David said, both sighing and rolling his eyes, "your therapist is prohibited from discussing your sessions. You are free to talk about them."

"Well, I'll have to research that and get back to you."

Long pause.

"Why is it that you dropped by again?" David said, sounding tired.

"Oh yes. I remember," I said, remembering. "Why did you have some woman call Maggie and ask her survey questions?"

David turned to pour himself a drink so that I couldn't read his expression.

---

[4] Including all twelve Dr. Ira sessions.

"I didn't," he said, sounding believable. But he is a Spellman; he knows how to lie and he *was* lying.

"I might believe you if it weren't for that embarrassing question about the Monkees.[5] Fortunately, she wasn't sure whether you were referring to the band or the primate."

David paused briefly, debating whether he felt like fessing up. He did.

"I could never date a woman who had a crush on Davy Jones. I just couldn't. Everyone has their standards," David said, repeating something I had heard at least a dozen times before.

"I certainly wouldn't date a man with a crush on him," I replied.

David turned to me. He had a serious question on his mind. I wanted him to ask, so I planted an expression on my face that I've learned comes off as friendly and nonjudgmental.

"I *really* like her," David said as if it were a deep, dark secret. He wore his guilt like a Christmas sweater.

"Dude, I figured that out already," I replied.

"What do I do?" he asked.

My response suddenly seemed really important to me. I don't remember David ever asking me for advice. And when I say ever, I mean, like, never. I felt a sense of responsibility to get it right. My first reaction, oddly enough, was that it would be kind of fun to have Maggie around more often. But then I had to look at the big picture. Was there any inherent conflict in David dating Henry's ex-girlfriend? I thought about it—quickly, because David wasn't going to wait all day for me to mull it over—and came up with something that I have to believe was a sensible response.

"Nothing just yet," I replied. "You let Rae continue whatever bizarre matchmaking schemes she's got planned, and in a few weeks you can ask Maggie out."

"What about Henry?"

---

[5] David was, in fact, referring to the 1960s' original boy band. His disdain for this group is both legend and incredibly tiresome.

"Don't worry about Henry. I caught him on a date the other night."

"You don't see a problem?" David asked.

"Nope," I replied with great conviction.

The only thing that mattered in this picture was that Henry and Maggie were no longer together and from all accounts were going to stay that way.

"Let me just give you a piece of advice," I said. "If you and Maggie start going out, don't check her pockets, even if you think you're going to find candy in there."

"Huh?"

"Just remember those words," I said.

My work at David's was done. I just needed to decide whether I would risk a quick dart around the house and into my apartment or if I'd kill time elsewhere until I had a safer entry.

"Any plans tonight?" I asked.

"No, I'm just staying in reading my book about blah, blah, blah."

Sorry, I should really pay more attention when people talk, but I had the information I needed six words into the sentence.

"Sounds like a fun night," I said. "I'll see you later."

Once again I took a huge risk: I strode down David's front steps, scoped the area for nosy neighbors, and circled his residence, stealthily entering through the back door.

When I checked my e-mail later that evening, fairydust611 had kindly replied.

To: Izzy Ellmanspay [I.Ellmanspay@gmail.com]
From: Fairy Dust [fairydust611@gmail.com]
Re: Re: Re: Linda Truesdale
Message:

Hi Izzy,

I remember Sharon Meade. She was a sweet girl. Two classes behind me, I think. You should e-mail some of the alumni from 1983. They might have her contact information.

I sent a quick thank-you e-mail to fairydust611 and then hunted for the most active profile from the Benjamin Franklin alumni from 1983. Lavae Aldrich (burbmom28@gmail.com) was my most promising informant. She also had a MySpace page and a blog.[6] I sent her an e-mail and went to bed.

My phone rang in the middle of the night. It was jarring, but not as much as it would have been if I'd been asleep. My habit was to keep my phone on vibrate, but I was getting sloppy, as you've undoubtedly noticed. I dashed toward my jacket pocket, removed the phone, and inadvertently opened it instead of silencing the ringer. Remember, I was tired. The call was connected and when my eyes were able to focus on the caller ID, I saw that it was my mother. So I figured I should take the call. Besides, even on her worst day, my mom is more interesting than David's ceiling.

"Hi, Mom. Is there an emergency?"

"Not really," Mom replied, sounding more awake than one should at 3:15 A.M. "I can't sleep," she said.

I slipped into the closet, which I'd come to think of as my own personal phone booth, so that I could speak freely.

"I hate to break it to you, Mom, but few people find conversing with me soporific."

Dead silence.

"Mom?"

---

[6] I went to her MySpace page hoping for some explanation for her name, Lavae. Apparently, her father named her after an ex-girlfriend, only the ex-girlfriend's name was Ravae. Thanks, that clears things up.

"I can't believe you know that word," Mom said.

"How insulting,"[7] I replied. "I should just hang up the phone."

"I'm impressed. That's all," Mom said.

"Feeling sleepy yet?" I asked.

"No."

"Would you like me to sing to you?"

"I'd like you to listen to my confession," Mom said, and suddenly I was wide awake.

---

[7] I should admit that I learned the word while Henry was quizzing Rae for her PSATs six months ago.

MOM'S CONFESSION

At first I had no idea what my mother was talking about. She rambled, not using proper nouns, avoiding full disclosure, but eventually I got the gist.

I gathered that Rae's PSAT cheating scandal, followed by her throwing-the-test scandal, troubled my mother to an unprecedented depth. For years, my mom's desperate-mother energy had been focused on me and all my brushes with serious delinquency (and/or jail time). Rae was one of the good kids—a delightful, warm, cheery child who was aggressively self-directed and maybe a bit bullying. However, all of that in the package of a five foot two adolescent who always looked a few years younger than her age came off as adorable. Until recently, that is.

In sixteen months, my sister would be eighteen. At that point, whatever sway my mother had over her would be lost forever. My mom was suddenly flush with the realization that her daughter was out of control. While it was true that there was something to admire about Rae's uncompromising sense of what she wanted, there was also something ruthless about the way she went about making sure she got it.

As far as my mother was concerned, Rae's going to college was a non-negotiable edict. However, you can't make someone of legal age do anything, and since Rae wanted to protect her massive savings and, frankly, had no interest in a college education—I'm assuming this was based on the fact that she felt she could learn whatever she wanted for free—they were in a very uneven standoff. Rae had a gun; my mother had a water gun. And so my mother started doing what any concerned, dedicated, and crafty mother would: She began playing a single-minded game of *Gaslight*[1] on her daughter.

This was the game: In order to encourage my sister's high school work ethic, my mom had her grades doctored during her junior year to make it appear that she was not doing as well as she really was. When my sister actually took to studying and found that her efforts were in vain, she worked even harder. The reasons were twofold: 1) According to the Spellman bylaws,[2] if Rae didn't maintain a B-plus average (used to be B-minus) she would lose all non-life-sustaining sustenance, and 2) Rae has a healthy sense of her own intelligence and has always believed she wasn't an A student only because she chose not to be. When she started putting in effort and began receiving scores in the C-minus range, it made her rethink her perception of herself.

Keep in mind, the grades that Rae was receiving on her papers and tests were not the ones that would go down on her high school transcripts. At the end of the year, Rae would be clued in to the deceit and receive her actual grades, which for the first time ever just might surpass a B average, if my mom's ruse worked according to plan.

How did my mother have Rae's grades—or at least the appearance of them—doctored? Excellent question. There are two camps of instructors at Rae's school. Below you will find samplings of quotes from both camps, taken from a variety of parent-teacher conferences throughout the years:

---

[1] The 1944 film, starring Charles Boyer, Ingrid Bergman, and, most importantly, Joseph Cotten, in which a husband drives his wife mad by altering her environment.

[2] Yes, there are bylaws.

Pro-Rae

Mr. Sputter (chemistry instructor): "I appreciate that Rae has a distinct preference for lab work vs. lecture classes, but before she starts experimenting willy-nilly in class, it would be prudent if she paid attention when I mentioned which properties are combustible when mixed."

Ms. Baxter (AP English): "Her papers are entertaining, insightful, and well written, if a little on the short side. Having her in class for ninety minutes every other day is a complete delight. Yes, ninety minutes is about my limit."

Mr. Peabody (see previous document for further details): "Other than that one incident last term with her obsession with my desk drawer, I find her class comments perceptive and unique, and I think she contributes well. An unusual child, but I'm sure I don't have to tell you that. She's not working up to her potential—no news there—but she's still one of my better students."

Anti-Rae

Mrs. LaFaye (second-year French): "I don't care if she speaks in English or French—I refuse to negotiate my lesson plan with your daughter."

Mr. Blake (U.S. history): "As far as I can tell, the only part of history that interests Rae is digging up dirt on our founding fathers."

Mr. Wayne (calculus): "Every day she goes out of her way to make sure I know that I'm boring her. Constant yawning, nodding off in class. Oh, and tell her to stop counting my 'uh's. I know she's the one doing it and writing the number on the board every afternoon. I will not tolerate that kind of disrespect."

The next question you're probably asking yourself is how my mother got both camps on board with her scheme. Another excellent question.

She didn't. Mom knew after the cheating incident that the anti-Rae camp would still believe she was a cheater and be naturally biased against her, lowering her marks on any subjective exam. The pro-Rae camp, however, was all for a moderate push in the right direction and willing to play this little game with my sister.

The question my mother posed to me was this: "Am I doing any real damage to Rae? Is this inherently wrong?"

Well, what do you think I said? I had my own *Gaslight* game I was poised to play. I cleared my mother's conscience with the skill of a priest and returned to bed, finally clocking in a few hours of sleep. Rest was what I needed, since the next night I would hardly sleep at all.

STUNG

I waited three weeks for my sister to repeat her crime so that I could enact my revenge. Henry and I didn't plan the kind of sting operation that involved a "gotcha" moment when we'd jump from behind the curtains and reveal our evil identities. No. Our plan, our purpose, was more subtle than that. We wanted Rae to endure a night when Murphy's Law was illustrated with the heaviest hand nonfiction would allow.

The following evening, the alarm that indicates when my car is moving went off at 12:30 A.M. I got up, threw on a pair of jeans and a sweatshirt, and exited David's house, stuffing my laptop in a shoulder bag. I walked four blocks to Van Ness and Broadway and tried to hail a cab. I phoned Henry, waking him from a deep sleep, and said, "Subject's on the move. I'll be at your house as soon as I hail a cab."

"I'll pick you up," he said.

"No," I replied. "It'll be faster this way."

Honestly, I hadn't thought about this glitch in my plan. I should mention that San Francisco isn't like New York in terms of hailing cabs, but it can be done. Fortunately, that night taxi luck was on my side. I arrived at Henry's house and we briefly reviewed the variety of plans we could put into effect, opting for flexibility over careful orchestration. This is how the night went down:

Phase I

Fifteen minutes later, Henry drove as I directed him toward the current location of my vehicle. It was parked on Baker, near McAllister (in the vicinity of the Panhandle, near Golden Gate Park).

Henry slowed his car as we approached the area. I spotted my car blocking a driveway in front of a single-family home.

"If she's blocking the driveway, they might not be staying too long. What do you think?" I asked.

"I'll keep watch," Henry said. "Let the air out of the left back tire. They won't be able to see you from the house."

Henry turned his lights off and remained double-parked a few doors down. I exited his vehicle and crouched down as I approached my car. I unscrewed the cap on the tire and stuck a pin in to release the air. A few minutes passed, the tire deflated, and my cell phone buzzed. I looked up to find the front door of the residence open. I quickly put the cap back on the tire, ducked past a few more cars, and sprinted around the corner. I hid behind a tree until Henry picked me up a few minutes later.

Henry made a quick U-turn and raced down the block in the direction we'd come. In a few minutes, we were approximately fifty yards behind my sister's vehicle as she drove south along Divisadero.

"She's driving like there's nothing wrong," I said.

"Sometimes people don't notice flat tires," Henry replied.

"Wait. She's passing a gas station. Maybe she'll pull in."

I'm sure you're biting your nails with anticipation right now, so I'll cut to the part where Rae doesn't even notice that she's driving on a completely flat tire. Nope. She turned right on Fell Street and continued west, turning onto Lincoln and heading into the Outer Sunset. Then she somehow found a legal parking space right away. She and two other adolescent females and one adolescent male exited the vehicle, none of whom noticed the flat.

Subjects entered a nearby house from which muted sounds of music and laughter emanated.

Whatever excitement Henry and I felt at the beginning of our caper had washed away. Gloom was starting to set in already, and we were only in phase I.

"What do I do?" I asked. "If she doesn't put air in the tire, she'll ruin the wheel and I'll have to pay for a new one. That result would be in complete conflict with what we're trying to do here."

"Let me think," Henry said, and since it looked like he was thinking really hard, and since I trusted that he wanted revenge as much as I did, I remained silent.

"There's an air pump in the trunk," Henry said. "Reinflate the tire while I disconnect the battery."

"You have an air pump in your trunk?"

"Battery powered," Henry replied.

"Wow. You think ahead," I said, feeling a swell of affection.

Henry double-parked again. We jumped out of his car, raced across the street, and completed our assigned tasks. We checked the perimeter as we returned to his car to lie in wait.

Phase II

An hour later, subject exited residence alone, got in my car, and tried to start the engine. Approximately one minute later, subject popped the hood of the car and checked the engine. Subject left the car with the hood open, knocked on the door of the residence subject had previously entered, and a few minutes later returned with an unknown male and a flashlight. Both subjects studied the engine out of view of the investigators. Shortly after that, they entered the vehicle. The engine started and subject pulled the car onto the road.

"They sure figured that out fast," I said, sounding—I'm sure—defeated.

Henry refused to lose focus on the task in front of him. He was a cop, after all, and his surveillance skills were impeccable. Henry and I maintained a tail on subject, who may have foiled some of our plans but at least remained unaware of the surveillance performed on her. Subject drove to a residence in West Portal and double-parked while Unknown Male #1 exited the vehicle and knocked on the door of a nearby residence. Unknown Male #2 answered the door and both returned to the car.

Ten minutes later, all three subjects returned to the Outer Sunset residence where they were previously seen. Subject parked the car a few blocks away, and all three subjects walked together back to the party.

Henry parked in a driveway a few doors away from my car. From that location we couldn't view the party, but we agreed that the best way to monitor Rae was to keep an eye on my car.

"Now what?" I asked.

"Phase three," Henry replied.

Phase III

When I was sixteen, Petra's cousin Hugo taught me how to siphon gas out of a tank. It's not that hard, but Henry made it clear from the get-go that he would not partake in this activity.[1] He simply purchased the supplies.

"The hose and the gas can are in the trunk," he said, popping the lid. "Use the end of the hose that's marked with masking tape."

"Why?" I asked.

"Because I washed it in dish soap."

"Thanks. That was sweet."

I tried to look inconspicuous carrying a six-foot garden hose and a gas canister through this relatively quiet residential neighborhood. I had to duck in the bushes for a few minutes while some revelers seeped from the

---

[1] You'll soon learn why.

house and disappeared into the distance. Then I ran as fast as I could to my car, unlocked the door, opened the gas tank, swirled the hose in a single loop, inserted one end into the tank, and began sucking on the other end until I could hear, smell, and almost taste the gasoline bubbling through the hose. Then I lowered the hose below the level of the gas tank and inserted it into the canister.[2] I knew there wasn't much gas in the tank earlier that day. We had simply hoped that we could siphon enough to make Rae either A) run out of gas, or B) at least have to pay for some.

Ten minutes later, I returned to Henry's car with the fuel and the hose. I returned the supplies to his trunk and sat down in his vehicle, where we waited for fifteen minutes in silence.

"Are we just going to sit here in the cold?" I asked.

"It's a little pathetic, isn't it?" he replied.

"Yes."

Long pause.

"I have something to tell you," Henry said.

I felt my heart jump for a second—just once. I thought that maybe the only thing that would make this night less of a disaster was if Henry confessed his undying love or something like that. Don't get too excited. His follow-up sentence was a letdown on all fronts.

"There's a good chance," Henry said, "that the car won't run out of gas."

"I know," I replied, once I'd scanned his words and accepted there was no hidden meaning in them.

This could go down as one of the worst nights in my history as a PI. Worse than that night three years ago when my dad slept through his alarm clock and failed to relieve me from my post outside a North Bay residence. At 2:15 A.M., when the subject decided to move, I was relieving myself behind

---

[2] These aren't instructions. Don't, like, try this at home. That would really annoy me.

his shrubbery. The only worse night I can think of was when I was forced to team up with Joey Carmichael (ex-cop, acquaintance of Dad's) and he kept asking me to pull his finger all night long. My point is I had to do something to alleviate the pain.

"There's a diner around the corner," I said. "Let's wait there. I can have my phone beep when the car moves again."

Five minutes later I was eating cherry pie à la mode, minding my own business, when Henry said, "Do you have any idea how much high-fructose corn syrup is in that pie?"

"Do you want a bite?" I asked.

"Yes," Henry replied, stealing my fork.

The bright neon lights of the diner did nothing to boost our spirits. The night had been an epic disaster.

"Is she always going to win?" I asked.

For a moment Henry looked defeated, but then he wouldn't allow that emotion to take over.

"No. You can't think like that," he said, like a soccer coach in a Disney movie trying to rally the team's spirits. "We'll never win if we don't improve our attitude."

"I should remind you that so far, all of our plans have been foiled. What happens when she drives straight home and the car doesn't run out of gas? What's phase four?"

Henry thought for a moment: "The silent treatment."

It was as if Henry and I were suddenly watching ourselves on a giant movie screen. Two full-grown adults, professional sleuths, trying to take down a teenage girl by the most amateurish means.

"If you think about it really hard," I said, "this is kind of insane."

It didn't take Henry all that long to agree. "It's not my finest hour," he replied.

It could have been the massive jolt of caffeine in the early hours of the morning, or the exhaustion that had set in, or the sense of failure about this entire charade, but when we started laughing, we couldn't stop. And when I say we couldn't stop, we *really* couldn't. It was convulsive, uncomfortable laughter, tears dripping down our faces. The embarrassing, I-hope-nobody's-watching-me laughter. And people *were* watching. Especially our waitress, who dropped off the bill and suggested herbal tea might be in order. The laughing didn't stop until my phone buzzed.

Henry left $20 on the table and we raced out of the diner and hopped into his car. Within minutes we were in hot pursuit of my Buick, filled with the subject and at least four unknown subjects. One in particular had his head out the window.

"That one better not vomit in my car," I said.

"She better not be drunk herself," Henry commented, suddenly finding the situation far more serious. "Maybe I should have a squad car give her a sobriety test?"

"Yes!" I said enthusiastically. "That would be great!"

Henry phoned the precinct and made his request, providing the license plate number and the vehicle's current coordinates. Within ten minutes a squad car closed in on the Buick and signaled with its loud buzz for the car to pull over.

From a distance, I watched through binoculars as the officer gave my sister a sobriety test.

"Let me see," Henry said, taking the binoculars from my hand.

"She's sober," I replied soberly.

Don't get me wrong, I was happy my sister wasn't drinking and driving. Best as I could tell, she was using my car primarily to drive drunk people home from a party. However, it was *my* car and she never asked *my* permission!

It was late. It had been late for hours. Henry and I were tired. Maybe our minds weren't as sharp as they ought to have been, because suddenly Henry stated the obvious.

"I have another idea for phase four," he said.

"What?" I replied, not too hopeful.

"You could report a stolen vehicle."

RAE ARREST #1

Henry and I celebrated our victory by taking a three-hour nap at his place—different rooms; thanks for asking—while we waited for Rae to call me to bail her out of jail. (We assumed I would be her first choice.) Three hours later, we realized we were wrong.

My mother was the first person I saw as Henry and I entered the police station on Valencia and Seventeenth Street.

"Do you want to tell me what's going on here?" my mother asked.

"I believe," I said, "if I have the facts straight, Rae has been booked for driving a stolen vehicle."

"She borrowed your car without asking," Mom clarified.

"Where I come from that's called stealing," I replied.

"You're dropping the charges," Mom said.

"No, I'm not," I answered.

"Isabel, be reasonable," my mother said, not sounding reasonable at all.

"She can do whatever she wants and there are never any real consequences. What's the harm in making her meet a court appearance and do community service or whatever else they give her? She's turning into a monster!"

314

"She's testing her boundaries," my mother replied. "That's all. You did exactly the same."

"And I paid!"

My father now approached the nexus of the drama. "What's going on?" he said to no one in particular.

"She doesn't want to drop the charges," Mom said.

Henry finally came to my defense. "I could have had her arrested two months ago for trespassing and vandalism when she changed the locks on my door."

"Once again, Henry, we're very sorry about that," my father said in his most sincere mode.

"I *will not* have two daughters with a juvie record," Mom said.

"Come on, Isabel," Dad continued, tag-team style. "She was driving drunk kids home from a party. Her blood alcohol level was zero. It's not like she was dealing drugs."

That's when I lost it. *"I was a pothead; I was never a drug dealer!"* I shouted in the middle of the police precinct.

If you'd placed a wager against me in this battle, you probably would have doubled your money. Just when I dug my heels in and adamantly refused to negotiate, my father whispered in my ear: "Drop the charges or I'll tell David where you're living."

When Rae was released, she looked rested and chipper—not at all the way someone is supposed to appear after she's been graciously sprung from a holding cell.

"Sorry about the misunderstanding, Isabel," Rae said after she embraced both of my parents.

"It wasn't a misunderstanding, you little rat. You stole my car."

"No, I borrowed your car," Rae replied. "I just forgot to mention it to you."

"That's called stealing, or at the very least, conversion."[1]

"How about I pay for a tank of gas and we call it even?" Rae suggested.

"You can't be serious," I replied as I felt the inside of my head start to overheat.

"Rae," my dad said slowly. His tone was *Watch yourself*; she didn't.

"I know you're low on funds these days, being jobless and all. How about I give you a cut of tonight's earnings?"

"I'm going to kill you," I said as calmly as I could.

"In a police station? How bold."

In an instant, I leapt at Rae, my hands reaching for the hood of her sweatshirt. Henry reached his arm around my waist, lifted me up, and spun me around. His arm was still holding me in place as he turned to my father and shouted, "Just get Rae out of here!"

As my parents ushered my sister out of the police station, I shouted the following threats, among others (sorry, I can't remember in what order):

"You're dead!"

"You think you've won, but you haven't!"

"I really am going to hunt you down and kill you!"

"Just wait until you get your first car! It better be pretty to look at because I can guarantee it will never run!"

"You will pay! Mark my words!"

"Are you done?" Henry said to me when the family was well out of earshot and I was still screaming.

"Yes," I said, beginning to feel the emotional crash of injustice coming on.

---

[1] A legal term, basically saying that the defendant (Rae) deprived the plaintiff (me) of the use of my property. Punishable at the very least with compensatory measures.

But speaking of injustice: *Rae* stole *my* car, but *I* had to wait two hours for it to be processed and released through the impound lot.

"We still have the silent treatment," Henry said. When my car was finally released, we said our tired, defeated good-byes and agreed to reconvene later to come up with a follow-up plan.

On my way home, I ran out of gas.

GOOD-BYE, MORTY

Ruth and Morty had a three P.M. flight to Miami. All their household goods had been boxed and shipped. They had been staying at a downtown hotel for the past week. My mother invited the Schillings to brunch Sunday morning; Mom has always had limited contact with Morty, but ever since he handled my legal defense last year, in that matter I'd rather not mention yet again, she'd felt indebted to him. Like all of us, she was sorry to see him go.

I arrived at 1799 Clay Street earlier than the other guests to help my mother prepare. This involved putting food from delis and bakeries onto a serving plate, if it was not already on a serving plate. My mom tidied up and shouted for Rae to set the table. Rae raced downstairs and said, "Hi," in my general direction.

I ignored her, but she didn't seem to notice.

Rae asked me how many people were coming. I didn't answer. "Set the table for ten," my mother said.

Within minutes the entire guest list arrived: Henry, David, Gabe, Petra, and of course the guests of honor, Morty and Ruth. I cornered my mother in the kitchen and said, "Could you have arranged a more awkward brunch if you tried?"

"We're all adults here," she said as Rae was passing through my peripheral vision.

"Not all of us," I replied.

When Henry arrived, he tossed a jacket at my sister and said, "I found this in my hall closet."

Rae looked over the jacket and spotted a missing button.

"Where's my button?" Rae said, puzzled that it hadn't been replaced like all her previous missing buttons.

"It's in the pocket," Henry replied.

Rae stared down at the jacket. Henry entered the kitchen and asked my mother if she needed any assistance.

As the rest of the guests arrived, an unappetizing blend of moods took shape. Some guests were sad, some were uncomfortable, some were cranky (Dad was extremely hungry), and some (Rae) were clueless. Morty was perhaps experiencing a mix of all of the above. His coping mechanism was to consume as much food as humanly possible.

Eventually, Ruthy said, "Morty, they got food in Miami, too."

Even among such a crowd, at times I was certain that I was the most uncomfortable. Petra and my brother shared some awkward glances, but it almost seemed as if my mother had warmed to my old friend, knowing that she was now with another man. Oddly, the only outright hostility at the table was directed at Rae, and it took at least an hour for her to notice.

"Henry, pass the cookies," Rae said.

Henry did nothing of the sort.

Rae, misinterpreting his unresponsiveness, said, much, much louder, *"Henry, will you please pass the cookies?"*

My brother, hoping to avoid any blatant conflict, passed the cookies, although Rae had lost interest in them. She stared at Henry for a long while, trying to unnerve him, but it didn't work.

"Oh, I get it. You're not speaking to me again," she said.

Then she turned to me.

"You, too?" she asked, making eye contact, but I didn't respond.

Rae scanned the table. "If you're speaking to me, please raise your hand."

Everyone else in the room raised their hands.

"You should all be ashamed of yourselves," I said.

Two hours and a pound of lox later, the guests began to disperse. I walked Morty and Ruth to the door and suddenly felt the full impact of his departure. Morty would be a postcard or a phone call away, but that was it, just handwriting or a voice.

Morty sucked some item from brunch out of his teeth. That wasn't how I wanted to remember him.

"Remember, Morty, it's going to be hard to make friends in Florida if you keep doing that."

"Give me a hug, Izzele."

When I hugged my short old friend good-bye he whispered in my ear, "Be good." But then he went on to say that if I wasn't good and happened to get myself arrested again, he'd be happy to fly back and take care of things.

"You're not suggesting I break the law, now, are you, Morty?"

"Bah," was his last word to me.

I felt a wave of sadness take over as he left. Morty had some good years left in him; I knew that. I also knew that I probably wouldn't ever see him again. I held on to my tears as I waved my final good-bye. As I watched Morty shuffle to his car, I noticed that his shuffle had gotten slower in the past few weeks. Just getting into his car was an ordeal. I watched and kept a smile on my face. I waved good-bye until the car disappeared in the distance. Then I lost it.

When I turned back into the house, tears dripped down my face.

"Why are you crying?" Rae asked in a casually insensitive tone. I would have snapped at her, but I had no energy left. On the other hand, Henry did.

"Go to your room," Henry said, practically seething.

What was odd was that Rae didn't challenge him or turn to my mom or dad to challenge Henry's authority. She merely followed his instructions.

GOOD-BYE, MILO

That night I showed up at the Philosopher's Club for Milo's good-bye party. The bar was packed beyond the fire limit. It was hard to move or breathe or even find Milo, and yet, in that mass of people, Bernie found me. Yes, Bernie. Don't worry; he's not back for good. He happened to be in town to deal with his apartment, which Milo was now vacating.

I was locked in a brutal bear hug before the voice bellowing my name completely registered.

"Izzzeeee!" Bernie shouted right into my ear as he held on tight.

When you're talking into someone's ear, you actually don't need to shout, no matter how loud it is in the room. I twisted my head away from Bernie and tried to claw my way out of the embrace.

"Hey, Bernie," I said.

"How you been?" he shouted. "Tell me everything."

"I'd rather not," I replied.

The thing about Bernie is that you can be rude, abrupt, and directly hostile and he remains friendly. Tonight I needed that.

"You want to move back into Casa Bernie?"

It sounded dirty when he said it.

"Maybe," I said. "It depends."

"On what?"

"Are *you* planning on moving back to Casa Bernie?"

"No, no. I might visit every once in a while. But things with Daisy are good."

"Let me think on it," I said.

"Think fast," Bernie replied.

I swam through the crowd, searching for Milo. But it was Connor who found me.

"Isabel, I got another letter for ya," he said.

"Oh yeah?" I replied unenthusiastically.

"It's in the office. Come with me."

Connor took my arm and parted the crowd, guiding me into Milo's office, which I guess now was technically Connor's office. He shut the door behind us, which quieted the unnerving din that was starting to scrape my nerves. He passed me an envelope from the desk, which I opened, hoping nothing too culturally challenging was in my future. As usual, I was wrong.

ThIs ISn't OVEr
SeE a PLaY @ acT
OR UR SeCREt wIlL
B rEvEALed

I stared down at the note longer than necessary. Connor watched me carefully.

"Bad news?" he asked.

"I don't know," I replied. "I'm currently unclear on what good news is."

"Don't be sad, Isabel."

I turned to leave, but then I felt an arm around my waist turning me back around. Before I found the word for what was happening, Connor's lips were on mine and his arms were holding me tight. It took me too long to break away. It was a nice kiss. Soft and warm. It was the kind of kiss that made you forget things, like where you were and that there were other people you'd prefer kissing. Once I figured out where my arms were located, I placed them on Connor's shoulders and gently pushed him away.

"I have to go," I said, and quickly left the office.

I scanned the room for Milo and caught him by the pool table. Once again, I fought my way through the crowd.

"I was wondering if you were gonna show," Milo said.

Milo and I hugged for a good minute. We both knew it would be a while before I saw him again. There wasn't much to say, so we didn't say much. I knew I'd see Milo again someday, so I refused to let sadness take over. This was "See you around," not "Good-bye."

"I'll miss you," I said.

"Try to be good," Milo said.

Then I skipped out through the emergency exit and made my way "home."

HELLO, BED

When I returned home, I checked my e-mail and finally had a message from burbmom28. She vaguely remembered Sharon, but like fairy-dust611, she had no recollection of a Linda Truesdale. I sent her a picture of Sharon to see if it would jog her memory. I cropped a surveillance photo to make it look like a snapshot. Burbmom28, AKA Lavae, responded later that night.

To: Izzy Ellmanspay
From: burbmom28
Re: Sharon Meade
Message:
Wow. She has had some work done. Thanks for sharing. I think I'm going to cancel my Botox appointment for next week.
Cheers,
Lavae

I sat up for a few more hours, trying to figure out the next step, only I couldn't really think of one. I had two women, complete opposites, some-how connected, although not connected in the way they claimed to be. I also had a morally bankrupt detective and a deep-pocketed political consultant all trying to get to the bottom of the matter. And, to refresh your memory, I had only five days left before I was supposed to make a decision about my entire future.

Somehow I got it into my head that if I couldn't solve this case before Harkey did, I shouldn't be solving any cases. In the past, I'd stumbled upon the answers, often misreading the evidence, getting to the truth only by sheer doggedness. I wanted to solve this case without my usual bullying tactics. The answer was in front of me, only I couldn't see it.

When the last bit of energy drained from my body, I went to bed. And I stayed there for the next three days. During that stretch of time, I watched bad TV at the lowest volume and ignored the rolling waves of voice mail messages that piled up on my cell phone.

Just to be clear, it wasn't only my unsolved case that drew me into this funk, or my impending decision, or my sister's minor victory, or my departing friends, or even the kiss from a near-stranger that I enjoyed just a little too much. No, something else was at work that I couldn't quite put my finger on. It was vaguely like I had a sudden glimpse, a snapshot, of who I had become—a single, unemployed squatter in court-ordered therapy. No little girl dreams of growing up into that.

I alternated between real sleep and half sleep, but both were more than welcome. Semiconsciousness is underrated. After three days I was mostly out of food and my head throbbed from lack of caffeine, but still I didn't budge. I'm not sure how long I would have lasted on my own, but my escape came to an abrupt and jarring end.

While I was watching a travel program in the late hours of a morning— no, I didn't know what day or exactly what time it was—there was a knock on my door. Okay, if you are not fully comprehending the shock value of this loud knocking, let me remind you of this fact: This was the first knock at the door. *Ever.* Instantly, my heart started thumping. I felt my face flush, my hands go clammy, and my legs get weak. Shit. The jig was up. I took several deep breaths and waited. Maybe I'd imagined the knock. Maybe someone wasn't knocking on my door but knocking on some other part of the house . . .

Then there was the knocking again. I was closer to the door this time, so I can say with 100 percent certainty that the knock was for me.

What was I supposed to do? I had only two options: 1) Ignore the knock and let unknown events unfold as they might, or 2) answer the door. Frankly, I had been living in a state of uncertainty for so long, I don't think I could have taken much more. I answered the damn door.

David stood there in his bathrobe, holding a cup of coffee.

"Hi," I said, because, really, what else can you say under this precise set of circumstances?

"Hi," David casually replied. "Do you want some coffee?"

Dumbfounded, I took the offering. I took a sip of the coffee to kill some time and think of something, anything, to say.

"How long have you known?" I asked.

"I've known all along," David replied.

Long, long pause.

"So, are you my blackmailer?"

Twenty minutes later, David and I were sitting in his kitchen drinking coffee and eating breakfast while I grilled him about the details of my secret sublet. It wasn't entirely true that David had known all along. It took him approximately three days to notice my presence below him. Here were his clues: The sound of footsteps in the middle of the night, the occasional drop in water pressure when he took a shower, and the time his neighbor Tom asked him how his new tenant was working out. Also, my soundproof closet phone booth apparently tunnels conversations directly into his kitchen pantry.

It had been over a month since David's return. I had to ask the obvious question:

"Why didn't you kick me out?"

David shrugged his shoulders. "It seemed like you were going through a rough time—no job, the therapy, who knows what else? I figured you were broke or would be soon, and your only other option was to move back in with Mom and Dad. That didn't seem like a good idea."

His response was so out of character it was jarring; it took me some time to form words.

"I'm sorry, I'll get out of here soon. I promise," I said.

"Don't worry about it," David replied.

"You're being suspiciously nice," I said.

"I'm your brother. I'm going to be nice on random occasions."

"Thanks. But I'm trying to understand why this time you were so nice."

"Honestly, because you were so, so . . . pathetic."

"True," I replied.

"You need to take a shower," David said.

It had been three days. I couldn't argue with him.

"Right," I replied.

And then I noticed that while David appeared clean and well—his health and arm repaired from his wilderness adventure mishap—he was still home in his bathrobe at 11:55 A.M. on a weekday.

"What day is it?" I asked.

"Wednesday," David replied.

"You're still not at work," I said, begging for an explanation.

"A natural detective, you are," David replied. I think he was debating whether to speak the truth or concoct an untruth. I think we were all coming to the conclusion that the truth was actually easier to live with.

"I quit my job," he said.[1]

"No!" I replied.

"Yes."

"Why?" I asked.

"Because I didn't care about it. If I'm going to work seventy hours a week, it should matter, right?"

---

[1] David informed his clients of this fact, but to keep the news quiet from his family, David had the main receptionist tell callers that he was out.

"Right," I replied. "Do Mom and Dad know?"

"Not yet. So keep your mouth shut."

"Sure thing," I said. "It's the least I can do."

"More coffee?" David asked. He didn't wait for a response; he just poured me another cup.

"So, are you or are you not my blackmailer?" I asked.

THERAPY SESSION #20

[Partial transcript reads as follows:]

ISABEL: Sorry I missed my session Monday.

DR. RUSH: Would you like to tell me why?

ISABEL: I was depressed.

DR. RUSH: That's a good reason to come to therapy.

ISABEL: I couldn't get out of bed.

DR. RUSH: Are you better now?

ISABEL: I'm out of bed.

DR. RUSH: What sent you to bed in the first place?

ISABEL: Friends were leaving. People are changing, but I'm sort of staying the same.

DR. RUSH: Are you sure about that?

ISABEL: I don't know. The great thing about staying in bed is that nothing happens then. You know?

DR. RUSH: Things still happen.

ISABEL: But I can pretend they don't.

DR. RUSH: Pretending will only get you so far.

[Long pause.]

ISABEL: My father left five voice mail messages on my cell phone when I was

330

sleeping or half asleep. The first time he asked me to lunch, I assumed it was so he could remind me that time was running out on my big decision. But when he called me again, he said we didn't have to talk about my big decision. But he still asked me to lunch. What is it with him and lunch?

DR. RUSH: What do you think it is?

ISABEL: Maybe he's really hungry.

DR. RUSH: [impatiently] You must have a theory beyond that.

ISABEL: Not really.

DR. RUSH: [sigh] Isabel.

ISABEL: Look, I know. People think I don't see things beyond the surface, but I do. I see it. My dad is getting older; he doesn't want any regrets. I know he loves me and I know he cares about what happens to me. I don't exactly dislike spending time with my father, but he always wants to know how I'm doing deep down. Sometimes I don't want to think about that.

DR. RUSH: What happens when you do?

ISABEL: For instance, my job. When I think about doing it for the rest of my life, it makes me think not just about the job and how I feel about that, but the rest of my life. And then I think, *Is this it?* And when I ask myself that, I'm not even sure I'm thinking about the job.

DR. RUSH: What are you thinking about?

ISABEL: Life and death and that sort of thing.

DR. RUSH: That covers a lot of ground.

ISABEL: I know.

DR. RUSH: Maybe you need to break it down.

ISABEL: I have. This week I'm only thinking about my big decision.

DR. RUSH: Have you come to one?

ISABEL: I just need to figure out this case I'm working on. If I can solve the case, I'll know what to do.

DR. RUSH: Why is this case so important?

ISABEL: Most of the job is pretty basic. I sit behind a computer and research someone's past, someone's criminal record, or I follow a person around and try to catch him or her doing something they're not supposed to be doing. But every once in a while a case comes along that demands more, and I need to be sure that I can handle it the right way. Sometimes the answer isn't everything.

DR. RUSH: Where are you on this case?

ISABEL: Nowhere. I'm certain there's something to figure out, but I don't know what.

[Long pause.]

DR. RUSH: Is there anything else you'd like to discuss?

ISABEL: My secret has been exposed.

DR. RUSH: Oh, good.

ISABEL: It's a load off my mind.

DR. RUSH: You're referring to the secret about where you were living, right?

ISABEL: Right.

DR. RUSH: So?

ISABEL: I guess I can tell you now. I was living in my brother's secret basement apartment.

DR. RUSH: Why would that be a secret?

ISABEL: Two reasons: A) At first, I didn't know this apartment existed, and B) because he didn't know I was living in it.

DR. RUSH: You were living in your brother's apartment without his permission?

ISABEL: Yes. And he wasn't as angry as I thought he'd be. He was pretty decent about the whole thing. I apologized, in case you were wondering.

DR. RUSH: It sounds like an apology was in order.

ISABEL: It was.

DR. RUSH: I hope you've stopped investigating him.

ISABEL: I have. But mostly because I ran out of steam. It turns out David just sort of changed. There was no big turning point behind it, besides his divorce, which I already knew about.

DR. RUSH: Why do you seem so surprised? People change all the time. You've probably changed more than you think.

ISABEL: I don't know about that.

[Short pause.]

DR. RUSH: Something else on your mind?

ISABEL: David wasn't my blackmailer.

DR. RUSH: Could it have been someone else in your family?

ISABEL: I questioned everyone and each one denied it, even after my secret was revealed. The Spellmans, like any fringe political organization, like to take credit for their crimes. There would be no benefit in denial. Besides, the terms of the blackmail never seemed to fit anyone's MO.

DR. RUSH: Could it be someone outside your family?

ISABEL: Morty was too busy and I don't believe he has the hand dexterity to cut and paste—

[Long pause.]

DR. RUSH: Isabel?

ISABEL: I know who it is.

TWO CAR CHASES AND A BUDDHIST TEMPLE

O n my way home from therapy, I was followed once again. Since my only scheduled activity was my weekly session with Dr. Rush, I had to assume that my pursuers had learned this fact and used it to track me down. Otherwise, if you think about it, I'm a pretty difficult person to find.

The vehicle shadowing me was a green Ford Taurus, driven undoubtedly by one of Harkey's men. He was good. I tried to lose him, but I couldn't without breaking some major traffic laws or getting into an accident. Allow me to cut to the end of the chase. Twenty minutes after the pursuit began, I parked in Lower Haight and entered Petra's hair salon.

"I need a wig, new clothes, and your car keys," I said to Petra as I entered.

Petra, without asking for details, tossed the keys to me from her pocket and said, "I'm parked around the corner on Steiner. You know where to find the rest."

I entered the back room of the salon, the smell of shampoo and chemicals burning my nostrils, and searched through the lost-and-found items and Petra's personal collection of wigs.[1] I chose an auburn

---

[1] For years I'd encouraged Petra to lose the wig collection—I think it sends a bad message to customers. I've quieted on this matter since discovering I can make some use of the collection.

shag cut and a faux fur coat with black sunglasses. When I entered the front room, Petra looked at me and said, "I think we found your next look."

I offered her my car keys in exchange and told her she could reach me on my cell.

I exited the storefront and walked down the street. My challenge was to ascertain whether I was being followed without appearing in any way suspicious. Regular people don't walk down the street looking over their shoulder.[2]

As I approached Petra's car, I looked into her driver's side mirror to see if the Taurus was anywhere in the vicinity. Nothing. After I drove away, I knew I was free. My escape was just the thing I needed to lift my spirits.

Two minutes later

My mother phoned.

"I need you to pick up Rae from a Buddhist temple in Marin."

I wasn't really sure where to begin, so I started with an easy question.

"Why can't you get her?"

"Dad and I are on surveillance right now," Mom said.

I moved on to a slightly more difficult question: "Why can't she return the same way she got there?"

"Because she doesn't want to come home," Mom replied. "She only called me so I wouldn't worry."

And then the hard question: "What's she doing at a Buddhist temple?"

Mom's reply: "Don't ask."

My mother text-messaged the address to my phone and I took Petra's car across the Golden Gate Bridge.

---

[2] Spellmans do, of course. After my first surveillance, at age twelve, I generally assumed it was possible I was being followed.

Thirty-five minutes later

I entered the Buddhist Temple of Marin, interrupting a beginning meditation class my sister was attending. The instructor, a warm and peaceful gentleman in robes, invited me to join the group. In a perfect world I would have said in a loud, abrasive tone, "Get your stuff, Rae; we're out of here," but I could tell by the way Rae was pretending to meditate yet peeking out of one eye at me and my wig, that she would have refused to move. I didn't want to disrupt whatever level of calm the other attendees had reached, so I sat down next to my sister, shoving her over just a bit, and followed the monk's instructions.

I breathed and stuff for the next twenty minutes, which I have to admit took the edge off my anger at Rae. When the class was over, I said to her, "You know, they've got places just like this in the city."

"Oh, so now you're talking to me again?" Rae said.

"No, I'm not," I replied.

"What's with the getup?" she asked.

We walked to the car in silence.

To be obnoxious, Rae then twisted her legs into a pretzel on the car seat, rested her hands on her knees, and began chanting, "Ommmmm . . . ommmmm . . . ommmmm," until interrupted.

"Meditate on your own time!" I said.

I delivered Rae to an empty Spellman house. She climbed the stairs to her bedroom, saying she was going to center herself.[3] I then phoned Petra to arrange our car swap.

We met at Crissy Field, in part because it was a nice-enough day and Petra wanted to see the water, but also because there are ample

---

[3] Of all the activities she could pursue on a whim, this had to be among the least perilous for everyone concerned.

parking spaces there. Without any fear of being followed, Petra and I strolled along the beach and caught each other up on our current events.

"I still don't understand why Rae was at a Buddhist temple," Petra said.

"She thinks her schoolwork is suffering because she's under stress. Hence the meditation class. At least I think that's why she was there, based on the conversation I overheard between her and the monk. I'm not speaking to her, so my information isn't firsthand. I'm tired of talking about Rae. Your turn," I said.

I'll spare you the sappy details, even though I was not spared. Petra and Gabe think they're in love. She's taken up skateboarding and he's taken up leave-in conditioner. It's been only three weeks since he got his first haircut. I think you need at least six weeks, or two haircuts, to know for sure. I'd like to say that my ease with Petra had reverted to that of our old partners-in-crime days, but it hadn't. We had grown up (sort of) and grown apart. I was never sure how to relate to her after the divorce. She was my best friend, but she cheated on my brother and it changed him. I had spent years being jealous of David's perfection, but I was always comfortable with my role, envying and resenting him. To see my brother sad and confused, well, I didn't know how to behave when faced with that. Petra changed everything and I found that our relationship became too sticky to dust off. If we were young and had a mutual enemy's car to vandalize, I'm sure we could have erased the tension. But today I wasn't sure when—or if—it would completely vanish.

Petra and I returned to our cars and swapped keys in midair. We said a vague "I'll see you around" good-bye. I told her to invite me to the wedding. I got in my car, took Bay Street up to Van Ness, made a right turn, and then noticed that I was being followed yet again. This was my own fault. I assumed that when my pursuers saw Petra get into my car, they would stop the tail. I guess they weren't as stupid as I thought, and apparently I must have been more important than I thought.

Car Chase #I-don't-know-anymore[4]

I'd love to tell you that I took Harkey's goon in the green Taurus on a *Bullitt*-style pursuit through the streets of San Francisco, culminating in a top-speed chase down Lombard Street, but I didn't. First of all, car chases are dangerous; second, there's usually a line backed up for Lombard; and third, I had another idea that I figured would save me some time.

I drove to my parents' house, parked in the driveway, and watched television until my mom and dad came home.

When the Unit came through the door, my dad looked at me and said, "We have company," nodding his head in the direction of the street.

"I know," I replied. "Mom, could you distract him for a minute while I skip out through the back?"

While my mom offered Harkey's surveillance guy a cup of coffee and chatted with him about the weather, I exited through a side window and cut across a neighbor's backyard to the next street over. I then took a leisurely stroll back to David's house.

---

[4] Sorry, I've actually lost my long-term count. But it's only the second one of the day, if that clears anything up for you.

ARE YOU MY BLACKMAILER?

C onnor had left a message on my cell phone while I was waiting for my parents to return home. He said there was another letter for me at the bar. I would have preferred avoiding the barman altogether, but I wanted the letter, just so I had one final piece of ammunition against my blackmailer.

I took a bus and train to the Philosopher's Club, because—if you recall—my car was still located at my parents' house. When I arrived, the bar had a modest crowd, a population unseen at this hour, on this day of the week, during Milo's long tenure.

Connor was tending bar by his lonesome. I wasn't sure what to expect after the incident, but Connor simply handed me an envelope, same as before. I avoided eye contact; he didn't.

"Ya can't blame a man fur tryin," he said pleasantly.

I smiled and said, "No, you can't."

I left the bar and hailed a cab to find my true blackmailer.

On the cab ride I opened the envelope and read my final note:

tHe SYmphOny IS NeXt
U mIGHt WaNT 2
Buy UR ticKets NOW

My blackmailer opened the door. I crumpled the ransom note and threw it at his chest.

"Isabel, to what do I owe the pleasure?"

"You can drop the act," I said. "I know it's you."

I pushed my way past Henry and checked the apartment to make sure we were alone.

"What are you talking about?" he asked with a perfectly innocent delivery.

"*You* are my blackmailer," I said, looking Henry in the eye.

It was my hope that he wouldn't deny it, since I had no hard evidence.

Henry smiled, full of himself. "You got me."

"Why did you make me wash my dad's car?" I asked.

"It was dirty and I wanted to throw you off the scent."

"Bravo."

"Thanks."

"But why?"

"You were living in your brother's house without his knowledge!" Henry shouted.

"What's it to you?"

"Someone had to stop you."

"But you didn't stop me. You made me go to the zoo and the museum."

"The zoo was your crazy idea. Who thinks that the zoo and SFMOMA are interchangeable?!"

"I asked my mom and she said it was fine!"

"Of course she did."

"Why make me go to the museum or the theater or whatever?"

"I thought you could use some culture."

"You are such a snob!" I said, looking for something to throw.

I couldn't find anything that wouldn't cause personal injury, so I kicked some magazines off of his coffee table.

"Really mature."

"That was just an accident," I replied. I walked into his office and emptied the trash on the floor. "But that was not."

"This is ridiculous," Henry said. While he was restoring the garbage to its place, I returned to the living room and began realphabetizing the books on his shelf.[1]

I managed to relocate at least ten books before Henry intervened. He grabbed *War and Peace* out of my hands and stuck it back on the shelf.

"You wouldn't like that one. It's really long."

"Ouch. That hurt," I replied, backing Henry into a corner.

"Now what are you going to do?" Henry asked. "Rearrange my furniture?"

I kissed him. That's what I did. He didn't have anywhere to go and I was pretty close to him. He's taller than me so I had to stand on my toes. I thought for sure I felt an arm slide around my back and I know at first I felt the kiss returned, but then he stopped and pulled away. He looked confused and sad, sort of, and he didn't make eye contact. I didn't utter a word because it looked like Henry had something to say.

"No," he whispered.

I took a few steps back.

"What?" I asked.

"No," he said more clearly.

"Okay," I replied.

"It's not that I don't feel anything—"

"Don't worry about it," I said, backing away some more.

"I can't wait for you," Henry said.

I was almost at the door, but then I had to ask.

"You can't wait for what?"

He sighed and cleared his throat and fought his own brand of discomfort.

"I'm forty-five years old, Isabel. I can't wait for you to grow up."

---

[1] Translation: randomly swapping them around.

What is there to say to that? I had nothing. Nothing. I turned around and walked out the door.

I spent the entire evening on David's couch, watching TV and eating an assortment of candy from god knows where. My brother didn't ask me about my troubles; he just sat there, keeping me company. He even let me drink the good stuff.

CASE #001

CHAPTER 12

It might seem like the case of Ernie's maybe-suspicious wife was far from my thoughts, but the truth was, I believed the case was the answer to everything. If I could figure out Linda Truesdale's secret, then maybe all sorts of other things would become clear. My last investigation—the Case of John Brown[1]—had me convinced that my instincts were off and maybe I was in the wrong line of work. I had to solve the Truesdale case or I had to quit. You might find my logic arbitrary, but it seems to me that someone should have at least a minor talent for his or her career choice. Setting out a shingle for the Lousy Detective Agency wasn't an option. I could never be like Harkey.

Never.

Ernie phoned me the next morning as I was sleeping off the whiskey I drank in my brother's living room the previous evening. Ernie said that his wife was meeting Sharon for lunch again. He wasn't sure where, so I'd have to start the tail from their place. She would be departing in less than

---

[1] See previous document, *Curse of the Spellmans*—now available in paperback!

forty-five minutes. Depending on traffic, I needed at least a half hour to get there, since my car was parked at my parents' house.

I dressed in my clothes from the night before and knocked on David's door. No answer. I took his spare key and entered his house. I shouted his name; I called his cell phone. Nothing. I saw his car key by the front door. I took it and I took his car.

There was an accident on the freeway. I made it to the Black residence just as Linda was pulling out of the driveway. I followed her back onto 101 North and continued the tail as she took 280 and exited at Nineteenth Avenue. Linda stayed on Nineteenth for over five miles. At first I thought she would head across the Golden Gate Bridge, but instead she made a right turn on Clement Street and began searching for a parking space. After parking, she entered, surprisingly, a casual dining establishment called Good Luck Dim Sum.

I was hungry and, for once, dressed appropriately for their restaurant of choice. Since Sharon and Linda had never laid eyes on me, I saw no harm in keeping a short leash on this surveillance and grabbing a bite. I waited five minutes and entered the restaurant.

I saw the women in the window by the street. I asked for a table along the wall. It would provide a clear view of both subjects as they dined.

I ordered hot and sour soup, a pot of tea, and some pot stickers. The women ordered off the cart, although body language indicated that Linda was in her element and was making all the ordering decisions. I could overhear snippets of conversation, Linda offering descriptions of the delicacies. I hadn't observed the women up close for this long. The observation that struck me most was how uncomfortable they seemed with one another. Before, I had witnessed Linda's discomfort in her friend's austere, pricey environments. But this time Sharon, dressed in a hugely inappropriate Chanel suit, looked positively silly trying to eat with chopsticks. And unlike my dad, she wouldn't use a fork and knife.

What broke the awkward lunch was even more awkward: Sharon took a small gift box out of her enormous handbag and handed it to Linda. The redhead opened the box and smiled appreciatively. I think it was jewelry, but Linda didn't display the gift. She put the box in her own more modest handbag and poured herself another cup of jasmine tea. A sadness—at least that's how I translated it from twenty feet away—appeared to wash over Linda's face, but then a moment later it seemed to disappear.

I assumed after lunch that the women would be returning to their respective homes, so I lingered and made sure that I got the caffeine equivalent of four strong cups of coffee from the less efficiently caffeinated tea. I finished my soup and departed about twenty minutes after the subjects did.

When I pulled out of my parking space, I realized I was being tailed yet again.

This time I tried to evade my pursuer, who was driving a black Ford Explorer. I should remind you that I was in my brother's shiny new Prius—an excellent vehicle, but not exactly a muscle car. I turned south down Nineteenth Avenue, thinking the freeway might be my only option of escape. When I merged onto 280 South, I immediately cut across three lanes and continued along by the center divider. I switched lanes only to pass other vehicles. I was speeding, but safely. The Ford was a few cars back and one lane to my left. I cut across three lanes to my right, consecutively, and exited the freeway. When I checked my rearview mirror, I had lost the Ford Explorer. On the other hand, I had gained a squad car.

"License and registration, please," the officer said. I didn't catch his name, because I was trying to find the paperwork in David's glove compartment.

I showed the officer my license and the paperwork from David's recent purchase. There were no license plates on the car, but I didn't see a problem.

"You're not David," the officer said.

"No, I'm his sister, Isabel. See, we have the same last name."

"Please remove your sunglasses," the officer asked.

I complied.

"I'll be right back," he said. "Wait here."

I waited about five minutes and the officer returned.

"Ma'am, please step out of the vehicle."

"Is there a problem, officer?"

"Ma'am, step out of the vehicle."

I exited David's car and the officer put my hands behind my back and cuffed them.

"Ma'am, I'm going to have to take you down to the station."

"Why?" I asked.

"Because this car has been reported as stolen."

Arrest Number . . . Whatever

If you've read the previous document, you may be thinking that my parents might let me stew in a holding cell all afternoon, but that was not the case. My father arrived with Rae just an hour or so after I was booked. Dad explained the situation and had the arresting officer speak to David on the phone. I was immediately released. I suspect my sister came purely for the entertainment value.

When my personal effects were returned and I met my father and sister in the waiting room, Rae said, "Talk about irony."

"I swear, I'm going to kill you," I repeated once again within the walls of a police station.

"If I am ever murdered," Rae snapped, "you should leave the country right away, because you will be suspect number one."

My dad then told us both to shut up.

Because the car was registered under David's name, he had to pick it up from the impound lot. When he arrived at the police station, I unloaded some hearty apologies.

David shook his head in bafflement. "All you had to do was write a note."

CASE CLOSED

ater that night, I solved the case. Well, most of it. As I looked through my file on Linda and Sharon, I noticed that November fifteenth was Sharon's birthday. The day of my arrest was November sixteenth. Why would Sharon give a gift to her friend one day after her own birthday and yet the friend came to the lunch empty-handed? They were also eating at an establishment that clearly catered more to Linda's whims. I checked Linda's birthday, just to be sure it wasn't closing in. She was born on May eighteenth. I had a hunch; maybe it's the same hunch you have.

I e-mailed burbmom28 once again and attached two JPEG pictures. I asked burbmom28 which picture most resembled the Sharon who attended Benjamin Franklin High. Two and a half very long hours later, I received my reply. Burbmom28 identified the photo of Linda as that of Sharon Meade.

Some other investigator might have tipped off Ernie at this point, but I just had one fact down; there was no meaning behind it. I had to understand what I'd learned before I revealed anything to my client.

The next morning, I jogged[1] over to my parents' house and checked under my car for one of Harkey's tracking devices. I found it and showed it to my dad.

---

[1] Not something I make a habit of.

"I have to go," I said. "What should I do with this?"

Dad smiled wickedly and took it from me. "I'll figure something out," he said.

I headed out on Van Ness, merged onto 101 South, checked my rearview mirror, and knew that for the time being no one was following me.

Thirty-five minutes later

I parked outside Ernie's muffler shop. I could see Linda answering phones through the window. I waited three hours until she exited the building and walked three blocks to a coffee shop. I followed her inside.

As Linda was about to pay for her coffee, I approached the cash register.

"Linda, is that you?! I can't believe it," I said.

Naturally, Linda looked baffled. I insisted on paying for her coffee and ushered her over to a table. (Yes, I'm that persuasive.)

"You don't remember me, do you?" I said.

Linda smiled a friendly smile and admitted that she didn't.

"I've had some work done," I whispered. "Sit down. I'll tell you all about it."

Most people can't resist dirt, even if it's on someone they suspect to be a stranger. Linda sat down. I dropped my act and pulled out a picture of Sharon.

"I need to ask you about this woman. Please don't get up and leave. I just want some answers."

Linda grew pale. Her eyes searched the room for assistance or an explanation or something I couldn't define at the moment.

"You don't need to be afraid of me," I said. "But there are some people out there that you do need to worry about."

Linda continued to stare at me without uttering a single word.

"Would it help if I told you what I know?"

She nodded her head.

And so I told her. I had to rat out Ernie, but I defended him as best I could. I told her that I knew she and Ernie weren't legally married; I knew that Sharon Bancroft had given her lavish gifts and some money over the years; I told her that I knew she was being followed; I told her how I was offered a bribe to keep silent when I knew nothing at all. And then I told her that I knew that she was the real Sharon Meade and I told her how I figured it out. I also told her that I knew that Sharon was born as Linda Truesdale. But that's when things got confusing and I told her the last thing I knew for sure.

"When I figured out that you were Sharon, I couldn't make sense of it at first. Why would you take on the identity of someone with a criminal record, someone with a past she would want to forget? What didn't make sense was why you would make such a big sacrifice, losing your own identity, for a friend. And then it seemed obvious. She's not your friend, is she?"

"No," the current Linda replied.

"She's your sister," I said.

Linda nodded her head. She almost seemed relieved to have someone figure it out. "How could you know that?"

"Because it's the kind of sacrifice you can only make for family," I said. "What happened?"

This is the real story: The current Sharon was born Linda Truesdale, three years before her sister, Sharon—now Linda, the woman sitting with me in the café. Their mother was a drug addict. When the older sister was seven and the younger sister was four, they were placed in the foster care system.

Within a few months, an older couple named Meade adopted the younger sister and raised her. They were kind, attentive, and made sure that she had a proper education. The older sibling, on the other hand, drifted from one foster family to the next until she landed in an orphanage. She got into some trouble with the law in her teenage years, and when she was in her early twenties, she was convicted for check fraud and spent four months in a minimum-security prison. With a record, she found it almost impossible to get a job once she was released. The sisters stayed in touch, but their relationship at the time was strained. Their lives had become so different. And the older sibling found herself harboring some resentment.

After two years of college, the adoptive parents of Sharon Meade (now Linda Black, Ernie's wife, remember) died in a car accident. She was left their modest savings, and after handling their affairs, she decided to go to Europe for a year.

In her absence, the older sister applied for a catering job—a job she really wanted but had a feeling she wouldn't get because of her record. On a whim, she filled out her application as Sharon Meade, using all of her sister's personal information. Her sister had a clean record. Linda Truesdale, under the assumed name Sharon Meade, got the job.

A few months later, "Sharon" met Charles Bancroft at a party she was catering in Detroit. He was going to law school in California at the time, but they began a long-distance relationship. The older sister waited for a time to tell Charles, but she never did. When the younger sister returned from Europe and the older sister knew her sibling would be looking for employment, that's when she told her the truth.

"That's quite a sacrifice to make," I said. "My sister would *never* do that for me."

Linda Black refused to portray herself as a generous soul. She explained that for years she didn't speak to her sister when she realized how complicated her life had become in sustaining this deceit. But she also felt guilty about how differently their lives played out, and eventually she found some peace in being Linda Truesdale. Now, it seemed, most of the guilt rested on Sharon's shoulders—hence the lavish gifts. Linda's only regret was that she and Ernie were not legally married. She never filed the license because it would be a forged document.

I had hours' worth of questions, but I ultimately had learned what was necessary for my client's case. Besides, Linda had a few questions of her own.

"So, Ernie hired you? Why?"

"He thought there might be another man. He was afraid of losing you."

Linda then laughed. It wasn't a mean laugh of mockery but more along the lines of *How could he be so foolish?*

"This explains a few things," she said. "I thought *he* was having an affair when he started doing housework all of a sudden."

"You should tell him. Tell Ernie everything. He can handle it," I said, and I believed she would.

"The question is, are you going to tell anyone?" she asked.

"No," I replied. "That's not part of the job. It's unlikely you'll see me again. I don't want any trouble."

"Neither do I," Linda said.

That was the last time I saw her.

I could have told Linda about the mess of investigations surrounding her and Sharon's relationship, but I decided against it, hoping that I could put the problem to rest and maybe they would never know. If you think about it, all the interested parties would want to keep silent. The only loose cannon was Harkey. There was no telling what he would do if he discovered the truth.

On the way home from my impromptu meeting with Linda, I was followed yet again. It was time to nip the problem at its source. I called information and got the address of Frank Waverly's[2] office. I arrived forty-five minutes later and was greeted with a cold reception by his secretary. I sat down in his vast, unwelcoming waiting room and let his secretary know that I would sit there until Mr. Waverly was willing to speak to me. Twenty minutes later, I was guided into his slick, chrome-filled office.

---

[2] Remember, the political consultant who tried to bribe me?

"What can I do for you, Ms. Spellman?" Waverly said as he sat down behind his massive, yet mostly bare, desk.

"It's what I can do for you," I replied, staying on my feet. I did this because my visit would be brief, but also because I knew it would unnerve him.

"Have a seat," he said.

"No, thanks. Listen, call off your goons. I'm tired of being followed."

"I don't know what you're talking about."

"One more lie and I walk out of here. I'm not a problem now, but I have the ammunition to become one."

Waverly said nothing.

"Good. I like you better quiet. The truth is, no one who can hurt Congressman Bancroft has any desire to talk. Tell your client to go home and ask his wife the questions he needs answered. You, fire Rick Harkey now. Pay his bill in full, and make sure you never do business with him again. In your effort to smoke out a secret, you've hired someone who has broken the law on your behalf. You want to get as far away from him as you can."

"What do you want?" Waverly calmly asked.

"Get Harkey's men off my back now and then you and I can live peacefully. That's all."

Frank sat behind his desk in stunned silence.

"What are you waiting for?" I said. "Pick up the phone."

I waited until I was sure that Waverly had Harkey on the line. Then I exited the office without another word.

When I pulled out of my parking space, I noticed I was still being tailed. I counted to ten, looked in my rearview mirror one more time, and I was free.

LOOSE THREADS

Forty-eight hours later, I arrived at 1799 Clay Street and knocked at the door. I have a key, but the knock seemed more dramatic.

My father looked at his watch. "With two hours to spare, no less."

I followed Dad into the Spellman offices, where my mother was seated behind a small mound of paperwork.

She looked up at me. "Do you have a decision?" she asked.

"I do," I replied.

"Well?" said my dad.

"I'd like to come back to work," I said.

The Unit's collective sigh was at the volume of morning traffic. My father slumped into his chair. I could almost see his relief erasing the lines on his brow.

"Under these conditions," I added, handing them an envelope. "You can read it and get back to me," I said. "I have a few other matters to take care of right now."

"Lunch on Friday?" Dad asked.

"I think I can free up my schedule," I replied.

. . .

Forty minutes later I was knocking on an all-too-familiar door at an apartment in Richmond.

"Izzeee!" Bernie bellowed as he opened the door to the vacant one-bedroom that used to be Milo's, used to be mine, and used to be Bernie's.

"Give Uncle Bernie a hug," he said.

"I'd rather not," I replied, "but perhaps you'll take a check instead."

I passed Bernie a check for the first month's rent and the security deposit.

"This time, you can't move back in. Got it?" I said.

"Not even a visit?" Bernie asked, trying to be cute.

"NO!"

Bernie—a big man—had to take a step back.

I held out my hand for a businessman's shake.

"Nice doing business with you again," I said.

Bernie shook my hand and pulled me into a bear hug.

"Mi casa is *su casa,"* Bernie said.

"Stop saying that," I replied. And then I left.

Next up: I phoned Maggie and asked her to meet me at the Philosopher's Club. It had been a while since I saw her last and, I have to admit, I missed having her around.

When I arrived, a new guy was tending bar. His name was George and he was a graduate student at SF State. I had no problem with George other than that he was new. In case you're curious, Connor was nowhere in sight.

Maggie arrived ten minutes after me. She ordered a beer and snacked on some chocolate-covered almonds from a half-eaten bag in her pocket.

A few sips of beer seemed to banish whatever stress had been written on Maggie's face.

"Thanks for inviting me. I didn't feel like going home," she said.

"Me, neither," I replied, already thinking about how I could postpone my next move. David already promised that he wouldn't help.

"I haven't gotten any more survey calls," Maggie said.

"I think it was Rae," I said.

Yes, I'm aware that was a lie, but a mild stalking incident doesn't usually make for an auspicious beginning for a relationship.

"Really?"

Maggie didn't seem all that concerned anymore.

"Yeah. I think she just had a few more questions she wanted to clear up."

"Let's play pool!" Maggie said as if it were the first time the idea ever popped into her head.[1]

I followed her to the back of the bar.

Usually people who suggest a game of pool actually have some idea of how to play the game, or at least how to rack the balls. She didn't know a thing and I didn't let on that I did.

As we picked out our cue sticks, I said, "You've met my brother, right?"

Brief pause.

"David? Yes, I've met him. He seems really nice," she said. She said it like she was holding back, so I knew I was onto something.

"You want to make this game interesting?" I asked.

"Sure," Maggie replied.

"If you win, I'll make sure my sister never demands your chauffeur services ever again."[2]

"And if you win?" Maggie asked.

"If I win, you ask my brother out on a date. Deal?"

"Deal."

And then I proceeded to kick her ass.

Five easily won pool games later, Connor entered the bar. When he saw me playing pool, he winked and went into his office. I like a man who can

---

[1] I would later learn that it was.

[2] Yes, I was aware that I couldn't make such a promise.

accept rejection. That's the kind of man who suddenly becomes unbearably attractive.

"Excuse me," I said to Maggie as she eyed the table, trying to find a shot she could make. "I'll be right back."

I knocked on the door of Connor's office.

"Come in," he said in that foreign language he speaks.

I entered and shut the door behind me. Connor was seated at his desk, paying bills. When he saw me, he put down his pen.

"Can I help ya, Izz-a-bel?" he asked.

I nodded. Connor slowly got to his feet and stepped closer.

"Are you sure?" he asked.

I nodded.

He placed his right hand behind my neck, his left behind my back, and he kissed me. It was the kind of kiss that makes you forget people. Connor was there, all handsome and smelling sweet like whiskey. But the most perfect thing about him was that when he kissed me, he didn't hesitate.

The kiss could have gone on indefinitely, but I broke away, remembering I had a "game" of pool to finish.

"So, uh, I'll see you around," I said.

Connor smiled. "Don't be a stranger."

FOILED LUNCH

My dad studied his menu, debating whether to get a salad or a soup and a salad. I told him that while I found his dilemma compelling, I thought he should make his decision on his own. Mostly I was tired of hearing, "I just don't know what I'm in the mood for."

His mood and lunch decided, Dad put down his menu and said, "Mom and I agree to your terms."

In case you have short-term memory problems or are an incredibly slow reader, Dad was referring to the provisions of my new work contract.

"I like how you think," Dad said, tapping his head for effect.

"Thank you," I replied. Dad was referring to a particular stipulation in my contract, which I'll explain in just a moment.

"Did you tell Rae?" I asked gleefully.

Dad smiled, enjoying himself almost as much as I was. "Not yet. We're waiting for the perfect moment. Who knows when that will be?"

The terms of my employment negotiation were, in fact, fairly reasonable. I wanted a raise and a retirement plan and a clearly mapped-out shift in ownership between me and my parents over the next ten years. But my coup de grâce was an explicit understanding that no matter what ultimate percentage of ownership my sister shared in the business, I would always be the acting principal. Essentially, I would be Rae's boss for all of eternity, unless she decided to find another line of work.

There was one not-so-small matter that I had to mention.

"Dad, what are we going to do about Harkey?"

"We'll get him," Dad replied.

"When?" I asked.

"Be patient, Grasshopper. We'll get him when the time is right."

Like some cosmic interruption, my cell phone rang. It was Mom.

"Isabel, you need to pick up Rae from the hospital," she said.

"What's wrong with her?" I asked.

"She's fine," my mother said, speaking slowly for emphasis.

"Then what's she doing at the hospital?"

"Trying to get them to run as many expensive tests as they can on her brain."

"I see," I replied.

"Our insurance will not cover recreational MRIs. Got it?" Mom said.

"Which hospital?" I asked.

"San Francisco General."

"It might be better if you went," I suggested.

"I'm at the hair salon," Mom replied. "If they rinse out the dye now, I'll have to resort to a wig. Deal with this, Isabel."

Sigh. "Okay," I said.

"Oh, and Dad doesn't know about my . . . intervention," Mom said right before hanging up. "Let's keep it that way, and don't forget: Record everything."

Twenty minutes later, my dad, Rae, and I clustered in a tiny, curtained-off section of the emergency room, discussing Rae's "condition" with the delightful Dr. Gupta.

[Partial transcript reads as follows:]

DR. GUPTA: Are you having headaches?

RAE: My head feels weird. Like there's something in it.

ISABEL: Marbles?

ALBERT: Quiet, Isabel.

ISABEL: She's fine.

RAE: My short-term memory is all but gone.

DR. GUPTA: Since when?

ISABEL: Since just a minute ago.

ALBERT: Let the doctor work, Isabel.

RAE: I'm going to need a CAT scan, an MRI, and some snacks.

DR. GUPTA: I think we'll start with some blood work.

RAE: That won't be necessary.

ISABEL: Dad, I think I'm in love with Dr. Gupta.

ALBERT: Shhh, you're embarrassing me.

ISABEL: *I'm* embarrassing you?

RAE: I'll meet you halfway, Dr. Gupta. We'll start with a CAT scan and go from there.

ISABEL: Can I speak to you in the waiting room, Dad?

[I pulled my dad by the wrist out of Rae's earshot.]

ISABEL: Dad, she's fine. She's faking it to rack up a medical bill.

ALBERT: Why would she do that?

ISABEL: Revenge. Just tell the doctor we'll bring Rae back if the symptoms persist.

On the car ride home, my sister cradled her head in her hands and said, "I'm almost one hundred percent positive I have a tumor."

"Shut up," I said.

FAMILY THERAPY
SESSION #1

[Partial transcript reads as follows:]

DR. RUSH: Who would like to begin?

RAE: I would.

ISABEL: No, don't start with her.

RAE: Why not? I have some things to say.

OLIVIA: We all have things to say, Rae.

ALBERT: I know I do.

DAVID: Why am I here?

DR. RUSH: You're part of the family.

ISABEL: He thinks he doesn't have any problems.

DAVID: I *never* said that.

ISABEL: Correction, you think you have fewer problems than the rest of us.

DAVID: [sigh] I sort of do.

RAE: I'd like to talk about my brain problems.

ISABEL: You don't have any brain problems.

RAE: You're a doctor, right?

DR. RUSH: I'm a psychologist, not a physician.

RAE: If I suddenly lost some mental acuity, wouldn't you send me to the doctor?

DR. RUSH: Yes, but you—

OLIVIA: I confess, okay?!

RAE: Confess to what?

OLIVIA: I had your grades altered so that you'd try harder in school.

RAE: Duh. I know that.

OLIVIA: Who was the rat?

RAE: Mr. Peabody. I hid his lunch and he squealed like a pig.

OLIVIA: I should have known. He looks weak.

ALBERT: What exactly did you do, Olivia?

OLIVIA: She was playing us because she doesn't want to go to college. I've got news for you, Rae. You're going.

RAE: You can't make me do anything.

DAVID: Since people are confessing things, I'd like to make an announcement.

DR. RUSH: Go ahead, David.

DAVID: I quit my job.

OLIVIA: You didn't.

DAVID: I did.

RAE: Since David doesn't have to go to work, why should I go to college?

ALBERT: Rae, be quiet. There's no parallel there.

OLIVIA: David, what are you going to do?

DAVID: I don't know. I'll figure it out.

ALBERT: You'll be fine, I'm sure. You always land on your feet.

ISABEL: Oh my god, you would never have that much faith in me.

ALBERT: Isabel, give it a rest.

DAVID: Since we're on the topic of Isabel, don't you have a confession to make?

ISABEL: What?

DAVID: Where you've been living.

ISABEL: Dad already knows.

DAVID: [to Dad] *You didn't tell me?*

ALBERT: You have way too much space for one person.

OLIVIA: David, we all knew.

DAVID: You people are not normal.

ISABEL: "You people"?

DR. RUSH: I'm not a fan of that word, "normal."

RAE: Me, neither.

ISABEL: Quiet, car thief. No one asked you.

ALBERT: I don't see how we can accomplish anything in an hour.

DR. RUSH: Yes, this might take more than one session.

OLIVIA: I already need a disappearance.

ALBERT: Me, too.

DR. RUSH: Excuse me?

EPILOGUE

D r. Rush was right. The Spellmans needed more than an hour to untangle the web of deceit that we'd been weaving over the last decade. Some truths were uncovered that are not surprising but worth mentioning nonetheless: During the time after my sister's dual PSAT scandals, my mom agreed to trim Rae's punishment if she helped play matchmaker to David and Maggie. However, I can hardly blame my mother, considering my own role in uniting the couple. Since my first and last game of pool with the pastry-pocketing attorney, she and my brother have gone on six dates and show no signs of letting up. However, David is mute on the subject, so all of our information is secondhand.

I moved back into Bernie's place the following weekend, and I'm happy to report that I no longer take the bus for rest. Connor did the bulk of the move for me. That's when he met my mother. She refers to him as the Irish thug and has looked into his green card status. (Mom has always had an irrational hatred of bartenders and dentists and bankers, since we're on the subject.) The next week she withheld my paycheck until I signed a document (drafted by David) in which I promised not to marry Connor. Ever. I signed the document, took the check, and had David draft another document forbidding all Spellmans to practice any form of blackmail. David tried to explain to me that a contract in which you promise not to break the law is ultimately redundant, but I didn't care.

My sister finally managed to track down the file containing my newly minted employment contract. I can't prove it, but I'm pretty sure, post-discovery, she keyed my car and then stuck a piece of chewed-up gum in the ignition. After that, she showed up at Henry's house, looking for sympathy. Henry called me for a Rae extraction, but I let the message go to voice mail and never returned the call.

Ernie phoned me after the dust had settled. Linda told him everything.

"I sure didn't see that coming," Ernie said.

"It was more complicated than we thought," I replied.

"And *you* figured it out," Ernie said, sounding unduly impressed.

"I guess so."

"You're a natural-born detective, Izzy."

"Why, thank you."

And that was the last I ever heard from Ernie. I'm going to imagine that he and Linda lived happily ever after.

Morty sends me postcards from Florida. He's found a deli by his house. The pastrami is out of this world. He played shuffleboard once and he's pretty good, so he might play again. He told me he looks terrible in shorts, but he wears them anyway. Sometimes he takes a dip in the pool.

My father and I continue to have lunch. Dad asks the hard questions: "What do you want out of life?" I ask the soft ones: "Were your eyebrows always like that?"

Some things change and others remain exactly the same.

APPENDIX

Dossiers

Albert Spellman

Age: 64

Occupation: Private investigator

Physical characteristics: Six foot three, large (used to be larger, but doctor put him on a diet), oafish, mismatched features, thinning brown/gray hair, gives off the general air of a slob, but the kind that showers regularly.

History: One-time SFPD forced into early retirement by a back injury. Went to work for another retired cop turned private investigator, Jimmy O'Malley. Met his future wife, Olivia Montgomery, while on the job. Bought the PI business from O'Malley and has kept it in the family for the last thirty-five years.

Bad habits: Has lengthy conversations with the television; lunch.

Olivia Spellman

Age: 56

Occupation: Private investigator

Physical characteristics: Extremely petite, appears young for her age, quite attractive, shoulder-length auburn hair (from a bottle), well groomed.

History: Met her husband while performing an amateur surveillance on her future brother-in-law (who ended up not being her future brother-in-law). Started Spellman Investigations with her husband. Excels at pretext calls and other friendly forms of deceit.

Bad habits: Willing to break laws to meddle in children's lives; likes to record other people's conversations.

Rae Spellman

Age: 16½

Occupation: Junior in high school/assistant private investigator

Physical characteristics: Petite like her mother, appears a few years younger than her age; long, unkempt sandy blond hair, freckles, tends to wear sneakers so she can always make a run for it.

History: Blackmail, coercion, junk food obsession, bribery.

Bad habits: Too many to list.

David Spellman

Age: 34

Occupation: Lawyer

Physical characteristics: Tall, dark, and handsome.

History: Honors student, class valedictorian, Berkeley undergrad, Stanford Law. You know the sort.

Bad habits: Makes his bed every morning, excessively fashionable, wears pricey cologne, drinks moderately, reads a lot, keeps up on current events, exercises.

Henry Stone

Age: 45

Occupation: San Francisco Police Inspector

History: Was the detective on the Rae Spellman missing-person case three years ago. Before that, I guess he went to the police academy, passed some test, married some annoying woman, and did a lot of tidying up.

Bad habits: Doesn't eat candy; keeps a clean home.

Mort Schilling

Age: 84

Occupation: Semiretired defense attorney

Physical characteristics: Short with scrawny legs and small gut, enormous Coke-bottle glasses, not much hair.

History: Worked as a defense attorney for forty years. Married to Ruth for almost sixty years.

Bad habits: Sucks his teeth; talks too loud; stubborn.

Bernie Peterson

Age: Old

Occupation: Drinking, gambling, smoking cigars, annoying sublet tenants

Physical characteristics: A giant mass of a human (sorry, I try not to look too closely).

History: Was a cop in San Francisco, retired, married an ex-showgirl, moved to Las Vegas, moved back to San Francisco when she cheated on him, reconciled with her, moved back to Las Vegas.

Bad habits: Imagine every bad habit you've ever recognized. Bernie probably has them all.

And, for the hell of it, I'll do me:

Isabel Spellman

Age: 31

Occupation: Private investigator/sometime bartender

Physical characteristics: Tall; not skinny, not fat; long brown hair; nose; lips; eyes; ears. All the usual features. Fingers, legs, that sort of thing. I look okay, let's leave it at that.

History: Recovering delinquent; been working for Spellman Investigations since the age of twelve.

Bad habits: None that I can recall.

Surefire Ways to Kill Time in Therapy

- Start with small talk. Mention the weather or traffic, or comment on the office décor.
- Think long and hard before you answer any questions. Make sure you look pensive during the silence.
- Ask therapist personal questions.
- "I see you're reading [insert name of random book on bookshelf]. How is it? Is it good?"
- Arrange for someone else to knock on the door and then make a run for it. (Never tried it myself, but I'm sure it would work.)

Transcript of Petra's Visit to Harkey's Office

PETRA: Thank you for agreeing to meet with me.

HARKEY: It's part of the job.

PETRA: I assume you've had your office debugged.

HARKEY: Of course.

PETRA: Today?

HARKEY: I personally debug my office every morning.[1]

PETRA: You can never be too careful.

HARKEY: I agree.

PETRA: I like to debug twice a day, but I understand that you have a busy schedule.

HARKEY: What can I do for you, Ms. Shvelde—

PETRA: Call me Agatha.

---

[1] Actually, not true.

HARKEY: Agatha?

PETRA: Yes.

HARKEY: You don't look like an Agatha.

PETRA: That's because I'm not one. I just want to be called that to throw them off the scent.

HARKEY: I see. What exactly can I do for you, um, Agatha?

PETRA: I'd like you to find my husband.

HARKEY: When did you see him last?

PETRA: About a year ago.

HARKEY: Have you contacted the police?

PETRA: They can't help me.

HARKEY: Do you suspect foul play?

PETRA: Oh yes.

HARKEY: What do you think happened to your husband?

PETRA: He was taken by *them*.

HARKEY: Who?

PETRA: You know.

HARKEY: I'm afraid I don't.

PETRA: [mumbling] The aliens.

HARKEY: What kind of aliens?

PETRA: I'm afraid I don't have enough knowledge about extraterrestrial life forms to narrow them down to a particular species or culture. Frankly, I don't know how they think of themselves. I know you debugged the office, but in case they're listening, I don't want to offend any of them by using a derogatory term.

[Long, long pause.]

HARKEY: So, you're talking about aliens from outer space, right?

PETRA: What other kind of alien is there?

HARKEY: Illegal aliens.

PETRA: Why would someone from another country want my husband? That doesn't make any sense. He doesn't have any special skills.

HARKEY: So you believe your husband was abducted by aliens.

PETRA: You're kind of slow for a PI. Are you sure you found your calling?

HARKEY: I've handled my share of alien abductions, but I have to be honest, it's an expensive operation. It requires special equipment and I can only assign this work to my seasoned investigators.

PETRA: How much money are we talking about?

HARKEY: Around five hundred dollars a day.

PETRA: Would you take fifty?

HARKEY: Fifty dollars?

PETRA: Yes.

HARKEY: A day or an hour?

PETRA: It's just a little alien abduction case.

HARKEY: I'm afraid I can't help you.

PETRA: I'm so sorry to hear that. Do you validate?

Theories on Why David Got Fired (Hypothetically Speaking)

- Interoffice romance
- Money laundering
- Abusing Free-Bagel Friday
- Not showing up at all
- Too much swooning by the support staff

A Brief Explanation of the Spellmans' Misuse of the Word "Disappearance"

A few years ago, Rae vanished herself in a misguided attempt to reunite the family. She was fourteen at the time and her absence seemed unlikely to have anything but a tragic outcome. Needless to say, it took the family some time to recover from the incident. Rae, in an attempt to rewrite history, would refer to that time as her "vacation." My parents, in retaliation, swapped the word "disappearance" for "vacation" so that Rae wouldn't forget.

Regrettable Meals à la Rae

- Chef Boyardee on Toast (canned ravioli on white bread)
- Tater Tots Casserole (tater tots, Velveeta, and hamburger meat)
- Peanut Butter/Pop Tart Sandwich (exactly what it sounds like)
- Chili in the Bag[2] (canned chili poured into a Fritos bag)
- Marshmallow Surprise (marshmallow fluff and Nutella on Wonder Bread)
- "Fruit" Salad (fruit cocktail and vanilla pudding served in an ice cream cone)

Magic Punch Recipe

- 1 part vodka
- 2 parts limeade
- 1 part sparkling water
- 4 packets LifeSavers[3]

---

[2] Apparently a Texan delicacy and not Rae's original recipe, as she had claimed.

[3] If it's a holiday party, use only red and green.

ACKNOWLEDGMENTS

As usual, I am very grateful to everyone at Simon & Schuster for their continued support of the Spellman books. I must first thank my brilliant, funny, and patient editrix, Marysue Rucci. A massive thank-you to Carolyn Reidy. David Rosenthal, thanks for not heckling me at my reading. I would also thank you for dinner, but Marysue paid, yet again. Also at S&S, Aileen Boyle, Deb Darrock, Michael Selleck, Victoria Meyer, Leah Wasielewski, Jackie Seow, and Dana Sloan. You all have been way too good to me. Thanks to my hardworking publicists, Kelly Welsh and Nicole De Jackmo; my genius production editor, Jonathan Evans; and Marysue's new and fabulous assistant, Sophie Epstein. If I have forgotten anyone, please forgive me. These acknowledgment pages are due today (well, last week) and I'm writing in a rush.

Equally important is my incredible agent, Stephanie Kip Rostan. I don't know what I'd do without you. I am also extremely fortunate to have the wonderful people at the Levine Greenberg Literary Agency on my side: Daniel Greenberg, Jim Levine, Elizabeth Fisher, Melissa Rowland, Monika Verma, Miek Coccia (still pronounced "Mike"), Sasha Raskin, and Lindsay Edgecombe. Thank you.

I would also like to thank all the booksellers I've met on the road for their hospitality and generosity, and to apologize if I happened to have stolen one of their pens. Please know that it was probably the only thing I stole. I would also like to thank the media escorts who took care of me when I was sleep-deprived, cranky, and suffering from a particularly unattractive head cold.

Since I'm talking about being on the road, I'd like to thank all the actors who helped me with my readings and all the regulars who show up again and again, even though no one is paying them. I'd especially like to mention the Rucci clan, who once again came out to show their support—Debbie and Joe Rucci, and, of course, my actor Ted (if I can book you now for next year, that would be great!). Virginia "Ginny" Smith, thanks again. A giant thanks to my San Francisco regular, Steve Kim. You never let me down. Also, Anastasia Fuller, Eric Etebari, Dave and Cyndi Klane, Hayley Dox, Craig Fox, and [insert your name here if I've forgotten you].

Now let me thank my family. Okay, I'd say stop reading here if you don't know me. Seriously:

My mother, Sharlene Lauretz, thanks for all the support and free book promotion you've done on my behalf. Also, thanks to my mom and my aunt Beverly Fienberg for that terrific party you threw. I've decided not to thank uncle Mark Fienberg.[1] (Should a very tall CPA in Beverly Hills ever ask you to house-sit for a chocolate lab and a golden retriever, named Bebe and Xena, respectively, under no circumstances should you say yes.)

More family to thank: Anastasia Fuller (again) and Jay Fienberg for their fabulous work on my website,[2] reading early drafts (in Hawaii, no less), and offering expert advice on brutal computer geeks (thanks, Jay). I depend on you both for way too much. Dan Fienberg, my cousin and my financial advisor,[3] thank you. According to the terms of the deal, I mention him in the acknowledgments if he *reads* my book before the next one is

---

[1] I think you know why.

[2] Also Jason Fuller!

[3] Now located in Santa Monica, not Beverly Hills (sheesh, I'm going to start charging for ad space, Dan).

finished.[4] Once again, thanks to Uncle Jeff and Aunt Eve Golden—these books would never have existed without your generosity.

I'd like to thank Morgan Dox[5] for all her help along the way and give another shout-out to the rest of the Dox-Kims, the aforementioned Steve, and, of course, Rae Dox Kim. Thanks to Dave Hayward, employee of the month and captain of the Spellman Enterprises softball team.[6] Also, Gretchen Rice for all her research and assistance, and my friends from Desvernine Associates, who continue to show their support and welcome me with hugs, crazy stories, and valuable information—Des, Pamela, Pierre Merkl, Debra Meisner, Yvonne Prentiss, and not Mike. A few more thank-yous to the people who helped the book take form, or at least helped me survive the process: Julie Ulmer, Frank Marquardt, Stephanie Dennis, Peter Kim, Carol Young, Lisa Chen, Warren Liu, and Mayumi Takada. Thanks to Dr. Linda Lagemann for showing me that therapists can be funny, too. And to my French friend, Charlie: *S'il vous plaît prendre vos vitamines. Chacun d'entre eux.*

---

[4] This usually involves a half-hour conversation in which he retells the story in his own words to prove that he's read it. It's quite amusing and an excellent refresher.

[5] The mastermind behind Rae's unfortunate recipes.

[6] No, there's no team. But I'm not entirely opposed to the idea.

POCKET
BOOKS

Lisa Lutz

CURSE OF THE SPELLMANS

They're baaaack ... In the Spellman family eavesdropping is a mandatory skill, locks are meant to be picked and blackmail is the preferred form of negotiation.

When Izzy Spellman, PI, is arrested for the fourth time in three months, she writes it off as an occupational hazard. She's been obsessively keeping surveillance on her new next-door neighbour (yes, he's her ex-boyfriend and yes, she's tried to break into his home several times), convinced he's up to no good – even if Spellman Investigations Management (Izzy's parents) are not.

When her (displeased) management refuse to bail her out, it's Morty, Izzy's octogenarian lawyer, who comes to her rescue. But before he can build a defence, he has to know the facts. Over weak coffee and pastrami sandwiches, Izzy unveils the whole truth and nothing but the truth – as only she, a licensed 30-year-old professional can.

ISBN 978-1-41652-641-4
PRICE £6.99

POCKET
BOOKS

This book and other **Pocket Books** titles are available from
your local bookshop or can be ordered direct
from the publisher.

978-1-41652-641-4   **Curse of the Spellmans**   £6.99

978-1-41652-640-7   **The Spellman Files**   £6.99